WAR HAWKS

A novel based on true events

by Donald A. Gazzaniga

WAR HAWKS

Visit: www.arrowhead-classics.com

Cover design: The eGraphics Company
Editor: Tony DiMarco
Interior Design, Typesetting: The eGraphics Company
www.egraphicscompany.com

Gazzaniga, Donald A.
War Hawks

ISBN: 978-1-886571-16-7
ISBN (10): 1-886571-16-3

"They stuck it up our ass, so when it became my turn, I stuck it up there ass." — Frank Strickland, USMC, Ret.

CHAPTER 1

OVER A HUNDRED THOUSAND angry Chinese troops, pretending to be the "People's Volunteer Army," poured into South Korea with enough firepower and chaos to pulverize Texas. They came with screaming violence into an area known to the U.N. as the X Corps area of northeastern Korea. The battle at the Chosin Reservoir had just begun.

"Get the hell out of here," Frank Strickland yelled to his men through the pandemonium of hell. It was dark. Chinese weren't supposed to be in the area, but were in fact coming at them in numbers never thought possible. The temperature was in the minus zone by at least thirty degrees. Men were literally freezing in their ice-sculpted foxholes. No one was dressed for the weather. Rifles froze, trucks wouldn't start. Bodies now dead in the dark tripped others who tried to run at the enemy or away from them as though the dead didn't exist. As though the dead were just chunks of ice.

Strickland was a Marine Corps First Lieutenant platoon commander with the Fifth Marines. The Fifth was a regiment of the Marine 1st Division out of Camp Pendleton, California. He was tall, strong as an ox, not bad looking as poster boys went. He loved sunny southern California. He hated this goddamned ice and snow. He carried two pistols always. The Corps issued one, he issued the other. Strickland was not really in the Corps demographics of the most obedient of their infantry officers. He was a leader, and a fighter, and he had his own World War II experiences, which had altered a few of the "by the book" procedures. Carrying only one small Colt 1911A1 forty-five caliber pistol just wasn't enough for the big guy, so that part of the rule book didn't exist in his life.

Like most of the Regiment during that first night at Chosin Reservoir, Strickland's platoon was stretched out to the max. They couldn't cover the ground the way they should have. The Taeback mountain range just didn't lend itself to defending their position efficiently. Nothing in the area was like Bridgeport where they'd gone through cold weather training and nothing here resembled sunny Camp Pendleton. Neither was anything like the islands in the Pacific where he'd already gone through more than one hell.

Worse, in Strickland's mind, MacArthur's latest blunder was unfolding, and the Marines were taking it in the shorts. Strickland never liked working under army snobs, especially MacArthur. Both had served in the Pacific during the big war. Mac was a famous general, Strickland a nobody sergeant who ended that war with a piece of Japanese metal buried deeply in his left hip.

What Strickland and his Marines didn't know at Chosin was that the Army to the west of them was also in deep shit. Over the mountain and closer to the coast, the 7th Army was suffering as badly as Strickland and his men. The 7th would soon sound the call of retreat and head south along a 275 mile route, a withdrawal that would cause more than 10,000 American casualties.

Even if Strickland knew about the Army's plight, he wouldn't care. He'd lost too many men, and was about to die along with them. He tried to catch sight of his men through the night's blackness but could spot only the backblast that poured out of each rifle. Silhouettes bounced around like ducks in a carnival. The horror was that he couldn't tell if they were his or theirs.

He knew holding ground was probably hopeless. There were just too many goddamned Chinese out there. But to run? Without a fight? The concept was frying his brain and he knew it.

A total of one hundred twenty thousand Chinese had laid in wait for them just north of their position with a surefire plan to attack a handful of what were now referred to as U.N. Forces.

It was so goddamned dark. His Marines were being split up and no wonder. A few hundred Marines against a hundred thousand-plus Chinese in an ass-cold black night.

War sure is hell he reminded himself, but someone's got to do it. They'd faced down straggler outfits before this night and thought little of it. They had learned that nighttime was when the Chinese liked to attack. And always during the coldest point of the night.

Bugles and horns and loud music added to the din and confusion. True to form, the chaos right now was coming from everywhere, bouncing off mountain walls, ricocheting down upon them as though they were under siege from a million-man armada. Because this had happened before with smaller units, much smaller units, too many of them—including that goddamned MacArthur—assumed the force up north was small. But the accurate rumor mill of S-2 had been more on target. Too late for that. His men were now the only target he was concerned about.

"Jesus H. Christ, Skipper," four-striper Ernest Shipley shouted through the cacophony of Chinese hell, "how many gooks they got up there?"

Strickland liked Shipley. He'd been a reliable sergeant for him. A good man. He was a proud graduate of the twenty-two-student high school in Centennial, Wyoming and longed to return to his hometown where the only shooting he wanted to do was at elk. His grit was borne of hunting alone through the Teton mountains while carrying heavy backpacks loaded with ammo and food and empty saddlebags on his mount; bags large enough to pack away most of the meat he'd get. And he'd always fill his backpacks with deer or elk meat on his return trip. He was taller than you'd expect for a cowboy from Wyoming, but shorter than Strickland who stood the tallest of any of his men. Shipley's biggest gripe since moving so far north was simply that the United States government hadn't issued them cold-weather gear. The rest of nature's elements didn't seem to haunt him or bug him as much as it did others. Hell, he'd been caught in colder weather in the Tetons with less clothing, but at least back then he could hunker down for protection without being shot at. He once told the story of getting trapped by a storm and not being clothed for it. So he killed an elk, skinned it and wrapped the fur around his body. Two days later searchers found him hearty, healthy and cooking elk meat.

Now, like so many others, mountain-man Shipley was suffering from first-stage frostbite on his feet, his hands, and his goddamned nose. It was either fifty degrees below zero no matter where you were or it was a hundred. That was topped off with a fifteen knot wind that forced human bodies to stiffen like giant ice cubes, especially if they stopped breathing or moving for just a few moments. Like Strickland and a few others in the outfit, including Fraker and Drier, and that irritating captain who'd just been killed, Shipley was a World War

9

II vet. Some of the officers and NCOs among the first Marines into Korea were older veterans from the big war. Many weren't.

Strickland nearly laughed at Shipley's question about how many Chinese were at their picnic. "Ask Almond or MacArthur," he fired back.

Strickland, a former enlisted man with a big enough thirst for survival for each of them, pushed his men through the heavy ice and snow to keep them moving. He was strong, he had long legs with powerful muscles. He'd played football before he'd joined the Corps after Pearl Harbor. He'd had few friends; his parents had died in a United Airlines crash over Saugus Newhall, California. His best friend Tommy also died when they were out riding their bicycles on a Sunday morning. They'd just left Chapman's ice cream parlor on San Fernando and Glendale Boulevard when a drunk ran over him. And Strickland had watched it. The imprint of that disaster was with him even on this blasphemous night.

He could feel his strong legs giving out tonight though. Running in snow and then over icy slopes took a toll. Especially with boots that didn't have cleats or spikes. That's why most of the men had bottle caps hammered into the soles of their boots. First you drank the beer, then you screwed the cap into your boot sole. He wondered which drunken Marine had first thought of that. It wasn't regulation, but it worked.

The ice and snow, the whole goddamned terrain of "glacier ambience" he called it, humbled each of them. Now it was bringing death to many. In fact, the cold weather did account for a high number of casualties for both sides. It was to blame for the deaths or maiming of nearly 35,000 Chinese. The U.N. forces for this battle alone would lose nearly 7,500 to the freezing climate. That amount was nearly half of the total casualties, which included 2,500 dead.

Strickland was pissed for more reasons than the weather. He'd lost too many men to the Chinese and too many to the cold. But it wasn't just the Chosin freeze that had affected many of them. He knew from his experience that a corrupt arms and equipment supply system was also to blame. If he ever got out of this alive, he'd deal with that later. He'd do his own investigation and then rap the assholes responsible for it. He wasn't sure where the fault lay, but he thought he had a damned good idea.

The gunfire around him continued while his mind sought

solutions. Men were still moving hurriedly, some were dropping, others were screaming for corpsmen. Now, more than adrenaline was keeping him going. Anger did that to you. Drove your mind, your heart, your muscles. But, he knew you had to manage it so that it would work for you.

It was hard to picture now, but only a few hours ago they had crawled into their sleeping bags with their buddies zipping each other in. The zippers worked only from the outside, not the inside. To keep from freezing each of them had to zip all the way up. What they had never experienced in these bags before, was a sudden surging attack from thousands of well-hidden and well-armed enemy, and never in freezing conditions. For god sakes hadn't the Marines always been in hot weather zones? Who would ever think the damned zippers would freeze up?

The problems with the bags would be solved later, and solved directly because of this battle, but that wasn't going to help his dead Marines. They'd been trapped. They couldn't get their zippers down on their own. Someone else had to get them out of their bags. For many the lost time and inability to defend themselves cost them their lives.

Hell, it had been just a few days before hadn't it? MacArthur stated flatly to America, "We'll be home by Christmas." Was Thanksgiving just yesterday?

Reality was brutal. Their fate had been scribed earlier when America, a country that had won the big deuce and saved the world had stood down, depleted its military, sent most everyone home. Everyone that is, except the Marines. Only the Marines were prepared for combat when the North Koreans headed south to destroy, conquer and take possession of South Korea. Oh sure, they'd gotten a lot of new recruits, many of them now dead even though they'd received the best training known to any military. But, many were still alive. He had to find them, pool them together, and attack into the center of the Chinese. Disperse them. Blow them out of there.

Private Polanco, a shorter man than Shipley, a very strong youngster with a "ton of guts," was hightailing it behind Strickland when he slipped on the ice, fell forward and slid ten yards until he hit a pile of snow. An overhead flare that just exploded a hundred feet above them lit his way, brightened the area for everyone more than they wanted. The flare was supposed to show the enemy, not them. But now they could see that the enemy was within their ranks.

The world had quite suddenly turned upside down.

Polanco's rifle trailed behind him while he slid down the steep bank. "God damn it," he bellowed. "I'm so goddamned cold I can't even move my arms." He got his rifle. Saw a Chinese soldier coming down the slope toward Strickland who had been directing his men. Polanco moved quickly, suddenly. He aimed his rifle just to the side of Strickland. Strickland whirled around just in time to see the Chinese soldier grab his own throat where Polanco had shot him. The man crashed to the ice in a heap.

Strickland turned back to see Polanco grin with pride. But Strickland wanted Polanco and everyone of his men to survive. "Move it Blade, move it," Strickland yelled over the gunfire. He headed for Polanco to get him off his knees, the position he'd fired his rifle from. Crap, his feet hurt.

"Get out of here," Strickland yelled. "Join the others."

"Yeah, right," Polanco shouted over the din. But how in the hell was he going to get to his feet when his knees were so fucking frozen to the ground?

Marines were shooting in one direction and taking cover in another. Still, Strickland had trained them well. Those close by hadn't yet broken apart. Too many had been killed or wounded, but the living among them knew what to do.

Get the hell out of there and regroup.

A corporal whose name slipped his burned out mind, hauled his crazy ass past him, "I told ya' Skipper," he shouted. "I said this friggin' place was no fuckin' good f'r us. Fuck'n cold, fuck'n ice, fuck'n frostbite, and now the fuck'n Chinks. Sir!" The corporal, his name was Hank Beauchamp, his hometown was Elk, Minnesota where his ass also froze every winter, got to Polanco first, pulled him up to his feet, shoved his rifle into his hands and urged him on.

"C'mon Blade, we can make it outta here."

Polanco followed him slowly at first, then quicker. He wanted to fight, but for chrissakes he emptied most of his clips on a sea of Chinese and no matter how many he dropped, they just kept coming. He decided he had no other choice. Run.

Here, was the north-end outpost for the 7th Marines at the west side of the Chosin Reservoir near Yudam-ni, Korea. They'd come from Inchon, maybe too quickly, where they'd been referred to by the American press as some kind of heroes. Now look, they were ice cubes and being shot at like ducks in a shooting gallery. Two regiments of Marines. The 5th and the 7th. The First Marine Division was in trouble. They were fighting their way out of a monster trap sprung on them not by great tactics, but instead by a mass of gun and rocket toting human flesh and a couple of ancient American generals.

Waves of human flesh. And tanks. Goddamned, hadn't they heard tanks, too?

Strickland felt it had taken him too much time to gather his own senses. He'd been separated from his company. His platoon had been isolated. It was as though the Chinese had split up the pie and now wanted to devour each piece.

They'd done a lot better at Inchon and the march up here. But now, just fifteen whole-body survivors of his original forty-four man platoon seemed to have made it. Trucks from battalion had stalled while others rolled out of there. None were now in sight or within audible range. He wanted cover fire, but there wasn't any. Fox Company? Where was Fox Company? Strickland soon decided without informing his ass-frozen Marines that either they, or Fox Company, must be disoriented. He had no radio anymore, it had all but turned into an icebox.

Another challenge faced them as well, like they needed another challenge. The narrow and very ancient road they'd moved up on was going to be the same narrow road they'd have to take south, and it was one crappy winding mountainous trail. It hadn't been built for the trucks that came up and tanks didn't do much better. And there were Russian tanks, manned by Chinese in the area. Strickland was convinced that if those came down that road, they'd all be in a big death trap.

The mystery for the moment for him was, "Where are we?" All he could hear was gunfire where they had been. Howitzers, or were those Chinese artillery? Mortars? Bullshit mortar fire from the Chinese. Coming from where? Above us? The horns and music and other crappy sounds had disappeared. Thank God for that.

He knew from the sounds around him that they were on their own. Just like when that airplane went down over Saugus Newhall, a farming community north of Burbank in San Fernando Valley. The one that killed his mom and dad. He'd been left alone. So alone. Even when the church put him into their orphanage and got him through their school he was alone. Just Tommy as a friend. Then he too, was killed and Strickland was alone again. Loneliness had become his life. The sound of battle suddenly pierced through his psychotic reverie and he realized that maybe he liked all this.

Shit, that's nuts.

Sergeant Shipley must have flown through the air to tackle him. What the hell was this? A football game?

"Down, down, down," Shipley yelled. The noise of war had elevated again. Mortars, tanks, rifles, rockets. Machine guns from the Marines in reply, and tracers everywhere. A flare. A goddamned flare again.

A rifle propelled grenade sailed over them and exploded about twenty yards farther on, killing a Marine they considered one of the best riflemen in the outfit, and wounding another. The wounded man got up, staggered on down the hill into the blackness of night.

Strickland jumped up, pulled Shipley up with him and yelled to two Marines near the now out-of-sight wounded Marine, "Get someone to help Osborne," he yelled.

Craig Osborne. From where? Shit, Strickland couldn't remember. Dammit. He turned back to find two Marines who appeared out of nowhere and shouted, "Move it! Get down into that gully and set up covering fire."

The two Marines took off for Osborne, glad to get away from the pressure of impending death. They left behind their Skipper and their Sarge who had three stripes and one rocker. Shipley longed to become a Gunny. That was his goal and he figured before they got out of this piece-of-shit country he would.

Strickland needed more ammo or another weapon. He yanked an M-1 off the snow pack where a Marine had died earlier and continued shooting at the oncoming Chinese. "Get out of here, Ship. We'll regroup at the bottom."

Shipley headed off in the direction Strickland pointed. Three steps. That's all. Then a fusillade of bullets from a Soviet PPSh 41 Submachine Gun, the gun that became famously known as The Burp Gun, smacked into him. What seemed like hundreds of rounds chewed Sergeant Shipley and the complaining Private who had joined Shipley for the move to the road, into a single pile of clothing and human burger. The private's name was Rodriguez, Strickland remembered, the kid from El Paso. Had a sister who sent him Hot Tamale cookies with red-hots in them. Different as hell. Good cookies. An upright boy, suddenly, maddeningly, vaporized.

Strickland's gaze fixed on Shipley's remains. Polanco had returned and killed the owner of the burp gun. Polanco then pushed on Strickland to move out of there.

"Damn it Skipper, I'm gettin' tired of pulling you out of this fire. Let's move it."

But Strickland wanted Shipley to rise up.

"He's a goner, Lieutenant. He ain't even makin' no noise," Polanco yelled. "Them arm's aren't attached to nothing. He's gone, sir. Move it. Move it."

Strickland had seen men die like this in the Pacific. It always hit him hard. War was so goddamned stupid.

Polanco shouted into his ear again as though his mouth was within millimeters of his ear. Strickland whirled around to face two Chinese coming at him, one with a jammed gun, but the other guy was shooting right at him. He fired all eight rounds of a clip from his hip and knocked them both down. Each collapsed straight ahead with their rifles pushed into the snow. Strickland dropped on his knees next to Shipley.

"God damn it Sarge. You can't die on me now!"

But Shipley was as dead as the ice he lay on. Four huge impact wounds showed in his chest alone, three in his shattered jaw. His arm's were gone. Blood was everywhere.

A flare popped above them.

"Oh my God," Polanco muttered.

Strickland's stomach gurgled audibly. The flare told them more than flashes in the night could. The pile that used to be Rodriguez was as horrible as anything either man had seen. He was very dead in a large patch of reddened snow and ice.

Strickland's mind was trying to catch up to reality, but violence had a way of causing one's brain to retreat. For a moment his only thought was, "No more red-hots?" It was an absurd passage through his mind, he knew that, but it was like all those absurd thoughts he'd had on Peleliu and Okinawa. Weird shit. Football! It was like a big game of football at his high school. They'd huddle, call out their play and go out and get their asses kicked, over and over and over. Their only fame had been that they'd never won a single game during his years there. It wasn't his fault either, or his friend Tommie's. They were the best and the local papers said so. But they were surrounded by teammates who just didn't care whether they won or lost.

He mashed his teeth together. Goddamn, now I got a great team and we're still gettin' our asses kicked. He stood right into the line of fire and shouted, "We have to win this one."

No other choice was acceptable.

Polanco realized during the light of the flare that his skipper was considering taking the remains of Shipley with them. It was a Corps tradition. Take the dead with you. But body snatchers were usually around to do that. Not this time. Not now.

And Polanco knew the look in the man's eyes. He'd seen it before. Now, it was scary.

"No sir, no sir. We can't be doin' that. I know it's the Corps, but this ain't no fuckin' standard battle, sir. No sir."

Lieutenant Joe Hughes, an officer with a combat history similar to Strickland's, scrambled on his hands and knees toward his friend. Hughes was as strong as they came. His legs were pier posts and his upper torso was built like a suspension bridge. He had eyelashes like John L. Lewis the union leader, and a mouth shaped like the half moon on an outhouse. He had a weightlifters tuned muscles and body shape. He grabbed his boss by the epaulet of his field jacket and tugged him away from Shipley as though Strickland was a rag doll.

"C'mon Frank," he yelled over the gunfire. Hughes had served in the Corps since December 9, 1941. It was the same day Strickland had signed on. Hughes had made Gunny sergeant on Okinawa where he'd also saved Strickland's life. The two of them had been serving together as sergeants for a lifetime as far as Hughes was concerned.

After that war the two of them had gone to college on the G.I. education bill, got their degrees and commissions and now, without asking for it, they were here. Dumb move Hughes thought. Just goddamned idiotic. Should never have gone to college.

His fist gripped tightly around Strickland's field jacket. "The body-snatchers will have to get 'em, Frank. If we take them, we'll die doin' it."

"No," Strickland shouted. "All out. We take 'em all out."

Hughes clenched Strickland's field jacket tightly and pulled him to him to make sure his friend unerstood. "Get your ass out'a here Frank. We take the living, not the dead. Move it, 'fore those assholes kill all of us."

Polanco couldn't believe he was watching two officers haggling during the middle of a firefight. "Crap sakes, sirs. Let's hucklebuck." Polanco raised up hunch-high and took off down the slope.

Many who sign on to fight during a war or just as one cranks up, do so believing things will move along quickly. They figure that the odds are they'll be right there to win it for the Gipper in their life and bang, the war ends. Nobody would go into battle willingly if they didn't believe they would be the ones to exit alive on the other side. That's the way it was, right?

When Strickland signed on early that December morning in '41, he figured a few weeks of training and then off to the Pacific to fight for glory and "all that." He quickly found himself at San Diego Recruit Training Depot along with a large group of others, most of whom were reacting to the attack on Pearl Harbor, some simply trying to escape the Geat Depression, none, including himself prepared for what was ahead. His induction also became his new humility. He had considered himself overpowering on the football field, and his size generally gave him strength against any wold-be antagnoizers, but now he was under attack from a tough-ass Marine D.I. The drill instructors had just explained how useless he "really was."

He would have to prove them wrong.

In the beginning, many fell and many crawled. But it wasn't that way for Strickland. Boot camp, he'd tell you, was much easier than the Nuns at the Catholic orphanage where he ended up after his parents had died.

He figured it out quickly, too. When a drill sergeant ordered them to do something all he had to do was perform. But with the Nuns, even if you performed well, it didn't matter. They'd still climb all over you with God fearing messages no matter how well you did. At boot, all the drill sergeants did was swear a lot and wave their swagger sticks like rat tails when you complied exactly as ordered. Some of the guys got knocked around with those sticks, but the D.I.s never touched him.

He graduated first in his boot class, a position he had not consciously aspired to but one that brought him his first stripe as a PFC, and very shortly after that he was promoted to corporal. It was a giant leap from private as far as he was concerned. But more than earning his boot camp honors, he had learned a bit about leadership. The lessons would pay off later.

His first assignment was Camp Pendleton, where he was staged for an immediate trip to a place called Guadalcanal. It was at Pendleton that Hughes and Strickland had first met. The next time they saw each other was on Okinawa, when Strickland dashed into a death zone to pull one of his wounded men away from a sea of machine gun fire. Just as he got back to safety, he plopped down to stare straight into the eyes of Joe Hughes.

"Fancy meeting you here," Hughes had quipped.

Strickland acknowledged Hughes by tapping him on his shoulder while calling out as loud as he could, "Corpsman."

"Still mother'n your men, huh Frank?"

Strickland's expression didn't change although he was excited to see Hughes. "Yeah, guess it never stops. Where you been? Could have used you a few times."

"Got busy killin' Japs. What about you?"

"Same. Need a job?"

"Got one." He pointed to his double rockers. "They made me a gunny." He grinned broadly. "Guess I outrank you now."

Strickland was still a staff sergeant.

"I figure it's temporary."

"There's a whole platoon over there without officers or NCOs. You could borrow them for a while."

"Hughes, we got bullets flying around, grenades poppin' off every which way, napalm and flamethrowers burning flesh and you still got that shit eatin' grin on your puss. What gives?"

"They call me Smiles, now. New nickname. Not sure I like it."

"You love it."

"I'll get those guys for you." Hughes tucked and ran down the lava ash slope to order the leaderless platoon up to the fight."

"Hey," Strickland yelled after him. But Hughes couldn't hear over the chaos of war. Strickland shrugged, "Never mind. I'll find Fraker myself."

He discovered he was still stanching the bleeding of the private in front of him when a corpsman finally arrived.

"You seen Sergeant Fraker," he asked the medic.

"You mean that guy over there?"

The corpsman pointed to a man standing directly in the field of fire while commanding his men.

"Yeah, that would be him."

Strickland shook off his past and then splattered snow on Shipley and Rodriguez as though to protect them from further harm. "This is nuts," Hughes barked. "I'm runnin' out of ammo and we got more Chinks headed this way."

Strickland's voice was as acrid as the burned gunpowder around them. "Nobody kills my boys and lives. Nobody."

Hughes tugged at Strickland's jacket one more time. "I know Frank. I know. We'll be back. We'll get 'em."

Strickland faced the enemy he couldn't see and shouted, "You mother'n bastards, I'm comin' after you."

For a moment, Hughes thought his friend had flipped, gone nuts. He'd seen it happen in the Pacific with others. Hell, for that matter so had Frank. Perfectly sane, perfectly brave men just all of a sudden lost it.

The living were already down the slope, anxiously waiting for them. It was still too dark to see any distance, or to tell exactly where they'd landed.

Hughes and Strickland moved quickly with Polanco down the icy trail, ducking right and left, praying now that their small band would make it back far enough to be covered by other Marines. Their lungs ached from the cold with each breath penetrating deeply as though they'd just swallowed a dagger. Their strength was gone; their feet had lost all feeling. Their ears were plugged with thick layers of ice. They would keep running, moving, crawling, whatever it took to get the hell out of there or they would never have a chance to fight again. Their field jackets, trousers, and boots were not made for cold weather fighting. To sit, to lie down, to hunker under would only be like shoving themselves into a freezer and slamming the door shut forever.

Hughes shouted over the gunfire, "You ever wonder if we're gonna ever have quiet barracks duty?"

Humor always helped to get them through the tough moments. But not now. Not for Frank Strickland. "Knock it off, Joe."

When they made it to an area in the road where they could duck out of gunfire they stumbled into a pile of ice-coated brush and rocks and human flesh. They found themselves alongside the men who'd outraced them, who had protected them. Just when they arrived four more Marines rushed around the bend in the road just north of them and dove into the same mess. One of these carried one of the new 3.5 rocket launchers. Everyone was there now, all thirteen of the survivors.

Strickland realized that he could see the new men who had just joined them. In an hour full sunrise would penetrate the clouds and give them more light.

For now, though, each man understood they were in a lot of trouble.

"You got any rockets for that?" Strickland called out over the gunfire. He was still unraveling himself from Joe Hughes.

"One, sir. But the tube's frozen."

The tube belonged to Corporal David Drier, who held tightly to the 'zooka.' Good looking kid. Lots of spirit. Showed no fear. From some place in Oklahoma, Strickland remembered.

"It's the trigger. It won't pull." Drier was a bit older than the other young Marines. He'd been in the Corps a few years more, having also served in the Pacific. His experience included Okinawa. He'd made it to sergeant and back to Corporal and up to Sergeant and back to Corporal three times since then. It wasn't because he was a bad ass, either. It was because, as his officers knew, he was psychologically built for war. And the period between the Big Deuce and Korea was peacetime. "That's when the true warrior gets into trouble," Sergeant Peletier at Camp Pendleton, had told him. "Now, keep your ass out of trouble or next time you'll get booted." Drier had paid attention to advice, and was now eligible for his sergeant stripes again. This time he swore he'd keep them.

"Trigger, your ass," Gunny Sergeant 'Snake' Fraker growled. "Hand that tube to me."

Drier handed the gruff, bull-nosed sergeant the 'zooka. Fraker's red beard was covered with ice. His permanently stubby cigar was missing, and that always put him into a bad mood. Fraker was nevertheless loved by the men who served with him. He personified courage and bravery and psychotic warriors. He stood only five feet ten-inches tall in his boots, but he sounded and worked as though he were a giant.

When Drier handed over the tube, Strickland noticed something in the corporal's eyes. The early morning light had opened up and what he saw just then nearly put a smile on his face. This youngster has no fear. He wasn't going to buckle under.

"Round's in my pack," Drier said calmly.

He reached back for it, but it slid out into the open. He glanced to Fraker, then to Strickland. Strickland raised a brow as if to say get it. Drier looked up the road, heard the Chinese coming. He rolled out over the embankment that was made of rocks and boulders and brush and ice and snow. He grabbed the round and then rolled back. Clouds of condensed breath from his nose and mouth exposed the energy that seemed to evaporate from him in the freezing air. Strickland spotted the man's boots. He wasn't wearing the gawd-awful rubber galoshes the Marines had issued them as thermal protectors, the same gawddamned rubber boots that caused everyone's feet to sweat then freeze. He had on only his leather Endicott Johnson boondockers, and better yet, with his own specially cleated bottle-cap soles. This was a smart kid as well. And he drank beer. Good on him.

"There's a tank pushing down on us," Fraker yelled. Fraker always swore he could hear a rattlesnake crawl across an open plain. A tank he'd tell you was a bit more obvious.

Chinese foot soldiers appeared up the road rounding the bend. Fraker handed the 'zooka to Strickland and then settled his M-1 firmly into his shoulder and started shooting like a sniper would. He squinted into his sights, the wrinkles of a thirty-five year old gunny sergeant letting everyone around him know it was time for Fraker to retire, to get the hell out of the war and the Marines. Fraker was your basic gunny, too. One who appreciated younger men like Drier, since Fraker himself had made corporal three times, private twice, and staff sergeant at least twice. He didn't like peacetime either. "Get your rifles up Marines, we got business," he said. He fired a shot and dropped one of the enemy.

"Give me your Zippo, Snake," Strickland shouted over the gunfire.

Fraker stuck his left hand, bare and cold and purplish into his glacier lined pocket while still holding his rifle up toward the enemy with his right, and brought out a Zippo with a Marine Corps emblem carved into it with the year 1938 engraved under the emblem. That was the year Fraker entered the Corps. He handed it to Drier to pass along while explaining, "He's the best, kid. We were at the Canal together. Bloody Ridge is where. Then Peleliu and Oki-knock-knock." He grinned, "South side of the island, not north side where you was. Skipper kilt hundreds of Japs at the Canal with the two-point-six," he said, referring to the earlier model "bazooka." The 3.5 was introduced sometime mid-1942, just in time for the rest of the war in the Pacific.

Fraker fired two more rounds at two brave Chinese who appeared at the bend of the road. Two other Marines popped off rounds at the same time. The Chinese ducked back. Fraker's clip ejected. Damn, he thought. Bad shooting. Not now, dummy. He reached to his bandoleer and frustratingly pulled a new clip of eight out. Quickly it was into the M-1 with the familiar sound of the bolt crashing down, driving the first round into the chamber. "Crap, I think I could shoot icicle bullets with this right now."

Drier handed Strickland the Zippo. Strickland opened it, whisked the flame up to the trigger housing mechanism of the 89 mm launcher, moving it back and forth to heat the unit while the rest of the men picked up the shooting. More Chinese took the big gamble and appeared around the bend.

"Steady men," Fraker said. "Aim, then squeeze."

"Always the gunny," Strickland said, smiling inwardly. Then louder, "Load it." He raised the tube to his right shoulder. At that moment the Chinese tank that had been making so damned much noise appeared around the bend.

"Holy mother of Jesus, we got a problem," Polanco shouted.

Quilt-clad Chinese foot soldiers, seemingly well dressed for the cold weather appeared behind the tank. Their clothing the Marines learned later, turned out to not be much better than the light garments worn by the U.S. Army and the Marines.

"Kill those bastards," Strickland ordered.

The Marines continued to fire with as much destruction as they could muster from their very limited supply of ammo. Strickland jammed his right eye into the bazooka's sight.

Drier shoved the shell into the tube but it refused to seat. "It's jammed," he cried out, his first display of angry emotion. "Goddammit, it's jammed," he said in a lowered more matter of fact tone.

"Push hard on it," Strickland shouted. "We got about ten seconds before that son of a bitch melts all of us."

Drier stood and kicked the round into the tube. It clicked. He got to Strickland's right side and tapped Strickland on his helmet. "Loaded. Ready. Clear."

If the area behind the tube wasn't clear, whoever was there would die as quickly as anyone at the front of the tube.

Strickland paused, aimed as carefully as he could. He squeezed the trigger, it was hard, didn't want to move. He grimaced, squeezed harder. The tank was rotating its giant gun directly toward them. The machine guns mounted on the front of the tank were firing at a high cyclic rate and the bullets were walking down the slope behind them.

Whoosh! The rocket left the tube and hurtled toward the tank. It exploded right where Strickland wanted it to. Where the turret met the tank. The tank's fuel exploded, sending the tank into the air, flipping it on its side and taking some of the Chinese infantry with it. It rolled off the embankment into the gully that paralleled the road. Flames spewed upward, causing snow and ice to melt while it tumbled.

Fraker shouted, "Now they's good gooks."

The Chinese foot troops lost half of their men with the explosion. Drier rolled back to his position alongside Fraker. The living Chinese were trying to run back around the bend. Marines shot after them trying to pick them off but most got away.

"You guys got buck fever," Fraker shouted. "Settle in."

"My rifle's jammed," Polanco called out. He slid down the parapet into the ditch. He kicked on his M-1's bolt. The M-1 had proved itself during the WW-II in the South Pacific. However, this was the frozen Chosin and without a good hunk of lubriplate to keep the mechanism working, a bullet would not quite enter the chamber when the back pressure on the bolt was finished with its job and the bolt prematurely returned forward in the cold air. The gas cylinder rod just couldn't handle the freezing conditions if the rifle had been left to sit or had waited too long between firing.

"Man," Polanco complained, "fucker works just like my bowels. Neither one wants to eject."

Fraker yelled out over the shooting. "Pull hard on the bolt, Blade. Eject the bent round. Hurry man, we need your firepower up here." Then he laughed, "And don't worry about your gut. When there's time you can squeeze off a round there, too."

Drier slid down to help. Polanco wasn't succeeding. When the Chinese came back around the bend and started shooting again Polanco's hands started shaking, making his efforts useless. Drier grabbed the rifle, put the butt on the ground and his boot on the bolt. He stood on it, driving it backward. He reached down and with ice-numbed fingers pried the jammed round out. He let the bolt go and a new round entered the chamber cleanly. "If you live through this goddamned battle, Blade, grease this son of a bitch," he said sternly while handing it back to Polanco. "Now get your ass up there and kill some gooks."

It took them just three minutes to kill another dozen Chinese and drive the rest back around the bend.

For a while things were quiet. Sitting on the ice, taking a breather while they quickly greased their rifles and pulled more eight-round clips out of their bandoleers and belts, Strickland mapped their way out of there. His goal was to keep them alive, keep himself alive if he could, and kill as many of the enemy as possible.

Meanwhile, Fraker had found a cigar butt in his jacket pocket. Old and frozen but workable. He rolled it from one side of his mouth to the other while he explained to Drier a bit more about Strickland.

"I trust he'll get us out of this alive." He grinned, spit, pulled the butt from his mouth, eyed it curiously, and then returned it. "On Peleliu we pulled together a motley crew of a platoon and made a charge that nearly won the war." He grinned broadly, his cigar seeming to laugh along with him. "Both lieutenants done real good there."

"Both?"

"They weren't officers then. But, when you get to know someone in a few battles, you glue together for life. You earn a trusted friend and you become one. It's the nature of the game."

They were in a roadside gully that was probably a spring and summer stream now packed with ice and snow. Large rocks and boulders grouped around them and ran to the north and the south. Each was covered with a cap of snow and ice as though sculpted rock-soldiers frozen in time. Blue and red hues from the snow pack clashed with the olive drab color of Marine utilities, blankets and ponchos. Their backpacks, if they still had one, were nothing more than twelve by twelve inches with straps that were slung up and over their shoulders. A small collapsible shovel hung from each backpack and it was over the top of these packs each Marine would strap his bedroll. Their heavy steel helmets once covered with camouflage cloth but now just metal, were World War II surplus. Craggy mountains surrounded them. The hills were mostly treeless although they had a green hue when snow didn't blanket them.

Joe Hughes lifted his head above the protective rocks. The Chinese had bugged out, leaving their dead behind. That's when he spotted the corpses of Marines off to the side of the road across from them, about 20 yards up. "Holy crap," he muttered, "where did they come from?"

Strickland and Fraker rolled up alongside. Fraker frowned. "Gotta be our boys."

"Golf Company moved out ahead of us," Strickland agreed. "They were probably covered with snow until the tank melted it."

"They ain't all dead," Fraker said.

One of the Marines moved his arm slightly. Hughes gasped, "He wants help, Frank."

"Ain't a smart thing for 'em tah do," Snake growled into what he considered a very irritating wind. "Chinese can hear 'im, too."

Strickland glanced from Snake to Joe, then back to the other Marines. "Might be one of the Chinks playin' games."

"Like the Japs done," Snake added. "One of theirs in one of our uniforms. 'Member those three on Oki, Skipper. Damned bastards nearly tricked us to death."

"This guy is one of our men," Strickland said.

"Else they got another tank hiding behind the bend, just trying to see what we got here," Fraker said. "We run out, blam, we gone."

"Oh my God," Hughes groaned. "He's not from Golf Company. It's Barnett. PFC Barnett. A B.A.R. man. He's one of my men."

"I'll go, Lieutenant," Drier said. He jammed a fresh clip of twenty rounds into his B.A.R. The B.A.R. stood for Browning Automatic Rifle. It weighed nearly twenty pounds. Heavy for a rifle, it had a bipod attached to the front of the barrel. It was there for the shooter to lay it on the ground and hold it steady while cranking off in machine gun fashion twenty armor piercing .30 caliber rounds.

"Dumb move, boy," Snake chided. "Get yourself kilt and then we lose two of you."

Hughes shook his head. "He's my responsibility."

Strickland grabbed him by his field jacket. "No. We can't afford to lose you."

"Bull crap," Hughes boomed. "This is when the rules don't count." He rolled over the rock they were behind and landed in the road. Before they could stop him, he was gone. "Cover me," he shouted.

The sound of a low flying Marine recon plane overhead drowned him out. Strickland looked up. It was snowing for god's sake. They could barely see fifty yards. Sure, he thought, it's getting a bit lighter, but the pilot had to be snow blind up there and either goddamned stupid or brave as hell.

CHAPTER 2

IN THE BACK SEAT of his Cessna OE-1, known by Marines as a "Bird Dog," a lean and silver-haired World War II commander from the battle at Peleliu, a man his friends called "O.P.," strained his eyes through wind-driven sleet in an effort to find Marines, or their enemy, on the icy road below. The falling snow created vision problems more because they were moving too fast for it than because of how much there was. O.P. Smith, the Marine General in charge of all Marines in Korea, knew he was in the hands of an expert pilot, but this crappy weather could snatch even the best of pilots out of the air and end their lives abruptly.

Which was against his principles. His pilot, he noticed, wasn't a bit nervous but was instead doing a great job of going as slow as the plane would allow. There wasn't much of the damned white-flake moss out there, but their movement made it look like a wild-assed sleet storm. Crap, was all he'd allow himself to say aloud.

Oliver P. Smith's gut pressed achingly against the bulkhead of the small plane while he looked down on the narrow road leading to the Chosin reservoir. One very narrow twisting road in, and the same damned road out. Not wide enough for one vehicle to pass another.

He hated being so right when it involved the lives of his men. Being right that is, against a wave of higher commanders who were terribly wrong about things involving this war, but very much in charge.

As the road climbed through the mountains it was channeled by steep hills on each side with just a riverbed or large gully offering the only additional space. It was a trap. And, damn it, depending on which side you were on, it was a gorgeous or an awful trap. He dripped with sarcasm when he decided earlier that he'd have to thank Mac someday for his monstrous error in judgment.

Mac had a lot of fans, but Oliver Smith wasn't one of them. Sure, Mac was credited with planning important battles, and his record was unlike any other in the military, but each man finds his time, "gets his due," as Smith would say to others. "You can't live on P.R. alone," he would tell you. And now it's Mac's time. Too many errors here, too many deaths. Mac should go home. And with him so should Generals Almond, a man Smith considered the antithesis of his own careful planning—and take Walker with you, he urged to himself only.

O.P. had at least been smart enough to move northward slowly, to build supply caches and medical support teams along the way. He had ignored the pressure from Mac and Almond to move "full speed ahead." He had done his best to protect his Marines.

It had been called a "race to the Yalu" by the commanders in Tokyo. But O.P. blew that off saying it would cost more lives than necessary. To leap ahead of your own supply and support systems was suicidal. "Napoleonic," he told them. So, against their wishes and command, he spent extra time to build defensive positions along the high ground of this narrow, winding and idiotic road. And a few supply depots. Only problem was, supplies were in short. His caches were running low for everything from munitions to food and first aid. And attrition of personnel was just running too goddamned high.

O.P. also understood he would have far too many wounded, so he'd built small airfields along the way to fly them out. The nearest to the calamity now was at Hagaru-ri. The same airfield he'd left just a half-hour ago.

The challenge he faced now was to get the wounded out of here and to safety. More than that, he cussed to himself, if he could just get the goddamned army commanders in charge of this war to understand that the Chinese were damned good fighters, then he might make enough inroads to regroup and counterattack with success.

Unfortunately, Oliver P. Smith wasn't in charge of operations in Korea. Almond and Walker were, and they took orders from Mac.

Chain of command, he groaned. It seemed to only work correctly when you were at the top. He laughed to himself, he still had a sense of humor. He stuck the binoculars that he fondly called field glasses to his eye and gave Mac one more thought. Maybe the powers in Washington would wake up and take his encumbered commander out of theater.

Smith was known as a "gentleman." His long face, and his perfect manners were a huge part of his reputation as a refined and sophisticated man.

Until Peleliu.

Peleliu was where his planning and perfection mattered, and where his manners were set aside for a while. After 27 years in the Marine Corps, Smith's very first test came at the small Island in the Pacific. Peleliu was a horrendous engagement and O.P. stood out as a heroic Marine who feared no one.

He passed the test.

His career fast forwarded to Korea after that. It was Major General O. P. Smith who led the surprise invasion into Inchon on September 15, 1950.

O.P. was given the job of carrying out an amphibious landing deep behind the North Korean lines. The operation had its challenges, some of which Smith doubted in the beginning. The assault, more complicated than most in the Pacific Theater, would take place in a narrow harbor with extremely high tides. But Smith was the epitome of a Marine. He was gung ho, well trained, full of esprit. After working out the details with naval commanders, he successfully landed his division at Inchon, where he caught the North Koreans and the American press completely by surprise.

Early on he had become fully aware that he'd have to keep the press in the dark. Emperor Napoleon had taught tactics long before Smith arrived and one of his greatest lessons was that, "Surprise was half the battle." Include the press and the world would soon know what he was up to and where they were headed, and even more dangerously, the press had begun to create pathetic cliché phrases for battles.

For O.P., that would have been the worst thing that could happen to his men short of injury or death. Morale was vitally important in combat, and having a bunch of newsies target his troops with phraseology could prove disastrous. He had forcefully pressured

Army command in Tokyo to keep the mission a top secret event. "Nobody knows," he argued. "And that includes our press guys. Even our own PR guys. They cannot be allowed to inform the enemy what we are up to."

His forced urgency paid off. He had been absolutely right and Mac had at least bought into it. One good notch for the man.

From Inchon, the Marines, including Strickland's unit, pushed inland to Seoul, the capital of South Korea. After heavy fighting including bombardments that killed thousands of civilians, they secured the city by the end of the month.

Smith's success was darkened however by his difficult if not impossible relations with his Army commander, Major General Edward M. Almond, whose official title was Commander of X Corps.

Almond was well known as a forceful, energetic individual, but also as a rude and high-handed officer who was disliked in nearly every corner of the Marine Corps and much of the Army. He treated Smith as though he were camel dung. Almond's reasons were based wholly on what he considered to be military immaturity.

Smith was from Texas, had graduated from the University of California at Berkeley, "as an ROTC candidate of all things." He did not, in other words, graduate from Annapolis, nor from West Point, as the arrogant Almond had.

Almond complained constantly that Smith was too sluggish in advancing on Seoul, as though there were no enemy in his path to slow him down. It was Almond who wanted to leap ahead of reserves, supplies, and medical aid.

Part of Almond's complaint rang true, but for the wrong reason. Smith was a cautious exacting commander who favored careful tactical maneuvers not only to win battles, but to keep his men alive as much as possible.

The Marines were gutsy in battle. Always. But they had also developed battle maneuvers and fire teams that the army had not worked out. Marine infantry worked with teams. Each team was trained to work with other teams in their platoon, companies, battalions, regiments and divisions. The bottom of the totem pole in other words, often worked with the top and all the elements in between. And squad leaders were expected to make decisions in battle when necessary. To be flexible, to bend the rules if victory was to be the ultimate outcome. Not so for the army.

"Fire and Maneuver" became the basic infantry philosophy for the Marines. Each platoon had 9 Browning Automatic Rifles (BAR), while each army platoon had only three such weapons. Marine platoons were broken up into squads. Each squad was broken down to fire teams. The design had proved to be successful not in just defeating the enemy, but in keep as many Marines alive as was possible even in the worst of battles.

Unfortunately for the army, they were still pretty much fighting like they did in World War I. The infantry operated with one set of rules, and nobody was expected to adapt, even if such creativity was necessary for victory.

One other thing bothered O.P. He believed that Almond and Mac were reckless and too concerned with personal headline-grabbing triumphs. In that regard, Smith was on the money. Smith had also argued, weeks before he'd gotten to Hagaru-ri, that, "there are six to ten divisions of Chinese at the Yalu." Meaning, they simply couldn't do anything about that with the few men he had available.

Almond fired back, "That's impossible. There aren't two Chinese Communist divisions in the whole of North Korea." He was reiterating MacArthur's conviction.

He lowered his glasses. From his seat in the tiny Cessna, Smith looked down at the disaster that Almond and Mac had created. A mess he feared that he may not be able to salvage. His mind raced with thoughts concerning a victorious conclusion to what appeared to the American press as a defeat. He couldn't help but flash back to the beginning before he could figure out the conclusion.

In October, Smith's division was ordered north toward the Changjin (Chosin) Reservoir, with the ultimate goal of driving the enemy back to the Yalu River to complete the conquest of North Korea. They had pushed right up to the Manchurian border, which as far as they were concerned, was China.

That was when Smith and Almond got into a donnybrook of words. Mac's instructions, according to Almond, were to make a rapid advance to the Yalu along roads that showed up in EUSAK's supply of maps. Unfortunately most of the roads didn't exist and the maps, known as charts, were fraudulent.

Smith argued that the planned movement would lead to disaster. In his opinion it would leave his men widely dispersed far inland in the mountains in the dead of winter, without adequate flank protection, and they would be dependent upon a single, narrow serpentine road for supplies. It was Napoleon at Waterloo, where the famous emperor met his first and only military failure, which everyone knew, did the man in.

MacArthur's and Almond's drive north was, in other words, "Insane." Nonetheless, Smith was ordered northward. Almond and Walker each believed there were "Scads of roads up there."

With very little confidence in success, Smith moved slowly north from Hungnam, a port city along the coast, through Koto-ri to Hagaru-ri and Yudam-ni in the vicinity of the Chosin Reservoir. His final argument when accepting the orders was that he could only move as fast as the slowest equipment and no faster than the supply and food that would have to follow.

He was pleased while looking down at the road from his plane that he had been so ornery about stockpiling ammo and rations along the way. Those rations might be what saves these men now, he thought. If only I could get the damned stuff up here. Quickly. If not, then they were all in deep shit and very few of them might survive.

Only yesterday he had ordered an airstrip be built near the reservoir to ferry in supplies and take out casualties. It was at that time that Smith's personality became "boss O.P." and when it mattered that he become thusly respected. But it had been too late.

The Bird Dog bounced hard against something, air pocket he figured, then settled into its droning slow flight again. Cessna had built a hell of an airplane, he thought. Got to write them a note of thank you.

He continued to search the ground below. He had to find either his men or his enemy. One would tell him where the other was. He remembered right then that Almond had suggested a retreat. "Leave the equipment behind, just bug out," he had said. Smith was still raging inside over that message. Cut and run? Bullshit.

Smith had refused. He knew his Marines could break out, fight and kill the Chinese who had blocked the only road out of there in four or five places. He grimaced. His 5th and 7th Marine force, along with the 11th Marine artillery, was on the wrong side of the trap. They had moved forward two days after Thanksgiving and they'd taken Yudam-ni and the ridges surrounding it. Mission accomplished.

Colonel Harold Roise, an outstanding World War II officer set a perimeter by the book, and then reported to him his plans for the attack the next day. Smith blinked, held his eyes shut for a few seconds. His face glistened with sweat while the wind whipped through the cockpit. Colder than a well digger's ass and he's sweating. He laughed at the incongruity and then applied his thoughts to his men below. Body heat he thought, that's the only thing keeping my men from freezing to death. Keep 'em moving and they'll survive the conditions. That and the challenge.

Sweat from fear, sweat from hustling, enough to freeze the lips and ears and shut their eyes. But also enough to keep them warm under whatever garments they have.

Smith was angry. His Marines had fought a losing battle with a winning attitude and had damned near accomplished the impossible. But a hundred-thousand or more Chinese against two-thirds of a division of Marines had finally taken a toll. The textbook was gone, only blood and guts remained. "To hell with the book," he muttered into the noisy engine of the plane. "We'll rewrite the damned thing."

The plane banked to the right, bringing him back to reality. He had to solve his immediate problem. In the very early morning hours his Marines had come under fire in temperatures far below twenty degrees Fahrenheit. It nearly decimated his forces. Along with human life, way too much ammunition and C-rations disappeared. An enemy led by a general called Sun Shin-lun, a man he thought to be either craftily intelligent or just damned lucky, had really done a number on them.

He watched while a pocket of Marines below them appeared trapped in a ditch, poised at the embankment of what was probably a stream or a river now hidden under ice and snow. They looked prepared to fight. Up the road and around a bend he saw Chinese ground troops preparing for an attack.

"Drop down, Hawk," he ordered his pilot.

Lieutenant Colonel Trevor Hawk a former Corsair fighter pilot was at the controls. He was the only flight officer in the area when O.P. wanted someone to take him aloft to find the goddamned enemy and their own valuable Marines.

"We've got to warn them."

They were only a hundred feet off the ground, hanging there like a kite with full flaps down and the plane riding on the edge of a stall. The only other plane in the U.S. military that could fly like that was the OY, a plane built by Stinson. Of the two, Hawk preferred the OE.

Hawk searched the road for his bearings, wondering at the same time if they'd really get through the day alive. He dipped the wing while adding a touch of power to prevent a stall in the turn. Full flaps would do that to you if you weren't awake. With the general aboard Hawk was intentionally cautious.

"Right over them, Hawk," O.P. shouted over the engine noise.

"They shoot these toys down just for the fun of it." It was cautionary statement only, just to remind the general where in a world of reality he was.

Lousy timing. The engine coughed and Hawk was forced to straighten the plane and push it's throttle in a bit more while making sure his carb heater was still on. The Continental engine roared back to life. "Just the left tank running dry," he called out. The right tank was on the down side of the bank, so Hawk had to bring the plane around in a tight left turn. O.P. adjusted his body in the tight cabin and worked out of the left side.

O.P. nodded to his pilot's skill. Hawk had been right about getting the commander out of harm's way, but today he'd have to let O.P. work things out even though they were assuredly an inviting target for the Chinese. "Can you slow down a bit more, Hawk?"

The Marines below them would be slaughtered if he didn't do something. He'd begin rewriting the staid old tactics book right now.

"Make one low pass," he urged.

Hawk slowed enough to let the plane drop down fifty feet. He pushed on the right rudder, brought the plane back to level flight. He had gotten too far south of the men on the road. He pulled the stick back a touch to keep the nose up and dropped his flaps to twenty degrees. They were vulnerable now. More than ever before. He found himself gripping the stick hard and his ass began to sweat, waiting he supposed for the explosion from a Chinese rocket or even a few heavy caliber rounds.

When they got over the Marines below, he defied aeronautical physics and put the plane on its wing tip. That would give Smith the best look at the men below.

"Aww crap," Smith yelled, "there's a Marine running across the road." It was Hughes going for his fallen Marine.

Smith popped open his window. "Pull your power back, Hawk." Leaning out the open window, he yelled, "You've got Chinese around the bend!"

* * * *

Strickland waved to the plane, his long fingers appearing more like icicles than human digits. "I don't know who that crazy Marine is, but he's got my vote for being gutsy."

"Wouldn't want my ass flying 'round in this crap," Fraker quipped. If you took his helmet off and stripped Snake Fraker of his field clothes and the cigar stub that forever protruded from his mouth, shaved his facial growth and gave him a shower, he would look like your average American government issue Marine drill instructor with his own bulldog voice. Only thing was, Fraker wasn't average. At least that's what the men around him figured. He had a killer's instinct, the right amount of bravado to get him through hell, and the outward compassion of a warthog, even though, like most veneer-tough Gyrenes, he cared for his men like he was their mother. Strickland also thought Fraker grinned too much for a guy who had spent his youth in Okeene, Oklahoma catching rattlesnakes.

"You're just mother'n again, Snake."

"Picked up the habit at Parris Island," Snake snapped.

"The mother'n or being a warthog?"

An explosion in front of them pierced the air. Shrapnel flew past them, except for one small piece that smacked into Blade's heavy-duty bayonet sheath. "God dammit," he yelled. He was knocked down by the impact but he was all right.

Hughes was returning across the road with the wounded Marine when a shell from a Chinese rocket launcher ripped his helmet off and then exploded about twenty yards farther on. Hughes was flattened to the icy road. The wounded Marine he'd been carrying died before he hit the ground. Three Marines down from Strickland's position, young men who'd raised their curious eyes above their protective parapet also perished either from shrapnel or the concurrent machine gun spray of bullets that rained down from the Chinese at the bend in the road.

"I'm hit, I've been shot," Corporal Craig yelled. He sounded surprised, as though he never expected it. Then he slumped down into the ditch and died. The three freshly dead Marines slid on the ice along the ditch as though logs down a flume.

Strickland jumped up and ran to Hughes. "Get your ass outta

here, Joe," he yelled. But Joe was unconscious. Strickland yanked him up in a fireman's carry and dashed back sliding into the ditch without much control. Drier, Snake, Polanco, and two other surviving Marines were quickly engaged in a tracer-bullet fight with Chinese soldiers who had brazenly appeared around the bend. Ten Chinese collapsed. Dead. Four who came with them dashed back for cover. Strickland set Hughes down and leaned back to inspect his friend. "Aww, God," he moaned.

Hughes was alive, but the back of his head appeared to be shattered or fractured or missing a piece of his skull. Blood flowed but froze, cauterizing in a lump on Hughes's exposed skull.

"God damn it," Strickland yelled.

"We gotta get outta here," Polanco shouted over the gunfire.

Fraker kept shooting at the few Chinese who were brave enough to continue to probe around the bend in the road, which now seemed to them to be a lot closer than they had thought it was.

"They're gonna get on the hill behind us Skipper," Drier shouted. He dropped a Chinese soldier with three successive shots from his M-1. The empty clip flew out with a loud ping noise. "Shit, Blade, gimme a clip."

Polanco tossed Drier a clip and he quickly jammed it into his rifle. He raised it and continued shooting. He was beginning to believe that there were more Chinese on this road than there were people in his home town.

Marine corporal Washington came alongside Strickland. "Lieutenant, we gotta get outta here. Too many of 'em."

Strickland was still trying to help Hughes. "Give me a hand here, Washington." They lifted Hughes and tried to move him out of the line of fire, but their boots couldn't hold on the ice and they went down, sliding together while hanging on to the wounded Hughes. They slid for about ten feet down the flume.

"Shit," Strickland yelled out.

"They's pulled back, Skipper," Fraker said.

Drier came to Strickland and tugged at his skipper's jacket, keeping his eyes turned away from the awful sight in Strickland's arms. "Lieutenant, we gotta bug out, or we're all gonna be dead."

"Nobody else here but us," Polanco shouted out. "And I'm getting' low on ammo."

Fraker came to help with Hughes. "C'mon Skipper. We'll get him down the road a piece. More 'n likely safer there." Then as though he had to explain it, he nodded to the dead Marines with them and said, "Don't think we can take them with us."

Strickland lifted Hughes to his shoulders. "We're taking this one. Take off," he ordered.

Farther south and still flying low in the Bird Dog, General Smith missed catching the action on the road. Hawk had pushed the throttle to the firewall and dug them out of the hole they were in and headed safely south.

Smith's attention returned to putting his 1st Division back together. He remembered that just two days before, on Thanksgiving Day, Commanding General of the Army's 7th Division, Major General David Barr, met privately with him and confided, "I am seriously concerned about the future, Oliver. We are in trouble." When Smith asked him why he was concerned, figuring he already knew the answer, Barr surprised him with, "Because we have only one day's supply of food and ammo on hand."

"And we've reported this to command?"

Barr nodded, "Almond himself," he said.

"We have stored some supplies at Hagaru-ri."

"They're gone, General. Used up. Some were blown up in the trucks used to get them north. Army and Marines. We're stripped, sir. Haven't had any fresh supplies for a few days now."

Smith remembered turning to his plot board and thought, we are there. Out of supplies, troops, and quite possibly the ability to fight. So much for a five star army general's overwhelming ego.

When the plane touched on the airfield it took Hawk all of twenty feet to stop the OE. Smith, his sharp nose turned an odd dark purplish hue from the cold hissing air that moved through the plane, ordered Hawk to report to him at his CP in an hour. "I want you available to fly me at all times, Hawk. You showed me some spunk on this run." Then he smiled a little grin and added, "Mixed with the right amount of caution of course. I like that in a man. Shows he's got respect for life."

Twenty minutes later Smith sucked down a lung full of stale C-ration cigarette smoke created by his staff of weary Marines, and stared at the situation map in front of him, a map that had not gotten better during his absence. His staff remained quiet. That's the way he liked it. It was time to think this through, time to come to terms with hell. Smith's helmet remained on his head. His thin frame appeared to be a pencil with a huge eraser at the top. Yet no man, no Marine had any more strength of character or physical endurance than Oliver Prince Smith.

His men already understood that Smith disagreed with Almond and Mac on how the Marines should handle this fight. The Army generals wanted the Marines to retreat immediately, leaving their equipment. Even though badly damaged, the Marines thought differently.

"Retreat? Retreat, Hell!" Smith had yelled. Smith's reaction had caused the top general in the world to reel backwards.

"We'll take everything and everyone with us that we came in with and it won't be a retreat," he continued firmly. He glanced around and then continued into the phone, "We'll attack in another direction." They would kill more enemy than they would lose of their own—and by a large ratio.

No matter which way they headed, they would be fighting Chinese. How in the hell could it be a retreat if the Chinese army had them surrounded? "We're heading south and we'll tear them a new asshole." The move would later become legendary as a "retrograde," but by any Marine's jargon, it was still a goddamned helluva fight.

Smith couldn't help but reflect that it was General Almond who had earlier emphasized to him that MacArthur wanted the 1st Marines to make a "Pincer movement right up the middle. Pull the Eighth Army and the Koreans together; trap the Chinese. Pinch the bastards." Now, it was Almond who felt the gripping tightening effect of the Chinese, and Almond, and Walker, and MacArthur who wanted to cut and run.

Ironic.

"General?" Colonel Ballstrop broke in. Ballstrop was Smith's G-2, his Intelligence commander. And he looked the part. He stood medium height, had a familiar balding head and thin mustache. The man could play the role in a movie, Smith thought. "The ROK II Corps has disintegrated and the Eighth Army has come to a standstill," Ballstrop said calmly. For him it had always been a chess game, one where lives could be saved or lost. He was a calculator, a planner. And he'd been with Smith for a long time.

Smith looked into his G-2's eyes. "They haven't joined up?"

"No sir. There's a 25-mile gap in the lines."

Ballstrop didn't like the cliché term "hole in the lines." He rather preferred to define exactly what was happening. And the word gap did it for him.

"For chrissakes, just what in the hell were we supposed to pincer?"

O.P. didn't like the word pincer, which in army terms meant going up the middle of the enemy and pushing them to the sea left and right. It was one of Mac's favorite words, which made O.P. wonder if that's why he hated it so.

Before Ballstrop could respond, a bleary eyed Captain Karoly, the paunchy guy with the unlit Cuban always sticking prominently from his breast pocket, called over from the radio bench.

"Colonel Litzenberg's demanding more food and ammunition, General. They're running out fast, sir."

"Order up everything he needs and get it there immediately. Strip our mess hall of chow. Get them all the munitions we have around here in reserve," he paused, then added, "Get the army reserves into this now. Call the Brits. 'Bout time we got them involved."

Karoly took off with orders in hand.

O.P. dropped his chin and closed his eyes for a moment in prayer. He had the Brits and his army combat teams had a few trucks of food and ammo. He wondered if their chances of getting there in time were good, or if getting there at all was just a coin toss. God help them all.

As soon as Oliver Smith's staff could put it together, Lt. Colonel Drysdale headed north with a new force made up of units from other battle groups including 41 Commando, a unit from the 1st Marines, and a tank group. They moved out under protective fire from howitzers.

Donald B. Drysdale was a long-legged, tightly reserved and proper British officer. He was commander of the Independent Commando, Royal Marines known as 41 Commando. Some historians would later call Drysdale's force "Task Force Drysdale," but army purists never referred to the units with that general term.

Drysdale had fought in the Big Deuce with Montgomery, helping to quell the ferocity of Rommel. Now, he was being asked to run supplies up to beleaguered Americans.

"Piece of cake," he responded with his trademark thin-lip smile. "Done, as it were," he added with solemnity.

Lorries and armored personnel carriers loaded with British commandos roared up the long nameless MSR toward Yudam-ni. A contingent of Marine Corps six-by trucks carrying Marine headquarters and service personnel also joined in with them.

Marine F4U Corsairs swooped low and spread newly killed Chinese across the landscape with fiery tracers laid out neatly in wide swaths of steel and copper shrapnel. Occasionally a huge ball of fire from napalm would explode, sending shock waves of terror and agony through the Chinese.

Corsairs were designed for low level ground support during World War II, and the pilots who flew them knew just how to strafe for effective kill ratios. While their guns blazed away they'd kick their rudder pedals, right, left, right, left, until they were through with their pass. By doing so, bullets didn't just walk along the ground in a straight line like you'd see in a Hollywood movie. Instead they criss-crossed like a huge broom sweeping the landscape, ensuring that anyone in their wake was killed.

The sounds and heat and fireballs sent notice to those at the rear of the Commando 41 column that the Brit commandos at the front of the convoy were more into the war than they were. They also understood that it would be only minutes before they dove into hell along with their comrades. Tyros were eager, the veterans weren't.

While Drysdale's force proceeded northward, Navy and Marine R-4Ds along with Army C-47s, risked ground fire from all directions when they flew into the airstrip at Hagaru-ri and Koto-Ri, bringing quickly gathered medical supplies and some ammunition. Once off-loaded, they waited to retrieve the wounded for a quick flight back to Japan. Farther up Bird Dogs and Flying Jeeps also known as the OY, struggled against a heavy snowfall and nearly zero visibility to retrieve some of the worst cases of wounded.

"Everything seems to be going as planned," Drysdale's second in command reported over the radio to his leader. Lanky British Tank officer Major Hague was at the head of the column where he commanded the force of tanks that led the group northward. Drysdale's own opinion of Hague was not especially complimentary. "He is an opinionated young man."

Hague had refused Drysdale's order to distribute his seventeen tanks along the length of the convoy in order to offer protective cover for the foot soldiers, trucks, and personnel carriers, insisting instead that they should, "Punch through as a unit at the front of the column." It was a classic military mistake.

A tank driver could reverse course or turn back by leaning heavily on the control of his right or left track, braking one and running up the other or reversing one while jamming the other forward. This would allow him to "rotate" his tank. But still, having done that he would not be able to escape past the vehicles behind him, especially if one of them had been put out of action. It was in effect, a potentially chaotic trap and Hague drove right into the hellhole it presented.

"Not exactly as I had planned," Drysdale murmured coolly.

Were it known, Drysdale's biggest problem with Hague was that in spite of the man's arrogance he liked him. Liked him for his coolness, his history, and the fact that he had been a good tank commander back in the "Panzer battles."

"Quite by the book," Hague responded while scratching at his mustache. He sounded indifferent although Drysdale knew him to be unbendable.

"Hmmm. So it would seem," Drysdale said more distinctly, not meaning it.

Hague, stood alone with his upper body out of the turret of his vehicle. He frowned. They were just north of Koto-Ri now.

"Hold on there, Colonel," Hague shouted over the radio.

Drysdale stiffened. Hague had spoken with a sound of fear not heard in his voice before.

"Something's happening," Hague continued. He ducked down into his tank, pulled the hatch cover over him and with wide eyes motioned to his tank commander to take a look ahead. Something terrible was happening, something not in the book.

Without warning, heavy mortar, machine gun fire, and a few rockets rained down on the convoy like fiery pellets of exploding steel. Quite suddenly, seventeen tanks were facing a hugely difficult challenge. They were targets, yet had no targets in sight to fire back at and besides, they were single file on an especially narrow road.

"We're under heavy attack, Colonel," Hague shouted into his radio. A newfound humility swept over him. He could hear the explosions through the steel walls of his tank, and he didn't like them one damned bit. It seemed to him that it was better to fight other tanks. Bunkered or hidden mortars and rocket launchers were something totally new for him.

Drysdale jumped from his lorry and ran hell-bent to the head of his column, passing all the tanks his officer had jammed together on the road.

He jumped up on Hague's tank and pulled open the hatch. "Get out of there, man," he shouted. "You can't fight a war tucked into your goddamned tank."

Hague stuck his head out, glanced around. It was calm for a moment. The Chinese were reloading or regrouping or something. He was sure of it. He looked into Drysdale's eyes, his own a blur of confusion and panic.

"Sorry sir," he said. "But the Chinese have a rather heavy barrage of mortars. We don't know where, sir. We have no way at all to fire upon them."

His enemy was out of sight, and as far as he knew, out of range. Then, returning abruptly to his recognized character, he asked with his best British demeanor, "Should we press on?"

Drysdale wasn't dumb. He could see the dangers up ahead in his tank commander's eyes. This was a normally brave man he'd remembered from the past, one who had just smartly ducked out of death's way in order to command again. At the moment he didn't care about the young man's personality or his momentary withdrawal from the heat. He had his own troops to think of.

"I should rather think this is General Smith's call," he answered stiffly. "Do bring him up on the radio, Major."

"You must push through to Hagaru at all costs, Colonel," Smith replied loudly to Drysdale. "If you don't get that road open, thousands of Marines will die at the reservoir." Unseen by Drysdale, Smith tapped Koto-ri on his situation map with his pointer. He nodded to his understanding G-2.

Ballstrop, now working in more than his official role, fired up more adrenaline than he was accustomed to and jumped across the room to another field phone.

Smith continued speaking to Drysdale. "I'll get some tanks up there to help."

He hoped promised support would motivate the Brit. He wasn't lying, but neither was he sure he even had any tanks available.

Ballstrop pulled his field phone from his ear and motioned to O.P. that they had a few and they were headed up there.

Smith listened a moment to the anxious voice at the other end then said, "Right away. They're leaving as we speak."

A few miles north Strickland collapsed to his knees. He'd been carrying Hughes over his shoulders and it had finally taken a toll. He lowered his friend onto the snow. They were at the base of Hill 1120. His weary mind had chosen the hill because it gave them the advantage of overlooking the steep valley adjacent to the long road to Hagaru.

He was still trying to get a grip on what had happened to them and where they were. There were only five Marines remaining now, with one, Joe Hughes, about to die.

"He ain't gonna make it, Lieutenant," Snake snapped off like a shot from a rifle. "You gotta let him die like a Marine, boss." Snake understood the relationship between the two officers, hell, he'd been with them on Okinawa hadn't he? But that was then and this is now. Hughes was a good man. Strickland was a good man, but goddammit, none of us is gonna be a good anything if we don't get ourselves outta here. To Fraker, Corps history in the 'cific was tight back then. A short handed Corps begot many relationships. But, things gotta keep movin'. "We'll come back later and get 'im. If 'n we make it."

"He's not dead, Snake. And he's not gonna die."

Snake moaned audibly and fell back into the snowpack that had built up against the large boulder behind him. "Yes, sir," he moaned.

"Too many Marines already dead, Snake."

Strickland's voice sounded hollow. Snake too, was an ally from his past. An important one at that. Didn't matter though, Strickland wasn't about to give up on his closest friend. Hanging his head down, not able to look Snake in the eyes he added, "Look, I'm not holdin' you men to hang in here with me. You can bug out, no hard feelings." He spit snow out of his mouth, rubbed his painfully frozen chin to get some feeling, then added, "That road down there heads south to safety. You'll probably run into a bunch of Marines."

"Don't count on it," Snake fired back. "Thing's are lookin' a might fucked up."

"If he's breathing, I'm sticking with him."

His eyes came up and bored through Snake's own tepid pools that lingered under eyebrows that appeared more like horizontal icicles. Crap, Strickland thought. Snake looks deader than Joe. White and pale and dusty with powder as though about to be buried. His mustache was missing under an icepack although his beard had survived. His dark eyes are staring at me from the head of an ancient statue. Two friends gone if I don't get them out of here.

But the gunny wasn't dead. His mouth cracked the ice that covered his face, and his expression became the same as Dick Tracy's archenemy Prune Face. "It's a mistake," he said.

Strickland wondered if he appeared the same as Snake. He glanced around to Blade and Drier. Only Drier still looked human. How's he do that? The kid is one macho son of a bitch. He could barely get his head turned back it was so goddamned cold.

"Marines look out for each other. So do good friends."

Snake nodded but no one could see it. "We better move, Skipper. Turning into an ice cube ain't a good idea."

Strickland tried to move his legs but damned near couldn't. They were not just frozen, they had been used up. "Hell," he groaned as he rose, "it's like on Okinawa when I got it. If it hadn't been for Joe Hughes," he paused, then went on, "I'd of been dead a long time ago."

Fraker moved his arms outward and then brought them back in and then back out in an effort to heat them up. "Shit. Let's go. I'll carry 'im fur a while." He knelt down along side Hughes. "Maybe you'd a been better off if'n he hadn't saved you." Snake's teeth were chattering along with his words. He stopped. He reached up and repositioned his helmet on his head. More'n likely he'd just said the wrong thing and now the damned helmet felt heavy all of a sudden. Fuck'n war was the pits.

Strickland knelt down on the opposite side of Fraker. Drier and Blade now stood over the two of them, barely able to keep themselves from shaking apart.

"Yeah. You might be right," Strickland said.

Fraker looked into his officer's eyes. "You gonna carry 'im or me?"

"I will. But thanks for the offer."

Fraker started to rise but not before he said, "Seems like we always gonna be in a frickin' assed war."

It was the first time Strickland had heard the gunny say anything that wasn't upbeat or straight ahead. "Seems," he said quietly.

Strickland raised up with Hughes straddled across his shoulders. Keeping him balanced with one hand, he pulled out his half full canteen of Vat 69 and offered it to Snake. The Snake took it, gulped down a mouthful and handed it back to his skipper who took a swig for himself. When he was done he handed it down to Drier indicating to pass it along to Blade. Then he turned back to Snake and said simply, "Livin's a lot better'n dyin'. Even with all this inconvenience."

Drier handed the canteen to Blade, squinted through the snow that seemed to never stop falling, and blurted, "Inconvenience?"

"Loco," Blade said. "Muy loco."

The men glanced to each other, then back to Strickland. They started to laugh, one of those nervous chuckles that helped calm uneasy souls.

"Okay," Snake said cutting them off. "We're with you, skipper. I guess till hell freezes over."

Drier laughed . "Fuck Gunny, can't you see? Hell's already froze over."

"Not till your balls drop off, kid."

"Nice talk for a gringo," Blade put in.

PFC Polanco was a husky, bullish Marine from Southern California. They'd nicknamed him 'Blade.' Only Drier remained among Blade's Marine friends. All the others had been killed or seriously wounded. He patted the long-knife, his bayonet that hung from his belt. He felt at ease with it. Polanco thought often of his girl friend in L.A., and his old gang, just a bunch of street guys who liked to fight other gangs, drink beer, smoke Lucky Strikes and play Wurlitzers known as juke boxes in the local pub until past midnight. They were known by the neighborhood as the Machos. It was a good time back then, a hell of a lot better than where he was now. He'd also lost a lot of weight over here in Korea. His mama wasn't going to know him. From a ball shaped guy to a stick. And this permanent crew-cut on his head. Bullshit on that.

"Thar's somethin' 'bout you Blade, makes me wonder why God's let you come this far," Snake chortled. Spirits were rising with the sarcasm, the dark humor, moving bodies, and Strickland was glad to hear it.

"That, Sarge, is because I am one of God's chosen few."

"Listen," Strickland said, holding his hand up for them to pipe down. The tone in his voice froze each of them. What the hell was about to happen now?

They could hear booming howitzers, exploding mortars, and screaming Corsairs.

"Shitsakes, they're south of us, too," Fraker said.

"¡Mios Dios!" Blade said. "I knew L.A. was safer than this fucking place."

"Knock it off," Strickland ordered. He pushed his canteen back into its pouch. "We're gonna make it 'cause I say so. Those Chinese bastards aren't taking us down."

Snake grinned. "That's what I like 'bout you Skipper. You never did know when to quit."

It was known as the Naha-Shuri-Yonabaru line. It seemed every Marine still alive in May of 1945 was on Okinawa to fight the Japanese. There were the 7th marines, the 5th Marines, the 22d, and the 29th Marines. Before they arrived there were the 1st and 6th Marine Divisions who after a month of devastating combat had bludgeoned General Ushijima's defensive belt, killing more than 50,000 Japanese. Ushijima broke off the fight.

The Army was also there along with Naval bombardment groups that sat offshore providing on-call artillery. Marine Corps aviation and the Army Air Corps along with the Navy's great flying force were there. It was the entire Pacific Fleet, by now the most experienced battle tested Navy in the history of the world, and they had the Ryukyus surrounded.

The 1st Marines made the initial mid-island landing seem like a cakewalk. They rushed across the Yara Hikojo airfield from the west to the east. The airfield had been used by Japanese fighter planes and would later be known as Kadena Air Base, after American forces took over the island.

There were of course a few hotly contested firefights with their push, but the Marines worked through them quickly. With mission success, they stayed put, following orders to hold the airfield along with Army units. They would stay in reserve in case the rest of the Island proved more difficult than what they had already experienced.

Sergeants Strickland and Fraker were with the 1st Marines who were fighting along the Naha-Shuri-Yonabaru line.

They were feeling pretty cocky by now. They'd come through the Canal, Peleliu, and now Okinawa. What they hadn't figured on was the endless supply of snipers who the Japanese had planted in trees and caves along many of the hillsides. These independent operators were chartered to kill anyone at any time of their own choosing. Many of these snipers played possum during the hottest part of the battles. They would simply wait for their moment.

Even though Okinawa may appear small on a map, although geographically narrow, it's a long mountainous island for a foot soldier. It is comprised of seemingly endless hills and valleys, much of it with low brush. It wasn't always a part of Japan. Before the Japanese conquered the Ryukyus Islands, Okinawa was part of an independent nation known as Okinawa Kingdom.

The natives had carved terraced rice paddies into the hillsides as well as a catacomb of protective caves, each hidden by rich foliage fed every day by a consistent afternoon rainfall. Japanese soldiers used the native caves but also dug more of them during the war-years while waiting for the inevitable arrival of the Americans. They were so well camouflaged that too many Americans died before they figured out how to deal with the snipers and "cave dwellers."

Flamethrowers were brought in to help rout the small units of enemy from these "hillside holes." The flamethrowers would blast the voracious oxygen eating flame across the mouth of each cave they'd find, or directly into them. The flames would simply suck all the oxygen from the cave, leaving the Japanese soldiers inside to either suffocate to death or scramble for the entrance where they'd either explode in the ball of fire or be immediately captured or killed by rifle fire.

It was near one of these caves in the remote northern area of the island that Frank Strickland took two hits, one to his left hip and the other to his right shoulder just below the collarbone. He took a third hit in his abdomen. He collapsed first to his knees, then fell forward on his face. His helmet bounced off his head and rolled down the slope stopping in front of Staff Sergeant Hughes and the buck sergeant who was alongside him who referred to himself as The Snake.

"Goddamn it," Joe Hughes yelled. He raced across the open field to Strickland. He ran like a football halfback. He dodged to the right and then to the left. He bent down low and nearly found himself duck walking. He could hear bullets snap all around him like a hummingbird might sound when zipping around your head. Some were close enough to sound like popcorn in his ears.

Snake Fraker, who wished he had a flamethrower right then, flew past Hughes to the cave without the duck walk or dodging bullets. He fired his rifle the whole time into the cave that had been exposed when the sniper pushed the brush aside to fire at them. Then, one after the other he threw three shrapnel grenades into the cave. The explosions gave off a muffled sound telling him the grenades went in deeply or were jumped on by one soldier trying to save another.

"Frank," Hughes yelled into his ear when he got to Strickland. "Can you hear me?"

Nothing. Hughes ripped his first-aid kit from his belt and began to put pressure on Strickland's belly wound. He called out for a corpsman but no one else was near them except for Fraker. They had been on a search and destroy patrol and broken away from the main body to check the slopes. Fraker came back to them.

"If anyone's in that cave, Joe, they're dead now."

Hughes tied the bandage over Strickland's abdominal wound tightly. He then administered quickly to the shoulder wound. "Let's get him to a doc."

More battle sounds from Drysdale's convoy. Tumbling artillery followed by explosions along the road. A shell smacked into a truck in the middle of Drysdale's convoy, setting it afire. It created a serious roadblock for the vehicles behind. The column was suddenly split into two separate units and very much in trouble.

Drysdale continued to press ahead, leaving behind half his commandos, most of Company B of the 21st Infantry, and nearly all of the Marine Headquarters service troops. More than 700 troops that included 100 tank personnel were suddenly under the command of a reticent British officer.

Colonel Chidester was not thrilled with his new command position. "Let's get this convoy turned around, before we're plastered," he ordered over the horrendous sound of war.

They'd head back to Koto-ri he figured, back to safety. The road though, as he well knew, could become a bigger blockade than a division of Chinese. Turning the lorries around might prove impossible. Damn. Which one of those Americans got us into this wicket?

All along the column, admittedly frightened and pressured drivers worked their vehicles back and forth across the narrow strip in order to reverse direction. One truck went over the edge of the road into a snow bank that rose higher than the ditch. It became permanently glued there. Up and down the long convoy engines behaved like lunatics in a Charles Dickens prison. The sound of whining engines with RPMs that produced more noise than energy only caused truck tires to slip and skid on the icy road. The hands of the drivers became purple-numb from hanging on icy steering wheels that absorbed cold like a good beer in a fridge. Driver vision was minimized due to frosted or glazed windshields. The thick snowfall caused even more frustration and loss of vision. The trucks were barely able to move more than a few inches at each try. Death haunted them as though ultimate and soon. It was action without hope, a failed mission with no way out.

Then it happened. Before they were turned halfway around an entire infantry division of Chinese burst over the ridgeline and came down on them like mosquitoes attacking a campsite in late spring.

Chidester frantically ordered his survivors into the ditches. Marine Corps Corsairs appeared out of the clouds and zoomed down against the Chinese, piercing the air and the enemy with fire-blazing tracers and napalm. The Chinese swept through Chidester's men so quickly however, that the Colonel was captured before anyone knew he was in jeopardy. The Chinese dragged him off, towing him like a log in the snow. When they tired of that, a dozen of them stood around him while he tried to get up to his knees and then, without mercy, they bayoneted him until he was dead.

The ceaseless Corsair attacks finally caused the enemy to withdraw. Later that night when the air itself felt like a sheet of frozen crystals entering your lungs, the Chinese opened fire again. This time they increased their mortar bombardment, but amazingly they did not mount a full-scale ground assault.

U.S. Army Major John N. McLaughlin was in charge now. He'd had experience enough to understand why the Chinese hadn't attacked. "Their magic hour is when it's coldest, right 'bout midnight or shortly after," he explained to his troops. "They'll come then." They'd be ready this time, he insisted.

"We're short of ammo, Major," tobacco chewing Staff Sergeant Otto Jaks said. He spit into the snow when he spoke. He was tough, taut and always ready for a fight. His face had been carved out of granite, his jaw jutted out as though ready to start any brawl he might like. He stood like a utility pole, unbending, ramrod straight and wired. "It ain't gonna be a long fight." He sounded a bit like Gary Cooper, enough so that his men had nicknamed him, "Coop." If there was contradiction to this man, it was that he also exhibited signs of Arthur Godfrey's dry humor.

Just after midnight, McLaughlin was proved right. The Chinese first sent probes out. Then they began lobbing grenades and mortars into the American troops. Slowly, one by one, soldiers and Marines were killed or wounded while hurling back whatever ammo or grenades they had left in their arsenal. The kill ratio of four Chinese for every American wasn't high enough for the Americans to come out on top. It was obvious to the experienced that attrition by death would decide the winner.

Jaks crawled up to McLaughlin during a barrage of mortar shells. "We better get our asses out'a here, Major, or we ain't gonna have one."

"How's the ammo," McLaughlin shouted.

"We're down to knives and cold C-rations. I saw a guy throw a can of potatoes at a gook." Then, as though it were important he muttered, "The son-a-bitch ate them."

McLaughlin stared at Jaks a moment, always stunned at his deadpan humor, but more so at the realization that they were indeed out of ammo. They were, in other words, effectively out of action.

"Tell the men that I'm going to chat with that Chinese commander." There was a sudden lull. No sounds from either side. "No, wait. Call the men together."

Jaks frowned. For his money, speaking with the enemy commander seemed cowardly or treasonous. And calling the men together was suicidal. But, orders were orders so he raced off to heed his commander.

The survivors gathered around the major, their bodies more like chunks of ice from their mother's ice boxes than breathing humans, their desire to live only slightly stronger than their desire to die. McLaughlin rubbed the stubble on his gaunt face, his wool mask no longer effective against the endless Korean snow and the irritating wind.

"We're gonna vote on this one. We can give up, or fight to the death. The Chinese have promised to evacuate the seriously wounded."

He shifted his feet and kicked at loose ice with his boots. He wasn't a tall man, about the same height as his troopers. His shoulders were broad from having worked a lifetime on an almond ranch in Tracy, California. His chest was similar to a barrel, his arms once muscled, now seemed as gaunt as his face. And his face, usually tanned with a coarseness not unlike the almonds he worked with was now purple with splotches of white. He seemed more a corpse than a major.

"Liars," Jaks spit out. His voice came out as the sound of a man still ready to fight, a man who would never vote to give up. He was Sergeant York, or better McLaughlin thought, Randolph Scott. "You know they're liars, Major." The tone in Jaks's voice never changed. He was not a man afraid.

"It's a gamble," McLaughlin pressed. "I admit that. I suspect they'd just shoot the wounded. But I might be able to stall 'em long enough for a few of you to get to the others in the perimeter. Warn them. They can head south, return to Koto-ri. Regroup."

"Major's right Jaks," Gunny sergeant Morris growled, his voice not as crisp as it had been. The freezing temperature was playing hell with everyone, even the strongest among them. Morris turned to the group and said with the best he could muster up, "I want five volunteers."

Morris was stiffly straight up but for some reason also a bit bent over at his neck. His dark eyes bored through anyone he glanced at. He was always a soldier, never a jokester. He'd proved himself a great warrior while fighting at Bastogne, and then later near the Rhine. It was all snow and ice, he'd tell you. But it seemed hot all the time because of Jerry's persistent fighting and the grueling never-sleep atmosphere. He'd put on a few pounds since then, but Korea was taking them off. That was okay, he figured since his "five-eight" frame couldn't carry much anyway.

Every man stepped up. McLaughlin watched curiously while Morris chose his runners. When he finished, McLaughlin said, "We'll hold the Chinks down for about ten minutes."

"I figure there's about four hundred soldiers and Marines out there," Morris added. "You know where they are. Now, take off, and get 'em the hell out of here." Before they'd gotten five feet, the messengers were absorbed by darkness and snow and fear, their absence felt quickly, startlingly.

Sergeant Morris kept his eyes glued in the direction they'd headed while making clicking sounds with his mouth, a nervous habit when he grew impatient. When he figured they were out of earshot, he said, "Pray for 'em Major. They's on a suicide run and they don't even know it."

"Just stayin' here is a suicide mission," Jaks said. He had never sounded as resolute about his own death as at that moment. He pulled his bayonet from its sheath that hung on his web belt and seated it on his rifle. "Well, I'm takin' a bunch with me if I gotta go."

McLaughlin stepped on his words, trying to block them from the ears of the others. "They'll make it. Now if you'll excuse me, I promised to meet with a Chinese captain about our decision."

One hour later, McLaughlin and his remaining soldiers were taken prisoner. All the others he'd sent warnings to received his message and escaped the trap.

CHAPTER 3

DRIER TUGGED AT Strickland's field jacket. "Listen."

Strickland rose as quick as a jackrabbit wakened by hungry coyotes. He pulled himself up to the edge of the ditch and looked south along the road. He could hear the tanks and trucks, but he couldn't see them.

"When did it stop snowing?"

"An hour ago," Drier said.

"What day is this?"

Snake chuckled. "The day of, sir. You been sleepin' couple hours now."

"Damn."

"We put that poncho under ya, Skipper. Thought it might keep you from freezin' off your balls. And oh, I've gone without takin' my mornin' dump, Lieutenant."

"Funny."

"I missed my biscuits," Drier threw in. "And goldurn it, that ain't funny." He meant he hadn't eaten. And that included the hard-as-nails biscuits in his C-ration pack also known as John Wayne biscuits.

"Have a snowball son," Snake quipped with a somber tone that Drier had become accustomed to. Fraker would start that way but always end up making light of the subject. "Five snowballs a day, that's what it takes."

Fresh snow began to fall again as though on cue.

"They're comin' to save our butts, boys. We made it." Strickland stood, hoping to see farther down the road, but still he could only hear them. "The snow will provide us some cover."

"Better get your butt down Skipper, or you'll get us all kilt," Snake growled. Lieutenants, he thought, they're all the same, even though this one used to be enlisted. Gawd if only he, The Snake, could just run officers training school for just one year. He'd sure as hell change a lot of things in this man's Corps. He gritted his teeth, spit out tobacco juice, adjusted his helmet, picked up his M-1 and stood up against the agony of his older knees without complaining. What the hell, everything hurt, so why bitch now?

"I'll work myself down the gully and see if they're ours," he said.

Strickland turned his attention to Joe Hughes. His friend remained unconscious and yes, he looked nearly dead. But wasn't nearly dead also nearly alive?

"You okay, Skipper?" Drier asked. Drier was no dummy. He read Strickland's expression and thought his commander might be psyching out.

"Yeah. Like you. Just cold." What he didn't say was that he was putting them at risk because he'd made a promise to himself when his friend Tommy died. If he ever had a good friend again, and if that friend got into trouble, he'd do everything he could to save his life.

Hughes was covered with all the spare clothing they could muster, some from the dead, some from their own backpacks. He needed medical attention and he needed it quickly. Right then, Father Cavanaugh's consoling words after Tommy's death came back to Strickland.

"It's who you meet along the way . . ."

He tightened his lips, squishing them together to break the icy freeze that seemed to burn his flesh. His mission was clear. Get his friend to safety.

"Snake's comin' back," Drier said.

Fraker popped over the ledge abruptly. "It's the Brits, Lieutenant. And it looks like they've takin' a big-time Chink bath. Best part is they got a few Marines pushing the snow with them. Shit man, it's ass freezing cold," he added involuntarily waving his arms around again like he'd done before.

Strickland cocked an eye against the pain of his own frozen

brow. Fraker never complained. This had been his first complaint since Strickland had met him on Guadalcanal. Oh yeah, there was the normal bitching and all that, but never a complaint about what might be ailing him.

"You okay Snake?"

"Yes, sir. Just a bit too much of this white stuff. That's all." Snake frowned a bit. He knew he'd goofed. He'd keep his dumb mouth shut from now on. Keeping up the morale of the few men he had left was going to be tough enough without their gunny bitching. He reported what he'd gone out to learn.

"Long column. Tanks, trucks, troops. Couldn't see all of 'em. They're still under fire down the road. Want me to hustle a ride for 'im?" He nodded toward Hughes with a clear inflection for Strickland that he wanted a positive response.

"Sounds like they're headin' back to the reservoir. That might kill Joe."

"I figure we got a few more miles to get to Hagaru," Drier volunteered.

Snake was from the "old Corps." You didn't butt heads with a sergeant in the old corps and you wouldn't get away with it now either. He glared at Drier. "At this pace boy, it'll take another tour of duty to get there." He rolled his cigar from one side of his mouth to the other and quickly regretted his snappy words.

Drier nodded. Snake was upset, no sense making things worse. He'd let Fraker spit out his own form of apology, which he did.

"Harumph," Snake grunted. "That didn't come out right."

"Don't lose it on us now, Gunny," Blade quipped.

For Fraker, it was like he'd lost control of his outfit. "Son, you can get on a man's edge."

The clanking sounds of tanks increased beyond the bluff and below them. The men worked their way to the ledge of rocks and snow and peered down to the road. Icy crystal like snow was falling now, blowing into the eyes of the British soldiers in the column like tiny daggers.

"They've either lost quite a few or they got a whole gang of stragglers behind 'em," Fraker said.

Strickland turned his attention toward the rear of the column but the snow blanked it out. "Hard to tell."

The realization of conditions struck Fraker like slapshot against his head. The thought itself gave him pain but the prediction that came with it nearly knocked him out. "Lieutenant, if they ain't nobody back there, that means . . ."

". . . That we're completely surrounded and our neighbors are very close by."

"We're screwed."

"Just like L. A., man," Blade broke in. Nobody laughed.

Strickland spotted Lt. Colonel D. B. Drysdale, who had stopped the convoy and walked to the head of his column. He watched, unaware that Drysdale's Number 41 Independent Commando, a highly respected British outfit comprised of Royal Marines, was as tough as any Marine unit. Drysdale had also started his trip north with a detachment of 5th Marines at the rear of the column along with an Army infantry company. That's who Fraker had spotted.

On the road, Drysdale was concerned that they'd come this far too quickly and with surprisingly little resistance since the heavy attack north of Koto-ri. He'd lost a third of the Marines and most of the army infantry company, both given him by General Smith at Koto-ri. It had just struck him that the Chinese were gathering en masse somewhere nearby, possibly setting up a counterattack or an ambush to wipe them from the map. Without even drawing a line on his chart he knew he'd screwed up. He had walked them into a valley of death. They were on a narrow road, in freezing conditions, low on ammo and morale, and they were surrounded.

Drysdale's original orders were to move up the MSR with supplies that included heavy weapons. For ease of movement, all supplies and weapons remained in their shipping crates. He left Hungnam for Koto-ri believing the journey should be rather easy.

At the 4000 foot level, up the Funchilin Pass, the Unit arrived at Koto-ri where Marine Corps Colonel "Chesty" Puller's 1st RCT HQ was based. Drysdale was informed that the Chinese Communists (CCF) had blocked the northward road. Drysdale's Unit was then assigned the job of guarding the perimeter for the night.

Before sunup the next morning, General Oliver Smith ordered Drysdale to head north to help the beleaguered Marines at the Chosin. Drysdale's unit would be made up of 41 Independent Commando, G Company USMC, B Company 31st Infantry US Army, and elements of the Divisional train.

"You will fight your way to Hagaru, at the southern tip of the Chosin," Smith had explained.

The full complement of the Unit would consist of 922 men and 141 vehicles. During their first fight, near panic action took place with men having barely enough time to break out a section of 81mm mortars and A4 Browning LMGs, otherwise known by Americans as "light machine guns."

Drysdale then led his advance from Koto-ri at 0930. It was 29 November 1950. The snowing had stopped for a while, but the skies were still gray, dreary, and the temperature was below freezing.

Within two miles the Commando Unit and G Company were up against serious resistance, but at 1350 Drysdale was reinforced with 17 tanks from D Company 1st USMC tank battalion, which had moved up that morning thanks to Smith. Slow progress was resumed until at about 1615 when the column was halted about halfway to Hagaru. They had entered a defile.

A radio message from the Marines at the end of his column informed him that the Chinese had closed in and split the column into two sections. The radio was loud enough for Strickland and his men to catch the depressing report.

With his inimitable style Fraker recognized the complications ahead. "Crap, to get to the end of this column we'll need to break through those Chinks."

No one including Drysdale was yet aware that when the Chinese split the column, they had forced more than one unit of the force into complete disarray and confusion. The Heavy Weapons Section, the Assault Engineers and elements of 41 Independent Commando HQ, along with most of B Company and Division HQ were strung out in separate defensive perimeters. Each was surrounded on the Chinese army's terms alone.

The bottom line was clear. The Chinese had effectively broken the back of Drysdale's large force. Some units were lucky and returned with their survivors to Hagaru while others made it back to Koto-ri. Others negotiated a surrender to the Chinese.

Drysdale now stood alone. He radioed Smith and asked if he should continue on. The response from Smith was "at all costs."

Drysdale sighed heavily. For him, "All costs" usually meant "all lives lost." Drysdale's mission had been to break through to the divisional base 10 miles up the road at Hagaru. His earlier egotistic attitude hadn't helped his tactical maneuvering. He'd considered the battles between Hungnam and here a nuisance, even though he'd already lost about 600 men to KIA and WIA. A real pain in the arse he'd say.

Just as he was about to order the tanks to refuel before nightfall blackened the area, a thundering explosion from a Chinese artillery round smacked destructively into his lead tank, one he considered an artifact. It was a Churchill MKIV left over from the war with Germany. The tank blew up, sending Colonel Drysdale flying through the air, still alive, but wounded. His only thought before smacking into the snow packed ground was, "We've had it." His wounds would turn out to be minor.

"Damn!" Strickland yelled out. He pounded his fist into the ice crusted embankment. He started to get up but Snake yanked him back down with a tight grip on his belt.

"Lieutenant! You'll draw fire on us. I ain't chicken sir, but the reality is there's nothing we can do if we're going to save Joe, I mean Lieutenant Hughes. We got to push south. Use this goddamned snowy sum-a-bitch for cover. Let the Brits finish what they started here."

"That convoy's more 'n likely strung out a mile back," Drier said. "Maybe we can commandeer a truck and get the hell to Hagaru." He gently touched his slightly crooked nose, injured in a high school fistfight with Billy Bob Dumbshit. The fight was over Sally McCutcheon. Stupid fight since Sally McCutcheon wasn't interested in either Billy Bob nor Drier. Damnedest thing was every time he scratched his nose that's all he could think about. Except now. Now he was actually concerned that his nose would just fall off his face if he rubbed or scratched it too hard. But shit man, it was itching like hell and he needed badly to scratch it. Damn, no feeling. His fingers joggled the frozen snot on his upper lip. Damn. Damn. Damn. That hurt. He put his whole hand round his nose and mouth to warm them up, but his goddamned hands were just as cold. "Crap," he blurted out.

The snowstorm intensified, forcing slivers of ice to come at them as piercingly as those that took down General Custer. It cut their faces like tiny blades of steel. Fraker took control once again. It was time to move or they'd become ice statues. He aimed them southward.

"I prefer the scenic route to Waikiki Beach if you don't mind," Drier shouted into the renewed wind while following Fraker. "When this war's over, that's where I'm headed. Yessir, Waikiki. Mai Tais, pretty girls, the whole darned bit. I mean, if I still got a nose. Shit, I lose my nose I ain't gonna be good lookin' anymore."

Strickland scooped up Hughes while the shelling of the convoy continued. "Good," he grunted, mostly unheard. "I hate competition."

"Ya finally got it figured out Drier," Snake said. "We're all goin' to hell. And you'll be the ugliest damned Marine down there."

They began their trek southward along the monsoon ditch. They climbed above the road, moving parallel to it. The ditch was filled with snow and ice, too deep to push against it more than a few feet. They guessed it was one of the waterways that caught the spring runoff or fed the Chosin reservoir, which they hoped was falling farther behind them.

A quarter mile down the ditch, they paused to check out the convoy. They peered over the protective wall of snow and cringed at the destruction. "The Chinese are eating them alive," Drier said.

Polanco remained silent. Eerily so. He just shook his head. It was all such a waste. Damned waste. Fraker got to the point.

"I count fifteen kilt out there right now." He spit into the snow, adjusted his cigar and added, "Bastards!" He pointed to others who were trying to escape down the opposite slope.

"Man, let's hurry before they wipe out all the trucks," Polanco yelled, finally breaking his fast.

"Hey, you're alive," Drier chided. "Thought maybe you'd died on us."

"Fuck you."

"You wish. We could stay and fight," Drier urged not meaning it. He pushed the safety of his M-1 forward. He noticed his fingers were blue. Not yet gone, but getting damned close.

"Get your ass down the ditch," Snake ordered. "We got a wounded officer here. We'll be in the thick of it soon 'nough."

Drier and Polanco put their rifles at port-arms and pushed ahead in short, difficult steps through the heavy snow. It had stopped coming down. It was getting lighter even though it was later in the day. Something was happening to the weather.

"Sky's changin'," Drier said.

"Move it," Fraker yelled.

They'd try to get to the end of the convoy and salvage at least one vehicle for one very wounded brother. They also knew they'd get into a fight at the column's end. The Chinese had learned their lessons well from their ancestors. Attack the front, the middle and the rear simultaneously. Drier wondered if his skipper ever considered the enemy intelligent. They were, he had learned. Damned smart in fact when it came to fighting.

But Strickland didn't have time to think about all that. His heavy cargo continued to take a toll on his usually strong legs. He had gone a step beyond what other men might have done. He stumbled, crashed to his knees, slid a few feet on the ice before he sat on his butt to brake his sledding down the icy slope.

"Here, let me take him for a while," Fraker said.

Strickland handed Hughes over carefully.

"Ya know Skipper, you're a good 'un. But you're gonna get your ass kilt out here the way you do things."

"Keep moving," Strickland responded with a hoarse grating in his voice. In his own mind, Frank Strickland hadn't done enough. It wasn't just Hughes who bothered him. It was all the men he'd lost in the past few hours. They were under his command and he'd lost them. They'd never come back, never be found. Frozen corpses in a distant reservoir, skeletons of mankind's cruelty to itself. No, he wouldn't let this one get away. Joe Hughes would live or he'd die trying to save him.

Ahead of them, Polanco was the first to make it to the end of the convoy. The artillery hadn't worked its way back that far yet, but Chinese were firing rifles and machine guns from positions along the hillsides. The sounds of battle were loud, steady, boldly defining their scheme of death. Smoke filled the air adding an acrid odor that seemed to freeze in chunks when it hit them. Trucks burned. A tank was upside down and black from the fire that had engulfed it.

A half dozen vehicles had been able to turn around and get the hell out of there and head back to Hagaru. When Blade ran up to the last truck in line, the driver was furiously shifting from first gear to reverse and back, rocking the lorry on the narrow single lane road.

"Hey, we need a ride," Polanco shouted.

Three U. S. Army soldiers, themselves sunk into a snow bank while firing at the Chinese, shouted to him, "So do we, pal."

The driver was astonished to see the Marine. "Nifty. Just fuggin' nifty. How in the hell did you get here? Marines are supposed to be at the head of the column by now."

"We're not part of your convoy," Blade shouted over the roar of the engine.

"Aww, shit. Jump in mate, but don't ask me to stop."

At this point the driver didn't give a damn who rode his truck as long as they weren't Chinese. Rifle fire hit the truck. Two bullets passed through the windshield on the passenger side. The shattered glass nearly panicked the driver. Blade jumped up on the running board. "I've got a wounded officer and three others with me."

Just then, Drier jumped up on the other running board.

"Bugger off lads," the Brit exclaimed.

"Stop this truck," Drier shouted.

"Fuggin' Yanks. Where'd you come from? And can't you see we're takin' fuggin' hits?"

The Brit driver wore thick glasses, incongruous with his job as a driver. His nose barely protruded from under the rims and his entire head was covered with a green wool stocking cap. His body quaked from hard shivering due to the extreme cold. His cheeks were a deep purple while his nose looked like it belonged to Rudolph the reindeer.

"Yudam-ni. Separated from our outfit. Got any food?"

Artillery shells finally found the range. Rounds sailed overhead and crashed into the convoy a hundred feet up, taking out another truck. "Fuck!" the driver shouted in his best British tongue for his best invective. "You wantta ride? Okay, but I'm not waiting for anyone else."

Drier and Blade dove for cover while the Brit continued rocking his truck. Two more bullets penetrated the truck's windshield. The Chinese were getting the rifle range as well. The driver scrunched down in his seat as though doing so protected him more.

Strickland popped out of the ditch and skidded down the slope to the road. By now the truck was making its way fully around, its tires mostly slipping on the ice while trying to turn. All three axles were direct drive, but the tires still rotated without much forward movement, a process that also caused a bit of fishtailing.

"Pull up here," Strickland shouted.

The Brit shook his head. "No fuggin' way, mate." But then, after glancing at the American officer he said, "Gotta get out of here so me mates behind can move 'round. I'll pull up ten meters, slow for ten seconds. That's it. Be there."

Snake came out of the ditch with Hughes over his shoulders. "Comin' at you!" he yelled.

The truck slowed as promised but did not stop. The driver yelled, "Hurry."

The men helped Snake down and then loaded Hughes aboard. Just then another Chinese shell hit, this one only 50 feet away. It took out the second to last vehicle. Fragments hit the truck they'd just put Hughes into, some pieces driving all the way through the right side of the truck blowing out most of the glass. The driver freaked out. He gunned his engine and sped off, heading southward with only Joe Hughes loaded aboard.

Fraker ran after him. "You bastard," he yelled. "Get your ass back here." Fraker waved insanely at the Brit truck that bore a hand-painted number 69 on its tailgate. But the truck disappeared into the snowy white mass of frozen road and canyon and mountains, leaving Fraker, Lieutenant Strickland, Corporal Drier, and Private Polanco wondering what in hell was going to happen next. While the others ducked to the side of the road for protective cover, Strickland's gaze seemed frozen.

"Lieutenant," Fraker shouted. "Take cover."

Strickland couldn't move. His friend was on a fast moving truck headed south and no one knew what lay in wait down there. He'd let his pal down. He should have carried him the whole way. All he wanted to do now was die. Or get stinking drunk. Either one would work.

"Lieutenant!" Fraker shouted. "Get your ass out of there." Fraker left the protective rocks and trees where'd they taken cover and ran to Strickland who was still standing in the middle of the road where Chinese were doing their best to hit him with rifle fire. He shouldered his officer and returned to their tenuous protection.

Oliver Smith stared at his situation map as though he'd just recognized for the first time the massive problems ahead of him. He wondered who and what remained out there with the ability to fight. There hadn't been a full retreat order given yet, except that damned "drive" southward order that came from Almond. Like every Marine in Korea had expected, O.P. overrode the order after an abusive argument with the Army general. Nevertheless, some elements had been forced south and were now headed toward Hagaru for safety. It was not a retreat, he repeated to himself. Marines are a proud lot. We've never in our history run away from a fight. We sure as hell won't now.

He looked around at his staff, then back to the charts. Marines were also great historians he admitted to himself. Maybe that's why he fired back at Almond that, "I'll be damned if I'll go down in the history books as the first Marine commander to order a retreat."

Unfortunately, the army's 7th division, east of the Marines, had been torn apart by the Chinese and needed help desperately if it was to survive. They'd been told, as had Drysdale, that they "had to break through" to save and relieve the 5th Marines at the Reservoir.

Now two units were in trouble.

Help for the 7th Army and the trapped Marines near Chosin meant more Marines were needed. A tough call. "My Marines aren't doing all that well right now," he muttered quietly. O.P., was fully challenged now. But he was determined. Success would be his. He thrived under these conditions, but not without feeling the pain, the death of every single Marine he loved so dearly. Tough outwardly, hawkish faced Oliver P. Smith was actually a softy when it came to his Marines.

What Oliver Smith understood was that the cold, the snow, his planes, and the U.S. Army, and U. S. Marines were inflicting great pain and harm to the Chinese. It wasn't a one-sided battle although he fully understood his combat teams probably thought it was. But in his experienced heart he felt confident that if he could break out of the alleged trap the Chinese had sprung, then the morale on the other side would wane. The result would be that the loss of men and equipment on the Chinese side would saddle them with a much weaker army. This could give the U.S. counteroffensive a hell of a chance for victory.

He would need another three or four days. He glanced to the calendar. December 2 or 3. By then he thought he could turn this whole mess around. But first, let's get our men out of the trap into an area where they can regroup.

He walked slowly to the field phone. He would have to order the rest of the Marines held in reserve, the 1st Marines, and a newly arrived army combat team up the road to Hagaru. He knew that many of those living, breathing men would be dead within hours of his order. He would feel each death deeply, always did, but he could not run and he knew they would not want it any other way. He would pull the 5th Marines from the east side of the reservoir to the west, ordering the fresh relief regimental combat teams (RCTs) to guard the east side. He reminded himself again that he would lose lives, but he would also save many more. It was the toughest call of the roulette wheel of battle an officer could ever make. In this case, he had to go with the math.

"Colonel Faith here," the voice at the other end answered. Army Lieutenant Colonel Donald C. Faith commanded the 1st Battalion manned by 1,053 soldiers. He would soon be recognized for his new assignment, Regimental Combat Team 32 (RCT 32). Many later historians changed that to "Task Force Faith," but they were essentially in error with that phrase.

Faith's 1st Army battalion of the 7th Division had spent their initial days in Korea in warm barracks in Hamhung, where they'd heard a broadcast from Tokyo announcing the new UN offensive that would end the war. It was a boastful, publicity seeking prediction of being home by Christmas that excited everyone into cheering.

It was Mac's bravado. This was the home by Christmas promise. Mac himself had ordered commanders to "...tell the troops that when we get to the Yalu River they can all go home. You will be home by Christmas"

So much for bravado.

Instead, they found themselves at Hagaru about to be ordered to head up the road to the eastside of the Chosin Reservoir. They would relieve the Marines, who might not otherwise never be home for any Christmas, this year or future years.

Army Colonel Allen D. MacLean, commanded the 31st Regimental Combat Team (RCT-31) farther south. He came out of Koto-ri. His group would later be referred to by the same errant historians as Task Force MacLean. The phrase "task force" was never used in the army during Korea nor was it used later to reference any regimental combat team. RCT 31 would catch up to RCT 32 who would then become attached to MacLean's unit. They would meet at the east side of the reservoir to strengthen the defense of that area.

MacLean's force included the 3rd Battalion of the regiment, an antiaircraft artillery group with mounted .50 caliber machine guns, dual 40 mm guns, medics and a full force artillery battalion. Smith ordered him to secure the narrow serpentine road that ran around the east side of the reservoir to the Manchurian border. MacLean would be in charge of the overall actions of both RCTs.

Not too long after passing through Hagaru, MacLean's point guard ran into four obviously displaced and exhausted Marines trudging south. The advance men radioed back to the company commander of the point company, who in turn informed the battalion commander.

When MacLean got to the head of the column, the four Marines were sitting by the side of the road. They were tired, cold, hungry, but still Marines. Strickland alone stood when MacLean arrived.

MacLean was a straightforward sort. "Lieutenant? Where are you from?"

"5th Marines sir. Yudam-ni."

"What are you doing down here?"

"We were an outpost, Colonel. We were separated. A snow storm and a whole bunch of Chinese split us up. We put one of our wounded officers on a Brit truck heading south. We're searching for him now."

MacLean shook his head. His memory bank pulled up Almond's briefing about what lay ahead. "That doesn't fit with what we've been told."

"Have you seen the truck?" Strickland asked blankly. Crap, who was this guy? Hasn't he seen the damned Chinese yet?

Before MacLean could respond, Fraker came off the ground and asked, "Don't know what you were told Colonel, but up ahead you got a real fight on your hands. And your men ain't dressed for it any better 'n we are. S'fact, sir."

"Lost everyone," Strickland said quietly. "Many to the cold, most to the Chinese."

MacLean found the report unbelievable. But then they'd just come from comfort quarters, a euphemism enjoyed by the combat experience grunts. "Cold? You lost men to the cold?" The wind wasn't blowing where they stood, but ice was everywhere and a fresh powder base of snow had covered the ground with a smooth sheen broken only by the crunching of Army and Marine boots.

"Plumb froze to death," Fraker said. "Some got out with just losin' fingers and toes and a nose here and there. But sir, the Lieutenant here's right on the money. They was just too many Chinese. We kilt a bunch of 'em, but they were a human wave."

MacLean wasn't yet a believer. "And you're here because you're looking for someone?"

"We were taking Lieutenant Hughes, to Hagaru."

"Head wound. Purty near lost most of his head," Fraker said.

MacLean grew impatient. "On my chart that's only 10 miles. When did you leave Yudam-ni?"

"Two days ago, sir."

"Where's this Hughes chap now?"

"In a truck, hopefully at Hagaru, sir." Fraker said.

MacLean doubted the story. Hell, hadn't he run into men cutting and running before?

"You men will join us now. We're relieving the 5th Marines at the east side of the Chosin. We intend to tag up with Colonel Faith and his regiment. Lieutenant, you can fall in at the rear of the column, and join your outfit when we get there. My men will provide you with food, water and fresh ammunition."

Strickland's thoughts were only with his survivors and Hughes. This was his past, not his future. When he opened his ice encrusted mouth to speak, MacLean cut him off.

"That's an order, Marine. Straight down from General Oliver Smith."

"Order accepted," Strickland said brusquely.

"Move out."

But Strickland didn't move. He stared hard into the colonel's eyes. He had to get the truth of what lay ahead into that frozen army brain. "Would the Colonel like a report of what's ahead, sir?"

MacLean noticed peripherally that his men weren't unhappy about hanging out here. The longer they spoke, the happier they seemed to get. And now, with Strickland's request they were obviously curious, hungry for news. He nodded without speaking.

"There are at least three divisions of Chinese that moved in on the east side of the reservoir where you're headed."

"I'd say double that, Skipper," Fraker threw in. "Maybe more."

Strickland nodded slightly while he continued on. "On the west side, we couldn't tell how many. They swarmed over us with an endless number. Maybe ten divisions and more. Last word we heard was there were one-hundred thousand Chinese involved. We believe the mission of the Chinese on the eastside is to cut off the road, trap the 7th and 5th Marines. Straight up ahead you've got a column of Brits in deep trouble. Tanks, trucks, and a whole lot of wounded. Many killed, sir."

"And the snow's a lot deeper," Fraker said.

"We've been sent up here to relieve your people on the east side, Lieutenant. Don't worry about the snow or the column ahead. We can help them, too."

Strickland shook his head only a little bit but Colonel McLean caught it. It sent a chill up McLean's spine, one he hadn't had since Bastogne.

"Now off with you, Lieutenant. Take care of your men here."

"Would the colonel reconsider, sir. I want to find my XO and make sure he makes it back safely."

McLean had given his order and he wasn't going to change it.

Strickland stood his ground for a moment and then saluted. The unspeaking McLean had said enough. "I'll wait for the end of the column sir," he said.

MacLean returned his salute with a loose sort of wave and started off, but before going too far, he turned back and asked, "What was your job, son?"

"Platoon leader, sir." The soldiers had begun to move with MacLean. They stopped when he did, their ears perked to the Marine hoping to pick up the scuttlebutt they so desperately needed to keep their spirits alive.

"Well, where's your platoon now?"

Strickland glanced to the soldiers in line, then back to MacLean. "Here sir. These men. And Lieutenant Hughes."

"That's it? Where are the others?" It was the first time McLean had shown real concern and Strickland wasn't sure if it was for his men or the man's own safety.

"Most are dead sir." His voice cracked when he added, "Or wounded badly enough to be taken out from the Hagaru airfield before the Chinese surrounded us. All of them gone," he said in a lowered voice as though trying to explain it to himself. "Except us."

MacLean returned to Strickland. He stood within inches of the lieutenant. In a lower voice, one not to be heard by his passing army, he asked, "All of them?"

"Yes, sir. Some never got out of their sleeping bags, Colonel."

MacLean glanced to Fraker, Drier, and Polanco, who had remained as motionless as any man he'd ever seen, then back to Strickland. "Where's your company, then?"

"A lot of them are gone too, sir. Don't know for sure. When we got cut off, we were forced to head this way. That's when Lieutenant Hughes got it."

"I'm not sure I understand what's going on, Lieutenant, but none of this fits with reports from Command." He meant EUSAK, which stood for the Eighth United States Army in Korea command.

"MacArthur sent us into a death trap, sir. It's that simple."

That was the firing cap that finally set McLean off. He leaned into Strickland's space, nearly pressing his nose against the lieutenant's. "Are you nuts? MacArthur's the finest general this country's ever seen and you best not forget it."

"I hope you believe that after you get to the reservoir, sir."

MacLean's demeanor changed. His voice crackled with angry distaste for the man in front of him when he responded.

"Fine. Fine. You'll learn what it means to mess with the army, Marine. You'll be there with me, you hear. Now, fall in and join a man's outfit." With that, he wheeled around, raised his right arm as though he were Ward Bond in a western and commanded, "Continue the march, men. We have a war to win."

The soldiers continued on, but not without chanting while they passed Strickland and his men, "Hey diddle, diddle, right up the middle." The laid back army considered the Marines "nursery rhyme soldiers" because of the Marine approach to warfare, which in a phrase was simply, "straight ahead."

When a salty five-stripe doggie sergeant passed moments later, he teased them with a different tune. Singing to Hank Snow's "Train comin' down that pass," he bellered, "Sixty thousand gooks comin' down the pass, play the burp gun boogie up a Gyrenes ass, they're movin' on."

Fraker had to keep Strickland from shooting him.

CHAPTER 4

IT BECAME RECORDED HISTORY that neither Faith nor MacLean had realistic visions of the rough battles ahead. Their sole information source had been poor G-2 work at X Corps, commanded by General Edward Mallory Almond, and from MacArthur's headquarters. The 3,000 men of Faith's combined force were about to meet an estimated 60,000 to 80,000 angry Chinese of the CCF Ninth Army Group. Their mission would become known as, "the most ill-advised and unfortunate operation of the Korean War." They were, quite literally, lambs on the way to their slaughter.

Colonel Allan D. "Mac" MacLean was ordered to take his RCT-31 and attack north from positions they established west and east of the Chosin Reservoir. They were to help take the pressure off the Eighth U.S. Army units to the west and also to help the Fifth Marine Regiment who would move north to join the decimated Marine division.

Things came apart quickly and easily. Although Strickland and his men had been overwhelmed at the reservoir, so had MacLean and Faith's battalions. However, MacLean also had about six-hundred ROK troops attached to his unit. Many of these lost their lives during the first battles.

On his way to the east side of the Chosin Reservoir, MacLean, whose name generally described his physical appearance, ran into departing 5th Marines headed to the west side to reinforce the 7th Marines. The first Marine he spoke to was a young Pacific theater veteran from Truman's hometown in Missouri, Staff Sergeant Terry Hines. Hines had actually lived across the street from the locally popular Truman's home in a house "just a bit more modest than Harry's." He was a farmer's kid who was now a career Marine with clear opinions of this war, and they didn't agree with his neighbor Harry. He was taller than Harry, he remembered that, and much more adept at fixing things. Harry had often had Hines or his father "over to the house to fix up some pipes, or something."

In Korea, Hines had definitely been through a hell none of MacLean's men yet understood. He'd aged well past his twenty-eight years, had lost most of his hair but sported a three-inch reddish beard covered with a thick layer of icy Korean white.

"Three more Chink divisions just moved into the east side, Colonel," he said with his Missouri it's-a-matter-of-fact tone. "Best you keep your eyes and ears poked out there, 'specially at night." He knew he was stepping over the line telling a colonel what to do, but for "Chrissakes, the man seemed to need it." Without further discussion, Hines trotted on, moving quickly and wondering if he was doing so to catch up to his own men or distance himself from the crazy colonel who he knew to be marching into a valley of death.

At the rear of the column, Strickland watched while the 5th passed by.

"Where ya headed?" he called out to Hines.

"Gotta save the 7th Marines' ass, pal." When he caught sight of a bit of silver under Strickland's field jacket he added, "Nothin' personal, Lieutenant."

"Nothing personal taken. Semper Fi."

"Shouldn't we join 'em, Skipper?" Snake asked, pushing the words out as though an order. Fraker was close enough pals with Strickland to make it sound that way.

Strickland shook his head. His mind went back to his own unit. A unit that no longer existed. Maybe back then he would have. But not today. These guys were part of the 5th all right, but a completely different battalion. Besides, his curiosity had been tapped by the colonel. Oh yeah, he'd angered him, but down deep he saw something else in the man's eyes. He had put a call out for help and Strickland thought he could provide what the man needed. This time he wouldn't lose so many. This time he would show them how to fight and kill and stay alive. "Orders. Last I heard was we joined the army."

Snake shook his head. He didn't much care for the army or the officers in the army. "That rule don't matter here much," he said. He nearly added Strickland's first name, which would have put them back into the same foxhole they were in on Okinawa. But those days had passed, even though they were in the nakedness of combat again, respect due rank was respect given.

Strickland grinned with such gusto the ice on his face seemed to crackle. "We're gonna play this out their way. Might prove interesting. Besides, that's Sergeant Hines. Signed on 'bout the same time we did. He was on Peleliu. Ran into him last on the Rock before I got hit. Man's as good a you are. He doesn't need us, but his troops will need him. Good man. Good man," he repeated in a much lower voice.

Snake wondered if his lieutenant's energy for fighting had vanished. Strickland's voice never tapered off. "You okay, Skipper?"

Drier frowned, didn't liken to questions that challenged the man in charge. "We may need them ourselves, sir," meaning the Marines who'd just passed by. Oh boy, he gulped. He'd stuck his boondockers into his mouth again. "Well, you know what I mean, Skipper. We'll have a better chance of surviving with our own kind." Then with a tone clearly defined to show he wasn't telling his skipper what to do but only making useless noises he added, "Wouldn't we, Lieutenant?"

"Pay attention to the lieutenant, boy, and you'll live longer," Fraker scowled. Good, they were both out of their holes. Fraker's frozen cigar stub danced across his lips while he spoke. "Fur chrissakes, how many times I gotta tell you tyros to pay attention."

Strickland chuckled, which was a first since they'd been chased off the reservoir. He seemed totally pleased by what he'd heard.

Drier glanced to Blade wondering what the joke was. Blade only shrugged. They kept on walking. They were at the tail end of the army column and could bug if they had to.

"The Gunny's right," Drier said. "I'd rather stick with the Skipper."

"Kissin' ass, Drier?"

"Don't gotta kiss nobody's tail. Just keepin' my lips warm."

"They looked beat up. A bad fight like we had, maybe." Blade nodded back where the Marines had already disappeared.

"Yeah, I s'pose like us."

"Life's a bitch," Snake said philosophically. "We all gonna get beat up now and then."

"My dick has froze off. Nothing matters now." Blade sounded as though he was in pain. "A man loses his dick and he's 'bout as beat up as he can ever get."

Drier laughed. "That'd make a good country song."

Blade lightened up and tried to sing. "My dick is falling off, my nose is next to go, my dick has fallin' off, it's lyin' in the snow." He laughed hoarsely, "Naw. It don't work."

"What the hell you doin' in Korea Blade? Man, you belong in Nashville."

"Shit. You always pickin' on me."

"I actually heard a note in there."

They walked a while longer, then Blade said, "They told me to join up, or visit Folsom. That's up the state from L.A. Not a good place. I had a bad day. Went to the recruiter place. Bingo, here I am."

"That was a terrible day."

"But you, what the hell happened to you? Man, you could 'a been a ossifer."

Drier shook off the comment. Instead he said, "What'd you do? Folsom. That."

"Paid back a debt."

"Knock off the chatter," Fraker ordered.

When the column got to their new position, Colonel MacLean ordered everyone to dig in and to get busy cutting open their fields of fire through the scrub brush on the hillside. They could expect company any time.

Across the way, Colonel Faith located a farm compound just below a ridgeline and set his command post there. The Chinese would come from the other side of the ridgeline. For him the sheen of the surrounding ice and snow would be enough to see anyone who might try to approach. Then he sent word to MacLean that his unit was dug in. Would MacLean like to meet at Faith's camp or at MacLean's. MacLean was in charge, Faith's RCT-32 was attached to RCT-31. The word came back that MacLean would show up at Faith's CP that evening to discuss their tactics. He was bringing along a Marine officer who'd "been here" as well. MacLean explained the Marine's familiarity with current events more completely to Faith. Faith wasn't a dumb man. He'd had enough experience to listen to anyone who'd been on the same real estate fighting the enemy, especially just before his arrival.

MacLean ordered Strickland to his CP tent. "Lieutenant, I'm surprised you didn't join your Marines when they passed us."

"The Colonel offered us a challenge, sir. Can't pass that up. 'Sides, you got a sergeant in your outfit who needs some retraining."

MacLean let the comment pass. MacLean was known for his crisp, succinct nature. "We're going to meet with Colonel Faith at his CP tonight. All company commanders will be there as well."

"May I suggest you up that time? Later may be too late."

MacLean's expression tensed. "Reason?"

"The Chinese have their own plans, sir, and they never match ours."

"It's well-known they attack later at night. Past midnight I understand."

"Theory, sir. They've been hitting us earlier and earlier. Maybe the Colonels would like to meet now."

MacLean looked away, gave his troops a serious scan, saw that his men were digging in properly, that the fields of fire were being opened, that there was still some concertina wire from the 5th Marines defensive positions stretched out in front of them. He turned back to Strickland. "I don't think they will this evening. You'll be impressed with Colonel Faith's knowledge and experience in this area, Lieutenant. You'll see that Marines aren't the only soldiers capable of fighting the Orientals." Curling an unthreatening snarl he added, "And that singing sergeant you ran into? His name is Robert Dell. He's out of the old army. Served in Shanghai before the Deuce. He's a good man."

Strickland threw MacLean a salute and returned to his men who were with Company A. Drier and Blade were digging a foxhole through the snow and ice.

Fraker asked, "What's the skinny?"

"Colonel wants me to join them tonight for their planning session."

"He invite the Chinks, too? They'll be there."

"Damned right on that," Drier said.

"Could use some extra bandoleers from those doggies?" Blade broke in. He was panting heavily from digging in the rock hard ice. His sweat had frozen on his face and his feet hadn't fared much better even though wrapped in tightly strung boots.

"I'll get 'em," Snake said. He took off.

While checking his front lines of defense, a young wet-behind-the-ears army second lieutenant, Bernard Jones, a shorter than Strickland officer who was so green he was still wearing his gold bars, interrupted. "You men okay?" He was Alpha Company XO.

"Marines are always okay, Lieutenant, it's you we're concerned about."

Jones felt as though he'd been pushed backwards by the Marine. "A little testy aren't we, Lieutenant?"

Strickland regretted his curt response, it was not a good idea right now to piss off the Army guys. "Apologies, Lieutenant. Nothing meant by it." He motioned to Jones to walk with him. When they were away from the troops, Strickland said, "Look, your colonel's ordered me to join him tonight for a meeting with your company commanders and another colonel."

"That would be Colonel Faith. He's, ahh, not easy to argue with."

"Right. Anyway, it's a mistake for them to meet that late. You know the saying 'one round will get 'em all? The Chinese will attack during that meeting as sure as we're standing here."

"We'll be ready."

"I doubt it."

"More sarcasm?"

"Reality, son."

"Hm. Well, we're trained as well as the Marines, Lieutenant. We'll handle it."

Strickland changed his tone. He was dealing with the army he remembered. They were different. They had trained differently and they used different tactics as well. He would have to go slowly.

"I assume you want to survive through the night."

"That's my plan. Name's Jones. Bernard Jones. Enid, Oklahoma. And goddamned proud of it. We drink oil for water and chow down on hay. That tough enough?"

Strickland smiled. Enid wasn't far from Drier's hometown. And Drier was cool under fire and tough as nails. Maybe there was hope here with Jones. He shook the young Army officer's hand, which Jones had offered up at the end of his spiel, and quickly noted the great strength of the youngster. Good looking kid. Too bad. No matter whether or not Jones survived, he would not return to the states with such innocence.

"Frank Strickland," he said.

They walked up and down the line of new foxholes, far enough away from the troops to not be heard but close enough to appear as though they were inspecting the terrain. Strickland began his Chosin 101 course. The inexperienced Jones turned out to be a human sponge. When Strickland explained how the Chinese would probe, Jones listened carefully. Then Strickland referred to similar battles in the Pacific.

"You were in World War Two? So were Sergeant Dell and Colonel Faith. MacLean, too. But they were in Europe."

"Dell, huh?"

"The man's all army."

Strickland let him by with that declaration. After a few beats he said, "The Japs were excellent at night fighting. On the sea and on land. At night they'd infiltrate our positions and create all kinds of havoc. The Chinese are not any different. They'll stick it to you at night and you'll never see 'em. They'll infiltrate. They'll fire salvos to try to learn from return fire what you've got. They will figure out how many men and where all your positions are by getting your men to return fire. They want to know how many weapons you have and what kind. Once they figure they've got all the info they need, they'll come at you with the numbers they think it'll take to win. You fire a ton of shit at 'em and what do you get for a reply? Hordes more. Not human walls, but sure makes you think they are. No tactics, no strategies. Just thousands of bodies. But, if you play possum and if they can't figure you out, they either won't attack or they'll continue to probe by throwing only a small battalion at you. An hour before dawn, they'll withdraw. They are incredibly patient, Jones. You can only beat them by remaining patient yourself."

"I'll see to it we don't broadcast our full strength."

Strickland nodded, glanced back to Fraker and the others, then added, "Keep an eye on my men. They're all I've got left. And Jones, go speak to your men now. We really don't have much time left."

Jones nodded that he would.

"And if you need a good ass kicker," Strickland added, "the gunny passing out bandoleers? He'd just soon eat your sergeant Dell for lunch."

Just after sunset when the American commanders met in Faith's

CP, two Chinese soldiers slipped through the underbrush until they located the communication lines the Americans had laid down at first arrival. The first man, Lin Ching, a printer's assistant from Nansa, China, and now the leader, signaled to his pal to keep an eye out. The soldier, Lam Man, a conscripted tomato grower from the Kung Pao Province, a youngster with four sisters and two brothers tucked safely away at home, knelt up into the night and searched the area carefully while Ching cut the lines. He severed all communication between MacLean's outfit and Faith's. They were good soldiers. They worked well together and now they succeeded in yet another mission. They slipped easily back to their outfit.

Faith's radioman detected the loss of communication immediately and called over to his C.O. Captain Abrams. "Lines are down."

But it was too late. The Chinese came with their usual probes. Mortar rounds pounded along the Company A line where Bernard Jones ran from man to man ordering them to cease fire. Ducking into a foxhole, he shouted, "Stop shooting!"

"Bullshit Lieutenant," the corporal shouted. "Those fuckers mean to kill us."

The entire outfit let go with everything they had. Jones immediately ran back to the Marines and pleaded with Fraker to help him.

"Aww fur Chrissakes, Lieutenant, why don't you army guys get a grip on your troops?" He left his hole and ran up and down the line with Jones, kicking butt with his size thirteen thermo boots.

Back into the same foxhole Jones had left, Fraker grabbed the corporal's M-1 and ejected all the unfired rounds, sending the clip sailing out into the night.

"What the fuck you doin'?" The soldier scrambled to collect the rounds.

"Stop shootin' into the dark. They's nobody there yet. And that's an order, soldier."

The tone of Fraker's voice would have frozen the man's brain if the weather hadn't already tampered with it. The corporal glanced up to Jones able to see him because of fresh blue flare that popped above them. Then he looked back to Fraker and finally plunked back into his hole.

"Fuckers are gonna get us all killed."

One by one Fraker got the soldiers to stop shooting. They were amazed to discover that when they stopped, the Chinese soon stopped.

Fraker explained why. They would be back, he said to them, but now with fewer men.

The Chinese continued to probe other units. Fraker figured the Chinese had established the size and firepower of Company A as medium strength. They would be back he repeated to anyone who'd listen and yeah, with fewer men that meant fewer than a division, which meant, of course, a couple of thousand could show up. "By midnight."

Back at the CP, MacLean and Faith broke up the meeting at the sound of the first shots. They sent their company commanders back to their positions. "We'll pick this up in the morning," MacLean yelled over the noise of war. He hoped he was right.

By the time MacLean returned to his outfit, they were under heavy attack. His artillery was firing endlessly into the night while scattering their shots in a wide sweep in front of them.

Colonel Faith on the other hand had no artillery. Instead, his soldiers fired only their rifles into the enemy patrols, unwittingly sending the Chinese the message that Faith's Battalion might be armed better than expected when the truth was just the opposite.

It seemed that Company A of RCT-32 was taking the brunt of the battle. The A platoon commander, Lt. Ray Denchfield was wounded so badly at the beginning of the attack that he was hurriedly carted out of there, hopefully to be taken to Koto-ri. He was replaced by the company commander, Captain Scullion, who had just returned from the Faith meeting.

"I've got command," Scullion shouted in his rich southern accent. But just then, only moments after Denchfield had departed, Scullion was killed by a Chinese mortar.

Scullion's death had a devastating affect on the troops. Shooting seemed to pause while each man wondered what in hell their own chances were. Sergeant Dell came to their rescue. Behaving similarly to Fraker's style, he ran from position to position bolstering the troops, urging them on. He was out there in the line of fire, moving without fear from man to man. His men rejoined the fight with renewed commitment.

Faith quickly sent his assistant operations officer, Captain Haynes to replace Scullion.

Haynes, a wiry fellow with an eagerness for battle worked his way along the icy trail that had been carved out by others until he came upon a shadowy form in the night. He called out.

"I'm Captain Haynes. Take me to Company A."

The gunshot that rang out took his life instantly, knocking him back into the snow where his blood turned the Christmas white powder and ice into rapidly frozen pools of red. Lin Ching had just killed his first human face to face. Working at the print shop was definitely a better job, he decided. Killing was not fun.

Faith was incredulous. "Goddammit, is that company jinxed?" he yelled to his executive officer, Lieutenant Cecil Smith, "get your butt up there and get it there alive. Put that Company back on line and do it quickly."

Smith sprang up and dashed off into the night wondering which bullet or mortar round would take his life on the way. He weaved his way through the lumps of ice and fields of snow until he got to Company A's position. When he arrived, the troops were shocked to see him alive.

"Jesus Christ," Corporal White shouted. "A livin' fuckin' officer."

"You bet your sweet ass," Smith shouted back. He was as surprised as they were. "Now turn around and kill me a bunch of those commie bastards."

Smith immediately went from foxhole to foxhole, encouraging his new command to rise to the occasion. When he crossed paths with Sergeant Dell he chalked a new medal up for him in his mind and kept on. The troops came together and laid down enough firepower to cause the Chinese to waffle. Surprising everyone, the Chinese backed away, at least for the moment.

Back at MacLean's Company A, Strickland was helping Bernard Jones. Challenges were large and small.

"This goddamned BAR is jammed," a silhouetted corporal screamed through the noise. The Chinese had finally committed to Alpha Company's line.

Strickland jumped into his foxhole and immediately fixed the weapon. "If you live through this crap corporal, strip this in the morning and pour buckets of lubriplate into it. Got it?"

"Ain't got none, Lieutenant."

"Get it from your armorer."

"He ain't got none," the corporal screamed over the noise of the firefight. "I been using axle grease. But now we don't even got any trucks left."

"Then use the goddamned grease from your colonel's jeep."

"Get Wild Root Cream Oil Charlie," the private next to the corporal sang out. "Does a rifle really good!"

Strickland didn't let them see him laugh, but he couldn't help it. The kid with the sing song rhyme was on the money. Hair slick would work for a while, and some of the guys actually had some.

When he stopped laughing he told himself these guys would be okay. They would make it. His quick temper had only been Marine mantra at work. But if they've got kids with that humor while fighting, then they were good kids. Not trained like his, but still good boys.

It was so damned cold that the men were fighting with most of their bodies tucked into their sleeping bags. They propped themselves up over the ledge of their holes with just their arms and heads and weapons sticking out. They also figured that if they were killed, they would simply fall back into their holes, already wrapped for the body snatchers.

"How we doin'?" Strickland yelled over the ear-splitting gunfire when he returned.

Fraker spit out some chew.

"These guys ain't exactly commandin' my respect. We'd be better off if we were doin' this by ourselves, Skipper. Four of us against a Chinese Division or two wouldn't be fair to the Chinks, but it'd sure make me a fuckin' lot happier."

"They'll do it. Just help 'em."

He wanted to say he was sorry he didn't duck MacLean's order and keep on plodding southward to Koto Ri but the timing wasn't good for that. Sorry? Hadn't that been trained out of him? Sorry! Never. Make the goddamned decision and then live with it. Even if you find yourself facing death.

He moved on to help others.

The Chinese withdrew a few hours before daybreak in order to regroup. What Faith and MacLean and Strickland didn't know was that their newly baptized U. S. army troops had killed a huge number of the Chinese. The fight put up by a bunch of greenhorns that night would have a major impact on the rest of the war. That night would make it into military history books. So would the end result of battles to come.

Back at Chinese headquarters, General Song Shilun was having fits. Not only was he losing more than half his army to the Marines and U.S. Army, the severely cold weather was killing off a bunch as well. Whole Chinese divisions had been decimated by American aircraft, and American Marines, and American soldiers. And now he had to participate in a change of tactical plans ordered by his immediate superior, Mao Zedong, who figured it would be a fatal error for the Chinese attempt at trapping and killing all the Americans if they continued on like this.

Mao Zedong ordered General Shilun to move south, to consolidate his divisions and try to stop the Marine and Army breakout somewhere near the Funchillin Pass. In the annals of war history, it would become a textbook example of what not to do.

Nonetheless, the Chinese change of tactics would not benefit MacLean's nor Faith's units. But the two forces had unwittingly played a big role in forcing the panic at Chinese headquarters. For that, their names will live long in military history.

Colonel Faith appeared without notice at Private Ferguson's foxhole. Ferguson was still in his bag, his gaze locked on his M-1 with its shattered stock. Faith became immediately depressed. "Private," he said, "what happened?"

But there was no answer.

"He's dead, Colonel," a voice from the next hole called out. It was Corporal Jenkins, a farm boy from just north of Fargo, North Dakota. "Mortar round. His buddy is dead, too." Faith looked to Jenkins curiously. Jenkins pointed to Ferguson's hole. "He's under him, sir. They're frozen together. They were my friends. Gone now." His voice trailed off as though sailing to another world.

Faith nodded to Ferguson, "You okay?"

Faith could barely speak. It hadn't been too long ago that he'd seen similar death in Europe. Why so soon? Why now? Why these boys?

Jenkins wanted to nod he was okay but instead he just asked, "Are we staying here?"

Faith nodded against his will to shake his head no and said, "I believe that's the plan."

"I need more ammo."

"I'll get ammo up to you."

Jenkins sank back into his hole without responding.

Faith moved on.

"Half my men are dead or wounded," he said to his executive officer, Major Perry, when they found themselves alone. "I'm sure that wasn't part of General Almond's plan. I know it wasn't part of mine."

Perry wasn't exactly pleased either. He understood what Faith meant. Almond wasn't known as a tactician.

"The men are huddled mostly in their bags, praying they won't freeze to death." He wanted to say they felt they were waiting for the inevitable: Death by bayonet.

Faith bowed his head. Perry feared the man's chin would freeze to his chest. He thought his colonel looked as though he might be in his barnyard just before heading his cows to the slaughter house.

"We need more than our light garb under these freezing conditions."

"C-Rations and canteens are also frozen."

Faith looked up slowly, with agony displayed in his expression. "Same as Bastogne."

"The men have nothing to eat. Their feet, fingers and noses are suffering the first signs of frostbite. And we have no warming tents available."

Faith patted his officer on his shoulder and then left him with the men. He returned to his CP, where MacLean met with him.

"We've lost ground and too many of our young officers. Two platoons were pushed back."

Faith dropped his finger on the chart indicating a hill across the road they had taken once and now needed.

"And the high ground?"

"Lost." MacLean said.

"Let's get it back, Mac" Faith said without making it sound like an order. MacLean was his boss, after all, and a good one. But sometimes the obvious has to be spelled out. He was reconciled to fighting the rest of this war with half his army, few working weapons and a lot of empty stomachs. "Before noon. Or we'll lose all of us tonight."

"We lost a lot of officers last night, Don."

His meaning had been clear. Who in the hell could they afford to lose now?

"The Marine?"

MacLean grimaced. "Turns out he fought in the Pacific. Hines knows of him. Says he was a former enlisted. A sergeant. A bit arrogant but duty bound."

"He just might succeed."

"I'll send A-company. They came through the night with the fewest casualties."

"How's that?" Faith seemed doubtful.

"Lieutenant Jones informed me the crazy Marine was up and down the line all night with his sergeant. Never took a break. Never sat down, never quit. Just kept prodding, fixing weapons, jacking up spirit."

Faith squinted toward the hill he could taste now.

"Let's see how our Sergeant York does it in daylight." His usual enthusiasm was gone and MacLean could hear it missing in his voice.

MacLean looked deeply into his eyes for a brief moment, then headed back to his outfit. Maybe the Marine could help. Maybe. When he called out for Strickland, Fraker knew instantly what was happening.

"Aww shit, Lieutenant. They gonna get us kilt now. Do me a favor, sir."

"What's that?"

"I'm out of cigars." Snake grinned.

Strickland chuckled and took off. When he got there, MacLean was searching the target hill with his field-glasses. He didn't have to look away; he could feel Strickland's presence. He had always admired men who had such chemistry, such energy. Their minds, and their bodies seemed to speak with a calm aggression, if those were the right words. He thought he could be blindfolded, bound in a dark room and know if such men were in there with him. He lowered his glasses and turned to the Marine.

"Would you do us a favor, Lieutenant?"

"Sir?"

MacLean pulled a chart out of his map case. He knelt down to the icy surface. Strickland joined him. "This knob, right here." He looked up and pointed to the hill. "We've got to get it back. They're up there Lieutenant, and most likely have our range for tonight's mortar and artillery attacks. I don't feel like being their target any more."

Strickland looked from the high ground back to MacLean. "Lieutenant Jones can do it. He's a good man."

"I'm sure he could make it. But, because you're the most experienced junior officer here, both Colonel Faith and I want you to lead a detachment of volunteers up there to take it back."

Strickland scanned the map carefully, looking for the best route up the mountain. "That road right there," he said, pointing to the map," but before he could continue MacLean spoke.

"It's probably secured by the Chinese."

"No sir," Strickland said politely. "It doesn't exist. These maps are all inaccurate, Colonel. We have the same issue, sir. Best you not trust them." Then, looking intently into MacLean's eyes he added, "It's another one of Mac's blunders, Colonel. Beggin' your pardon, sir."

MacLean's new respect for the Marine wouldn't allow the lieutenant to pick apart his army commander. "That will be enough of that, son. Will you do it?"

"Is that an order, sir?"

MacLean didn't like games. "Is that what you want?"

Strickland nodded. "That's how we work, sir. We follow orders, and we do it damned well."

"Then it's an order." Keeping his gaze glued to Strickland's, MacLean shouted to his executive officer, "Major Petri, Lieutenant Strickland here will command a volunteer group to take back Hill 1430. Give him all the support he needs."

Strickland caught Petri's eye. "That should include one very good cigar."

Bernard Jones would go along too, because he volunteered to do so.

"You're nutty as a fruitcake," Strickland said to him, hiding a touch of newly born pride he had for the man.

"Makes two of us," he answered. "I learned from you last night. I couldn't have done it without you. Actually, I couldn't have done what you did. I probably would have died."

"Dying isn't creative enough for me." Strickland's eyes were on the troops. He turned to Jones and said, "What we did last night was standard platoon commander leadership."

"I suppose that's why we believe Marines are crazy bastards. You just added one more notch to the legends."

"Okay. You're in. Maybe you can put a notch in your pistol grip tonight."

"Ready, Skipper," Fraker interrupted. He glanced to Jones. "Best you leave the backpack behind, Lieutenant. We're just goin' on a little hike."

Strickland nodded agreement.

When Jones dumped the pack, he muttered, "Why do I suddenly feel naked?"

"And get rid of that Carbine Lieutenant. Piece of shit, sir, and 'sides the Chinks know only officers carry them. Get yourself an M-1 loaded with plenty of lubriplate. Ain't regulation for officers, but it'll help you get back alive. And, please remove the gold bars. They're an invite to get yourself shot." He grinned and added, "Sir!"

They moved out of camp, forty of them in two columns, each man walking about ten paces behind the other until they were directly below the knob they volunteered to retake. Strickland figured the Chinese had kept an eye on them, knew they were coming.

He also figured they would have to expose themselves to get a look down the steep slope to see what was going on when he got closer. Once they were at the base, he selected eight men, including Drier and Polanco.

"Get within view of the Chinese up there," he directed He pointed to a section of the mountain that was somewhat clear of brush and trees, "Set up as though you're spotting for us. Drier, make it appear as though we're climbing up this side. Stay visible to the Chinks. They won't shoot until you make 'em nervous. That gives us plenty of time. Use your field glasses. Start by looking from down there, at the bottom. Work your way up slowly to the ridgeline like you're watching us sneak up. Point once in a while and wave us on. Be real dumb."

"That'll be easy." He grinned that damned infectious grin again and Strickland almost copied.

"I want you to sucker them in."

"Like William did to King Harold," Jones said.

Strickland glanced to Jones. "You're over-educated for this kind of work." Back to Drier he said, "Keep doing that until you hear gunfire on the other side. That will be ours. When Chinks come running down this side, you'll be able to start picking 'em off like ducks in a pond." Squinting toward the hillside, he added, "You're lookin' at about 25 clicks on your M-1 to the top." To his men he stated flatly, "Ten clicks on your rifles, gents." He clearly meant they'd get a lot closer to the enemy before they started shooting.

Then he led his contingent through the scrub brush around to the back side of the hill. It began to snow, covering their shoulders and bodies with a white powder that nearly made them invisible.

"They won't see us through this snowfall, and they sure as hell ain't gonna hear us in this powder," Fraker said. "These guys buy into the same tactics they hand out. Kind of like a salesman's the easiest guy in town to sell something to. Once't you learn that Lieutenant Jones, you got 'em boogered."

It stopped snowing. Strickland raised his hand to stop the column. He approached the men one at a time, the first being Pfc. Jamie Harper, a sheet metal apprentice from Wichita, Kansas. "You set, son?" he asked.

"Yessir."

"We'll be going up the mountain shortly. It's icy."

"I'm ready, Lieutenant. Lieutenant?"

"Yes?"

"Last night was a bitch, sir. Are we gonna get out'a this mess alive?"

Strickland smiled tightly. "Plan on it Harper. We'll raise a toast to these bastards at the Top of the Mark."

He then moved on to the next man Pfc. Barry Morgan who was from Seattle, Washington. Morgan was a full foot shorter than Strickland and nearly a foot wider. He didn't look like he could make it up the mountain, but he'd volunteered and, by God, Strickland would never argue with that. Morgan held a tight grip on his BAR. "Those haven't been working too well in this cold, private."

"This one, does Lieutenant."

"Why is it different?"

"I don't use issue, sir. It freezes."

"That's true."

"No sir, I use a mixture of axle grease and that crap that comes outta our C-rations. You can't get either one to freeze."

"Burns like hell though," the corporal next to Morgan volunteered. "It splatters everywhere each time he fires the weapon. Shit's hot."

Strickland glanced over to the corporal. "You are?"

"Corporal Highsmith, sir. Reginald P. Highsmith, from Boston, sir. Signed into this war July 4th, 1950." His enunciation, his grammar, his whole bearing was different than the others.

"You sound educated, Corporal Highsmith."

"Yessir. Harvard. Second year."

Jones stepped up. "Shouldn't we keep moving, Lieutenant?"

Strickland shot Jones a dagger-laced stare, then returned to Highsmith. "Why, Highsmith? Why sign up for this god-awful war?"

"My somewhat isolated New England family never talked about why we fought wars. So, I had to find out myself. And try to figure out why. I don't know why sir, just had to figure it out."

"You're as nuts as us," Burns moaned. "One chalk mark for the blue bloods."

"We're about to attack a hill full of mean-assed Chinks. That's what the class of people who fight our wars are about to do," Strickland said. "And none of us have ever figured out this war. So, what have you come up with?"

Highsmith stuttered at first, then calmed. "I, I'm not sure," he said. "But seems to me we're fighting some bad guys who believe freedom is a bad thing."

"And when this war's over?"

"I expect to return to Harvard, sir. I intend to go on to law school, run for office and work to put a stop to wars."

"Stunning stuff, Smitty," Burns blurted out. "Bullshit of course, but really impressive coming from a grunt."

"Crap! Can we get on with this before this BAR freezes?" Morgan complained. "Shit, that would be a first and I don't want it to happen here."

Everyone chuckled. Strickland had accomplished his purpose, to release the tension, to put them at ease, to make them feel alive enough to run up a mountainside on what could turn out to be a suicide mission. He chuckled inwardly because it was the first time he'd ever heard any of them attempt to justify crappy war. Well, that was okay. They could climb this hill, attack the Chinese and beat the hell out of 'em now. They were ready. He turned to Jones and nodding to him he said quietly, "Now, Lieutenant Jones. Now, we are ready to move on."

Jones stepped back while the men started out again. He was dumbfounded by what he'd just witnessed. It was a piece of leadership he told himself, that he would tuck away for a long time. At least, he reconsidered, until a Chinese bullet got him.

They started up the mountain in a by-the-Marine-textbook fire and maneuver tactic, which was completely foreign to the army guys. Strickland gave it to them in freshman lingo. Basically they relayed the covering fire from one squad to the other while each leap-frogged ahead. When they got halfway up, the Chinese were still not aware of them.

When they finally heard a shot ring out Fraker hoarsely said, "Chinks. Firing at Drier." They paused.

Strickland waved to everyone to remain still and not open fire. "It's working. Their attention is to the other side. Let's hucklebuck."

They moved through the fresh snow more quickly now, rising to the crest of the mountain without a single Chinese soldier catching on. When they got there, Strickland and Jones put their men in position and then, with a wave of his arm, Strickland launched their attack.

Across the road and at his CP, Colonel Faith strained to see through the light fog and snowflakes that drifted across the high ground. He held his field glasses tightly to his eyes while the battle raged on. He could barely see the hill, but was able to imagine the battle just from the sounds.

Soon, out of the fog came the Chinese. "Well, I'll be go to hell," he muttered. He was amazed to see the Chinese soldiers bugging out, coming down the mountain toward his camp. Believing Strickland hadn't prepared for this event, he lowered his glasses and called for Major Perry. But, before Perry could get there, the eight soldiers placed below the mountain by Strickland opened fire on the retreating Chinese with their thirty-caliber light machine guns, picking them off neatly.

Faith quickly brought his glasses back to his eyes. "Son of a bitch," he muttered plainly.

"Sir?" Perry asked, catching his breath.

"We got us one crazy son of a bitchin' Marine up there, Major. And I think he just took back our mountain."

"Yes, sir."

"Now, if we can just recover the rest of the lost ground."

"Working on it, Colonel. Job nearly accomplished. So far we've sixty WIAs and thirty KIAs."

Faith whirled around. "Dammit, Major. Can't we do this without so many losses?"

Perry shook his head, as if to say he wasn't in control. "It's the best we can do, sir. We're strung out a long ways."

The radio squawked. It was Strickland. "Bingo, Colonel. You've got your mountain back."

Fearing more bad news, Faith asked, "Casualties?"

There was a long pause, apparently while Strickland took count. Then the radio squawked again and Strickland clearly said, "None. Sir. Except for Fraker, sir. He lost his damned cigar again."

Faith allowed a tight smile. "That, Major Perry," he said firmly, "is the best we can do."

CHAPTER 5

AN HRS-1 SIKORSKY helicopter, known as a "Chickasaw," approached Faith's command post. It popped into sight just above the brush on the hill below, and climbed like a heavy bird barely able to keep distance between its feet and the icy ground.

"It better have ammo and medical supplies on board," Faith muttered, "or a bunch of flight guys are gonna turn into infantry soldiers."

When the bird touched down, Mac Arthur's senior sidekick, as well as Oliver Smith's nemesis, General Almond, stumbled out with a cartoon smile plastered across his cherubic face. Faith knew Almond. He didn't like the arrogant general and he felt confident that this visit wasn't going to improve that relationship.

Almond headed straight for Faith. He was dressed in army fatigues, most likely pressed that morning in the local Tokyo laundry. He wore an oversized fur-lined topcoat over his fatigues and Faith noticed that it was not government issue. He seemed to be in a big hurry. For Faith, that simply meant the general was here for a PR reason and that he wanted to get the hell out of this hellhole before anything serious flared up again.

When he got to Faith, Almond reached into his pocket and pulled out a Silver Star medal with a ribbon attached.

"For you, Colonel. For heroism in battle."

Almond beamed his photo-op grin, as though he was completely unaware of the blood visible in the snow or the frozen American corpses under canvas ponchos just a few feet away.

Faith could barely contain his anger. Through clenched teeth he said, "Forget the goddamned medal, General. I want your chopper instead."

"Not funny, Colonel."

"We need to get my wounded out of here and to bring supplies back."

"I'm here on serious business, Colonel. "

Faith bristled. What in the hell did this pip-squeak think the men of the two RCTs were here for? It wasn't his first run-in with Almond. "Good. Our medic is freezing his ass off because he's under clothed. Give him your coat so that he can be of even better use than he is now." He reached up to the front buttons of the large coat, but Almond swatted his hands away.

"Behave, Colonel Faith."

Faith glanced to the chopper. An army photographer had jumped out. He was grabbing any picture he could take.

"Get your butt over here, son," Faith called out.

The bird's blades were still swooshing overhead, but the photographer, Bill Danner, had learned a long time ago how to read lips and understand body motions. He'd followed Almond around now for five months and had also gotten use to the reactions of others in his presence. His boss was not liked it seemed, by anyone.

Faith waved him over again.

Danner had been in combat zones before, but this time he felt especially nervous. He'd kept up with the news, and the men he was looking at had been headlines just the day before. Dead he thought. All of them. Now, standing under the whooshing blades of the Chickasaw he could see the obvious. Lots of dead, but still lots of living, who, he thought, didn't look so distant from being dead themselves.

"Sir?" he mouthed.

Faith could read his lips because Faith had seen hundreds of men react the same way in combat zones. "Come take a picture of the General and me."

Danner moved tenuously from the chopper's belly toward the two officers. His camera felt like it had just gained a hundred pounds. Faith stepped to the row of corpses. "C'mon General, here's what this war is all about. Let's pin medals on these men. Just think of the PR."

Almond laughed him off with a huge guffaw. "Nonsense," he bellowed. He waved to Danner to stay where he was.

Danner stopped, happily.

Almond stepped up to Faith and pinned the Silver Star to the Colonel's breast pocket. "You're the leader here, Colonel," he blurted out, sticking to his nearly memorized medal awarding speech. "It's been a good show. You and Colonel MacLean have kept the Chinese from destroying the Marines. 'Sides," his words seem to click with his chattering teeth, "the publicity this will get us is badly needed stateside. We gotta show 'em we're kicking butt. The press at home is telling the folks we're losing this war. Poppycock, I tell 'em."

"One more battle like last night and we're not going to stop anyone," Faith said, hoping to tweak the general into leaving them alone.

"I tell 'em that our boys are pushing Chinese northward right now." Almond was in his own world. He tightened up his smile and leaned closer and added, "Besides, there's not enough room in the chopper to take anyone back."

Faith felt the anger spread through his body. It showed when he said, "That chopper can carry eight stretchers, General. Look around here, dammit. What in the hell do you see? Dead and wounded, that's what. You can take at least six of the wounded in that damned bird to safety."

MacLean had earlier informed Almond that they faced two huge Chinese divisions. That his forces were strung out too thinly. And Faith remembered well that it was this major general, Edward M. Almond, who had reprimanded MacLean for his report as though MacLean had perpetrated a lie.

"Nonsense," Almond said without looking around. "I'm here on a mission and the mission is what's important." He didn't even glance around to survey the area.

The tone of Faith's voice became sepulchral with a steady monotone that would have frightened most men. "Colonel MacLean and I have taken big losses here General. If you can get that bird up here then the flyboys can get more of 'em up here and rescue our wounded. You have an obligation to these men."

Almond leaned into Faith and with is own version of the same tone said, "Don't spoil this moment Colonel Faith. There aren't any other available choppers. I'm here for publicity. Mac needs us to look good."

Almond saw what looked like rocket's flaring up in Faith's eyes. Any fool could see that. Faith's battle-weary fighters who had circled them, did not overlook Almond's behavior. It was one of those moments of magic for battlefield leaders when his soldier's build legendary respect for their commanders. They were witnessing the worst of the army and in Faith, the best.

Throwing off any further conversation with Faith, Almond turned to Lieutenant Everett Smalley, Jr., who was sitting on a fuel can next to the aid station waiting for the evacuation that he long ago had given up on. Smalley had had much of his left arm shot off and his hip drilled by at least one round of heavy caliber metal.

"Here ya go, son," Almond said, pinning a medal to his chest.

Smalley was surprised. He turned to the man nearest him and muttered, "I got me a Silver Star, but I don't know what the hell for."

"I guess for sittin' on that gas can and not blowing up, Lieutenant," Corporal Whitey Briggs chuckled. "Hell, the old bastard probably thinks you're takin' a shit." They laughed together. "It's Beetle Bailey at work, is what it is." Beetle Bailey had recently made his first appearances in a few newspapers at home and families were sending the comic strip about a college cartoon character who accidentally enlisted in the Army when the Korean War started. The troops loved him.

Almond moved on, pinning a Silver Star on Sergeant Stanley, the current mess sergeant. He just happened to be walking by. Then he ran into Frank Strickland and pinned one on the Marine. Strickland glanced to Faith, and then back to Almond. "What's this for?"

"Heroism in battle, Lieutenant," Almond announced loudly for all to hear.

Fraker snarled, "The heroes are dead, General." He motioned to the row of corpses. "They's the guys who you might want to pin those on."

"Not true son," Almond blurted out. "We need living men to wear these. America needs to understand you're winning this war."

Fraker spit into the snow. "You for real?"

Almond glanced to Fraker's sewn-on nameplate, memorized it for the moment, and the future. The Marine had not addressed him properly.

"I understand Marines can be tough, Sergeant, but this? You can take this medal to the bank. Get a promotion later on." He pinned the medal on Fraker's jacket.

Fraker growled and turned away scrunching the snow with his kick-ass boots leaving a rooster tail of ice crystals to fly upwards behind him. He wondered what would happen to him if he shoved one of those boots up the general's ass.

"What's his problem?" Almond asked Strickland.

Strickland turned away without speaking and headed off with Fraker.

"They're Marines, General," a soldier near him said. "Don't much regard medals until war's over. They jest like the fightin'. That's all." More quietly he added, "They don't seem to like army generals either, sir. Beggin' the general's pardon, sir."

Almond grunted, turned back to Faith. "Colonel, please call your troops together. I have a speech directly from General MacArthur to give them."

"Look around you, General. These are the troops. Maybe you can give the speech to that row of KIAs there."

Almond nearly crumbled from a sudden attack of yellow-back. He recovered enough to raise his arms and give the speech he'd come to give — one that would ultimately affect his own career enough to drive him out of the Army. Just as he spoke, another army public relations type jumped from the Sikorsky. He had a scrubby looking pencil and a pad and he wrote down Almond's words while the general spoke.

"The enemy who is delaying you for the moment is nothing more than remnants of Chinese fleeing north. We're still attacking and we're going all the way to the Yalu. Don't let a bunch of Chinese laundrymen stop you."

Pompously he puffed out his chest, walked to his Sikorsky, got back into it and returned quickly to his warm quarters at Hungnam with his nearly empty bird. Faith had been correct. The chopper could have lifted at least six of the wounded out of there with them.

"Asshole!"

Fraker jerked the Silver Star off his jacket and pinned it on an army private who'd lost an arm, an eye and lay on a stretcher paralyzed, quite nearly frozen to death. "When you get home youngster, tell 'em for me that you fought like a son of a bitch'n Marine."

The soldier couldn't speak, but he was able to grab Fraker's wrist and squeeze it. Fraker knew he meant thank you. Tears welled up in Snake's eyes, making him at least momentarily in the eyes of the others, human. It proved to be contagious among the others. They walked away, each in their own private awakening, each abruptly understanding that they might never get out of this place alive.

Strickland tossed his medal as far as he could. "Bullshit army bastard," he yelled into the air from the ridgeline where his silhouette outlined a once bold, now angry Marine.

While Faith watched the helicopter disappear into the whiteout in the valley below he slowly and purposefully unpinned the Silver Star and dropped it into the snow, flicking his gloved fingers as though to rid himself of something sticky or bothersome. "Next time send me someone with balls."

"And ammunition," Lieutenant Smalley added from his gas can seat. He handed his medal to the new corpsman who had joined them just days before. The corpsman, a short fellow whose name he didn't know, smiled when Smalley said, "Patch me up good doc. Ain't no way I'm goin' back now. Shoot my shoulder with some morphine. And give that to a man who deserves it next time you pull one out of the fire."

The corpsman did have a name. It was Peter Fever. It was just that he didn't like using his name since it always invited really bad jokes. "You got it, Lieutenant. Best I can do for you is get you hooked."

Smalley nodded. "Do it."

Later, when the four Marines gathered around an alcohol heater to get their hands warm, Fraker said to Strickland, "I 'member you tellin' me about going to college 'fore the Pacific, Lieutenant. You played football and all. So, tell me again why the hell you re-upped?"

"Don't really understand it myself, Snake," Strickland said. "After the war I returned to finish college, then went off to Basic School and here I am again. Gettin' my ass shot at just like you. It's like I've never had a life since leaving high school." He wouldn't tell them he felt his life ended when his parents died.

Drier piped up. "So, why the hell are you still here, Gunny? You made it through the Pacific alive and well jest like you asked the Lieutenant, what excuse do you have?"

Fraker laughed. "You lived in Oklahoma, boy. Nothing to go back to but a dried up Canadian river. Lots of snakes, bugs and oil. Corps was good to me. Same for you, right?"

Drier could only nod. Snake was right.

"And now?" Strickland asked.

"Corps is still good Skipper. It's the goddamned Chinks that's a pain in the ass."

* * * *

"Walk with me to Faith's compound, Lieutenant." McLean was already moving.

"Yes, sir." Strickland glanced to Fraker as if to say, here we go again.

Even though messengers and scouts had pretty well worn a trail into the ice, it had become a twenty minute hike through the rough terrain from MacLean's CP to Faith's. Fraker and the others remained behind to dig into frozen C-rations. The same C-rations he'd had in the Pacific. The rations he held in his hands were dated February 1943. So was his ammo, he noted.

"Crap boys, we're fighting a whole new war with nothin' but army-surplus."

Faith, still a bit unsettled by Almond's visit, led them into his dugout. "Gentlemen, please, at ease. I've taken the liberty to have some coffee brewed."

"Here ya go, sir," a wounded sergeant said to Strickland handing him a filled canteen cup. "Kind of weak, Lieutenant. Been through the grinder more'n once."

"Thanks. What happened to you?" Strickland motioned to the sergeant's bloody gauze-wrapped head.

"Last night, sir. It's not bad. Helmet looks like hell though."

"Gents," Faith interrupted, "With your help, I'd like to develop a plan for tonight's battle."

"It's kind of up to the Chinese, isn't it?" MacLean said.

"What's your response to that, Lieutenant?" Faith said to Strickland.

Strickland set his cup down on the hardpan of blue ice that served as the deck. He eyed Faith's charts quickly and carefully.

"I don't care to lose any more men, sir. But the Colonel's not far off target. It depends on how many Chinks are thrown at us, and whether or not they probe. I believe they will. We should use the time between now and then to get the word to our men to turn their usual tactics back into their faces by confusing them about our strength while learning about theirs."

"We may not have enough men for that," Faith said.

"They probe us to figure out where we are strongest and where we are at our weakest." He turned to Faith. "Let's fake it. Let's seduce them into our strongest position." He meant MacLean's unit.

"Exactly how," MacLean asked. He'd not spent the night on the frontlines with Strickland and Fraker.

"When the mortars start, we give them the appearance of a hole in our line. When they bring on the attack at that point, we'll hit them straight on and with crossfire."

"Sounds good," Faith said. "Although a bit out of the ordinary."

Welcome to the Marines, Strickland said to himself only.

It was a good plan, but sometimes plans are never given a chance. During their absence the Chinese had quietly surrounded MacLean's unit.

"You can kiss our plan goodbye," Strickland said.

"Back to Colonel Faith's CP," MacLean ordered without humor. They would have to chase the Chinese out utilizing both RCTs.

"To paraphrase your general, sir, looks like we're being taken to the cleaners."

"Not funny, Lieutenant," McLean replied, but he could barely hold back a smile. "Do Marines always joke about pending disasters, Lieutenant?"

"No sir. Sometimes we just kill 'em straight out."

MacLean paused a moment. "There's something peculiar in the way you summarize things, Frank. Almost like you're a bit nuts." It was the first time he got personal with Strickland.

"Colonel, I thought you understood. We're all a bit nuts. Why else would you and I be standing here on a frozen mountain surrounded by a bunch of goddamned people who want very badly to kill us?"

That did it. That drew the chuckle he was looking for from the taut army commander. "Okay, you got me. Now, let's put this show together so that it works."

"Absolutely, Colonel. Absolutely."

Faith's reaction was that they apply basic army tactics. "We'll take them to the high ground east of the roadblock," he informed them. "Major Perry will be in command of the CP during my absence."

MacLean and Strickland went with one of the company's, while Faith went with the other. Once there, he explained to them, "We can outflank a swath of the enemy in this area. Move in on them and disperse or destroy them."

"Giving us a hole to breakout."

"Exactly."

Faith dispatched his heavy weapons to the hill overlooking the roadblock. "We can see the perimeter of Colonel MacLean's outfit," the voice coming over the radio said from the heavy weapons location. "There're Chinese all around them, everywhere. Hundreds of 'em," the voice shouted. "Jesus, man, it's a whole friggin' division."

"Mac," Faith called into his radio, forgetting codes.

There was no answer, except for static. The radioman tried again. "Thirty One . . ." But nothing.

"Damn! He has no idea how many Chinese surround his position."

The radioman continued to try, but finally looked up into Faith's eyes with frustration written across his gaze.

"C'mon," Faith shouted to his men, "we've gotta hightail it over there. We've got to help him."

Plan Two died right there.

MacLean's men were ready to attack with bayonets set at the muzzles of their rifles. Ammo clips were loaded and rifle safeties were off. They knew from learned instinct that things weren't right. They were prepared to throw care to the winds, to fight to the death just to get out of there. Their asses were frozen, their fingers dead sticks on the trigger, their systems working off dying adrenaline only. Ice hung from their noses and unshaved faces. They were so bitterly cold that some felt getting themselves killed might even be a treat.

"They'll do okay, Colonel," Strickland said.

"You're always upbeat Lieutenant."

"Not always."

"How many? How many Chinese we got out there?"

Strickland sniffed. "North Koreans as well, sir. We've got Chinese and NKs out there. Swear to it. That could mean you got a whole division up there, maybe more." Even Strickland didn't fully understand that the Chinese had two divisions about to attack them.

MacLean looked at him curiously. "Are you serious Lieutenant? Do you think you can sniff the air like a birddog and figure out who our enemy is?"

"Faith's column coming," a voice shouted out.

MacLean ran up the trail to the ridge and spotted Faith's troops coming toward them. Then he heard shots. Faith's column stopped moving; it was taking fire from Chinese soldiers.

MacLean however, believed the shots came from his own column. He glanced back to Strickland and yelled, "Our men are shooting into Faith's ranks." He dashed away before Strickland could stop him. Strickland ran after him. "Stop, Colonel. It's the Chinese."

But MacLean couldn't hear him. Strickland chased after him, but before he could reach him, Colonel MacLean took a direct hit from the Chinese. He jerked around, hit four times in the chest by a burp gun, and looked back wide-eyed to Strickland. He was hit again. The slugs knocked his body back with each impact. He worked himself to the other side of the icy trail, but disappeared over the ledge down the gully just as Strickland got there.

Bullets flew all around Strickland, but none hit him. He raised up his pistols and fired at the Chinese soldiers closest to him, so close he could definitely smell the familiar NK body odor. Garlic. One by one he killed them, drilling his bullets right between their eyes with his uncanny marksmanship. He had become known as one of best with a reputation bordering on the legends of the Corps. But that reputation came during his peacetime team shooting that took him all the way to Camp Perry just before Korea became a war.

But this was not a shoot in the park. This was different. This was close up combat, face-to-face, and eye-to-eye. Life or death.

Strickland had learned in the Pacific to carry more ammo than he thought he'd need. So, naturally, he was always loaded up with a lot of .45 caliber rounds for his two Colts. He always figured that his life would ultimately depend upon his .45s. He'd fired standard issue copper rounds in matches. But not here. Here, he'd broken all the laws. The shells were standard but his bullets were made of lead and it was he who made them. The cross he cut into each bullet at the flattened front insured that when he hit someone, they would go down quickly.

His ammo was preloaded into nine-round clips. His right hand pistol had a special grip he'd had carved out of monkey wood. The art included a bald eagle at the center of the grip with a skull and crossbones at the base.

His legend wasn't just about his shooting though. And neither were the pistols. In Korea something else was happening to him. The "mad man" from the Pacific had returned to war in Korea to kill "pinko commie Chinks." It was a new phrase, a new enemy and a whole new purpose for him. And the "Commies" were killing his men as though there was only the purpose of killing in the air.

He was also convinced that he was going nuts or had gone nuts, and he had kept it to himself. Or had he? He wondered if the others had figured that out, or whether they too were becoming as crazy as he felt. The perfect shooter, authorized by a degree of combat insanity to kill, to murder as many men as he could, one at a time, cleanly, neatly, definitely.

"It's pay back time you assholes," he shouted after the first three Chinese dropped into heaps in the white crystal ground.

To the amazement of the soldiers in the two columns — who now joined in the firefight — the 'madman' fired each round purposefully, as though he were on the pistol range back at Pendleton.

Bang! Another North Korean soldier died. Bang! Another. Then a Chinese soldier. It didn't matter who they were, when they appeared in front of Strickland, they died before they could fire their own weapons.

And all the while he was doing this, Frank L. Strickland, a First Lieutenant of the United States Marine Corps, a man commissioned an officer and a gentleman, was yelling at the top of his voice, "Take that you mother'n sons of bitches." Bang! "And that!"

Bang!

All his anger and frustrations propelled out the barrels of the guns in his hands, taking their message of death accurately to the enemy in front of him. He was temporarily blinded by hatred and anger, enough to feel completely impervious to retaliation by the Chinese. Nobody could kill him. He was safe because he was in charge of the shooting.

The targets moved neatly for him like ducks or deer or geese all in a row. The fairgrounds. He remembered the little bunnies that bounced up, ran along a line, then curled down at the end. Just like these guys.

He was Sergeant York in Germany, Ghengis Khan in Manchuria. He was the master, the killer. He was God delivering his verdict for each of the enemy! And damned if he wasn't enjoying it.

And that's why he figured, he had gone unofficially nuts.

And the proof of his immortality to the soldiers around him was that bullets kept coming at him, whizzing and snapping by his head, passing between his legs, but never hitting him. He seemed to them, totally immune to the return fire. Clark Kent was dressed now as a pissed off Marine.

Then, once again amazing the American army behind him, the Chinese dropped back. They withdrew rapidly. The American Marine could not be killed. They would have to come back later and hope he was not around. The Chinese were once again made wary of the legends their fathers had passed down to them. Legends of the very giant United States Marines.

And the flares, that he had not noticed faded when the Chinese faded. Strickland however, was not finished. He continued to fire after them, shadows that only he seemed able to see. He never missed, always squeezed his trigger as though he were squeezing a sponge. By the time it was over he'd killed twenty-eight of them with twenty-seven rounds of ammunition.

The men at Tun Tavern would have been proud of him.

"Not bad for a day's work," Snake growled into his ear when it got quiet. "Too bad so many run away."

Strickland remained momentarily frozen in his stance. The crazed mind that had possessed him needed time to ease off, to shake the hot blood from its feeding frenzy. His eyes had to refocus on reality. What may or may not be his sanity must subdue that ugly, crazy part of him that came to the surface when he felt himself cornered.

Like, with those nuns, his teachers in grammar school. The ones who always wanted him to do something that he would never have otherwise done and always out of fear of God.

"Snake," he said after a few moments, "I think it's about time we get the hell away from this army. These guys keep gettin' us into deep shit."

"Yes, sir," the snake catcher said, wondering if possibly rattlers might be a bit safer than his own skipper.

A few moments of silence passed before Strickland spoke again. Then, gently, in a quivering voice he said, "That colonel was a good man, Snake. I was just getting to like him."

"Yes, sir." Fraker twirled his new cigar around in his mouth slowly. "Lieutenant?"

"Yeah?"

"We can't leave just yet, sir."

"Why not?"

"'Cause Drier and Polanco are over there in that trap. They're still with the other outfit. Far's I know, they might be dead by now." He spit into the snow, shoved his cigar back into his mouth. "But they's our kids, and we gotta get 'em. One way t'other."

"Still mother'n, huh, Snake?"

"Bet your sweet ass."

An hour later F4U Corsairs came to help rescue MacLean and Faith. They blasted, strafed and bombed the Chinese all day, helping to keep them off balance. They didn't let up. When darkness swept the area, the night fighters continued the attack, releasing napalm, bombs, rockets and more fifty-caliber cannon fire.

Communication had been lost with RCT-31. Faith had no way of contacting them. Two patrols had been sent out to sneak into their perimeter, but each was pushed back by the Chinese.

"We need help here, General," Faith pleaded over the radio to Brigadier General Hodes, assistant 7th Division commander.

But Hodes was also frustrated. "We're bogged down at Hudong-ni," he replied through heavy static. "Didn't those airdales help at all?"

"Yes, sir. But we're still trapped here."

"Sorry Colonel. That's all the power I had left."

Faith's demeanor changed. He became angry. He was completely aware that Hudong-ni was too far away for Hodes to do any good in time. "Give me an ETA on getting unbogged." He reeked with sarcasm, but what the hell, in his mind he was about to be pushing up daisies.

"MSR's blocked. We sent the 2nd Battalion from the 31st out. But they're fouled up. Ten (X) Corps is in shambles. No trucks. They've gotta walk." After a breathless pause, Hodes added, "You're on your own."

When Faith set the field phone back into its cradle, he pinched the bridge of his nose with his thumb and forefinger while staring down at his feet.

"Problems, Colonel?" the radioman asked.

Breathing heavily, pressing away the surge of electricity that streaked through his head, Faith simply muttered, "We've been had."

That night, the Chinese attacked in waves of human fodder. The cacophony of battle was as deafening as a train running over your head. No one could hear anyone shout, no one could think clearly. All you could do was shoot and pray and shoot some more. The Americans ran out of mortar rounds, light machine gun belts, and the automatic rifles were down to manual load. But they prevailed, and the Chinese were repelled one more time. The high cost to both combat teams signaled an end was coming. They could not repel another attack.

Strickland fought like a grizzly sow protecting her cub. Fraker put in his two bits, too. Drier and Polanco at their location were exhausted and began to count the minutes before their demise.

All around them good men died.

The next morning a few helicopters arrived to pick up the severely wounded, but no relief column came. A few fighter bombers came to keep the enemy awake and disorganized during the day. But still, no salvation from fresh ground troops.

Night came too quickly for the two teams who were still on their own. The enemy attacked again, and even though it was impossible according to the best of them, the Chinese were thrown back once more. The Americans had very few grenades, and no mortars nor artillery. They were also out of air support. And bullets were in extremely short supply.

Four more attacks came that night. By sheer guts and a few bayonets, the Chinese were thrown back after reaping a deadly toll on the Americans. By dawn, the Chinese had captured a hill in the middle of the surrounded perimeter.

Faith had accepted his fate before the battle and came through it surprised that he was still among the living. He marveled at the esprit of his troops. Wondered what force kept them going. Surely it had nothing to do with him. He was a good man, everyone had agreed to that, but this? This was pushing against a wall and he'd never been good enough to lay claim to this new found fierceness his troops exhibited.

Lieutenant Robert D. Wilson, with MacLean's RCT, a not so gutsy kid when attending high school in South Dakota, bravely volunteered to counterattack and retake the hill. When he assembled his men, Corporal Drier and Private Polanco joined in. "We've only got three grenades apiece, Lieutenant," Drier complained. "That's gonna make it a damned short fight."

"And just a few clips of ammo," Blade added. "We can make that work Lieutenant, but only if we attach our knives." He meant bayonets, but this was Blade speaking.

Wilson ordered bayonets attached and then checked the compound for more ammo and grenades. He went from man to man, from foxhole to foxhole. He checked at the CP and with the supply sergeant. "I know it's depressin', but we ain't got a single grenade anywhere. And Lieutenant," the staff sergeant added solemnly, "we ain't got no bullets left either. Matter of fact sir," he added with a wink, "It's so bad, I applied for a bartender's job at the Pusan O'Club just this morning."

"Funny, Sarge," Wilson said without laughing.

Without more than minimal ammo and a handful of grenades, they headed out for their mission. "Corporal Drier," Wilson said, "I hope two Marines really are worth a battalion of dogfaces like you say."

Drier grinned. "Sir, Blade's worth a division."

"Good, then we can't lose this one. My fresh out of the box bride back home will be happy to learn that." Both men also understood that taking the hill meant being able to rejoin Faith's RCT.

"Where's home?" Drier asked, not really caring.

"We're from Rapid City, South Dakota. Home of Mt. Rushmore. But she's still at Oceanside."

"You're the second South Dakota man I've met here."

"Yeah? Who's the other?"

"A corporal. From Pierre as I remember."

Wilson squinted, "I think he got it."

Drier blinked, thought he said a quick prayer, turned away leaving the lieutenant alone. Wilson shifted the pack on his back. "All right, let's go," he said with little enthusiasm. "At least we'll get warm."

They headed directly up the hill, straight at the Chinese. Mortar shells began dropping all around them. Machine gun fire was thick as sleet. The crescendo was ear shattering, the confusion instant. Wilson pointed to Drier. "Get your people up there and take out that bunker," he ordered. He wanted the machine gun quieted.

At the same instant Drier acknowledged the order, Wilson was struck heavily in the chest by three Chinese bullets. He collapsed, dead, his feet pointing downhill, his arms held out along the snow as though he was directing Drier. Sergeant First Class Fred Sugua jumped alongside him, pressed his forefingers against Wilson's carotid, looked up at Drier.

"Well, get a move on Marine. We don't got all day." Sugua was now in command.

Drier nodded and started up the hill. Sugua screamed out, clenched his throat, then fell to his knees and collapsed dead. Drier was now the senior non-com on the battlefield. He was now the commander. "Move out," he ordered over the din.

His men charged up the hill, angry they'd lost their commanders, angry because they were short of ammo and damned well pissed off because each man knew he was about to die.

Their attack was so ferocious that the Chinese turned and ran as soon as the Americans got to the top of the hill.

"Cowards," Private Hemphill shouted after them, still firing his M-1.

Drier glanced at the army man, nodded with an imperceptible grin. Then he noticed another soldier, one with a BAR still firing at the retreating Chinese, one shot at a time. He smiled now. It was Pfc. Barry Morgan, the kid Strickland told him about, the one who used axle grease and meat fat to lubricate his Browning. "That's enough, Morgan," he shouted over the firing.

Morgan was surprised the Marine knew his name. He stopped firing, gave off with a sheepish grin and then immediately sat down and started to work on his rifle.

Drier glanced around to take count of the dead and wounded. "Hey, Blade, where are you?" he called out.

"He's dead, Corporal," an exhausted soldier said to him coldly. Pointing back down the slope about fifty yards, he added, "That's your friend there. Got it just before the gooks split. Poor guy. He damned near made it."

Drier stared at Blade's corpse for a few moments, disbelieving the news, waiting for his friend to rise and come to him. "Blade?" he said, his throat was parched, his voice cracked in the chilling wind.

There was no response.

Drier blinked slowly. He had guessed this would happen sooner or later to one or both of them. Often, he thought it would be easier to be the first one to go down. Then you don't lose friends, you don't cry or worry. You just die. And you don't even know it.

He took in a breath of shivering cold air and headed down the slope to Blade where he knelt down. Making the sign of the holy cross with his right hand, he touched Blade's forehead and pulled his eyes closed. Then he drove Blade's rifle into the snow, butt up, and hung his friend's helmet on it. He reached down and unbuckled Blade's Buck Knife. He put it into the pocket of his field jacket and said, "Rest now, Blade. And if you can, please watch over me."

Then he sat next to him, and cried his heart out.

CHAPTER 6

"WHERE'S STRICKLAND?"

Faith wanted Strickland at his CP immediately.

"Here we go again."

Strickland was sure he appeared to the men around him like an old man in the city plaza, one of those guys he'd seen back home who was hunched over, had a cane and could barely walk. It always seemed to him that they were just sitting there waiting for death or rigor mortis.

"Just got a report from a Marine recon pilot. He says there aren't any friendlies within miles of this place. Hagaru is the first sighting of any U.N. troops. Marines." Faith seemed a bit more anxious than Strickland had seen before.

"That's the 1st comin' up to help." Faith paused. After a moment he said, "Sorry we couldn't get together with thirty-one."

"My men will be okay," Strickland said. He knew what Faith was getting at. But his voice had cracked. Emotions that he thought he'd lost long ago surfaced and it showed.

Faith recognized the reaction. He'd had it many times himself. But right now, they had to center on their own survival. "I've asked for and gotten an air strike to cover us at thirteen hundred hours."

Strickland's heart quickly pumped enough adrenaline for him to become alert again. The army was about to change course again and he wasn't sure he was up for that. His expression must have said it all to the colonel.

"Look, I'm going to need your help. You seem to understand the Chinese better than we do. We're going to make a break for it."

"In daylight?"

"Yes. We'll take all the vehicles we can, destroy the others. Fire off all the artillery rounds. We've got one working half-track with 40 mm guns. We can take that."

Strickland found himself searching deeply into Faith's eyes. Was this guy as nutty as he was? You just didn't attack a gazillion Chinese with a dozen men in broad daylight.

"Think we can do it." Faith wasn't asking. He was ordering.

Strickland glanced around at the survivors, then back into Faith's eyes. The Army officer looked about ten years older than when the battle had started. The man had also seemed taller before. He was obviously intelligent, well trained and eager to save his men. But more than the tone in his voice had changed. His physical stature had also been altered. It had become gaunt, as starkly naked of body meat as a wild turkey. It was the sign of the toll that battle takes from each of them. They could kill the enemy, but they couldn't stop the ravages of war from stealing from their own living future. He wondered about himself. Probably close to death very much like Faith.

The walking dead. They would not be remembered, nor ever appreciated for the disaster that shouldn't have been. "I've tasted defeat," he said to himself, "and it's bitter." He would have to go along with the army guy's request, of course. What other choices were there?

"We can fight our way out of this, meet the First Marines and then come back at the Chinese and kill 'em all."

Bravo! his inner self cried out. All Marine, right? He shook his head only for himself. Something was still very wrong here. The Chinese were probably watching them as they spoke. Probably ready for them no matter what they decided.

"Okay," Faith said. "I'll put two soldiers through the Chinese lines into Thirty-One's position and relay that message. We'll do this together."

When both units understood the plan, Faith ordered the artillery to commence firing. "Shoot until you're out of rounds," he commanded them. "Then blow up the pieces and fall in at the rear of the column."

Lieutenant Mortrude, a youngster with the pluck of a Bronx born Irishman, which he was, and the wily ways of an elf, would ride the half-track at the head of the column.

"We'll push through, Colonel," he said to Faith. "There's never been another thought in my mind."

Faith smiled. He liked the curly haired Irish kid. The man had proved himself a true warrior more than once. Faith was also aware of Mortrude's motives for getting out alive. "If you play heads up Lieutenant, you might make that wedding. We'll start out as soon as the fighter cover arrives."

Mortrude took off to gather his men.

When cover came Mortrude headed down the narrow road that would lead them over the Toktong Pass, and into Hagaru-ri.

In the cockpit of his F4U Corsair, Marine Major 'Stumpy' Decker, a taut, blue-eyed fighter pilot known to his men as "Pappy" because at the age of 32 he was the oldest in the squadron, looked down at the column of troops along the road below. He checked his coordinates, then looked again. The squadron consisted of four planes. "I can't make out which are ours and which are theirs."

A few moments passed before a very experienced and hawkeyed Lieutenant Brooks replied. "The guys on the road are ours."

"You sure?" Lieutenant Hogg asked from his cockpit. "Man, they look like Chinese."

Decker had to make a decision. They circled twice, all the time checking the ground. Armed men were scattered on the hillsides, on the roads, in the gullies. From their altitude the colors of uniforms seemed the same – white, the weapons appeared to be the same. The British tank models were new to them, but the Chinese also had similar tanks. Confusion ruled. "Jesus, there's so many down there that blood's gonna flow all the way to Hudong-ni."

"There's a half-track. Army. Ours. It's moving."

"Stumpy, that's gotta be theirs. G-2 says our troops are out of everything from ammo to trucks."

"Where's their FAC?"

"Dead."

"Try them one more time. They probably have Prick Tens."

He meant PRC-10s, made by Phillips Radio Company.

"Red Charlie One," Decker called.

On the ground the colonel's new radio man, Corporal Charles Ledbetter, was taking a leak into the snow. His radio was on the snow pack, his hand receiver buried underneath it. He could not hear the call.

"Nobody there, Stumpy."

"We're here to help the army guys, Hog man. Some of those men have to be ours." He called again. "Red Dog One, are you there?"

Ledbetter buttoned up his trousers with his nearly frozen fingers and recovered his radio pack. He jostled it on to his shoulders and then pulled the receiver up. "Red Dog One," he said.

"We're overhead," Stumpy Decker said. "What are your coordinates?"

"Uh, this is Red Dog One. Uh, don't know the coordinates. Will get the colonel. Hang on."

"Is he kidding?" Hogg asked.

Decker punched his mike open. "We're running low of fuel up here pal. Are you on the road yet?"

Ledbetter was having trouble locating Faith. "No," he answered. We're just now heading that way."

Decker made his decision. "Let's go. The road is our target. Hold fire until we're close in." He rolled over on his side in a steep slip and headed down.

Each pilot held off their red trigger buttons until they got close enough to see the troops. They fired, squeezing the gun buttons on their joysticks. Stumpy toggled his bomb switch.

Instead of hitting the Chinese, they dropped their bombs on the head of the Faith column. One slammed into Mortrude's half-track. Fire was everywhere and all at once.

Men with hope in their hearts died horribly.

Three of Mortrude's men screamed in fatal agony, but mercifully only for a few seconds. Mortrude was thrown clear of the wreckage and the intense heat. He landed nearly eighty feet away possibly more he thought. The mound of snow that caught him protected his crash landing. He stood quickly like an acrobatic athlete would, but all he could see were damaged vehicles, fire and dead men.

The explosion had taken off Corporal Smith's left leg. He fell, tumbled backward into the flames that had punished the half-track. He died where he landed. Corporal Bob Henderson, the half-track's long-legged driver, a kid from Indianapolis, who'd worked the 500 dreaming that he could one day himself drive the race, made it to the icy road, stumbled a few feet and then dropped dead from severe burns.

Mortrude was unable to help his men. A sense of guilt rushed through him when he discovered he'd been blown out of the fiery vehicle unscathed. The burned corpses of his men brought up his C-rations while he fell to his knees and buried his head into the snow all the while screaming above the sound of the explosions, crying enough to cause his tears to freeze to his flesh.

The column had gone into disarray immediately, trying to escape both the Chinese, who'd begun firing at them, and the American pilots.

"Pull up. Pull up!" Faith screamed into the PRC strapped to the dead Ledderman's back. "You're killing Americans."

His men were running away, off into the ditches and behind walls created by ice-covered boulders and dirt. The Chinese were picking them off one at a time.

Colonel Faith stood bravely in the center of the chaos and waved his .45 in the air demanding that his men return to fight on.

It had become classic battlefield pandemonium.

Decker rolled to the right and pulled straight up until his Corsair nearly stalled. Where in the hell did that voice come from? Killing Americans? Blood drained from his brain, his mind suddenly blanked out from the horror of the scene he'd just created. From instinct only, he pushed the stick forward, flattening the plane's attitude and waited there for his men while moving 350 mph straight ahead. Sticky sweat rolled off his hands and forehead. He thought seriously of running the plane into the enemy's position, a suicide dive. He jerked off his lightweight helmet, wiped his brow and sucked in air as though he'd been suffocating.

"My God," he shouted into the emptiness of his cockpit, "I've killed my own boys."

He leaned forward and vomited on the deck of his plane. He tried sucking down more fresh air. He wanted to rip off the canopy; he wanted to jump. A huge lump grabbed him at his heart and settled in his throat. He choked, coughed it out. Someone was screaming into his earphones that he'd just murdered Americans and wouldn't he for god's sake stop? He began to cry uncontrollably.

The others, unspeaking, fell into formation. Finally, gathering all his training together, but regretting ever having signed up for the Corps, Stumpy said in a barely audible voice, "Let's go home."

On the ground, clearly unsettled and feeling useless, Mortrude stumbled along the road trying to pull together his ten living men. His mind grasped the impossibility of his position. He still had a mission to accomplish and he'd made a promise to the colonel who was now waving his pistol at his own men while shouting to them to get back into the fight.

Mortrude knew that he must clear the road ahead.

Faith caught sight of him a few moments later. He was amazed to see Mortrude and his survivors back on the job. They were working above and beyond their training, doing it all on foot, doing it he knew, to help forget the horror they'd just lived through.

Mortrude's guys pushed aside dead vehicles and the frozen cadavers of old friends — men they'd come to know too well in such a short, short period of time. They had become automatons, something Faith had witnessed in Europe. It was the best way to escape the absurd conditions they were in. They would continue on he knew, so he returned his pistol to its holster and continued urging his living to press on.

When Mortrude's group came to a bombed out bridge two miles down the road, they were joined by Company A. That meant that RCT-32 and 31 were now together. Mortrude's nearly defeated countenance said more than his words. But he was a leader, and he'd do his damndest. He spoke weakly, but tried to be lightly cavalier. "Fancy meeting you gents here," he said, then stopped. He couldn't carry on the joke that had crossed his flamed out brain.

The combined unit of foot troops only, continued on under the broken bridge, and headed southward. But the Chinese had other ideas. Without warning they opened fire immediately with big-bore rifles, and burp guns. The goddamned Chinese were everywhere.

"Spread out, spread out!" Mortrude ordered. "Don't bunch."

He was cut short by a Chinese mortar. It exploded near him, knocking him back about fifteen feet. This time he wasn't as lucky as before. A piece of shrapnel clipped him in the head, knocking off his helmet and cutting through his skull. He fell to the ground alive, but unconscious.

When Faith's operable vehicles finally got to Mortrude's position, they were forced to stop. The survivors of Mortrude's group and the A Company members who joined them had driven off the Chinese. Nevertheless, the bridge was not usable and Faith had vehicles that needed to cross the deep although narrow gap in the road. Continuing on without a bridge-replacement would be impossible. They would have to build a bypass.

Faith had Mortrude placed into a six-by truck. Then, searching the hillsides with his binoculars he asked Strickland, "Where the hell are the goddamned Chinese?"

"They're looking back at us, sir," Fraker volunteered. "They'll wait until they think we're vulnerable."

Strickland, like his men, was exhausted, once again driving himself with adrenaline only. His legs felt like soft rubber especially at his knees, his arms like lead weights. The colonel had to be feeling the same way.

"Fraker's right, Colonel. You can bet they're watching."

"From where?"

Strickland's gaze ricocheted from one hillside shadow to another while he turned his head from the steep mountains to the valley, then back to Faith. He appeared to be sniffing the air. Faith found him to be a "most curious man."

"I'd have to say, all around us. We got 'em surrounded."

"Don't get corny on me now."

"They're close, too. Garlic is in the air. I think they drink that stuff."

"Thing of it is, Colonel," Fraker said, "this man can smell the gooks a mile away and count 'em too."

"Christ, you Marines are packaged and wrapped in bullshit." He sighed heavily, "But I love ya. You fight like hell. Okay. All around us it is."

"They'll start shootin' after the trucks get into the middle of the bypass." Fraker said. "Always that way, Colonel." He pulled the stubby Cuban Faith himself had given him from his mouth and spit into the snow. "Maybe we should set up a couple Trojan horses for 'em." Glancing back up into Faith's eyes he grunted, "Think so?"

"Crazy."

"Well, sir, 'tis that. But it's the only suggestion I got, other than running like hell."

Faith ordered two patrols out to confirm Strickland's estimate. They waited while the bridge was being built and while the patrols were out. Strickland and Fraker explained that the patrols would more than likely return empty handed. He'd been right. When the patrols returned, Staff Sergeant Lucas Philbin, the shortest but best damned football player in Covington, Kentucky history, reported, "Nothing sir. No Chinese, no NKs, no friendlies."

Faith released the patrols and seemed to pout, although it was Strickland's guess that he was really exhibiting exhaustion.

"You ever hunt mountain lions?" Strickland asked.

Faith didn't want to lose his Marine's interest in helping them. "No."

"Well sir, a mountain lion can never be spotted. You have to hide, cover your scent and wait for hours and hours for one to come to you. Problem is the mountain lion may be waiting for you, too. First one to move, or let's say, if the chase is on, first one to falter gets it in the ass. Chinese are the same way. They wait until we're tuckered out or just plain cashed in. Like now. You think they aren't out there? They are. Like the lion, they have lots of patience. Just let your guard down and poof. The lion lunges at you."

"It's just best you believe they're there," Fraker added.

Strickland could tell from the tone in his voice that Fraker was getting a bit jittery. He glanced to him, let him know with his expression that everything was okay; at least he and Fraker would make it out of there alive.

Faith was torn between his trained and mandated army doctrine and the reality that this crazy Marine, this former enlisted man now an officer, this character of a mix of insanity and sanity was his 'trusted' guide; a nutty Marine had become his personal intelligence officer. He couldn't remember how that had happened even though it occurred only hours before or was it days?

"I guess I'll have to rely on you Lieutenant. You know, back home we have a saying. It goes something like this. If you don't know something, but your neighbor does, bend the fence a little and ask."

Fraker furrowed his brow. "What's that mean, Colonel?"

"Well, in this case, it means the army and the Marines better get together so we can all survive. I bow to your Lieutenant's knowledge of the Chinese in Korea. Look, I have very few officers left in working condition. Actually only one is not wounded, Major Jones. Good man. I hope he makes it all the way. So, I'm counting on you —"

"Colonel," Strickland said with urgency, now wanting to be away from this melancholy man, "I hope we all make it."

"Ready, sir," the burly sergeant in charge of the engineer group constructing the bypass reported.

Colonel Faith rubbed his chin, pushing ice from his stubby beard. "Load one of the lead trucks with riflemen, Lieutenant," he ordered. "We'll try your sergeant's Trojan horse."

What were known as multi-fuelers, or deuce and a half trucks, roared to life, belching out black diesel smoke that rose with dimensional depth against the whiteness of the snow and ice. Drivers inched their way across the freshly made bypass. Icy river water, open enough for chunks of ice to float southward, jostled the makeshift detour, causing the drivers to proceed with extra caution. Then it happened. The Chinese opened fire right on Fraker's suggested schedule.

"Aww goddamn it," Faith screamed. He wanted to grab his patrol leader by the neck, but that urge passed through him quickly.

Fraker came to life. "Turn this truck upstream!" he ordered the driver. The truck entered the low water and headed upstream. The truck went about fifty yards over the icy rocks, pushing itself closer to the Chinese, but the Horse didn't have the legs for the river so it stalled.

"Open fire!" Fraker shouted.

The riflemen and one team of .30 caliber light machine gun operators threw off the canvas covering and started firing into the hillside, blowing away the rest of the canvas and a helluva lot of Chinese with their first bursts.

"Bastards," Fraker yelled over the gunfire. "Kill all of 'em."

He stood against the fusillade, challenging the Chinese with waving arms, not understanding whether he wanted to live or die. The rest of the trucks continued along the road they'd left behind them, safely crossing the stream as rapidly as possible, protected to some extent by Fraker's small force having drawn the complete attention of the Chinese.

A truck stalled in the middle of the convoy. Mortrude, now spread out in the back and conscious, realized his vehicle had just gotten stuck. He rolled out of the truck and staggered toward the head of the column where he found a ¾-ton.

"Mind if I join you?" he called out through his agonizing wound. Even though he had lost a lot of blood and a piece of his head, he had drawn on unknown phantoms in his still-existing mind to move, to run, to help himself to safety. He climbed into the vehicle and continued on his way.

Strickland, at the tail of the column, ran toward the stalled truck to see what he could do to get things moving. All around him along the road he saw dead Americans, most laid in stacks or piles on truck hoods or across smaller jeeps. At one point, he picked a wounded soldier up from where he lay in an open field of bluish ice and helped him into the back of a truck. Then he continued on, searching for more living among the newly dead. The Chinese had taken their attention away from Fraker and now were taking on the convoy. He had become numb to the shooting. For him this had become normal. This must be what life really is.

Fraker continued his attack on the Chinese who were scrambling back up their mountain by the score. "Sarge," PFC Hall cried out. Hall was a black soldier from New Orleans the others called Dr. J. The "J" stood for the great Jazz that came out of his tenor saxophone. He liked the Selmer Conn he'd tell you and then he'd pick it up and play like no one you'd ever heard before.

"Lookee here, Sarge," he yelled. "Half the guys is hit. We're runnin' out'a ammo. It's time to bug-out, man!" Hall continued to fire his BAR and throw hand grenades up the mountain. A mortar round hit the hood of the truck and the vehicle bounced up, then settled. Another round came down just behind the truck.

"Get your asses out'a here," Fraker shouted. "They got us zeroed in!"

"Good 'nuff for me," Dr. J shouted. He jumped from the truck and high-tailed as fast as he could to protective cover.

The remaining living leaped from the truck and ran behind Dr. J. At the road they turned right and headed for the front of the column. Fraker headed the other way, looking for Drier and Strickland. He noticed the Chinese had slowed their shooting, but were still taking potshots whenever they found a target.

He got quickly to Strickland. "This constant bickering between us and the Chinks is gettin' on my nerves."

It was "Gunny" talk. Strickland nearly laughed. It was important for Fraker to be that way, important to himself and the others around him. True, he had shown signs of weariness, but now the blood flowed, the anger rose and he wanted to fight his way out of there and not into more Chinese.

Strickland was doing his best to lift a soldier off the icy road into a truck. Fraker moved in to help him.

"You don't look so good," he said to Strickland.

Fraker felt suddenly responsible for his skipper. First there was Joe Hughes, and only God knew what had happened to him. But Fraker did know where Strickland 's mind was, but it was his duty to get him home safely. They'd find Hughes he decided, probably between white sheets with a pretty nurse mother 'n him.

Strickland sounded depressed. "Want to upchuck it all. Terrible feeling. Too many dead, dammit. All dead." His hatred for the enemy and the endless combat was beginning to dominate his thinking. His anger showed by the way he lifted the men into the trucks. No longer was he careful about it. There were simply too many of them for that.

Fraker worked quickly, mostly in an eerie silence that seemed to clash with the crunch of snow and ice, and the mutterings of his skipper mixed with the screaming of the wounded they lifted.

They ended up strapping the wounded with the dead to the hoods of trucks, laying them across the canvas tops of jeeps, placing them one on the other. It was a scene that would not make it to Movietone news in your local theater.

"Heaps," Strickland muttered. "They're just frozen lumps. They never were anything else," he said, apparently trying to talk himself into accepting the chaos of so many frozen dead.

An explosion ripped through the air. It had come from the head of the column, which was now under attack at another Chinese roadblock. The column was stopped again.

"What now?" Faith shouted.

Strickland rushed past Faith with Fraker right behind him "We now have Chinese and North Koreans to deal with."

Faith caught himself sniffing. Ridiculous he thought. Nobody could smell what that guy smells. Gunpowder, yes. Garlic? "My God, it is garlic. And gun powder."

He got out of his jeep and moved angrily along the column, past Strickland, and toward the column point. At each vehicle he shouted, "C'mon men, let's get it moving. We can't kill time here. You, soldier, get out of that truck and return their fire."

He went like that, from truck to truck, pulling his men together, urging them to form up and counterattack. When he finished, he found he had only 200 fighting survivors remaining, and only one other army officer, Major Jones. He called back for Strickland to come forward.

While they waited for the Marine, Faith and Major Jones formed their remaining soldiers into two units and launched a two-pronged attack against the roadblock. Firing his .45 at the Chinese straight up the road, Faith hurriedly led his men right into the center of the enemy.

At the column's point, Faith's plan was working. The enemy dispersed, once again opening the road for the column to move. "Get that truck up here," Faith shouted back to the lead driver.

Major Jones called him on the PRC-10. "Colonel, we've cleared the left flank —" the radio went dead.

Faith, thinking the worst shouted to Sergeant Dell, the man Strickland had been searching for since he'd first met up with MacLean's outfit. "Dell, take a squad up and clear the rest of the road —" he heard something just then. A whistling sound, a sort of shrieking whistle.

Moments later, when Strickland got there, he found Colonel Faith mortally stretched out alongside the road where he'd just been killed by a mortar round. Sergeant Dell stood over him. Dell was exhausted and discouraged and not dead like Fraker had reported earlier. He looked up into Strickland's eyes, blinked slowly, said nothing. Neither man spoke. They didn't have to. Whatever it was between them before had just evaporated. A very good man had just died while showing them all the way to fight.

After a few moments, Strickland stumbled back against a six-by, his gut wrenching from the weariness of death. Fraker and Dell took up positions alongside him. Everyone had their rifle at the ready, but their spirit to fight had waned.

In the background of Strickland's fading mind, he could hear the continuing gunfire up ahead, and the pitched voice of the only remaining army officer.

Coach Justin M. (Sam) Barry stared hard at his players during the only halftime against UCLA he'd ever know. Since 1910, Coach Barry would be the only coach in USC history to serve as coach for only one year. He had to win this game. UCLA was USC's major rival, a game that loomed larger to students and alums than any other. Barry's season wasn't going well. Two wins six losses. USC was in the dumps and the alums were already calling for his head.

It was pep-talk time. One he wished he could deliver like Knute Rockne had just a few years before at Notre Dame. Stir these guys up into a machine, a playing, killing machine. He took a deep breath. He'd try.

"All year you've been playing behind. All year you've left something at home while suited up to play." He paused, breathed deeply and then went on. "Anderson. You're playing like you're still in high school. In practice you're great, in games you start out hot as hell then back off. Well, today you can't do that. Today, I may have to replace you with this new hotshot freshman here." He turned to Strickland, a freshman who was cleared by the NCAA to play if needed for this game only. "You ready to play, son?"

Strickland looked at William Anderson, who was a well-known USC quarterback. Anderson was having a bad year because the other teams were having great years and probably, he thought, because Barry wasn't a very good coach. He gulped and weakly nodded his head.

Barry turned back to Anderson. "Well, what will it be men? Are you going to go out there and play hard? Are you going to go out there and not quit on me? Are you ready to beat the pants off those Bruins?"

A roar went up, but not a very loud one. Strickland, whose own high school had never won a game while he was quarterback, felt a sudden queasiness in his gut. He was a freshman for god sakes. But because the backup quarterback had been injured, Barry had gotten permission to play him if necessary. Barry turned to him. "Strickland, if Anderson here can't pull it off, you get a shot. If you do, don't fall apart on me. Never quit son. Keep going straight ahead until you win. Do you understand that?"

Again all Strickland could do was nod in the affirmative.

"He won't have to play, Coach," Anderson bellowed. He turned to his team and yelled out, "Will he?"

They roared louder for Anderson than they had for Barry.

Time came and they headed out to the field. It was a grueling mess of a game. Toward the end of the final quarter the score was 7 to 7. A tie was in the offing. A tie meant Barry's job was as good as gone. Barry called Strickland up.

"You ready to fight? Get us on the board to beat those bastards."

Strickland's knees nearly buckled and it showed.

"Look son, remember what I told you. Straight ahead. Never give up. That's the only way to win. You can do it."

"Straight ahead," Major Jones shouted.

Strickland snapped around. He hustled toward Jones's position. Straight ahead! That's the only way to win! His mind went back to the game. It ended a 7 to 7 tie. It was a real bummer.

This was different, though. This was live or die. There was no such thing as a tie. He grabbed up an M-1 and a half loaded bandoleer from a dead soldier and made his way to the column's front. Fraker tailed behind him, wondering where in the hell Strickland got his sudden burst of energy.

Jones was trying to pull together the living, but it was proving nearly impossible. Three trucks had been rendered inoperable. They were packed with wounded who were now in grave danger. Strickland and Fraker helped the soldiers move them, piling them two and three deep into the operable trucks.

Then they pushed the wrecks off the road. And all during this the Chinese continued fighting.

When they'd finally got the road clear and the trucks moving again, Fraker found himself leaning against a blown out tree stump. Drier appeared next to him like an apparition from another world.

He'd been at the point of the column, right in the middle of the fire-fight since meeting up at the bridge. Fraker looked around for Polanco.

"Where's Blade?"

Drier's eyes welled up.

"Dead, Gunny. They killed him." He reached into his field jacket and pulled Polanco's dog tags out slowly, as though he were pulling on his own heart strings. "Here," he said, handing one of them to Fraker. He kept the other, as well as Blade's Buck Knife.

"You okay?"

"Yeah. Why does this have to be so shitty, Sarge? He was my friend."

Fraker sighed.

"That's what makes all this very, very hard."

"I cried."

Fraker rolled the scruffy cigar around in his mouth, and added simply, "'S'way things are, son. Best you let me break this news to the skipper."

The Skipper was having his own problems. He was fighting old worlds with new realities. Coach Barry's decade-old words woke him, but the sight of all the dead had numbed his senses. As though some kind of metamorphosis was taking place in his mind, the dead bodies no longer seemed to mean anything to him. He tried to think of them as fellow players sprawled out after a scrimmage but no, they weren't players and they weren't sprawled.

They were corpses.

His eyes roved across the chaotic results of maniacal war while his mind worked at football. The similarities were there; it was just that he failed to justify this world with his former world. The stone cold faces became cards in a gambler's deck. Their eyes buttons for the frozen earth. He tried to shake off the nightmare that seemed to have embedded itself in his mind. Was there supposed to be a payoff somewhere? It can't just keep on bein' like this without a reason. Straight ahead. Straight ahead.

But the bodies remained the same.

Stiff.

Cold.

Dead.

Jones broke into his lurid dream. "Let's move out," he commanded.

The column pushed ahead again. This time without enemy fire slowing them but instead the enemy seemingly pulled back, stopped firing. At least for now. A mile more and they were stopped by two burned out tanks that blocked the road.

"We can't move 'em, Major," Dell said to Jones.

Jones figured the Chinese had placed the tanks in the road to block them from breaking out of there. That meant they were nearby and probably ready to finish them off. He glanced back to Strickland who only nodded his head a bit to indicate he agreed with the thoughts running through the commander's mind. Jones turned back to Dell.

"Build another bypass, Sergeant."

"Yes sir." But dejection rang in Dell's voice.

"I know we're all beat, Sarge. But let's hustle or we may not make it out of here."

"Straight ahead," the arriving Strickland muttered. "Straight ahead."

It took a half-hour.

With Dell's new primitive but effective bypass they were able to push on.

Strickland took a tumble in the snow. It had happened so quickly that he was not able to catch himself. He'd stepped on a river rock that had been slicked over from eons of water and ice. He spread out alongside the war weary road as though he'd just been shot or tried to play Icarus from a tree. Fraker was at his side almost instantly. He grabbed Strickland's right arm and helped pull him up.

Fraker could feel the loss of strength in his friend's effort to recover, the same loss he'd experienced himself on Okinawa just before that battle ended. You just get damned tired, and that's when you also can get yourself killed.

Strickland was dazed. Fraker gave him a quick once-over to make sure the man hadn't been shot. No blood, that was good. But his skipper had become a zombie. He motioned to Drier to take Strickland's M-1 while he led their skipper back to the convoy and put him into one of the lead trucks.

"Take care of my friend here, driver. Ya hear? He's had a very bad week."

Around twenty hundred hours, they came to a small village. "We're gonna make it," the lead truck driver, Pfc. Brennan, a clean cut kid from Coeur d' Alene, Idaho, shouted into his PRC-6. "It's Hudong-ni." But a mortar round ended the communication and Brennan's life. Without warning, Chinese fired on the convoy from all directions. They hadn't bugged out after all. Instead, they had regrouped while keeping tabs on the Americans.

The remnants of RCT-31 and RCT-32 were still a long way from Hudong-ni. An explosion caused Brennan's truck to roll over on the driver's side, spilling out the wounded they'd worked so hard to save. In the process the truck crushed half of its occupants to death, including Lieutenant Mortrude.

The driver behind Brennan, in the truck Strickland was in, freaked out and spun his wheel to the right, causing his truck to slide on the icy road and crash into a tree. Now, the road was blocked by their own trucks, and their freshly dead.

When Strickland watched the wounded spill out of the first truck and be crushed by the vehicle itself, and then saw the wounded tumble from the truck he was in, he leaned out his open window and vomited dryly, his gut was empty. His mind raced with confusion and hatred. He flashed on a million things in his own past and none of them had to do with a fucked up war in Korea.

His thoughts returned to the Pacific where death was all too common and survivors were more likely maimed than simply wounded. He was now convinced that his own life would end soon. He'd have to gut up, suck it in and let it happen as a man, not as a coward. He glanced up into the snowpack that was now only a foot away from his window. The truck was jammed into the slope. He glanced back to his driver. The kid was dead. In a single instant, every emotion of fiery anger he'd ever experienced surfaced along with the overwhelming sickness he felt. He was suddenly unable to control himself. He had become, he realized, psychologically paralyzed. Then he heard Fraker. Somewhere in the distance, getting closer, coming to his truck.

"Get your ass outta there, Skipper!" Fraker yanked the driver side door open and pulled Strickland down past the dead driver. "C'mon, we gotta boogie. I told you these assholes would get us kilt."

Drier helped Snake guide his skipper away from the chaos. All around them soldiers scattered. Major Jones was leading as many as possible down the railroad line that ran north and south around the town.

Other drivers stayed with their trucks, deciding to make a run for it through the town. Fraker and Drier pulled Strickland up to a parapet of bombed out concrete and wood where they watched from behind a block wall. "Goddamned bastards," Fraker growled.

"Which ones?" Drier asked, meaning the Army or the Chinese.

Fraker glanced at him, snarled. "Look at that. Jones can't stop 'em. The trucks are trying to run the gauntlet. They'll die. All o' them. Chinks are just waitin'"

The trucks, most still loaded with wounded, were barreling into the village. It was obvious they thought they could run past the Chinese. But the Chinese came at them with mortars, grenades, and machine guns. The trucks blew up, spilling more wounded men into the snow. Those falling onto the ground first were crushed by the trucks behind them. The Chinese shot the others while Fraker, Strickland, and Drier watched helplessly in horror.

"Aww —" Strickland moaned. He leaned down into the snow and heaved up his dry stomach again. Nothing came out.

Fraker picked him up by the back of his jacket and yelled, "Move it, Lieutenant. Or we're gonna be as dead as them." It was time for Fraker to take charge. Time for the old sarge to save his skipper's ass.

They dashed back in the direction from which they'd come, this time tired, and angry, and possibly a bit scared.

The survivors who could walk, scattered. Those who could not were left behind and either froze to death or died from lack of food, or their inability to defend themselves against the Chinese, who systematically murdered those they found. In this battle, no prisoners would be taken. It was strictly a life or death engagement.

The two RCTs were finished. More than 892 of the original 1100 men had perished. They'd been through the worst battle of Korea so far, delivering to history America's worst combat debacle. And it wasn't even over yet.

Fraker led the way. Drier stayed to the rear where he would be responsible for checking the right and left flanks and behind them.

Strickland was recovering, but the trauma he'd been through

had weakened him greatly. "No way we're gonna make it through Toktong Pass alone," Fraker said. "Best we work our way back to our own battalion."

"You're nuts," Strickland groaned with a weakened voice. "We don't even know where they are."

"If they're smart, Lieutenant, they're coming down the road toward us. All we gotta do is go straight ahead through the trees, on their flank."

"Neither Smith nor Puller would bug out, Gunny. They'd die first."

"In which case, Mr. Strickland, Puller's men be comin' this way anyhow, 'cause this is where the Chinks are."

The snow started falling again.

Strickland shook his head. The cobwebs wouldn't go away. He closed his eyes tightly, then opened them again. "What we don't need right now," he muttered, "is more snow."

Fraker smiled. The man's humor was coming back. "We can move faster, Lieutenant," Fraker said. "No way the gooks gonna spot us at night in a snow storm. Said so yourself once't."

"You believe everything I say, Snake?"

"You bet your sweet ass I do. Now, sir, if you don't mind, let's hucklebuck."

They stuck to the east side of the road and worked their way north, back into the heart of enemy territory.

CHAPTER 7

IT SEEMED EVERYONE IN AMERICA was tuned in to MacArthur's straight-backed Army demeanor that always included a cocked hat and a corncob pipe. At least, that was his public image.

He was Douglas MacArthur after all, a man synonymous with unfamiliar names of places learned only recently by Americans, like Corregidor, Bataan, and of course they knew him mostly because he was the guy who had stated flatly that, "I shall return." Return as it were to a few thousand of his own troops at Corregidor, who he left behind for the Japanese to capture, torture and kill.

Much of his ado had been polished up by trained publicists as high-powered public relations needed for "the war effort."

According to Mac himself, his actions were based solely on an effort to help America get through the excessively high loss of life in the Pacific.

Ego was there. A high, tenacious ego was Mac's persona, as explained more than once by another general who never saw eye-to-eye with his former WestPoint brother. Ike had little use for Mac during World War II, and he let the politicos know it.

However, Mac's overwhelming ego helped him at times, although it also required a hi-test form of damage control now and then.

Korea was becoming for him one of those necessary times. A combination of events and changes in the homeland were making life tough for the dictatorial general. It was bad enough that the Chinese were smarter than he ever considered them to be, bad enough that North Koreans could actually fight. But now he was faced with a new enemy, one who wasn't playing the game the way Mac wanted them to play it. And his ego was about to explode on the world scene with a head-on collision with non other than Harry S. Truman.

Truman was president and that made him Mac's commander in chief. And HST was behaving like a real commander in chief, which upset MacArthur.

Oh for the good old days of FDR when Mac was the boss in the Pacific and Mac could do anything he wanted as long as he won the war. FDR gave him free rein. HST did not.

In his office at EUSAK Headquarters, in Tokyo, Japan where he planted himself during his Korean war tenure—never actually visiting Korea—MacArthur paced apprehensively from his large leather chair, along a row of U.N. flags, to the portrait of Harry Truman that hung alongside his own, although Harry's was lower. It was obvious that in the great General's office, he, Mac, was the commander, not the President.

After glancing with a bit of disdain at Truman's image, he returned to his spacious oak desk that had been made just for him and later carted around the Pacific at his whim. The desk had thirteen drawers. Six on each pedestal and one under the top. It was an impressive desk with hand carved designs of birds, military symbols and Mac's five stars, which crossed at the top of each side, designed with deep relief to appear with shadows and all.

He'd summoned his two field commanders, Generals Almond and Walker, to this meeting. He had a problem on his hands, one of magnificent proportions, and he had to work himself out of it if he were to maintain credibility with the American people and get Truman off his back.

He paused at the easel next to his desk. "You must help the Eighth Army," he demanded of Almond, pointing to the situation map that Walker had brought with him. It was clipped to the board on his easel. It showed X Corps and the Eighth split by a huge gap where the Chinese were filling the hole, circling both units; trapping them. "The way to do it, is to send the 3rd Infantry Division westward, here, along this road, across the Taebaek Mountains. They can attack the Chinese forces moving down the Eighth Army's right flank, and put an end to this whole goddamned snare." Turning to them he added, "Then, after that, we can push to the Yalu and on into Manchuria." He hadn't yet accepted the concept that they were getting the crap kicked out of their ground-pounding infantry units.

"That's a fifty mile gap in the lines, General," Walker said, wondering why Mac hadn't retired by now. He certainly was sounding like he should. Walker was a bull dog sort of man both in looks and actions.

Almond spoke. "The road you're referring to on the map, is not there. As a matter of fact, I've learned in the past two days that all the situation maps our commanders are using are inaccurate." He had actually learned it before the battles began, but blew off the revelation as not true simply because he wanted them to be there.

"We might as well have given them blank sheets of paper," Walker said.

Mac paid no attention to their pleas or situation facts. "I've informed Truman and the Chief of Staff that I intentionally left this gap here so that the Chinese could be sucked into that area and we could trap them. You, gentlemen, must work with that."

Almond came to his feet. Even he couldn't take much of this. "General Mac Arthur, it is we who are in a trap, not them."

"Frankly Mac, I'm surprise you made such a plan," Walker chided. He knew Mac hadn't done any such thing.

In fact, MacArthur was already searching for a scapegoat. He had guessed that neither general would salute his flag based a threat from him, but he had to confirm it for himself.

The bottom line for Mac was that inwardly he fully understood that he'd made a major tactical error when sending Americans too far north without adequate support or supplies.

"Multiple Divisions of Chinese have taken that area. General," Almond continued. "If we send the 3rd Infantry in there they'll be decimated."

MacArthur pulled the unlit corncob pipe from his mouth slowly. He gazed deeply into Almond's eyes. "Are you suggesting to me Ed, that you won't do this for me?"

"I'll do it if that's what you want, but I'll have to insist that Walton here," he looked over to General Walker, "keep them adequately supplied at all times. Right now, that's not happening."

"I can't promise that," Walker said quickly. "There is no way to guarantee it. Weather is dreadful. Trucks are few with too many not working. It's a logistical nightmare right now."

"The Chinese weren't bluffing," Almond said. "There were

600,000 Chinese soldiers across the border when we launched the attack a few days ago. And another 125,000 have been inside Korea since October."

Mac had refused to accept those numbers before the battles and he didn't want to hear them now.

"It was all a mistake," Walker stated flatly.

It was a defiant act for the two senior officers to point out to the mighty general that he had been "wrong."

But Mac was a politician more than a general. He always had been. He wouldn't disobey that need now. He shoved the pipe back into his mouth. If this was all true, he would not be able to push to the Yalu. He would not be able to drive into Manchuria like he wanted, hit China and finally destroy the Soviet Union with atomic bombs.

Truman!

That's who was to blame. The G.D. president was behind all this. In his mind he had pinpointed his scapegoat and it was the biggest name in the land.

And those goddamned spies. They were informing the U.N. of every move I've made. "I must inform Washington that we face an entirely new war," he found himself saying.

Walker stood, grabbed up his overcoat and cover. "That would be an accurate assessment, General. Now, sir, if I may, I must get back to Korea. We must do what we can to save our army."

MacArthur held his breath a moment, then said, "Pull X Corps back to the Hamhung-Hungnam area."

"Retreat?"

Mac flared. "Call it a goddamned movement in retrograde if you must use that Marine term, but get them the hell out of there."

"And the Eighth?"

"Keep them apart."

"General," Walker blurted, but he was cut off.

"Do it, Walton."

Almond rose to his feet and dared a question. "And the Marines?"

MacArthur wasn't a fan of the obdurate Marines. Oh sure, they'd taken the South Pacific for him, always outdoing his army, but they were just too difficult to handle. They were, in his mind, the only branch of the government he'd not been able to subdue to his will.

"General?" Walker pressed. "The Marines? At the reservoir?"

MacArthur seemed in denial concerning the total damage that both the 7th Army Division and the 5th and 7th Marines had suffered. Contrary to his public image, he continually failed to keep abreast of his daily reports, some thought to avoid bad news while others who were close to him simply explained it as one of his idiosyncrasies. Looking up from where he'd locked his gaze on the situation map, MacArthur answered his generals.

"The Chief of Staff insisted just hours ago that I pull the Marines out of the reservoir area. I don't know where he got the idea they had to do that."

"They're taking a beating along with our boys," Walker fired back. "May I remind you sir, that we sent two combat teams up there to help the Marines. And now those two teams are . . ." he stalled. It was too difficult to explain that he'd lost so many men.

Almond jumped in. "And the 7th Army, sir, especially the 31st Infantry. We must pull them back too. That is, sir, if there are to be any survivors."

Mac walked over and sat heavily into his dark leather chair. "Is it really all that bad, gentlemen?"

They nodded. Walker said, "Worse."

Mac frowned. "I've been defeated by poor air coverage," he said decisively. Then, thinking out loud, he said, "No, it's the administration. Congress. All of them. I've gotten no cooperation or I'd be in China by now." After a few moments that seemed like long minutes to Walker and Almond, Mac nodded to them and said, "The Marines too. Get everyone out."

Walker was at the door when Mac called him back. "Walton, what do you know about the CIA?" Mac knew who they were and had turned down their initial—and later proved correct—estimates concerning the Chinese at the Yalu.

"An offshoot of Ike's secret service."

"I know that. I want to know what's going on here with them. In Tokyo and in Korea. I understand they are led by a man named Tofte? Hans Tofte? Do you know about him?"

"Nothing."

"Look into it when you have time. He's in Korea. I'm getting some bad vibrations from headquarters. We don't need some civilian group messing around in this fight."

"Yes, sir."

* * * *

Oliver Smith dreaded the order, but the message from EUSAK command was clear. "Pull 'em back." At least Smith thought, that was better than, "Retreat."

When he turned over the piece of paper the message had been written on he read, "Regroup and attack to the south." He cut a proud smile. The Marine radio man wrote that message. Glory be to our Corps, he thought. No Marine liked the idea of running away from the damned Chinese any more than he did, and neither, he knew, would his Chosin Reservoir defense commander, Colonel Lewis 'Chesty' Puller.

He was a Marine. So he would follow orders without displaying the emotions he truly felt.

He quickly sent word to Puller that the 7th and 5th Marines were to operate under a joint operational command, a single commander. They would break out to the south, he explained. "Attack to the rear." And he wanted the high ground in unbelievably difficult terrain along the route south of Yudam-ni, protected by a composite battalion formed from the 5th and 7th and any other volunteers who could get there.

"It's going to be a long, hard goddamned war this week," Smith muttered.

Near Yudam-ni, Major Roach's biggest problem had been to build spirit among the nearly beaten Marines who gathered together as a composite battalion on the hill near Yudam-ni. If he didn't succeed, then chances were they'd all die and die pretty damned soon.

His new assignment was clear. "Hold the high ground along the route for the Marines to advance south."

Along the route? That meant forty plus miles of high ground. They would have to fight, reposition, hold the right and left flank, fight again then move again.

He'd have to do something to take their minds off the KIAs, off the cold and the futility of it all.

He was glad he'd taken possession of two green silk parachutes that were used to drop supplies that afternoon. He had his XO and two sergeants cut enough neckerchiefs so that every man in the new battalion would have one to display as a symbol of courage and victory. The sergeants kept another two dozen for stragglers who might join them on their mission south from Yudam-ni all the way to Hamhung.

The good news, if there was such a thing, was that the British Royal Marine Commandos were supposed to work their way up from Hagaru to help them by the time they got to Toktong Pass. They'd be supported by a dozen tanks, which Roach figured would be a welcome sight to a bunch of Marines fighting against tanks, howitzers, machine guns and mortars using only rifles and courage.

The men dubbed their suicide battalion, the Damnation Battalion. Wearing their new kerchiefs like soldiers out of the past, men who could barely pull together enough clothing to keep from freezing, now stood tall with new spirit and drive. Adrenaline flowed again while they marched southward through the ranks of those they were called upon to protect. They would leave first to get into position ahead of the convoy. They would be ready to serve and save. For the moment, the phrase Gung Ho seemed appropriate.

"The Chinese better look out now," Roach announced with renewed bravado, "'Cause the Damnation Battalion is on the way."

When they were dug into their first protective positions, trucks of the 5th and 7th Marines rolled down the narrow road carrying their wounded. They had been positioned in the middle of the long column of what remained of the 1st Division Marines. Artillery pieces followed at the tail end of the battalion.

Eighty-five dead officers and men were left behind after they were given a field burial with rites.

The 1st and 3rd battalions of the 5th were on the high ground north of Yudam-ni. They were so close to the Chinese when they were ordered to pull out, that their last battles were fought mostly with hand grenades and 60 mm mortars.

When at 0800 on the morning of December 1, the withdrawal began, bayonets remained fixed to every rifle. Five months and five days after the war began, American Marines were making a dash for safety.

And they didn't like the concept one damned bit.

CHAPTER 8

THEY WERE SUPPORTED by air cover from Navy Task Force 77. Marine and Navy pilots from aircraft carriers off Koto-ri bombed, strafed, and liberally dropped napalm on the Chinese and NKAs. It had all been so quickly intense that the enemy caught on to the new offensive too late.

On the American side, the 1st and 3rd battalions had disengaged and left the area more easily than they could have hoped.

The Marines moved southward slowly. They leapfrogged whole battalions from one fight to another, like they would do with smaller squad teams in a "fire and maneuver" tactic. From Hill 1294 to Hill 1542 they set down a line of defense that stretched from the arm of the Chosin down half the distance to Toktong Pass.

"Move 'em out," Roach commanded.

The Damnation Battalion started off, headed more than likely Roach thought, into yet another hell.

The 1st Battalion of the 7th Marines moved out with them, fighting their way across the road and the next range of mountains with the ultimate assignment to take the eastern slope of Hill 1520, which was heavily defended by the Chinese.

"We gotta rest 'em, Major," Gunny Van DerWenter said. "They ain't ate in three days. Water's too froze to drink and they all got frostbite."

Van as he was known, was one of those postcard Marines whose image was known to all war bond buyers of The Big Deuce. He was broad-shouldered with a body shaped like the butt-end of a whittled down cue-stick, much like the one he carried pressed hard against his ribs jutting straight out from his body with his left hand gripped tightly to the forward end. It came from the Main Street pool hall of his hometown and damned if he wasn't proud of it.

He could be caught nearly any time of the day thumping an errant Marine's helmet. No one ever argued. Not with him. Van wasn't fluff. Gunny Van was the real thing, the magic of the Corps. There was a mystical power in his being and in his actions. The others knew him as Gunny Square Jaw, or Gunny Starch. Van himself was an up front gent, but his nicknames were spoken only in the huddles of men who loved him or hated him. The straight-back sergeant was also a perfect likeness to his long time friend and mentor, Snake Fraker, except for the red hair and the long beard.

"We may not be able to do that, Van," Roach said, his voice giving way to his concern for his recent losses. "The column can't stop now. The Chinese would come down so hard we'd never get cranked up again."

Roach's instincts had been developed strongly in the battle for Okinawa. The enemy could get quiet, but that only meant they were grouping, planning, preparing for a larger counter-assault or playing a psychological game with the Americans.

But Van persisted. "We've lost too many Marines, Skipper," he said. "You keep pushin' 'em, we gonna lose 'em all. That ain't me talkin', sir. That's mother nature, pure and simple. I figure we've squeezed 'em dry." Everyone listened when Van spoke. The man wasn't a chicken. He'd never cut and run or laid down on the job. So, if he's asking for time off, then he knows something the others don't. "You've got to let 'em eat something and warm up their innards." He gritted his teeth with a sound, then added, "Chinese ain't above us right now, sir. We got the time."

Roach considered for a flash of a moment, then gave the order. "Give 'em twenty, Van." He meant twenty minutes of rest. Roach looked up the valley and then up the hillside to their column left. They had to take the hill. They had to setup an observation position for the battalions that followed. And they would have to lay down a defense.

"They're up there Van."

"If'n you're right Skipper, we'd hear 'em or smell 'em. My guess is they's on the other side of that ridge, smokin' stuff or waitin' for nightfall."

"Twenty minutes," Roach said with repetition.

Van understood from experience alone that men like Roach were driven to victory. Moving backwards was playing on the big guy's mind and Van had to carve a space for the officer to rest as well as his men. He also knew that if it were possible, Roach would drive them back up to the Yalu until the war was ended, or worse, until they were.

While the 1st Battalion rested with the Damnation crowd, the 3rd Battalion of the 5th Marines fought through Yudam-ni, which was only a mile up the road from Roach. They were led by a single tank. The 11th Marine artillery came with them, blasting Chinese during the entire trip. It took them until 1930 hours to reach the hill opposite the side of the road. Now, they too, needed rest. And supplies.

"Sergeant Van," Roach called out at exactly the twenty minute mark, "let's roll."

A squawk came over the PRC-10 strapped to the back of Roach's ever-present radioman. He grabbed the receiver, which closely resembled an old-fashioned telephone.

"Roach."

"Got three stray Marines coming up, sir."

"From the point?" he asked, sounding incredulous. "That's impossible." To Roach that meant the men came through enemy lines.

Strickland, Snake, and Drier appeared with one of Roach's men leading them.

Roach listened to their tale with astonishment.

"I'm amazed you survived," he said when they finished.

"It wasn't easy," Fraker explained. His cigar was in terrible shape, looking more like chewing tobacco hanging from his lips than a smoked stogie. But Fraker could make it appear as though the Cuban was still smokable, and he enjoyed that part of it. Fraker never tired, never changed, never even gave a moment's thought to resting. "Once you figure out the Chinese, you can pretty much skirt 'round them."

"Snake?"

Fraker looked beyond Roach. "Van? What the hell you doin' here man?"

"Same as you." Snake moved beyond Roach and up to his old friend.

"Old times?" Roach said to Strickland.

"Yes sir."

"Details," Roach said nodding in the direction Strickland had come from. But Roach's eye caught Fraker's look. Fraker had finally noticed that Roach's men had crapped out alongside the road and up into the trees and rocks. Van had not yet ordered them to the road as Roach had commanded. Fraker was eyeing them with enough concern to make Roach nervous.

"The big battle may come at Toktong Pass," Strickland said. "It's the last pass before heading to the sea."

"Your sergeant," Roach said returning his eyes to Strickland.

Strickland glanced around. "My guess is he wants to know why your men are slacking off."

Van came into the conversation. He had assumed the role. It was his job even though an unwritten assignment that gunny's were well aware of: Keep the old man clean. "I rested them. They're exhausted, Lieutenant. Just about to get 'em up and ready." He took off, calling for his men to fall in on the road.

"What're the parachute rags for?" Strickland asked Roach.

"Morale." Roach pulled three of the kerchiefs from his pocket and handed one to each of the Marines. "Here, you're now part of the Damnation Battalion."

Strickland nodded to his men and then tucked his into his jacket pocket leaving a piece hanging out. Drier pulled his around his neck for warmth. Fraker stuck his into his helmet, using the space between his pith and the metal pot. Strickland's expression changed and Fraker caught it.

"Sir?"

"Something's out of place." He looked to Roach. "My suggestion Major, is that we get your men ready right now. The Chinese magic hour is upon us."

"They'll be ready. They're exhausted but their spirit will carry them. They're out of rations as well. Gotta find food for them."

Fraker spit out tobacco, then looked into Roach's burning eyes. If he had to, he could be anybody's conscience. "Skipper and me, Drier here, we been at it for three maybe four days now just like you. Ain't had no food, ain't laid down once't that I can 'member. Feel like a goddamned zombie is what."

Van was moving up and down the line of men. His voice dominated while he shouted, "Rifles loaded, safety's off."

A gunshot punctuated the otherwise calm area. It rang out from across the road where Lt. Colonel Taplett's men were just getting into it with attacking Chinese.

Roach leaped into action. The Chinese would be coming from all directions. "Move 'em into position," he shouted to his officers and noncoms. They already knew where the Chinese were, so moving into position would be automatic although supremely difficult. The road was almost too narrow for three men abreast and the slope of the snow-plastered hill to their west was too steep for vehicles and most men.

The Damnation Battalion was barely alert when the first mortar rounds landed into the center of them, scattering living and newly dead Marines into the icy slopes.

"Fuck man," Snake shouted, "that weren't no standard mortar round. Them assholes is using the big ones."

Van DerWenter ran from man to man, pushing them up the slope or across the road into position. But the noise from incoming and outgoing firepower was too loud for his voice to be heard. No one noticed that it no longer mattered, either. A mortar round landed directly in front of Gunny Van and killed him and three other Marines who were struggling to set up their frozen machine gun.

For them, the war was over.

By morning, Company G and Company I had been reduced to platoon strength. Nearly 350 dead or badly wounded Marines lay in the I Company area. The 5th Marines were being decimated while trying to move southward. No matter which direction they fought, they were running into Chinese hordes as though the supply of armed enemy soldiers was endless.

It practically was.

Strickland moved through the field of dead Marines slowly, noting each man he came to carefully, memorizing his face or what was left of him. It had become an obsession. He needed to see what the Chinese had done to his brothers, to record it in his memory for all time. "Someday, in this fucked up war," he said to Fraker who walked with him, "I'll get a chance to pay the gooks back. In spades."

"That was the worst fight I've ever seen," Fraker muttered. "Man,

I thought island hopping was bad." After a moment of silence between them he added, "I didn't think it would ever get that bad again."

Strickland's mind was back in a small foxhole in a vacant lot across from the orphanage where his biggest battles before the Deuce were with nuns. He wondered now what it was that he thought was so terrible then. He glanced to Fraker, "They'll pay, Snake. Mark my words. They'll pay for this."

"We have to go Skipper," Fraker said. They'd been wandering through the battlefield of dead Marines for a half-hour. "The Major's movin' 'em out."

Strickland seemed distant. "Moving who out?" he growled. "For god's sake, who's left?" Then, stopping in his tracks, glancing furtively around the battlefield one last time he asked, "Doesn't it strike you as odd Snake, that we never find any dead Chinese in the morning?"

"They pick 'em up, Skipper. Most of the time. They take 'em with 'em."

"Yeah? Why do you suppose they do that?"

Fraker spit tobacco into the white and crimson snow. "You know the answer."

"Tell me again."

"So's we won't know how many we kilt. How many they got left."

Strickland sneered. "Then, shouldn't we take ours too?"

Fraker shook his head lightly. His friend was getting nutty again. This was not a good sign. "Body snatcher's be by soon's we leave, Lieutenant. That is if'n any of 'em are still alive."

They continued on like they had. Fighting hard while the long, serpentine column of men and vehicles continued coming. Taplett and his men battled Chinese on one side of the road while Lt. Colonel Raymond G. Davis and his men skirmished on the other. Davis would later be awarded the Medal of Honor for his "outstanding leadership and valor" in battle. He was destined to become an assistant commandant of the Marine Corps.

The remnants of the Damnation Battalion fought on either side, most of the time ahead of them, sometimes just alongside. Unfortunately for Roach and his men, there were nearly as many Chinese reinforcements as there had been originals.

Near the Toktong Pass, Marine morale climbed skyward when the 7th Marines forced thousands of Chinese soldiers to hightail it out of there, retreat was the word most often used, right into the field of fire of the 5th Marines.

Davis and Taplett called for air support and the Corsairs came with napalm, bombs, rockets and strafing runs. This time, they were on target. Within hours they'd completely slaughtered at least one Chinese battalion.

But the Marine toll had been high. Taplett's original battalion of 437 Marines at the beginning of the march had been whittled down three days later. By the time they reached Toktong Pass they had only 194 left. Nevertheless, the survivors were happy as hell to see the Royal Marine Commandos with its platoon of tanks waiting for them.

When Colonel Davis's battalion reached Hagaru, Major Roach's survivors with them, they formed into a snappy column and marched into town humming or singing the Marine Corps Hymn. They had been fighting intensely for a little more than a week now. They'd not had any sleep, nor food, other than a few dried "John Wayne biscuits."

General Smith greeted them with tears in his eyes. "Colonel," he said to the handsome and heroic Davis, "I've no idea how you endured the conditions you fought in, and neither do I understand how you stood it."

"We're Marines, sir," was all Davis answered.

"Take your casualties to the airstrip Colonel," Smith continued. "We've got planes there ready to fly 'em out of here. The rest of us will have to fight our way to Koto-ri."

Colonel Davis arranged immediately for the evacuation of wounded. He passed the word along to Colonel Taplett's outfit and down the line to the long column that was now arriving.

Later that same day Strickland found himself in front of Colonel Chesty Puller, who'd arrived earlier by helicopter to meet with the Regimental commanders.

"Before he died," Puller said to Strickland, who stared lifelessly at the Marine Corps icon, "Colonel Faith recommended you for the Silver Star. What do you think?"

Strickland's voice sounded broken, weak. His thoughts for both

Faith and MacLean were dominated by their deaths. His vision returned to when he'd first met MacLean and how they'd bonded after that. "MacLean was a good man, sir."

Puller's bulldog face scrunched up. "McLean? You knew him, too?"

"He was a good man, Colonel," Strickland repeated in the same dull tone. His mind wasn't working sharply.

"Do you deserve the medal?" the crusty colonel urged out of his officer. He could see plainly enough that the Marine in front of him had been through hell.

Sergeant Fraker spoke up. "Sir, if I may."

Puller, already a legend in every Marine's eye, turned to Fraker. "Go ahead," he growled.

"Straight out. The Lieutenant deserves the Medal of Honor. Sir, he might also be in line for a Navy Cross, a Silver Star and all the rest of 'em. Sir."

Puller squinted. "Not just the Medal of Honor?" He coughed, letting the sergeant know that Chesty Puller wasn't a loose man with medals. Lowering his voice he asked, "Just what in hell happened out there?"

"Dead," Strickland mumbled. "All dead. My men. The whole army. All dead, sir. Just the three of us left."

"The Lieutenant helped keep the army alive as long as he could sir. It was one of the finest displays of heroism I've ever seen. He personally kilt more than a hundred Chinese. Many of 'em with his pistol."

Puller nodded to his aide to join them. "Captain Duhain, get me a set of tracks." Turning back to Strickland, he said, "Captain, you've just earned your promotion. The Silver Star for sure, and I'll look into that Navy Cross. The Medal of Honor request will be submitted. Who's the corporal standing over there waiting for you two?"

Fraker beamed. "That's Drier, sir. A young pistol of a Marine who should be upped also. He's a good man, Colonel. Make a good officer."

Puller knew these men. Marines, good Marines always boasted about their mates. "We'll see about that promotion later," he said. He glanced to Drier and motioned him over. Drier came quickly, stood at attention. "At ease Corporal."

Drier relaxed. "Yes, sir."

"How was it up there, Corporal?"

Drier looked to his two companions, then back to Puller. "I have no idea why I'm still alive, sir. Other than these two who kept me going."

Fraker jerked the stub of rolled tobacco from his mouth. Puller chuckled at it.

"He fought hard, Colonel. We were surrounded the whole time." Then he smirked a bit and added, "Best conditions for a Marine, wouldn't you say, sir?"

Puller reached into his upper left jacket pocket and pulled out a six-inch Cuban. "Sergeant, I think you earned this." He handed a happy Gunny the brand new cigar.

"Why Colonel, I do 'preciate that. Sir. Beats a medal any day."

Puller who never was known for laughing, did indeed chuckle with that one. "Well Gunny, you just earned yourself a medal and another stripe. And Corporal consider yourself a three-stripper with a new medal. And gents, I'm not free with commendations. You more than earned them."

"Thank you, sir," Drier stuttered.

"No, Sergeant. Thank you." He accepted the captain's railroad tracks from Duhain when the man pulled up alongside, and pinned them on Strickland's collars. "Captain, I'd love to have you join us. We're about to move south to Hungnam."

"South? I thought we'd be headed north. Sir, I'm still searching for my friend," he blurted out, completely out of context. Fraker turned to him.

"Jesus, you think he's made it this far, Skipper?"

Puller tilted his head back. "Who's your friend?"

"Joe Hughes. Lieutenant. Took one in the head."

"Did he evacuate?"

"We put him on a truck. A Limey truck," Fraker responded.

Duhain coughed. "Only one of those made it back, Sergeant."

Strickland's demeanor perked up. "Where is it?"

"At the airfield. They're putting wounded aboard a flight."

Puller said, "Duhain, check on who the wounded are. Get back to us." Duhain took off.

Puller turned his attention back to Strickland. "If we can find him for you, we will." Then he snarled his famous Chesty curl and said, "As to your thoughts of heading north. You bet your sweet ass I would head north. But the G. D. army is running this show and we're gonna have to follow orders and beat our way out through the south. Mind you Captain, no matter which way we head, we've got a major battle on our hands."

"Yes, sir. Like I said, we're surrounded," Fraker said.

"Like you also suggested. That simplifies our challenge."

"If my friend is okay, then I want to help," Strickland said.

"Say again, Captain."

Puller had indicated that Strickland was going to join him, but Strickland had put a condition to it. That was not an expected reaction within the ranks.

Strickland looked into Puller's eyes. Chesty was shorter than he was, but as tenacious and tough as a pit bull.

"I want to fight with the Colonel, sir," he said, his voice crisply clear. "I want to kill communists, sir. A lot of them."

"But your friend comes first?"

Strickland nodded.

Puller eyed the new captain with respect. He'd seen this before. A man goes through hell killing scores of enemy, comes out unscathed, sees the dead of his own kind all around him and either goes completely nuts or begins to believe he's immortal, which, he ruminated, is a little like being crazy. Some of those men continue on in battle killing more enemy until either they are killed, or severely wounded or just get damned lucky. If they made it out alive, it was too often with a badly distorted viewpoint of the value of life.

The short, gruff colonel wasn't sure which of these conditions this new captain had acquired, but he guessed what great battles he'd fought and thought of the battles yet to be. More men would die. Too many good men. Analyzing the man in front of him, he thought possibly he didn't want to lose this one.

He glanced to Fraker. The sergeant had cringed when his skipper volunteered with a restriction on his commitment. He could tell now in the experienced NCO's eyes that the men before him had been together through more than just the previous week.

"That won't be necessary Captain, I can put you and your men on one of the planes heading to Pusan with the wounded," Puller said slowly, although he wasn't sure why. These men were Marines. Marines fought until they dropped.

"Colonel," Strickland said more firmly, standing straighter, fighting within himself to bring all his courage back. "Sergeant Fraker and Corporal Drier—"

"Sergeant Drier now, Captain," Puller said with a tinge of a smile.

"I'll, I'd like to find—"

"Yes, I understand that," Puller said stretching out his words.

"But I owe my battalion," he choked up. He couldn't speak.

"Captain's saying we'll gladly fight with you sir."

Puller called out, "Colonel Scott, see that these men are outfitted with fresh utilities, new weapons and feed 'em Colonel. Feed 'em all they can eat. And get this Gunny here some more cigars."

"Yes, sir."

"Has Duhain returned?"

"No sir."

"Assign these men to Headquarters Battalion and find out what happened to Duhain."

Scott left to take care of the arrangements.

Before Strickland and his two sergeants were released, Puller said, "You can get at least a few hour's rest Captain. When you get there, you can rejoin your old outfit at Hamhung. Deal?"

"Yes, sir," Strickland answered. "Thank you, Colonel."

"From what I've heard here Captain, I should pray for the Chinese who get in your way. Good luck, God speed."

With that, he left them. He'd been commanding this "break out" for only a few days but already he'd met more heroes than he thought he'd ever meet during his entire career. Puller himself had already earned four Navy Crosses, and become such a deeply ingrained legend within the Corps that no Marine existed who did not know his name or his history.

On their way to the mess area, Fraker told Drier, "You got yourself a real hero medal, boy. And you got it from a real hero."

"Yeah? Wonder what for."

"Beats me son, they cost about fifteen cents a month just to maintain 'em. Gets expensive is what it does." He smiled, added, "But I do think time will come when we might make a Marine outta you yet."

"Thanks, Sarge. Maybe after all this, I'll ship over."

Fraker looked upon the boy like he might look upon his own son. "God help us all."

CHAPTER 9

THE PLAN WAS TO MAKE it to the coastal port of Hungnam, and perform what MacArthur would later call a reverse amphibious assault. In other words, Mac was planning on a Korean Dunkirk.

The news hawks showed up too, most of them eager to write the story of what they believed would be America's first major military defeat. For sure, that would sell papers and maybe make one or two of the newsies famous.

"You boys should 'a been up the road with us," Fraker growled to a few of the parasites who called themselves journalists. He gulped down a cold potato from an olive green WW-II C-ration can, tasting a rancid flavor he was all too familiar with. "You'd 'a had enough material to write a 'cyclopedia of commie warfare if you'd a just been here."

Scoop Clifford wasn't impressed by Fraker's gunny-speak. He'd heard it all before. He'd been attached to Marines in the Pacific, an infantry unit on board a naval ship that cruised off Vietnam, referred to in their dispatches as Indo-China. That was back when Roosevelt and later HST wanted the French to know America was there for them.

Because Clifford had never stood alongside fighting men during the heat of battle, he was pegged as tail-end Scoop by the experienced reporters. Based at EUSAK headquarters thus far during the Korean war, he'd been one of those who had been trapped into believing Lin Piao's hoax news releases. That was, until General Walker spotted one of his negative oriented articles and went directly to Clifford.

"The story's in Korea, son," he said. "Not next door. You want stories, I'll send you off to the front."

Walker's suggestion was plain and simple. Get out of town or get to Korea. So, Scoop Clifford found himself on an Army C-47 headed to Korea with a group of EUSAK staff members.

Earlier, MacArthur had decided to use Hagaru as a field headquarters and staging site for the attack he'd launch into Manchuria, but now things were going the other way and it would be used as headquarters for the withdrawal. When Mac believed they would walk all over the Chinese, he had a base built at Hagaru with everything from thousands of Baby Ruth and Tootsie Roll candy bars for their PX to enough truck parts to reconstruct every vehicle they operated in Korea.

That was where Fraker, Strickland, and Drier met Puller.

"What the hell we gonna do with all this crap?" Drier asked, coming alongside Fraker. "We sure as hell not taking it with us."

But instead of Fraker responding it was the newly arrived Clifford who spoke up. "Maybe not," Clifford said, "Maybe all those candy bars we're seeing is why you're losing this war. I hear pogey bait can get you killed."

Fraker reacted like a wounded cat. "You want that pencil shoved up your ass, boy?"

"Hey, no offense. Just calling it the way I see it."

"Well you better open your fucking eyes asshole, 'cause we ain't lost nothin' yet."

A calmer voice joined them. It belonged to an older, more experienced field reporter named Max Store. Max was short and somewhat squat, not unlike a butternut squash. The men liked him because he wasn't owned by any newspapers or wire services like Clifford. Clifford worked for AP. Max worked for himself. He had deals with UPI and a few large newspapers, but he remained on no one's payroll. Better yet, he sold his material with restrictions. Buyers couldn't change the theme or the message or the article other than correcting some punctuation here and there. Max told stories. Good stories. "All true," he'd tell them. "So don't mess with 'em."

Max wore Marine utilities, and a green Marine cap. Pencils jutted out of his breast pocked just below his nametag. He was either dark skinned or deeply tanned, Fraker couldn't figure which. His accent was clearly New York.

"What happened up there, Sergeant?"

Max's question and his demeanor expressed his respect for the Marine in front of him and also served to shove Clifford aside. Max had earned honors for his photographs and his stories in the Pacific because he'd gotten into the trenches with the men. His photos were on the covers of Life, Colliers, and Time. He was one of the few reporters who told it the way it was. Like Ernie Pyle, his personal icon, he gave soul to each story. He knew what to look for, what to ask.

Strickland interrupted them. "Time to move out, Snake."

Max stuck his hand out to Strickland. "Max Store, Captain. War correspondent extraordinary," he said with a broad grin. "Mind if I come along?"

Before Strickland could respond, Clifford piped up, "He's a crazed syndicated reporter. But we love him."

"Independent reporter," Store said. "I write what I see. And so far I've seen a hell of a lot of heroes."

Fraker stepped next to Clifford. He pulled his fresh cigar from his mouth slowly and said. "You're welcome to come with us as well, if you think you can handle it."

Clifford shook his head as though it was a bobbing monkey on someone's car dash. "No thanks."

"You crazy like the rest of us?" Strickland asked Max.

"I believe that's possible," Max smiled.

"Okay, then. You're in."

"You really going with them?" Clifford asked. He was stunned. He'd stayed alive during the last war and so far this one by reporting from the rear.

Max nodded in the affirmative. "That's where the story is, Scoop."

"Nuts."

"How'd you get the nom de plume? Scoop! Seems to me you'd want to be with them."

"High school. While writing for the school sheet."

Max chided him more. "C'mon. Join us. Most that could happen is we get killed."

Clifford's expression changed. "You are nuts."

"Not really. These guys will give you a story even AP won't believe."

"You don't get it, do you? Why put my life on the line when the people back home will just rewrite what I send them?" He nodded toward Strickland and his men. "They okay?"

"They've been through hell and they're still alive. I think we have a better chance with them."

Clifford sighed deeply. "Okay. For a few miles up the road anyway."

Neither Max nor Clifford were physical giants by Fraker's standards, but they kept up with the Marines stride for stride, acts that won Fraker's admiration for both men. Max carried two cameras and a pocket-sized pad to write on. He wrote into his pad and snapped off photos while he walked and while the Marines rested. He was an obsessed reporter having learned through the years, "Not everything I write will sell, so I have to write like hell."

Clifford on the other hand disdained the camera. He swore he could write a better picture than he could take. His leather pad holder had become a familiar fixture for him. It had been made a bit famous by the New York Times in a photo taken of him during the Inchon invasion. An admiral had dared him to go over the side with Marines, down the netting known as a Jacobs ladder and join the men on the beach.

A Jacob's Ladder was a portable ladder made of rope and used primarily as an aid in boarding or disembarking a ship. Originally, the Jacob's Ladder was a network of line leading to the skysail on wooden ships. But the ladder used by the Marines to disembark a ship was a series of squares made out of rope and hung over the side of a ship, leading down to their landing craft. It looked like a giant fishing net.

"You mean fight with them?"

"No son, you're a reporter. Nothing like a first hand report."

Clifford recalled openly being, "Scared out of my drawers," when relating the tale to another reporter who did have a camera. That reporter had taken a picture of Clifford coming ashore with pad and pencil in hand, and a lot of fear expressed vividly on his face.

When the readers of the Times read his true confession they fell in love with him, at least for that week. An "honest reporter" they wrote in the letters to the editor section.

And then the readers wanted to know what kind of pad that

Clifford was carrying. So the Times printed a blow up of the leather pad, and of course Clifford's standard yellow number 2 pencil with an eraser that didn't appear to ever have been used.

But fame was fleeting and so were his heroics. The truth was that Clifford was only trying to keep his leather pad-holding pouch above the water line. And the paper dry. And more importantly, to stay alive.

Unlike Max Store, Clifford preferred to keep the sights and scenes in his head and write them down later. But Max was setting an example for him now so Clifford pulled his pad out and began writing right alongside him. After a while he began to wonder where Max found so much energy to do so much writing.

"What are you always writing about, Max? We haven't done anything yet."

"Right now I'm writing about you struggling through this snow and ice."

"That'll be a hit. You going to tell them I've been bitching about it."

"It might surprise you what I've written."

"Nothing surprises me any more."

"They already know you, Scoop. So, I'm telling them that even though you expressed trepidation on that landing, you have the guts to fight your way through bad conditions to get to the next battle with the Marines."

"Highly overstated. What else?"

"Ever hear of Lin Piao? Ah, I think it's pronounced with a B, however, like Bee-ow." When Max spoke he sounded breathless, paced more like a humming sewing machine than a drummer's steady rhythm.

"Yeah. He's the Chinese guy we'd like to ding."

"Commanding General of Chinese forces in Korea. Clever guy. He's actually got spies in Tokyo and in America, feeding the news guys junk stories they run as gospel." He paused, searched Clifford's eyes. "You one of those guys who fell for his stuff?"

Clifford found himself fessing up and it surprised him. "Yeah, I guess I was. General Walker ate me out for it and here I am. He wasn't' very nice about it."

"Gives me hope for Walker," Fraker said, then out of character he threw a smile to Clifford.

"Piao has already made a big mistake, Snake."

"Like what?"

"He reads the New York Times and Washington Post to see what's going on. But he got dumb. He's been reading his own lies and believing them."

"Well, shit man. Walker ought to be kissing my ass over that one," Clifford said. "You're not going to write that I fell for that crap?"

Max laughed. "No. Should I?" he laughed again.

Clifford saw the humor, he thought, anyway, so he laughed with Max.

The Marine units were ordered to capture East Hill where they took the position with little Chinese resistance, which surprised Puller and the grunt commanders. After securing the hill, resistance picked up quickly.

Along the rest of the ridge, while they continued their march south, the fighting became so intensely violent that Max wrote, "It was the most spectacular if not the most fiercely contested battle of the entire Chosin reservoir campaign." His syndicated column about East Hill would make it into every large paper in the U.S.

In his earlier reports, before meeting up with Strickland and the others, Max had avoided the usual reporter's description of Chinese mass attacks.

But not this time. Both he and Clifford wrote similar articles. It would be Clifford's first frontline story and it would make it into all papers, magazines and radio broadcasts.

"This battle," he wrote, "must have been important to the Chinese. This battle indicated to the Marines that the Chinese must believe that should the Americans break through this ridgeline, the Marines would make it out of the Chinese trap. Lin Piao threw wave after wave of Chinese elites headlong into the Marines. They advanced right into Marine artillery fire, flamethrowers, tanks, mortars, machine guns and bayonets. The Marines slaughtered them in such numbers that a human wall of dead built up in front of the weary Americans. The last waves had to climb over their dead comrades to face the angry Marines and they too, fell."

It was also his last report. He told his new pals that he would have to return to the base at Hungnam. He just wasn't physically prepared to last in the elements the way he was dressed and they had nothing to help him.

But one more firefight came up before he departed. So he stayed willingly to report it. While moving from one position to the other, trying desperately to stay alive while capturing the agony and sounds of battle, he was hit directly by a Chinese artillery round. He nearly evaporated, leaving behind only a few pencils, his famous leather pad-holder, and his boots.

Max Store was the only witness to his loss. For him Clifford's violent death became suddenly and surprisingly personal. His gaze and his mind were locked on the piece of real estate that had become so valuable to Clifford. This was not a fair war, as though any wars were. This was both personal and devastating. A fellow journalist, a man who had finally broken the mold of long distance reporting and come into the front lines had been killed for his effort. And Max felt guilt spread over him "like white on rice."

Max found himself dashing over for Clifford's pad. It was warm when he touched it. Even in this godforsaken cold air and snow-covered ground the pad still felt warm from Clifford's grip. He grabbed it tightly and raced back to his protective cover.

The battle was still raging around him. Other men were dying or suffering injury. He had to get his mind back to his own survival and, more importantly write the story of Clifford's demise.

He curled up in a shell hole and began writing about his friend. He titled it, "The Death of A Hero."

An hour later the battle subsided.

The Marines suffered sixty-three casualties for Company D and fifty-three for the 1st Battalion, which supported the defense against the Chinese counterattacks.

The battle enabled the 7th Marines to get out of Hagaru, moving farther to the south without a scratch.

Max rejoined Fraker and Drier. He told them about Clifford. Fraker made a familiar clicking sound with his mouth and then said, "Sorry to hear it."

"He was going to be an okay reporter," Max said.

Fraker wasted no time with advice. "Max, you gotta watch your butt out here. Take no chances, ya hear? You get your butt up in front again like you did and you gonna be a story just like your friend."

Later, Fraker directed Drier, "Boy, you keep an eye on that man.

He's a good'n all right. Tells things straight. No bullshit like some others."

The 7th Marines found themselves in a thick ground fog and in a steady hail of gunfire that came down on them from their right.

"C'mon, boy," Fraker shouted to Drier. "Grab some men and let's clean 'em outta there."

Drier led a squad of Marines into the fog toward the sound of the shooting. Max Store followed them. Half way up the hill they found their targets. Flashes from enemy rifles were barely discernible. Drier figured the thick fog was deadening the sounds and that the enemy was much closer than he might otherwise believe.

"Like drivin' on a two-lane back home with fog to boot. You know a car's coming but you can't make 'em out."

Fraker was busy positioning his men. "Just shoot where you see their flashes."

"What if they're ours?" Max asked.

"No fuckin' way." Then he pulled hand grenades from his belt. He always carried frags instead of the concussion grenades. He let the spoons fly off and threw them one after the other towards the Chinese. He was like a baseball-pitching machine. Drier joined in as though the two were in a competitive match. The explosions sounded muffled in the blurred air, but the effects of the grenades along with the squad of rifle-shooting Marines were cataclysmic to the Chinese. More than two-dozen Chinese were killed by the time gunfire stopped.

No Marines were injured.

"I can tell that you've done this before," Max said, hoping it would sound humorous.

Fraker whirled around surprised the reporter was still there. "You nuts, man?"

"It's what I get paid to do." Then chuckling, he added, "Just like you."

Drier laughed when he came past them moving down the hill toward the column on the road,.

"Gunny, I think you've just met your match." Then he added, "Welcome aboard Max. Nice to have ya here."

At dusk an OY-2 recon plane flew over the long column, disappearing into the night south of them. The presence of the OY-2, sometimes called a Sentinel or a Flying Jeep, meant that the Marines were getting an upper hand. The OY was a spotter plane and was used as a medevac plane when needed. It had been built by the Stinson aircraft division of the Consolidated Vultee Aircraft Corporation and later became popular among General Aviation enthusiasts, especially for its forward wing slot design, which helped the plane make very short field take-offs and fly low, slow, and safely.

"It's impossible to make out what they're facing, General," Hawk was saying about the same time they passed over Strickland and his men.

"Keep searching Hawk. They're down there. Nightfall's gonna be an awful time for our boys."

Smith searched the terrain below while he spoke. They'd left Hagaru for Koto-ri where Smith planned to meet with his commanders for the evacuation of the severely wounded and the final march to the sea. A march Smith did not want to make.

"Hold it. Circle."

Hawk didn't know if he was suddenly chilled or whether he was shuddering because this general had done this before and he'd been nuts back then and maybe he's nuts now. Circle an enemy this low to the ground in this slow flying lunker?

"Now, Hawk," Smith said with impatience. The fog was burning off or lifting, he didn't care which. What he did care about had appeared just below them and in huge numbers.

It looked like the entire Chinese army.

Hawk circled to the right. Below them thousands of Chinese soldiers were moving into position along the road at the ridgeline for what was obviously to be a mass attack.

A bullet hit the right wing of the plane, passing through the skin, barely missing the fuel tank. Hawk snapped his plane back into level flight and prayed the awfully small engine could get them the hell out of there.

"Gotta get out of here, General. Can't afford to lose you now."

"Any other time would be okay, huh, Hawk?" Smith shed a big grin that Hawk couldn't see. He liked this pilot. He'd find other work for this man once they had all his Marines safely ensconced.

The plane struggled for altitude and headed for Koto-ri.

The 7th covered about three more miles before nightfall. The 7th's C.O., Colonel Litzenberg, could have dug in and set up a perimeter but decided otherwise. The report from the spotter plane was accurate enough he knew, because he'd seen the Chinese along the ridgeline during the march south. He'd take the gamble and keep moving even though the night was a deep ivory-black.

The Chinese refused to cooperate with him, however. Somewhere near Hell Fire Valley, they lit up the dark theater of death with scores of flares and a barrage of tracer-laced gunfire. The red-tailed bullets with fire streaking from their butt-end pierced through the night from all directions while rocket exhausts glowed until they detonated on target. Mortar rounds exploded like firecrackers on the Fourth of July. Almost immediately Chaplain Cornelius J. Griffin was severely wounded in the jaw while administering last rites to a dying Marine. Then Drier's newly assigned platoon commander was killed. They were now down to two officers.

"Hey boy," Fraker shouted to Drier, "take those men up the hill and cover the colonel."

Drier rushed up the hill with his squad to the Battalion's commanding officer. Max Store tagged along behind, his camera reloaded with high-speed black and white film. He was ready for action. He didn't dare attach a flash. What a target he'd make. Max was clever though. He'd fashioned for himself a cue-stick like pole, about three feet in length that he could screw into his camera. He'd set the stick on the ground to steady the camera and open the aperture for a time exposure. The various lights gave special effects to each of his night pictures along with silhouetting his subjects. Many of his photos made it into the big magazines. This time would be no different. He would get the handsome Marine he knew as Drier and the other grunt they called Snake in some good photos this night.

Lt. Colonel William F. Harris and Major Morris were all that remained among the officers of the 3rd Battalion, 7th Marines, as well as Captain Strickland, who was damned busy and damned close to him. The popping sounds of bullets sailed past them, sometimes way too close, Max thought. He blindly scribbled into his pad, "This is indeed Hell's fire."

Drier spread his men into firing positions, pointed out their field-of-fire with a voice that was beginning to crackle. He had long ago given up washing himself or even brushing his teeth other than with his fingers. He wasn't dead yet, but in his mind, he'd already accepted its inevitability. "Fire at anything that moves," he ordered. "Except this nutty reporter." It was too dark for them to see his grin.

Then he dove down into the hard-packed ice next to Strickland who was covering the area to their left with his pistol.

Strickland pointed, "There," he said calmly. "There come the commies."

Drier growled. A bullet snapped near his right ear. "Shit. One of 'em shoots good."

"Wait a few more moments until they're close enough."

At that moment, Harris shouted orders into his radio to his artillerymen who were at the tail of the column. "Fire for effect."

The projectiles sailed overhead, hissing and thumping a trail through the night air. Then the explosions came, one after the other, landing squarely in the middle of the attacking Chinese.

Bodies sailed upward along with chunks of ice and snow, and then crashed bloodily back into the huge holes created by the explosions. The red dye of life spilled freely across the white sheath of ice, eerily visible with the help of the light from each new blast.

"Right flank," Strickland shouted, pointing to Chinese attackers who'd apparently broken through the line. Strickland screamed over the noise of gunfire and artillery, "Drier, get your men over there!"

Drier quickly ordered men to circle around and face off the attacking Chinese. Then he kneeled up and began firing at them with his M-1.

Harris called for more artillery. Max Store moved next to Harris, where he began snapping silhouette photos of the colonel in action while using only the flashes of explosions for light.

The Chinese were getting so close that Harris pulled his .45 from his holster and turned to fire on the enemy. Glancing to Drier he yelled, "Corporal, we're a bit short on officers around here."

"Yes sir, I noticed Colonel."

Harris fired two more rounds, dropping two Chinese in their tracks. "Okay!" He screamed over the gunfire. "I now commission you a second lieutenant in the United States Marine Corps. Sergeant Fraker, you hear that?"

"Yes, sir."

Drier nearly laughed. "Is that supposed to be a favor, Colonel?"

"No, Goddamn it! It's a necessity, and it's official. Now take your men and — "

A bullet entered Harris's heart, stopping him cold. He crashed forward, dead. Max Store's eyes bulged with horror. He'd actually gotten a silhouette of the colonel a second after the man had been hit. He could see his expression, although dimly lit and shadowed as though the man were a ghost in a battlefield of other ghosts.

Drier caught Max's horror with the sudden appearance of a flare overhead.

"Max, you all right?"

Max gripped his camera so tightly his hand felt frozen shut. His photojournalist's energized mind was suggesting how sick it would be to take a follow up picture of the colonel lying there now. He did it though; it was automatic. Then he felt nauseated. His throat lumped while trying to expel his gawdawful C-rations, but they wouldn't come. He sat back on his haunch and stared hard at the dead Marine until the flare petered out. Damn, he was getting too old for this. Every death mattered. Every wounded Marine sickened him. It was time for a desk job.

"Max, get your ass down," Drier shouted over the cacophony of war.

Max belched louder than Drier had yelled. His gut ached. His heart was broken and his spirit challenged. His mind raced with his own history. He'd been in battle before, but never close enough to smell the enemy, never close enough to feel the deaths he'd just witnessed. He'd been successful in holding back his emotions, the desire to make friends with men who he knew could die within hours of shaking their hands. But that was World War Two, and, and this is Korea. He'd made friends. He'd liked the camaraderie. He'd made a mistake.

"Oh my God," he moaned. He groped in the dark for a hole, something to crawl into, a place to catch his breath and rebound. But there was no place to hide, or duck, or run to.

Drier moved closer to Max to see what had happened. The flare had died out and his vision was unable to find the reporter, and besides, he'd been busy shooting in the other direction. How could he know Max was crawling around in some form of trauma or new fear.

As Drier got closer he began to understand. The colonel was

lying flat on his face in blood drenched snow that had already crusted from the irritating and goddamned unreasonable cold.

A blast nearby. Drier spotted Max who seemed frozen to his spot. He also saw Strickland who had just arrived. Another flare burst open above them. This was one of their flares. Dammit, dammit, dammit. Turn the goddamned thing off.

"Fuck those things," Drier yelled.

"They're Chinese," Strickland yelled hoarsely. "They must have captured a bunch of them at the reservoir." He sounded like he had laryngitis. Too much yelling, too much cold dry air.

Drier thought Strickland's complexion looked dreadfully pallid in the light provided by the bluish flare.

"Get back to work, Lieutenant," Strickland yelled. "The gooks aren't interested in dead Marines."

Drier left Max but not in time. A Chinese bullet smacked into his right shoulder. He crashed backward from the impact, rolled over, got back up and turned to face the Chinese with his rifle blazing. While all this was happening, Strickland crawled over to another dead Marine and yanked up his BAR and ammo pouch. He slammed the bipod down hard splashing snow up like a rooster tail stream behind a water skier. He sprawled out behind the rifle and began firing into the crowd of attacking Chinese. The BAR man had died before his magazine had emptied. Ten rounds had remained in the twenty-round mag. Strickland yanked at the ammo pouch only to find one mag remaining. He slammed it into the BAR and started firing single shot instead of rapid fire. He was in trouble and he knew it. Each shot had to count. Each shot had to wait for enough light to find his next target.

One by one he killed the offending soldiers with the same purposeful shooting he'd demonstrated during his stint with MacLean's RCT-32.

Max Store's consciousness finally returned. He scrambled through the snow to Drier. "You gotta get a medic for that wound," he shouted, but before he could continue, a bullet stopped him. He looked into Drier's eyes with shock registered in his own, and then fell forward. His face smashed down hard on his camera that had been swinging from a strap around his neck. His other camera rolled away a few feet before stopping. His right hand released its grip on his writing pad. He was dead.

"Get out' a here David," Strickland screamed. "I'll cover for you."

Drier continued firing until he had to change clips. The M-1 held only eight rounds of 180 grain, 30-06 AP. It was a bitch to reload in the freezing air, especially when his operative arm was definitely out of the strength needed to load the cumbersome Garand.

A loud phumpf from a Chinese rifle sounded damned close. No time to react. Drier was hit again, this time somewhere in his abdomen or was it his hip? He wasn't sure but the sound of it, the sensation of it hitting him twisted his brain into a contorted mass of chaos. He turned and looked for Strickland. "I'm hit," he cried out in disbelief. "Damn it, Skipper, I'm hit." His hand groped for the wound but all he could feel was warm blood turning cold.

He fell forward on his rifle. His body lay motionless alongside Max Store's corpse but for some strange reason he would never be able to explain, his left arm had reached up and gripped tightly to Max Store's writing pad.

It was all up to Strickland now. Survival for any of them was in his hands. He fought back anger and the temptation to lose control. But he lost that battle quickly. He jumped up from his prone position at the BAR and went totally, insanely berserk. He fired the remaining rounds in the BAR into the area in front of him. A flare popped overhead. "Goddamned it," he shouted. But his eyes caught sight of what he needed. The BAR man had neatly stacked three other magazines in a pile in front of his position. He went down to his knees and grabbed the top one.

He reloaded so rapidly you'd think the Browning held hundreds of rounds. He fired on automatic now, feeling the gluttony of wanton anger pulling at the trigger.

Fraker appeared. He plopped down alongside Strickland.

"Skipper," he shouted. "You gotta get outta here."

"No men left. They got Drier, help him," he screamed.

Fraker whirled around just as the flare died out. He spotted Drier and bending over at his hips he raced quickly toward him, the tears he wanted to shed for the boy not coming. When he got there, he could hear Drier mumbling. He thought Drier was probably bleeding too much. Fraker grabbed him by his feet and tugged him down the slope, sliding with him over the icy hillside to the road below.

"The colonel made me a lieutenant," Drier mumbled after they stopped.

"Boy," Fraker growled, his words tumbling from the depths of a Virginia coal mine, "that's the kind 'a thing that'll get you kilt."

Fraker looked back up the hill. It was too dark to see his friend. But he could hear the BAR still pumping out rounds only now they were one at a time. The skipper was back to manual firing. Fraker understood that meant his boss was about to become suddenly quiet.

He was right. Strickland ran out of ammo.

Fraker reached over and grabbed Drier's M-1 and took off up the slope. The rifle had Drier's last load of eight rounds in it. When he got to Strickland he handed it over to him. Strickland was a much better shot than Fraker was, at least that's what Fraker would tell you.

Strickland started shooting immediately. "You mother'n sons of bitches," he croaked out barely enough for Fraker to hear. He was on single fire again. One shot at a time into the last eight Chinese soldiers, dropping them the way a Marine legend ought to; flat, quickly, and dead. It was as though he could see in the pitch of night, but that wasn't it. The Chinese were firing at him, and each time he fired right back into the spot where the flash appeared, actually just a tad to the right of each flash, which fit perfectly into the range of the oncoming soldier's heart.

Then he ran out of ammo and luck. From his position on top of his dead comrades, a mortally wounded Chinese soldier fired his burp gun at Strickland and grazed him in the thigh. He was more than surprised to find himself spun around by the hit. It felt like he'd been corkscrewed into the ice. He had no ammo left. But timing was everything and this time neither did his enemy.

The Chinese soldier collapsed onto his own burp gun.

And then it got quiet.

Strickland tried to stand, but wasn't successful. "Snake? Where the hell are you?"

"Right here, Skipper." Fraker was already down the slope and back at Drier's side.

Strickland slid on his ass down the slope to them. When he got there he found Snake pressing hard against Drier's wound. "He's down but not out. Sure could 'a been worse. So goddamned cold his blood's froze up."

But Strickland didn't hear him. He had taken the hit in his thigh and lost a bit of his own blood. Without warning, the man who had become a legend with a pistol, passed out.

CHAPTER 10

NINETEEN YEAR-OLD Corporal Barry "Big-D" Dane drove the Marine captain from Iwakuni airbase where the Marine fighter squadrons were based, to the new Hardy Barracks in the center of Tokyo. Barry was larger than Strickland in frame, but not taller. They were a match when it came to altitude. Barry had the standard military haircut, a starched utility cap squared away on his hawk-nosed head and he sat perfectly upright. A well trained diplomat for the U.S. Army, Strickland thought.

"Captain?" the big man asked, "What's it like over there?"

Strickland disliked such questions. And he wasn't in the mood for this one, either. He sat quietly for a moment and then decided to do his best to tell the guy to keep his trap shut while he drove. "I'm not the first one you've asked that, am I, Corporal?"

"Yes, sir. You are, I mean. I just got here. 'Bout four days ago. Sorry if it sounds stupid."

Strickland shrugged inwardly. So the guy was innocent. "You don't want to be there," he said with a crisp snap to his voice. He closed his eyes and fought back the memories that would not go away. It had all happened so quickly yet had taken a lifetime. The Chosin, the road back, the loss of so many friends and the army colonel, MacLean. And then Faith. All too much, too quickly.

Damn it. He had really come to like McLean, too. Fierce, brave, and a damned good leader. He couldn't remember if it had felt as badly to see McLean go as when he lost his parents or his friend Tommy. He shook that thought off, closed his eyes and rested his shoulders against the Jeep's ill fitting seat back.

New questions had popped up since his release from the naval hospital. Oh the wound, yes, that. It hadn't been all that bad he'd been told. Two pints of blood, some flesh but his innards survived quite well. Turned out that whatever hit him, went through his full canteen and then his folded map that he'd shoved into the back pocket of his utility trousers. The impact was then reduced. He laughed a little inside. Poppycock. Sure looked like hell. Still smarts. He bet right there that in a month the scars would look like hell as well.

And why this trip now? Why was he going to an army base when most Marines ended up at the navy base while waiting for their ticket back to Korea, or if they were lucky, back to the states?

"Because that's what your R&R orders read," Marine 2nd Lieutenant Woszieski had explained. "Some go to the Navy base, others to The Barracks. Everybody wants to go to The Barracks. Not to worry, Captain. Everything's under one roof there. It's a choice place to be. By the way. You'll have to check in there before you go on liberty."

The word liberty had struck him pretty near as hard as the round that had knocked him on his ass. Liberty. When was the last time he was able to get drunk off base? And to be with a woman?

The Jeep made a sharp turn nearly throwing him out of his seat. The sentry at the gate checked the driver's papers, glanced to Strickland, saluted and passed them through. They went straight to the administration building. "Check in here, Captain," the driver said. "And Captain," Dane continued, "sorry if I upset you."

Strickland waved him off with a half salute.

"Captain Strickland?" The army clerk had spoken to himself more than to Strickland. He glanced through Strickland's papers. "I don't have you on my list, sir." He scanned a clipboard full of names. "No, sir, nowhere."

"What's that mean?"

"Means I don't got your name here. Mean's you probably b'long somewhere's else. Maybe navy barracks. Heck, we don't get many Marines through here."

Strickland bristled. "You have my orders. I'm to be here this date. Deal with it." He could feel his anger build. His face flushed some and his eyes began to burn. He would hold it back, he told himself. Don't lose it now. Especially in front of a dogface.

The clerk recognized what was going on in the Marine's head. He withdrew into an immediate defensive posture. "Army's got its list of who stays here and who don't. You ain't on it, Captain. That usually means you belong some where's else. And none of that is my fault. Sir."

Strickland grabbed back his orders. "Who's your C.O?"

"Sergeant Jones, sir." He pointed to a glass-enclosed cubicle. "There."

Sergeant Jones was a huge, burly black man with a hairless head that seemed to glisten like a bowling ball. His short sleeve khaki blouse was adorned with jump wings, expert shooting badges, and a mile high pile of ribbons for combat service in WW-II.

"Get him," Strickland ordered.

"Don't got to. You can walk right in."

Strickland glanced menacingly at the corporal. If a Marine clerk had responded with, 'Don't got to,' he'd be on his way to the rock pile.

Sergeant Jones saved him the trouble of breaking into his office. He opened the wood and glass door that someone had painted an off-military olive drab and invited Strickland in. "Please, Captain. Come in."

Strickland entered the office and Jones closed the door. "I've been waiting for you, sir," Jones said.

"Apparently you're the only one." He checked his attitude half way through his sentence.

Jones caught it. He looked into Strickland's eyes with a bit of empathy and said, "I dig it, Captain. Sorry about that. I'm not an admin type. Things tend to get screwed up around here and I'm the one responsible."

Strickland took a liking to the sergeant. "Thanks, Jones. Sorry if I looked like I was ready to spit."

Jones smiled. "Please, sit down, Captain."

While Strickland sat he checked the ribbons above Jones's breast pocket. Silver Star with a cluster, two Purple Hearts, Bronze Star and more. He was interrupted by Jones who had plunked into his own chair behind a large Steelcase desk trimmed with the same color as the door.

"You've been assigned the VIP quarters, Captain. The request arrived late yesterday. It's a special VIP assignment. Like I said, I neglected to inform the corporal. My mistake."

Jones glanced to the corporal, then back to Strickland. "Also, it's not my practice to include such requests in my noncom's list, no matter who they are. Those boys chatter too much outside the gates. Specially to those damned whores who work as spies for the Chinese."

Strickland's interest picked up. "I'm not in the mood to hear that's going on."

"The request for you to stay in the VIP quarters came directly from a Colonel Horace Taylor. He's U. S. Army. Do you know him?"

Strickland shook his head. "No. I understood my orders came from Colonel Bradford. My new Marine C.O." He'd served under Harrison Bradford at Peleliu and Okinawa. Good man. Glad to be going to someone he recognized and already knew. Same attitude as Snake's. Same demeanor as his own. Straight forward, all Marine. He looked forward to the tour.

"Must be a mistake on our part," Jones said with a shrug. "Well, sir. You're here and that's what counts." He picked up a folder from his desk and handed it to Strickland. "Map. Of The Hardy Barracks base. Your quarters are marked in red. There. See 'em?" He pointed on the chart.

Strickland nodded, his eyes saw 'em, but his mind didn't. His thoughts were already elsewhere. Not sure where, but sure as hell not here.

"Here's the key, and a packet of materials about where you are. You'll like 'em. They're isolated from the rest of the base with grounds 'round them. You'll have complete privacy. If you want to go into Tokyo, there's a Chevrolet staff car been assigned for your use." He handed Strickland two more keys. "It's parked at your quarters now. Have you been to Tokyo?"

"No."

"You okay, Captain?"

Strickland looked up. He'd drifted off again. "Yes. Fine. Thank you."

"Tokyo's right outside the gate. You might find the traffic more dangerous than the battlefield."

"Why the top notch treatment? I'm just a grunt captain."

The chair supporting Jones squeaked with a high pitched tone when Jones leaned back. "Apparently you're not just a grunt, Captain. Someone high up believes you're important. And I do mean, high up. I'd guess from what I've heard 'bout you, they're right. Anyway, that's it. The next two weeks are yours. By the way, officer's mess is open twenty-four hours a day. You'll find it on the locater chart in that packet. Please eat and drink all you want. We've got some pretty good chefs over there and some goddamned good beer and ale." He stood, stuck out his hand and said, "Welcome to The Barracks, Captain. Pride of the United States Army in the Far East."

The shower lasted for a half-hour before the hot water turned cold. After toweling off, Strickland scraped off his week old stubble with a Gillette that had been supplied by the army. After that he began to feel human again.

Finished, he stepped back into the large bedroom and dove face down on the king size bed. Five seconds later, he was snoring.

"They weren't Chinese."

"North Koreans. Some of those bastards were North Korean soldiers."

"We killed 'em by the thousands and they kept coming at us."

"Bodies. The road's lined with 'em."

"More ammo. Second platoon's out of ammo."

"Where's your platoon now?"

"Napalm comin'"

"Pull up. Pull up."

"North Koreans. They were all NKs."

"Lost his legs."

"Blade's dead, sir."

"We lost the colonel."

"My boys. Those are my boys."

"Gooks comin' down the pass, play a burp gun boogey up a Gyrene's ass."

Hughes. Joe? Is that you?

"We're out of ammo!"

"Out of ammo!"

"Out of."

"It's me Frank. Joe."

Strickland bolted up as though he'd just exploded out of a 'zooka tube. His face glistened with sweat that rolled down his cheeks as though he'd been splashed with a bucket of warm water. He inhaled deeply but couldn't catch his breath at first. He raised his arms over his head and sucked in air.

What the hell's happening to me?

He went into the head—the army called it a latrine—and grabbed one of the white cotton towels that hung over a short metal holder. The holder was mounted next to the mirror. He wiped the moisture off his face and from around his neck. He returned to the bed.

"Shit," he murmured, and then fell asleep again.

The following morning he headed straight for the Yokosuka Naval hospital where Drier was still recuperating. Yokosuka looked pretty much like it did after the big war except where the Navy had constructed new docks, support buildings, and the hospital. The orderly at the entrance pointed him to the ICU.

Navy Lieutenant Doctor Grimes, a young resident from Texas, was tall, muscular and refreshingly candid. His southern Texas accent lent itself to making Strickland feel at home.

"I won't kid you, Captain. The lieutenant next to your friend is in serious trouble. He belongs in an ICU ward but ours are chock full. So, tread lightly in there. As to your friend, his wounds will heel quickly. The pain won't. That will last a while. Right now we have him morphed up a bit. We take him off that tomorrow."

"Who's the other officer?"

"Lieutenant Dearborn. Seems to be a friend of the Lieutenant."

"Dearborn." He dropped his chin noticeably.

"You know him?"

"Yes. We were at The Basic School. Quantico. Before coming to Korea. He was a good man." His voice was trailing again and the doctor heard it.

"You okay?"

Strickland snapped out of it. "Why does everyone ask that?"

"Sometimes, Captain, we find ourselves injured even though the wounds aren't physical."

Strickland mulled that over a moment. "Psycho stuff?"

Grimes nodded. "Not always that severe. We have many challenges to deal with." He paused and in a much lower tone added, "Among other things."

"Dearborn's injury?"

"We would have flown him to San Diego, but we couldn't stabilize him. He suffered a trauma injury to his head. He also lost a lot of blood. He's in a coma. Do you know what that means?"

"Only that he's unconscious for a long time."

"It means in his case that his brain is not talking to his body. In other words, he's in a state where there is very little brain activity." Grimes could see Strickland's body tighten up. "He's hovering between life and death. I'm very hopeful that he makes it."

Strickland held his eyes shut for a period of time, enough to say a prayer Grimes thought. "Drier. How's he doing? I mean his mind." Strickland asked when he opened his eyes.

"His injuries are definitely physical and not all that bad. As to his mind, well, when he's conscious he wants to grab at the nurses. Seems pretty sane to me."

They entered the room and stood at the foot of Drier's bed. Dearborn was a few feet away.

"Light wounds you said?" He nodded toward Drier.

"Loss of blood was Drier's biggest challenge. But he's okay now. This is a classic Ripley's Believe It Or Not. When he's released from here, he'll be eligible to return to Korea. Unless of course, someone wants him assigned to duty in Japan or stateside." Grimes gave off a knowing smile, fishing Strickland for some help in keeping the young man from further combat.

Strickland found himself only nodding. "Thanks, Doc. Think I'll wait here for a while."

Grimes left him.

Strickland didn't know how long he continued to stare at the two lieutenants but it must have been a while. A nurse had come in, checked their blood pressure and temperatures and then left. Neither man had stirred.

He wished now that he'd explained to Grimes that he had known Dearborn when he was an instructor at Basic School before he'd been shipped off to Korea. Strickland himself had been a candidate earlier, but his Pacific experience was needed at the school. So, he was assigned a platoon of young officers and that's where he'd met Dearborn.

He'd known him as a student, a young lieutenant with courage and guts and a whole lot of smarts. Why he didn't explain all that he didn't fully understand. But he thought maybe it was because he didn't want to admit that yet another young man he'd trained was going to die. O'Hara. Green. Shipley. So many.

And Hughes. Damn. He darted from the room and up to the nurse station.

"Yes, sir?" Navy nurse Bledsoe, who looked like she could have been the mother superior of the fleet, responded.

"I, uh, I wondered if there's a way to find out if a friend of mine is here or came through here." He seemed more impatient to her than all the others who'd asked similar questions had appeared.

"I could ask records. Might take a day. Was he wounded in Korea?"

"Yes."

"Hmm. They don't all come through here, but I'll check. Here," she said, handing him a piece of paper and a pen. "Write down his name and if you know it, his serial number."

Strickland knew the serial number. He wrote down his friend's name and number and then returned to Drier's room where he stepped to Drier's bedside.

"Drier," he said hoarsely.

No response. He pulled a very ugly green Naugahyde-covered metal chair out from under the window and placed it between the two beds. He sat and stared hard at the bulkhead opposite him. He would wait. He would wait for Drier, he'd wait for Dearborn, and he'd wait to see if his friend Joe Hughes was still alive.

Two hours passed before Doctor Grimes returned and found Strickland sitting straight up with his gaze fixed on Drier. "You all right, Captain?"

"Yes, sir."

"Would you like to eat something? I can have the orderly bring a tray for you."

Strickland glanced to Grimes. "Yes, sir, that would be a good thing. Thank you."

Grimes smiled but only faintly. "Doc. You can call me Doc or by my name, Billy Joe. Around here we aren't used to the word sir." He was right. Navy doctors were generally always referred to as "doc." And so, it seemed, were all the navy corpsmen.

Strickland nodded. "Yes, sir. Doc. Billy Joe." He nearly laughed at his own clumsiness. "What part of Texas?"

"Deep in the heart of a small town called Paris."

Strickland nodded and said, "I know where that is. The boy here is from Enid."

Grimes said as evenly, "Oklahoma. I know where that is."

At twenty-hundred hours, twelve hours after he'd arrived at the hospital, a dozing Strickland leaped to his feet. Someone in the room had made an effort to speak. "Drier, it's me, Frank Strickland."

Drier said nothing. He remained motionless. Strickland glanced to Dearborn. Maybe it was Dearborn who spoke. He went to his bed. "Dearborn. Are you awake?"

"It's me Captain," Grimes said from the doorway. "Time to head back to your quarters. Regulations. You can return in the morning if you like. Oh Six Hundred."

Early morning sunlight creeped gently like a pet kitty along the wooden deck of Strickland's quarters. It pawed its way up the side of his bed and then moved lightly across his bare flesh. It brought with it the warmth of a sun he'd not felt in a long time. For him Korea had been snow or mud and always clouds and death. Now the sun shone and he was alive and he felt refreshed. At least, he thought, he felt a bit more human.

His eyes blinked at first then opened wide. His head was buried in a soft pillow, a feeling that he'd not had for a long time. He sat up, rubbed his cheeks with his open palms. He was naked, sweaty again even though it wasn't hot outside or inside. He thought for a moment about the day before. He swore lightly at the realization that he couldn't remember making it back to quarters from the hospital. Exhaustion. Maybe that's what Grimes was talking about when he said "Among other things."

He stumbled across the room to the shower. When he peered into the mirror he saw the reflection of a man who'd been beat up too many times. New wrinkles appeared on his face. Stranger yet, there was a gaunt look to him he'd never noticed before, and it wasn't just a loss of weight.

"Yeah," he said aloud. "If that's you, then get this. You no longer have a soul." To himself he added, I've been to hell and I think I've made a pact with the devil. Why else am I still alive? Everyone else is gone. He stopped the chatter. He felt his face. He needed a shave.

He reached for the tooth cleanser, a powder in an oval canister. With his forefinger he ran powder across his teeth. He'd have to stop at the commissary and pick up a toothbrush. He gargled with lukewarm water, and then stepped into the shower. With any luck, he could expunge the sickening memories of battle for a while. At least while he was awake.

When the water hit him his thoughts returned to Doc Grimes. He was right the first time. Grimes thought he'd gone nuts, but didn't know how to tell him straight off. He was pushing against something again. His internal conversations. He hadn't had these for a long time. Shit the last one was in the Diego navy hospital after Okinawa.

He ran the bar of soap across his shoulders and then washed his hair and head with it. When the spigot of water splashed the suds off, his mind raced backwards.

Hey, asshole. Check it out. I'm not dead inside or out. The body moves and the spirit lives. Then get your butt back to the hospital and pull Dearborn through. Got it? Yeah, I got it. And Hughes. Find him and help him stay alive. Keep Drier alive. Shit that's all you got man. You've lost everyone else.

He was kicking himself in the ass again.

The hot shower felt lusty. Sharp droplets pricked him in the face, poked at him with such driving force that he was obliged to tilt his short-cropped scalp into the flow. He grabbed the Gillette and raced it across his face until it was slick again.

He soaped down after that, rubbing every part of his body with the small bar of Ivory supplied by the army. When he was finished, he grabbed the towel off the rack and wiped vigorously. It all felt good. So very, very good. Maybe he could get it back he thought. Bring back the spirit for life that seemed to have dissipated. He must. He was alive. The others were dead. There was a reason, wasn't there?

He entered the bedroom and opened the closet door to grab up his uniform. He paused. What the hell is this? He plucked up a note hanging on a civilian suit and read it.

Dear Captain Strickland,

Forgive us for the intrusion. These clothes are for you. (Your liberty will go much better in these instead of in your uniform). You will find they are tailored to match the fit of your greens. Please wear them with our gratitude for all you have done for our country.

Horace Taylor, Col. U.S.A.

He crumpled the note in his hand and threw it into the small basket alongside the dresser. "Taylor!" He'd forgotten that Sergeant Jones had mentioned that a man named Taylor had asked for him.

He stepped deeper into the walk-in closet and found three white shirts, a pair of civilian shoes and fresh under garments.

Why not? This was R & R.

Once dressed in the cotton slacks and a white cotton twill shirt he headed straight back to the hospital.

"Good morning, Captain," Grimes greeted. "Good to see you more comfortable today."

"Do you ever go to bed, Doc?"

"Not in this hospital. I have to catnap. Good news. Lieutenant Drier is groggy but awake right now. Go right on in."

An ethereal sort of glow seemed to beam from Drier. "Skipper?" Strickland wasn't surprised at Drier's weak voice. He'd seen the same before and probably sounded the same after his fixer upper in San Diego back in '45.

"Good to see you alive."

Drier couldn't move his arm or even make a sign with his hand indicating a greeting. He was just too damned drugged. "You were here yesterday." It was a question although it sounded like a statement.

"Yes."

"Thank you."

"I guess they've got you patched up pretty well."

"Doc says I can get out of here in about a week. No bones. No organs gone. He says that all things should be good. Can't wait to get back. How's Jimmie?"

Strickland glanced to Dearborn. "I'd say he's going to take a bit

167

longer than you." He looked at Dearborn curiously. "Seems to have color in him today. Better than yesterday."

"Hmmm."

"Any pain?"

"Hmmm."

"Are you going to sleep on me?"

"No, sir." But he was groggy.

"Need pain killer?"

"No, sir. They give me too much of that stuff. Please tell 'em to stop. I can deal with pain."

"I'll mention that."

"How are the rest of the men?"

"Snake's in good shape, 'bout like me. The rest of our company took a hit, but those who lived through it are taking a big break from the war."

"Hmmm. Captain Hughes?"

"They're checking."

"Hmmm. How did I get here?"

"Fraker got us both to Hungnam after a corpsman patched us up. The entire United States military was there boarding MSTS ships. I was on the Ainsworth. Don't know which ship you were on."

"So, we bugged out after all?"

"Regrouped."

"Hmm."

Strickland already received his own orders after his R&R. He decided to clue Drier in now. "They're sending me up to Panmunjom. Something about moving the peace talks there from Kaesong."

Drier's philosophical mind kicked in. "We shoot and talk at the same time? Weird."

Strickland smiled. His boy was going to be okay. "Remember Bradford."

"Kinda. Where's that place?" He meant Panmunjom.

"About fifty kilometers, ah, thirty miles north of Seoul. Maybe this war will end soon. I guess they're going to try to talk them into submission."

"Hmm. Can I come with you?"

Strickland reached down and grabbed Drier's right hand. "I'd like that. When you're better. But you know you can return to stateside after this."

"So can you." Drier tried to laugh but of course couldn't.

Strickland glanced to Dearborn then back to Drier. "I'm going to leave you for a while David, but I'll come back. I'm here for two weeks. I intend to get fully, completely-out-of-control-drunk today."

Drier's humor was returning. "Get my clothes. I'll come with you."

Strickland felt good about his boy. He let the joke settle for a few moments then said, "We could have beat them back, you know."

"Uh, huh."

"All we needed was more ammo."

"Hmm. And a few more men."

"You did a fine job, son. We put you in for a Navy Cross for your actions. That'll put a star on the one you have. No C.O. in the future will ever screw with you. Except possibly me." He found himself chuckling for the first time in so long that he wondered where it came from.

"Hmm. I'll keep that in mind."

"Can I get you anything?"

Drier's eyes closed.

Strickland glanced to Dearborn again. Something was peculiar. When it hit him, he dashed for the doorway. "Corpsman. Get someone in here. Now!"

Two Navy nurses ran to the room. Strickland pointed at Dearborn. To the nurses, Strickland seemed so statuesque that possibly he was the one who might need help from them.

Grimes rushed through the door. Strickland's lips moved but no one heard him say, "Don't let him go."

He wasn't sure what they were doing to Dearborn. The only thing he could remember later was that the doctor bent over him for a few minutes, then stood up straight and said, "I'm truly sorry. I thought we could save him."

After they rolled Dearborn from the room, Strickland checked with the desk again to learn about Hughes, but the duty nurse said that she was aware they were searching the records. No news yet.

Strickland's familiar dull olive-drab Chevy struggled through Yokohama and then Tokyo, where he landed at an Americanized bar with a hand-carved sign over the door announcing it was the Bar New York. It was somewhere on the far end of the Ginza, where many American G.I.s hung out in bars or whorehouses. He parked directly in front of the Bar New York, stepped over the binjo ditch, a sort of exposed running toilet for the indigenous citizens, and available for any round-eye who wanted to try it.

Inside, he was led to a table along the back wall. There were no booths. The table had a small candle standing upright in a wax-filled saucer that was half burned. The saucer appeared to be a standard military issue Melmac plate. The candle's flame seemed expressionless, almost as though it were paper maché. Two translucent glass ashtrays with old cigarette butts squashed in stacks of burnt and stale tobacco caressed the candle as though supporting it until it's last puff.

Strickland recognized the discarded butts as C-ration Lucky Strikes. American military had been here. The bar had nothing else of interest. No cloth on the tables, no hardware, no napkins. The bare walls didn't even proffer a shadow from the lit candles in the room. This was where he wanted to be. His personal emptiness felt at home right here in this den of irrelevance.

"Asahi dozo, chee," he said in his best Japanese interpretation of asking for a locally brewed beer. He held up four fingers to the bowing waitress to enforce his choice of the number he'd spoken in the woman's native language.

"With the caps still on."

She departed.

He glanced furtively around. He was becoming aware of the total space of The Bar New York. It was dark throughout, probably intentionally. Perfect way to provide shelter for dark minds and dark intentions. The Japanese barkeepers had learned to keep their places that way twenty-four hours a day. His sensory system detected more than old tobacco. He recognized stale beer, old pretzels, and the sickness that came from too much drinking. And another odor! The binjo ditch outside was only a few feet away from a porous rice-paper bulkhead.

"Shit," he muttered. He wanted the quiet but not the septic river. His beers came.

The waitress bowed and asked, "Something to eat?"

Strickland shook his head, waved her away. Not a chance he'd eat anything in here. He pulled up his dogtag necklace. It also had the world's smallest beer bottle opener attached; a Marine tradition. It was a sort of a swivel design, much smaller than his tags and easily carried. With little effort the top popped off the first bottle with ease. It made a sound he enjoyed, one that started the process that he knew would either put him at ease or make him stinking drunk. He took a slug, then another, then another.

"A toast to each of you," he said clearly holding the bottle into the air. He visualized scores of men he'd known. Men now gone or badly injured. "I let you boys down," he said. "Damn it."

He downed a huge slug. The men were just boys he'd come to love. They became comrades long before they fought and brothers while in battle.

Violent death required drinking for the living witnesses. There was no greater toast to those who passed on than to have a brother raise a beer in the air as though sitting in Tun Tavern, and then down the son of a bitch.

He was feeling sorry for himself. He knew that. He also chastised himself for it. It was a weakness and damned if he'd open it up for others. Best to get drunk right here and have it over.

The cold Asahi felt good going down. It helped chase the war ahead of it, numbing the hatred for everything he'd done, including his failures as well as the redundant and senseless loss of his brothers. The second bottle went down nearly as quickly as the first but this time, instead of a toast, he burst out with a loud engulfing belch.

"Here's to you Dearborn and all the others," he said aloud while he popped off the third cap. He belched again and then downed the beer.

"Captain?"

He wasn't alone. A woman's voice. He twisted around in his chair to find the source and the source was a remarkably beautiful woman with what he considered to be incredibly sensuous lips and pure blond hair that swept behind her as though there were a breeze in the bar.

Burp. With just three beers he couldn't be drunk. Why this apparition? Damn. He looked at her again. Her hair seemed to flow behind her even while she stood still. Her complexion was uniquely model like. Yep. He had to be drunk. Women never turned up for him when he needed one. Never.

She sat down in the chair opposite his with a slight motion of her hand that it was okay to do so. "You don't mind." she said. It wasn't a question.

She sat erectly, perfectly postured, her shoulders in the right place. Strickland wondered if she was a woman Marine. He'd seen a few of those lately, but then again, none had looked like this beauty.

He noticed that her perfect chin was straight up, her body placed in the chair as though sculpted. When she spoke, her words flowed casually, like tools to be used for seduction or command. He held back an insistent belch to the point of causing pain in his esophagus.

He would have to be careful with this one, he decided. He'd not had the chance to experience it yet, but he'd heard about the round-eyes in the Far East. He wanted to know how she knew he was an officer. Hell, how'd she know he was a captain.

"It's not hard to guess," she said. "You are definitely an American officer. Officers stand out."

"I used to be enlisted. And not long ago," he said, more timidly than he liked. He worked at holding back another belch.

"Not now you aren't. You also look exhausted, I suppose you're on R&R from Korea. A Marine by the cut of your jib."

"Salty talk from a beautiful woman."

"You could have been a major, but I flipped my coin and you came up heads. A lieutenant is out of the question from the, well, the sagacious look in your eyes."

"Interesting word."

"Experience. Wise. It means that and other things."

"I know."

"You have a mystique about you. You've been through too much. Only a very young major would be caught in here and there aren't many of those around. So, I chose captain. You look like you might be a captain. Your age explains having been an enlisted man before." She smiled as though she had just won her high school spelling bee.

"You're a regular Sherlock."

"Conan Doyle was the most clever of writers during his time."

He finished off his beer and while she spoke he popped open another. Not even a good looking lady was going to stop him from getting smashed.

She tilted her head back sensuously, a motion that sent her straight hair out in a fan shape. It fell back gracefully to her shoulders just like the photo ads for one of those silly shampoos. She added, "However, and just in case you hadn't noticed, he did not often include women in his Sherlock Holmes tales."

"You have an accent," he said.

"I come from Denmark. But I speak many languages. English and French are my best. I went to school in London. Sometimes my tongue seems to forget where I come from."

"What's your name?"

"Juliana. My American friends call me Julie. You can, too. What's yours?"

The waitress arrived, bowed. Strickland nodded to Juliana. "A beer?"

Juliana glanced around. "This place? Can we leave it? Together? I know a better spot to, well, to get drunk if that's your goal."

"I think I'll stay here."

She stood and held her hand out. "Please, come with me. I have plenty of beer aboard our boat. And it's very private there."

Strickland gave her comment a moment to sink in. He glanced around the Bar New York and with a dash of clarity he thought a boat sounded better. Especially with a hot looking blond. "Do you have a bed on board that boat? When I crash, I go down hard."

"Of course. We have several accommodations. Do you smoke?"

"No."

She smiled. "That's good."

"Are you safe?"

She laughed loudly. "Oh, my goodness. You are different." She took his hand into hers. "Come," she said with her voice as smooth as cashmere. "I am much safer than Korea. We will enjoy each other's company and you can toast your men as many times as you wish."

They left the Japanese version of a slop-chute and she drove away with him in his Army Chevrolet.

Another Chevy, seemingly out of the same paint shop, pulled out behind them and followed them at a measured distance.

Strickland saw that it wasn't a boat. It was a yacht. It appeared to him to be about a hundred-feet long. It was anchored offshore in the Tokyo harbor close to half of the U. S. Navy. There were merchant marine ships, freighters, personnel carriers, and LSTs docked, anchored or tied to each other throughout the bay. Strickland could barely believe so much metal could float in one spot and not raise the ocean a few feet.

"Impressive, huh?" Julie said. They were standing amidships at the starboard rail.

Strickland nodded. The day was warm and he'd just downed four beers in a hurry. His head felt a bit heavy, cloudy maybe. Asahi had more alcohol in it than American beers. Kind of like that Cuban beer, Hatuey.

"Yeah," he said, "but it doesn't help us having them anchored here. The war's in Korea. The gunboats should be fighting and the freighters should be hauling supplies. The stuff we needed is probably sitting in one of those damned boats."

"Maybe not. If you'll stay here with me a few days you'll see that they are constantly moving supplies through here. Those boats are barely here for a day. New ones arrive empty, these leave full. Fresh troops arrive here almost daily on those transports. Then off to Korea the next day or so."

Strickland turned to her. She was his height, only more fragile. "You seem to know a lot about what's going on."

She nodded. "It's not a secret you know. The war I mean. And everything about it is in the American papers everyday. My father thinks that's stupid. You Americans seem to feel you can tell the enemy everything even before you do it."

Strickland seemed stunned. It showed.

She put her hand on his chest very lightly and said, "You didn't know, did you?" She grabbed his arm and led him into the spacious lounge. They sat at the bar while the steward poured them another drink.

"Well?" she asked waving her hand as though to fan the interior of the yacht. "What do you think?"

"I think it's out of place."

"But you like it?"

He nodded. "How could I not like it? Any beer on this junkie?"

She laughed and hauled him into the galley after dismissing the steward. "There. The reefer."

He opened the reefer door and his eyes brightened. Dutch beer? Lager? Wine?"

"Don't overlook the food, my dear Captain."

"Want one?" He held up a Heineken.

"Danka. I'll have ice water."

He turned and took her hand and pulled her close. "Something's fishy here. Tell me what this is all about. Nobody like you just drops into a grunt's life and swoops him off to a setting like this. What's up?"

She giggled and softly pushed away. "You're a real cornball. Maybe you think you're Bogie?"

"No. You're up to something but I can't figure it out. I mean one day I'm in hell and the next on a yacht with a gorgeous woman. Makes no sense."

"Thank you."

His look changed to curiosity. "For what?"

She tilted her head in a sensuous way and said, "You said I was gorgeous. Thank you."

He held up his hands. "That's it. I'm leaving. I just figured it out."

"And what did you figure out?"

"You're a commie spy. You're working for the Chinese or the NKs."

She laughed with a piercing guffaw that sounded more fun than ridiculous. "No, no, no. Not on your life." She walked to the rear bulkhead, reached up to the shelf and pulled a scrapbook down. "I despise communists. They aren't much better than the Nazis were. Look," she said. "Come. Look."

He liked the laugh, it was so honest and warming, that he knew he'd not nailed her reasons. So, he walked willingly with her. He hadn't been this close to a woman in so long he'd forgotten what it felt like. She sat on the sofa and pulled him down next to her and opened the book.

"This is my family. This boat belongs to my father. He is the Danish ambassador to the United Nations. He has close friends here. The war has been quite upsetting for us in Denmark, as much as it has been for your country. Father decided to come to Tokyo, to be here when and where things happen, to help if he can. I came with him."

"Where is he now?"

She glanced up. "In Korea. Pusan, I believe."

He looked curious. "For?"

She shook her head. "I never ask. You learn to be that way when you're the daughter of an important man. Do you understand?"

Strickland didn't understand and said so. The only men he

considered important were the men who fought so goddamned hard with so goddamned little.

He held the book with a tight grip and looked at each photo while she explained the pictures on each of the pages. The photos were real. They were mostly Box Brownie shots or more likely from one of those German folding cameras. She was a cute kid, he thought. She looked a lot like her mother. Her father was tall, slender, blond hair with pale complexion like her own.

"We hid from the Nazis," she said. "They were awful people. That's why my father feels obligated to help others. That's why he's a part of the United Nations."

Strickland found himself staring into her eyes. "If you're not working with your father, why are you here?"

She stopped turning the pages. "Difficult question."

"You can answer it though?"

"Not really. I've been here for six months now and I'm bored silly. Women don't cut it over here. The traditional Japanese men are awful to women. Have you seen them?"

He nodded. "Of course."

"It's not pretty. And I haven't found a single Dane over here other than my father. The French soldiers and the Brits are incorrigibly Chauvinistic. That's what it comes down to. So, today I went out looking for company. I have needs, you understand. Just as you probably do. So, when I saw you enter that bar I figured who I thought you might be and followed you in. Is that so bad? A woman seeking companionship?"

Strickland sat back into the sofa. This was unreal and if he were sober, he thought, he'd figure it out. He glanced to his watch. "In the morning I must visit a friend in the Naval hospital and check on another."

She snuggled up to him. "You can stay here," she said. "It will be perfect."

CHAPTER 11

HE'D HEARD IT BEFORE. Water slapping the outer hull of a ship. Troop ships. Hospital ships. The Ainsworth. But why was he hearing it now? Motion. The water wasn't just slapping, it was moving.

Slowly he came alive.

His eyes caught the chair where he'd flung his clothes the night before but now they were missing. And Julie was gone. Oh, God. Julie! He sat straight up just as the hatchway opened. Julie entered carrying an armful of fresh civilian clothes.

"Good morning Mr. Naked," she said cheerily. "I brought you some comfortable things to wear. That old suit would look asinine on deck."

"We're moving," he said more as a statement than a question.

She set the clothes down on the end of the bed and sat with him. "Yes, silly. We're sailing up the coast."

Strickland bolted to his feet, raw skin and all. "No! I have to get to sickbay."

She giggled. "Well, you could swim for it, but these aren't the safest waters in the world. Not even for Johnny Weissmuller."

Strickland grabbed up the clothes she'd brought and headed for the deck.

She laughed. "A naked man on deck my dear will only get the crew buzzing. And should I say, laughing."

He pulled on the pants and wrapped his shirt around his shoulders and worked frantically to button it. "We aren't out of the harbor yet. That's Yokosuka right there," he said. He pointed to the Naval Hospital. "Tie to or I'm overboard."

"Don't go crazy on me, Frank. You'd never make it in this water."

His passion startled her. "That's my boy in that hospital and I damn well mean to see him. Now!"

He looked to the flying bridge. The boat's captain was at the rail looking back. Strickland waved to the man to come down. Behind him Juliana nodded confirmation to the captain. When he arrived Strickland said, "Put it ashore Captain. Right there." He pointed to the Naval hospital.

The captain reacted as Juliana knew he would. "I can't dock anywhere near here, Sir," he said. "We'd have to return to our assigned berth."

Strickland straightened up with his brewing anger clearly obvious. "Put me over the side in your gig."

"Maybe you could dock at the Navy hospital directly," Juliana said to the boat's captain with a firmness that sounded more like she was the captain.

"Yes, Ma'am. I'll take care of that." He left them.

"You're spoiled rotten," Juliana said to Strickland. "Do you always get what you want?"

Surprising the captain more than it did Strickland, the boat easily obtained permission to dock at Yokosuka. When the yacht touched the wharf Strickland leaped to the dock and headed directly toward the hospital. He tossed Juliana a quick thanks but no thanks and yelled back that he could get his own ride to The Barracks.

She smiled the way only someone who knew differently could. "We'll see," she said, unheard by Strickland.

The corridor to Drier's room seemed deathly quiet. Only nurse Bledsoe was at the station desk and she was reading something. He pushed open Drier's door and found an empty room. Drier was gone, clothes and all. He darted back to the station.

"Where's Lieutenant Drier?"

"Drier?"

"That room," he pointed.

"Oh, yes. He's in surgery." She scanned Strickland quickly noting a rather loose civilian outfit. "You are?"

"Captain Strickland. His commanding officer."

She glanced to her watch. "He may be a while, Captain."

The tone in his voice displayed his concern, and his impatience. "What happened?"

She nearly grinned. "Your officer tried to get out of bed. He fell and dislocated his left knee. They've got to put your Humpty Dumpty back together again." She smiled, nearly laughed. "He was trying to grab one of our nurses, Captain. By the buttocks."

Frank Strickland, the tough Marine, relieved to learn that his boy was certainly a man, nearly laughed with pride. "He what?"

The nurse turned back to her desk. "You heard me. Damned Marines are all alike. Hard to kill 'em, and you can't fix 'em without a slap or two."

"Hughes," he said. "Did you learn anything about him?"

She turned back to him with a smile. "I thought you'd never ask," she chided. She flipped open a manila folder and read, "Lieutenant Joseph Hughes, USMC. In transport. Destination Bethesda Naval Hospital." She looked up. "He's alive, Captain, and headed for the best hospital in the country."

Outside in the parking area, Strickland threw his arms into the air and let out a wild shout of utter relief and happiness. Then, embarrassed, he pulled his arms back to his sides and searched for a military vehicle that he could hitch back to The Barracks. Instead, his eyes fell on Julie.

"Need a lift sailor?"

"That's really corny," he said, only now his voice had a much happier tone. He continued his search for a Jeep or a staff car.

"Something good must have happened in there. You've gone from Mr. Uptight to Mr. Happy."

He turned to her. "My men are okay. My best friend is alive and my boy in there is already chasing nurses. Now, I have another reason to get drunk."

A Jeep pulled up to him just then. It was Snake. "My God, look who's here," he said with a grin showing through his trimmed beard. A brand new cigar was locked tightly between his teeth.

"Another friend?" Julie asked.

Fraker stepped out of the Jeep. He gave Strickland a quick salute and then grabbed his hand to shake it. "Damned good to see ya, sir."

"And you, my friend. How'd you get here?"

"Puller hisself, sir." Fraker was clearly happy to see his friend. "Sent me to Jay land for R and R."

"Puller?"

"And our old buddy Bradford, sir. The two of 'em. Seems they're old pals."

"And you just happened by. Well, good timing."

"Came to see the lieutenant, sir. How's he doin'?"

Strickland flashed a shot of happiness that Snake hadn't seen in a long time. "Ya know, Snake, I think he'll be just fine." When he explained what happened, Snake burst out with his own laugh of relief.

"My main man, sir. Yes, sir. That's a good 'un."

"Now, why are you really here?" Strickland knew when Fraker was bullshitting him.

Snake glanced to the lady, then back to his Skipper. In a lower voice he said, "Truth is, I was sent to be your driver and to make sure you got back alive. Seems like a lot of people knew you'd be here. And Bradford's a bit concerned about you." He stepped back. "But hell's bell's skipper, you're lookin' good to me. White sailcloth civvies? Man alive, you got with it quick."

"I'm not done with the news."

Fraker stopped chattering. There was a familiar glint in his Skipper's eyes. Good news was coming. "Sir?"

"Joe Hughes is very much alive and on his way to Bethesda."

"Zowie, you did it." Fraker's voice reached higher levels again.

"We did it, Snake." They were shaking hands and practically hugging. "We did it," he said again in a softer voice as though convincing himself that Joe Hughes had really made it.

Julie stepped up. "Sergeant, you're welcomed to come along on our boat ride north if you like. Plenty of cabins aboard and lots of good drinks and food."

Fraker glanced to Strickland and back to the beauty who he just figured out. "Yes, sir," he said with a monster grin, "You got with it real quick."

"I take it that's a no," Julie said in a tone that told Fraker to lay off. "Well then, we'll return in two days, Sergeant. You can pick up your skipper right here if you like."

Fraker wasn't dumb. "Well, Ma'am, if he's just gonna be on the boat and then back here, I'll wait with the Lieutenant inside if ya don't mind. I don't s'pose Colonel Bradford would mind that. Accordin' to the way they talk back there, the captain here might just be needin' your trip."

"Enough, Snake. I wasn't going to go with her."

"You are now, Frank," Juliana said. "The sergeant here can keep your lieutenant company for a few days. Right, Sergeant?" Her piercing stare was enough for Snake.

"Right."

The yacht anchored in a quiet bay just west of Mt. Fuji. A short drive later Strickland and Juliana found themselves at Lake Yamanaka, courtesy of a Japanese touring cab.

The resort lodge with its individual cabins was nestled among a botanical garden of tall pines and a variety of shrubs and flowers below. Lake Yamanaka was where many Japanese visited for their own rest and recreation. It was unique, private, and by Strickland's standards more than impressive.

"Beats Drier's imaginary Hawaiian paradise," he muttered.

"Five lakes region," Julie said. "Yamanashi prefecture. The Japanese call this lake Yamanaka-ko. I think it's the most beautiful spot on the planet. Small, but beautiful."

Strickland perked up suddenly. "I think I'm hearing country music."

"Probably. The Japanese love two kinds of American music right now. Country and Glenn Miller."

Inside the lodge, in the bar-restaurant area, a 5-member American band known as *The Poorboys* was playing the Hank Williams tune, "Hey Good Looking."

"Perfect tune for now, isn't it?" he said.

"You are corny, Frank. You ever have a girlfriend?"

He wouldn't answer that. She was already getting too close.

They walked toward the lake for a moment. Nature had painted the lake a rich ultramarine blue hue with some smatterings of glistening whites and fire-red reflections caused by the setting sun and its effect on the cumulus clouds above.

Lake water closer to the shoreline bounced with images of cherry blossoms from the trees near the water. Two small boats crisscrossed paths on the lake about midway out. An unending breeze sent chill rolls across the water toward them, while Fuji smiled down with it's top-third covered in a white blanket of snow and ice. Its peak seemed sharply painted against the brilliant patches of a cobalt sky. Wind whipped millions of ice crystals from the mountain top into a horizontal wonderment, creating a line of frost from the peak, southward.

"It is a holy mountain," she said. "Some call it the calendar mountain. It's supposed to be 12,365 feet high, but I think it's a bit higher." She glanced to Strickland who seemed pensive at the moment. "The Japanese say that you must climb Mt. Fuji once." She smiled affectionately and added, "They also say that you are a fool if you climb it twice."

Strickland took a few steps toward the mountain. His eyes never came off the seductive cone of Fuji. "Then," he said, "we must not become fools."

"Meaning?" Julie asked.

He turned to her. "We will climb the mountain once. Tomorrow."

She smiled. He was loosening up. "That'll be interesting," she said.

"To the top," he added, his eyes still on the peak.

Early the following morning, a bit before dawn, they started up the mountain. A young Japanese guide who wanted to be called "Joe," explained that they were already at the five thousand foot elevation, so they had only seven-thousand to go.

By the time they reached midway up the mountain, it was noon and the seven-thousand was beginning to seem to Julie like seven hundred thousand. They stopped to rest at a small hut along the trail where a man came out to sell them Akadama wine. They turned him down with a polite "Arrigato."

When they looked down slope, they saw cumulus clouds below their altitude coming from the south. The clouds would surround Fuji halfway up the mountain, blocking their view of the lakes below. Joe pointed up hill. "More will come later, block out top, too."

"We better hustle," Strickland said. He started up the trail again. It wound back and forth in long sweeping arcs like a coiled snake, designed they were told to make the climb easier. Eight hundred feet from the top they stopped again. From where they stood, it was nearly a straight climb to the peak through solid ice. Looking behind them they could see two layers of clouds surrounding the holy mountain.

The sun was about four hours from setting. The light was eerie, breathtaking.

"Now what?" Julie asked Joe.

"There," he said, pointing. They saw foot notches dug into the ice by those who had preceded them. Joe went first, Julie second. Strickland followed. It was arduous work. Breathing became harder, the climb now required more energy than before.

Forty-five minutes later they reached the top.

"Incredible," Juliana said breathlessly looking out over the world of clouds that peaked and dropped as though they were actually millions of miles of rolling hills.

They walked along the rim, which seemed to Strickland to be in excellent condition, especially after the bloody ridges in Korea. Joe pointed to the interior of the volcano across what seemed to be a frozen meadow of ice that led to the chimney. "It's called a vent," he said. "Do not get close. Some people slide on ice, disappear in there. Never come out." And as though he had to, he added, "Bad. Very bad."

Strickland had become hypnotized by the inactive volcano. He was drawn into the crater's floor that led to the vent. He headed straight toward it as though he were about to sacrifice himself to his demon gods.

"Frank," Julie cried out. She took one step toward him and slid off the rim. She landed on her butt and began sliding uncontrollably toward the vent. Joe adeptly ran after her and drove his staff into the ice ahead of her. She rammed into it, stopping. Joe helped her to her feet. That's when Julie noticed that Joe had cleats on his boots.

"Why don't we have those," she said, pointing to his boots.

But Joe had only one thought on his mind. "Cannot go near there," he warned. "Can die."

"I must," she said. She glanced to Strickland then back to Joe. "He's a bit nuts, Joe. He's been fighting too long. He'll die if we don't stop him."

"You stay here. I go get him." He took off and she went right behind him. "Frank-san," Joe yelled. "Come back."

Strickland didn't hear him. Instead, the wind whipped up, kicking at his field jacket and civilian trousers. His cap flew off and sailed into the chimney, which was now only a hundred feet in front of him.

Julie caught up to him. She grabbed at his jacket. "Frank. Stop, you're scaring me." Her boots slipped out from under her and she crashed to her butt again.

Strickland pulled her up. "Stay here," he commanded. "I have to do this."

"You're behaving crazy Frank," she yelled after him. "You can't do this. Stop! Frank. Get Korea out of your head you dumb bastard."

He stopped and turned to her. "Where'd that come from?"

"I know," she said. "I know what you've been through."

"Crap. No one can know that unless they were there." He turned back toward the vent and continued on.

Joe pulled up in front of Strickland, his staff jammed into the ice pack. "No, Frank-san. No. We must go back. We will freeze to death up here at night."

Strickland pressed Joe out of his way. "I know what I'm doing, Joe. Leave me alone."

Julie covered her mouth with her hands, her eyes popped open like budding petals. Her only vision the impending death of Frank Strickland.

Strickland got to the edge where the sheer ice surface made it seductively dangerous. Joe stood with Julie, his hand gripping her jacket tightly. As a guide it was not good to lose a tourist. Two of them gone would be the end of his career. The American was nuts, that was for sure, and he decided, the American was also suicidal. They wouldn't hold that against him. At least he hoped they wouldn't.

Strickland stared down into the hole for a full minute, poised as though he would jump any second. Then he turned back slowly, keeping his feet right at the icy edge of the precipice. He faced his two companions. He spoke with a sepulchral tone. "That ancient pit is a reflection of all our lives. It is where we end up. In a hole like that, where hell forever burns. We cannot escape it. We are bound to hell for all the death, the killing, for all the wars we have fought. Each of us must do what we must to survive, and still we will end up down there burning with the others."

"Oh my God, Frank. Don't," she pleaded.

Strickland turned back to the hole, the toe of his boots hanging over the edge. "To stand at the edge of hell and not burn, to stand this high before the eyes of God and be at the doorstep of the devil without the sounds of war, only creates the illusion that we are safe."

Julie gasped.

Strickland turned back to her. His expression was peaceful, calmed. "Don't you see, Julie? Why should only the good be condemned to hell by those who pretend to be the angels? Let the failed statesmen and leaders carry arms, let them die while they argue. Let them stand at the edge of hell and see if they can survive the pull into eternal damnation like I have. Come here, please," he said, holding his hand out. "See for yourself."

Julie found herself unanswerably mesmerized by Strickland's unexpectedly calm voice and pacifist expression. She broke loose from Joe's grip and walked to him.

Joe freaked out. "Dami," Joe groaned. "No!" He stepped backward, slowly, moving purposefully back toward the volcano's outer rim. All was lost for him. His license, his income, his future. Shit, he thought with sudden contemplation, he might as well jump with them.

Julie kept on until she reached Strickland. She put her hand out and he guided her to the edge. When she looked down she nearly fainted. The chimney was sheer and the hole pitch black with an emptiness that must certainly never end. There would be no way out if they slipped and fell into it.

"It must reach to the bowels of the earth," Strickland said. "Fires of hell, indeed."

She moved her eyes slowly to his, fearing that if she moved faster, she'd lose her balance. "Everything's okay, Frank. You're alive. You're spirit is alive. You aren't going to hell." Barely able to breathe, she added, "We can go now."

Strickland returned her gaze. "Thank you, Julie."

"For what?"

"For waking me. Until now, I really had no idea what was happening to me. Now I know. Nothing really matters. Nothing. No matter what we do, it all ends up down there."

"Frank, that's not true."

He smiled. "Let's go," he said without changing his demeanor or tone of voice or his mind. "Before it gets dark."

"Captain Strickland?"

Strickland groaned with a deep guttural sound. Who in the hell was bothering him now? He reached out across the bed with his arms. Damn, Julie was gone again. Who the hell was this? He cracked open an eye to see who had broken into his sleep.

The subtle but firm voice had come from a short, fragile man who stood erectly at his bedside dressed neatly in a suit with a tie. Strickland buried his face into his pillow.

"My name is Horace Taylor. I've come to take you to dinner at the Imperial Hotel in Tokyo this evening. I believe you will enjoy the hotel. It was designed by Frank Lloyd Wright."

"Where's Julie?"

"Julie is on the deck enjoying breakfast. She's waiting for you. She told me you had a very good two days at Yamanaka and that you're probably well rested now."

"Who the hell are you?"

"Horace Taylor. I work for the United States government. Foreign Affairs department. A rather innocuous bureaucratic job, but I like it. I'm a Colonel in the army. As you know, we do the jobs we are assigned to do. That just happens to be mine."

Strickland was confused. "I don't get it."

"I'm the one who arranged for your quarters at The Barracks. Colonel Bradford approved of the arrangements. I dare say however, your using them for only one night has caused a frightful exclamation from the staff. They already believe you Marines are strange, but your absence has driven them completely over the cliff." He smiled, added, "So to speak."

"Sergeant Jones said you were a colonel." It was a statement, not a question.

"Like I said. U. S. Army. But now with a much different assignment." He nodded to the closet. "Bye the bye, the suits were gratis, also my doing. Therefore, it's rather obligatory that you have dinner with me wouldn't you say?"

"I didn't ask for any of it."

"Just the same. Even if it's just for one night out of your planned fortnight, I believe you will find an evening with Horace Taylor profitable."

Strickland rose from the bed, just as naked as he had been when Juliana awoke him. He rubbed his teeth with his forefinger, as though brushing them. "You sound British. Did you mean the British army?"

"Neither. I'm a military brat. My father served in India and China with the Brits. I picked it up then. Very young at the time. I'm an American citizen. I was born in Liverpool, however. Lived in the U.S. for a while. Returned to attend Oxford. Worked for the Americans there for ten years before returning to the states. And yes, I served as a liaison with the British army during the big war. Does that answer your questions?"

Strickland noticed his suit was hanging neatly from a hook on the bulkhead. His shoes were tidily under it. His shirt was freshly pressed. "Who did that?"

Taylor glanced over, then back to Strickland. "You've slept during your sail back to Tokyo Wan, Captain. Those are from your quarters at The Barracks. The ship's staff has very adequately prepared you for this evening. Efficient aren't they? About seven?"

"I'm on R and R, Taylor." Then, it struck him. "How in hell did you know I was on this barge?"

Taylor smiled. "You'll learn that tonight, Captain." He flashed Strickland his I.D. It looked official because it was. "Just in case you don't trust me."

"Okay, so you're with the government. So am I."

"Yes, I know. Would you like to cover yourself? Dress maybe, before we continue?"

"No."

"Right 'o. Part of my assignment has been to know where you were at all times. Unless of course, you return to the war. Then you'll be on your own again and they'll assign me another officer to watch over."

Julie appeared at the door just in time to interrupt the discussion before Strickland figured out what was going on. "I thought I heard you." She glanced to Taylor, frowned, then looked into Strickland's eyes. "Hurry, mein lieben sie. We have a delightful breakfast waiting." Throwing one last stabbing glance at Taylor, she spun on her heels and headed back to the deck.

Taylor looked back to Strickland. "She doesn't like me."

"Neither do I."

Taylor smiled tightly. "Seven it is. I'll be out here in the dinghy to pick you up. I dare say," he added with an inflection that irritated Strickland, "it'll be entertaining if nothing else."

"I'm bringing Julie along."

Taylor shook his head so slightly it sent a tingle up Strickland's backside. "No, you won't." Then he turned and departed.

CHAPTER 12

THE IMPERIAL HOTEL appeared natural and unobtrusive within its environment. It was meant to be that way. Its beauty was couched in terms of nature, more than architecture and that, of course, was due to the genius of Frank Lloyd Wright, its designer. The hotel, first commissioned in 1916, was really a hybrid of Japanese and Western architecture. It was intended to be a symbol of Japan having become a modern nation.

The hotel's restaurant was on the ground floor and it was impressively large. Booths at the side with tables in the center, enough tables to feed most conventions.

Even though it appeared to Strickland that no one else was in the restaurant save for one waiter, Taylor chose a private booth area where he could have his conversation with the Marine, ostensibly so that they wouldn't be overheard. Each ordered a platter of mushrooms, one of the only offered entrees that intrigued them.

"Can't trust their meat yet, Frank. I was here right after the war and their concept of beef nearly killed me."

The lighting was spy-shadow dim. Strickland was impressed that he was finally in a place that hadn't been built with rice-paper walls or tatami floor mats.

"Taylor san, welcome back," the waiter greeted.

After the waiter took their order and left them, Taylor said, "Now, Captain, we can speak."

"You're known here," Strickland said.

"Yes." Taylor's speech seemed abrupt to Strickland. It drove him to ask a question that had burned in him since Taylor first showed up.

"Who are you and what do you want from me?"

"To the point, ahh, that's good. May I call you Frank?"

"Yes," he returned the abruptness.

"Colonel Bradford did not mislead me about you."

"He hasn't told me about you. I doubt that you really know him."

"Rest assured, I know him. You are also considered a good man by your men."

"My men?"

"I know of Lieutenant Drier and Sergeant, oh my, what's his name? Yes," he answered his own question. "Fraker. I met them the day before I met you. In the Naval hospital at Yokosuka."

"He's important to me."

"And you seem awfully important to him and to the sergeant. More than that, however, you are considered essential by Colonel Bradford."

He pulled out an official document and handed it over to Strickland.

"Before I get started, I should very much like to give you some background of the results we seek." He motioned the waiter over. "Scotch, Frank?" he asked. Strickland nodded yes. Taylor ordered two Vat 69 drinks on the rocks. The waiter left them.

"We're growing, expanding. As you know Captain, the war's not been going well with the American public, nor among our international allies. Seems today's journalists have mucked things up a bit."

"Mac's Dunkirk mucked things up."

"Hm, yes."

"You took me away from a gorgeous woman for this. I don't get it."

Taylor smiled sharply. "The woman. Of course. She is definitely beautiful. Please have patience with me, Frank. When I am done, you may return to the beautiful Juliana."

"I've got a short fuse when it comes to mysteries, Mr. Taylor. Who is 'we,' and why am I here?" He glanced around the large room, already searching for an exit.

The waiter arrived with their drinks. After he set them down, he left. Taylor sipped at his a moment, eying the anxious Marine, wondering whether the man's unbridled energy was going to be good for them or just what they needed.

"All right. The results we seek include preventing another war of this scale, or potentially larger, while at the same time inflicting heavy and costly damage to the communists. The Soviet and Chinese communists want to take over the world Captain, that is not a secret. They even believe they will take over America from within. Without ever firing a shot, that is. The concept is not so distant. It's been openly expressed by Stalin and Mao Zedong and we must protect our nation from such thinking.

"Mostly, the Chinese communists want to destroy us. Ergo, we must defeat them everywhere they get a foothold. The general plan of our government is designed to accomplish just that. The plan also needs you and a few others like you if we are to achieve success."

Strickland leaned back and gazed hard into Taylor's eyes. "I'll fight for my country, Taylor, we know that. So, what's going on?"

Taylor pulled a small leather business card holder from his jacket pocket and handed one to Strickland. "This is who 'we' are, Frank."

Strickland read it quickly. "You're the bunch who grew out of the OSS. Donovan's boys."

Taylor stared unblinkingly into the eyes of the innocent Marine. "We have grown from a mere six agents in the Far East before this war to over 5,000 right here in Korea. It's now referred to as the Central Intelligence Agency or the CIA. And yes, we were born out of the OSS."

Strickland fell back into his chair. "Goddamned spies."

"No. We aren't spies. We are literally the Office of Strategic Services with a new name. And it's not goddamned. It may well be the only frontline of battle between us and communism."

Strickland felt a flush of anger rise in him like a spout of water, centered first in his gut and then splaying out through his whole system. He knew where the front lines were and they weren't in this goddamned restaurant or in a CIA office couched in an over-plush pack of buildings at Atsugi. "The Marines don't count?" he demanded more than he asked.

"Of course." Taylor thought he might be losing the Marine, so he added, "Although we deal in military intelligence for all branches, we are more involved today in political intelligence. An oxymoron I grant you, but a very necessary business. Because we are active in Korea, like you, we are fighting the communists."

Strickland's anger hadn't ebbed. To control himself he locked his gaze on his glass of Scotch whiskey. "And that's what you call the frontlines?"

"The whole war is a frontline, Captain. We each fight with what we have."

"And what do you have?" Strickland demanded.

Taylor studied the man in front of him. He would not directly answer that question, but he would provide a bit more information. "Thanks to General Stillwell and Harry Truman, we operate independently in Korea. We're authorized under Section Five of NSC ten-slash-two. We do not come under MacArthur's sphere of influence and command."

Strickland surprised himself. He was quite suddenly intrigued by this wire framed man with the clipped voice, but in no way was he going to let Taylor know that. If he did, it might appear as though he had backed down and now pride, that unholy of unholy mind game problems, had gripped him. He glanced up from his Scotch to Taylor's eyes. "Get to the point."

Taylor's smile was reminiscent of a Mafia Don saying goodbye to an enemy. "We're rewriting the intelligence book here, Captain. In Korea. We've been very active fighting communism, but it's all new for us." He coughed lightly.

Strickland squinted at Taylor warily. "There is a rumor over here about a third army. Is that you?"

"We aren't an army."

"Is the rumor about you?"

Taylor sipped at his drink then returning Strickland's hard stare he said, "I suppose."

"Tell me why MacArthur wouldn't accept the fact that a few hundred thousand Chinese were ready to come across the Yalu. Tell me why he threw my boys into their path without supplies or munitions. Tell me why my men died. Tell me where the GD intelligence was back then."

"In his hands."

"What?"

"We warned MacArthur. He rejected our warnings."

"He knew?"

"Yes, and no. We were slow at obtaining intelligence about the Chinese buildup before this war broke, Captain. The CIA was

191

allowed into Korea only two weeks prior to the start of hostilities. It was MacArthur who held us up. But we did know many things without being here in force."

"Like a build up?"

"Like a build up. He prevented us from entering the war because his arrogance, shall I say, got in the way of good sense. However, this is not a big plus for us, but once we were able to gather intelligence we were stinking lousy in passing along what we learned to the Secretary of State and to the President. It seemed to take forever to get the word to them convincingly. They just didn't trust us because MacArthur didn't trust us. Mac has always been too paranoid to trust anyone but himself."

Strickland fingered his drink, considered Taylor's words, then said, "So your guys got the information, but MacArthur blocked it."

"You could say that."

"I did say that."

Taylor gave him a look that suggested he settle down and stop arguing. He hoped Strickland got the message. "Since cranking up our activities, we've caught hell in all corners, especially from the New York Herald Tribune. But we faced that problem and now we're getting it together. Lately, things have been looking up for us. And as I said first off, we are expanding."

Taylor held his drink up as if to toast. "I don't need to tell you Frank, war's hell. I don't make wars. I work very hard to stop them. America's victory is always the goal." He sipped from his glass. "I suppose you could say your boys died for the 38th Parallel, which was designed you might say in a rather cavalier fashion by inept statesmen at Potsdam. The line makes no political, economic, nor military sense, yet you've been fighting to protect what it means."

"Which is?"

"Political geography. The commies live on the north side, while a tyrannical sort of democracy led by a closet dictator named Rhee, exists on the south. The north decided it wanted to control the south and apparently the U.N. and our country preferred Rhee. There you have it. A weak justification for war."

"Not worth the price."

"If it makes you feel any better, I happen to agree. About the war and about MacArthur. He was a poor general for this poly-sci war against communism. This is not at all like the Japanese in the Pacific.

The timing of that war was good for his career. But alas, Korea is different. He still doesn't understand the north's motives nor does he understand the international politics involved. When he dared to cross the Yalu in face of Truman's absolute orders to not do that, his actions brought him down. Communism is voracious, like he had said it was. It eats everything it can. It knows no borders, offers no quarter. Had we crossed over into China, they would have eaten us for lunch."

"They damned near did anyway."

"Your men gave it a good fight. But we have to understand this, the Chinese have already committed themselves to losing 300 million citizens just to defeat America. That will be their goal for the next hundred years."

That got Strickland's interest. He looked straight into Taylor's eyes urging, he hoped, more from the agent. "So, what's stopping them?"

Taylor glanced away, then back to Strickland. "Mao has said that the Chinese fear attacking America because our citizens are all well armed. They refer to our country as the largest guerrilla force in the world. As long as our citizens remain armed, at least the Chinese won't attack." He sipped at his Scotch, then continued on. "But for now, let me continue on about the OSS history and where this can take you and me."

Strickland nodded.

"We of the OSS had our own battles with Mac in the last war. First, he despised Ike. Donovan was Ike's closest friend. Therefore, Mac refused to accept the OSS into the Pacific Theater, and he fought to keep our Agency out of Korea. Truman over-rode him on that one. We're here, and we do more than spy. Agent Tofte, that's Hans Tofte, has a team that has established an escape and evasion system for our airmen who are shot down over North Korea and the Sea of Japan. The Agency actually occupies two islands offshore to achieve this. We man those islands exclusively with our personnel. We also have agents all across Korea who act as in-country guides. They have located or built hideouts and most important to us now, they radio us information on enemy troop movements. We pass those along to the military. Instantly. We also have our own air force. We operate a fleet of small boats all along the two coasts. We transport personnel, we ship war supplies and believe it or not, we even provide the ships, the planes, and when necessary, the people."

It was like listening to the most secretive spy in the world when Taylor spoke about what was going on. For Strickland it was getting too serious, too deep and a bit stretched. All he could say in response was, "Unbelievable!"

"No really. But we do hope the Chinese and NKs feel the same way. I believe that's why we get away with it thus far." Taylor was feeling stronger about his pitch, and believing his own salesman's pitch. "It goes further, Frank. Many freighters and other boats have become an integral part of The Company. These ships and small boats are also involved in smuggling materiel for us, which I'll explain later." He needed to wet his whistle. He lifted his glass up and swished some Vat 69 around in his mouth before swallowing it. "Our biggest coup has been to acquire over $700,000 in one-ounce gold bars for downed airmen to use as bribes and payments to escape. As you know by now, all of Korea is a very gold oriented country."

Strickland glanced around the restaurant. For the first time he noticed there were no other people there, except for the waiter. He was beginning to feel like a clandestine agent himself. "You're spies. They catch you, you're unpleasantly dead."

"You're a Marine infantry commander, Captain. They catch you, you're dead. Logic has it therefore, we are the same kind of animal. Which, when I get to the point here, is one reason you've been chosen to help us. I do hope you will accept."

"I'm listening," Strickland said, again surprising himself.

"We also operate our own planes. We fly supplies, personnel, and things like that."

Strickland felt suddenly out of place and definitely uncomfortable. One moment he was interested and then the next, after absorbing what he was hearing, he felt strained, pushed against a wall he thought. He twisted in his chair, glanced around the empty restaurant, fidgeted with his tie. "I don't think I want to hear any more, Colonel."

"You're cleared for top secret. You understand all of this is just that?"

"Yeah. Yeah. But this place. Nobody here. That waiter can hear us. Can we get out of here?"

"Don't worry about the restaurant. It's empty except for the staff. I bought it for the evening. And that waiter is one of our agents."

"Say again."

Taylor grinned. "Impressive, isn't it? The power of the CIA reaches its tentacles even into restaurants, Frank."

Strickland looked back to the waiter. "The waiter?"

"Yes. Anyone you see in here is an agent of ours."

Strickland had no choice. His shoulders dropped, and he fell back against his seat.

"You got me. But only because of Bradford." He shot forward and leaned over the table toward Taylor. "If you lied to me about Bradford, you're a dead man." It was the first time Taylor had seen real anger rise up in the Marine.

"I didn't lie to you. So, to the point. Last week, General Eisenhower appeared before the National Press Club and announced he would run on the Republican ticket for the presidency. It's our opinion he'll trounce Truman."

"That's what Dewey said." Strickland sat back again.

"Korea wasn't a war then. Remember, this is Harry's war. But for the fact that he and Acheson explained so clearly to the world that we would not honor our treaty with South Korea, this war may not have been."

He paused. It was clear that the Marine was not going to respond to political statements.

With good timing, the mushrooms arrived. Taylor gulped down the last of his Scotch while the waiter set the plates down and bowed to them.

"More Scotch?" the waiter asked.

"Dozo."

When the waiter left them, Taylor said to Strickland, "Please, enjoy your meal, Frank. They aren't exactly like C-Rations, but then, what is?"

"He's a Jap, Taylor. You got Japs in the CIA?"

"We call them Japanese now, Frank. He's actually from Los Angeles. Went to USC. Plays the role well, wouldn't you say? Ahh, he's also armed."

Strickland was suddenly very hungry. He picked up his fork. "What else?"

"The day after the press conference, Eisenhower was on the front page of all major newspapers standing with Bedell Smith."

"Don't know him."

"He is now my boss and was Ike's former chief of staff in Europe during the war. Remember, Ike is unequivocally anti-communist. He distrusted the Soviets during the war. He recommended to Truman after they defeated Germany that they march to Moscow and knock Stalin out of the saddle. You know how that went over. Yet, his fears were borne out at Yalta when the Soviets grabbed up half of Europe. Anyway, Ike offered Bedell a 'what if' scenario that frightened the hell out of the Director. We are now implementing a program to forestall the potential disaster of the communists taking over the entire Far East before Ike becomes president. He feels if we wait much longer, then he'll be forced to commit our troops to other wars like the one in Indo China. Ike doesn't like war, Captain. I understand neither do you."

"Neither does Truman." Strickland flushed a mouthful of mushrooms down with a drink of Vat 69.

"True. But the press is working against him. Truman's disagreements with MacArthur upset quite a few of the folks back home. Let's face it. Mac may not be a battleground genius to us, but he is a public-relations-created icon to the country and they like that."

"And Truman?"

"Truman has been characterized by the press boys as a malcontent. But make no mistake. He fully understands what's happening over here. And elsewhere. It's just that it took him too long to accept it. Ergo, enter Ike and the Republicans and Harry will lose. Too bad, too."

"So what makes you so strong? Ike's not the commander in chief yet, and he's not Bedell's boss anymore."

"The photo was old. After it appeared Smith approached Truman. He informed Truman of the problem in Korea and the solution. Therefore, it came from the Director of the Agency, not from a political opponent. Truman bought it as an Agency gig. He has no idea that it's coming from Ike. So far, the agency's latest successful operations in Korea have brought us favorable attention from the right circles in Washington. The plan I'm about to lay before you will help bring the military and the Agency closer together in the future. It's projected to cost about one-hundred and fifty-two million dollars. Considering that our fighter planes cost us twenty six thousand dollars apiece, that's a lot of money. Now, should we screw up, we would reverse all of that favorable attention and put the shovel in the face of the agency forever."

"Keep going."

Taylor speared a few mushrooms and chewed for a few moments. After he swallowed he said, "We want you to work in what we call Operation TP-Vampire. The TP precedes all Korea operations. It's there for administrative purposes. You'll see that code a lot. Operation Vampire moves war materiel through Korea, to Indochina. For the French in Vietnam. They're in a hell of a lot of trouble down there." After he swallowed he added, "Of course, if you pass along what I've just told you, the agency will deny it all, and well, frankly, you'll sort of fade out of everyone's memory."

Strickland had just been threatened. Hell, he'd just been trapped. Catch-22. If he did he was damned, if he didn't he was damned. His voice tightened, his attitude stiffened.

"I don't need this crap." He slid out of his bench seat and stood to leave. "And I don't like you sending arms to other countries when our guys need them in Korea."

"Sit down. I'm under the same constraints. And Bradford understands the ground rules as well."

"Bullshit."

"You're under orders, Frank. Read 'em again. There's more you should hear. Some of our boys in Vietnam who would be on the receiving end of your efforts have been there since '45. They are former OSS agents. Yes, they are now agents for the CIA. They have been working off and on with a Vietnamese leader named Ho Chi Minh. He's president of the Vietnam Democratic Republic. For whatever it's worth, he's kept us up to date on Mao Zedong's Chinese Communist Party in Indochina."

He'd gotten Strickland's attention all right, he could see that. The Marine sat down again, although quite a bit more stiffly.

"Right now however, Ho Chi Minh's threatening to form his own army. That's not good news."

"This tale of international intrigue has been interesting, Colonel. You've had my attention, threatened me, then grabbed my attention again. However, I'm a Marine Corps officer. I am not a spy. I'm not interested in being a spy. I'll put my twenty or thirty years in the Corps and fight commies wherever the commander in chief sends me, then I'll retire and go fishing for the balance of my life. Concerning your proposal: My decision is clear. I will not participate in your adjunct war."

Taylor pursed his lips, thought a moment, then said, "You'll maintain your Corps status. We can guarantee you'll receive your next promotion, maybe even soon. At least earlier than you believe possible. We will also guarantee you a minimum of twenty-years in the Corps if you want to serve them and with full retirement benefits of thirty if necessary. We've already done the same for other Marine officers who have joined with us. Retirement can happen when you chose it to happen. That is, if you elect, you can get out after this mission and still get the thirty year benefits. As to your current military duties, we've made arrangements of convenience for that, too."

"I'm to report to Colonel Bradford when I return. Those are my orders." He glanced to the transfer papers Taylor had given him earlier.

"Exactly. But first you'll meet our Far East director Hans Tofte at our headquarters at Atsugi Air Force Base. Then you'll spend a few days in Pusan. Tofte will assign you your mission. It's top secret. I would call it ultra top secret."

"Presumptuous! Do your people really believe that you can approach a Marine officer, make a pitch for some clandestine operation in a war zone, promise him the world and then we'll just say, yeah, yeah, I'm here for you, just tell me what I have to do to join your goddamned secret army?"

Taylor tapped the table with his finger nails, trying to make a tune but failed miserably. He was also trying to calculate the potential dangers of hiring a Marine like this guy. Yes, he was tough, honest, experienced and would be an asset. But his attitude was a bit over the edge it seemed, and the big question had to be answered. Would this guy make it through his missions without going nuts and then turning against the agency. He spoke carefully.

"Look, Frank. Try to understand how deeply serious this is. We have already positioned some Army generals into the system. And we have a very well known Marine colonel involved. All here. In Korea. Now!"

"Smuggling arms?"

Taylor threw off the question.

Strickland continued, "And Truman supports this Indo China thing?"

"Vietnam. Since '47 when he learned what was happening there. The dilemma there is that the French Army is having huge problems with their own people at home. DeGaulle wants the French to win the war in Vietnam so that he can dismantle and expunge the communists who riot and demonstrate in Paris all the time. Of course the U.S. wants to claim the destruction of communism, too. Ergo, we are helping the French once again."

"Why are the French people against this?"

"Dear chap, they aren't well known for not giving up."

"Is that British thinking?"

"Hmph. The French press is decrying DeGaulle'S effort as though they themselves are the head of the Party, much like the American newsies are doing in the states with this war. So, there you have it. A French army running low on munitions, a French president saying keep up the fight and a French populist-press saying, 'No, don't fight. We might lose. Bring the troops home. Send them no weapons, there will be no fight.' They are causing battlefield deaths of their own people! The French army is demoralized and so is the French citizen at home. If they lose their war, or quit, communism will take over one more country. Even though we want to be the nation that takes credit for destroying communism, we simply can't afford to allow that to happen. Frank, they need our munitions badly and they need them quickly so they can put down the war and dispel the bad news in France. With Congress rejecting all appeals from the French, this is the only way."

Strickland sat back into his chair as though he'd just been shot. "Two wars. Do you know what you're saying?"

Taylor nodded. "Afraid so."

"We've been fighting two wars and nobody understands one of them and they don't know about the other."

"Against communism, Frank. It's all against communism. Like one big war in two locations. We have to meet the challenge or the whole world will be plunged into a terrible fight."

"Damn it, we are in a terrible fight. And what the hell is this?" He stood from the booth and paced alongside it. "Makes no sense. Something fishy here. Bradford would not be involved in this. Why should I? What the fuck is the president doing?" He whirled around to Taylor. "Tell me that. Just tell me what the fuck the man is up to."

Taylor drained his Scotch glass, set it down easily on the table. After a moment of reflection he said, "Truman is betting his life's career and his personal history on this. It does not come from

Congress. He would never get this concept through congress. It does not come from the Pentagon. They would never allow the weapons out of their reach. This is not a public affairs event, they would bury each of us if they learned of it."

"Oh god damn it, and you want a bunch of Marines to jump into the pit so we can take the fall, right?"

"You will be working privately. There will be no guilt."

Strickland bent over and used his folded fists to rest his rigid arms on the table. This placed him face to face with Taylor. "Bullshit."

Taylor drew back against the booth and said, "Back away, Frank."

Strickland straightened but his tension remained in the forefront.

Taylor continued. "We need to get these munitions to the French and they must move through Korea. Your job will be to ensure they get out safely, and that they are not discovered by U. S. troops or the Koreans. That is why you are to be the PMO at Peace Village. Under Bradford. Will you join us?"

Strickland said, "You're speaking about illegal activities. Smuggling weapons straight out of the White House through Korea to another country's war? You'll end up dragging us into that war. That will be the outcome of your labor. We'll end up fighting two very different wars in two very different countries, each led by a dictator who's probably no worse than you and your god damned CIA. And you want me to join you?"

"Exactly."

Frank eased off a little. After a few moments, he returned to his side of the booth and sat. "I would be diverting arms and munitions from my boys. Young men who need them badly. Sending them to the French in a jungle war nobody's ever heard of. That's pretty stupid, isn't it?"

"Your men now have all the munitions they need. The military finally caught up with the war. Mac's terrible decision to send you into the Yalu was insane and the sign of an egomaniacal man. Thanks to his handling of the Eighth Army, you and they were starved for ammunition, food, and adequate clothing. It's different now."

"I'll believe it when I see it."

Taylor leaned forward. "Look, Frank. A special budget has been set aside for this project. That's the hundred-fifty million I mentioned. Nothing will be taken from our Korean war effort. And just to clear the air here, the NSC directive I mentioned, ten-slash-two, clearly authorizes this sort of activity. Clearly! Washington already refers to us as the ten-two-group. As a matter of fact, if it involves fighting communism anywhere in the world, we have no budget or authority limitations. We are free to fight them as we see fit. The CIA has, in other words, an open checkbook authorized by the President of the United States."

"Wait a minute. You just said only the president knows of this."

"True. True. But I stated 'this sort of activity.' We aren't exactly working within the meaning of the directive. You might as well know that we are stepping over the edge. The president was forced to make this public or disclose it to select members of Congress. He chose otherwise. With the current feelings in the U.S., moving arms to the French in Vietnam would clearly be trounced.

"It's all been planned by the deputy director himself. You alone will control the pipeline of arms that pass through Korea to the French. You will house them, ship them, inventory them. It will be your responsibility to get them out of Korea and on their way. You will of course have help. We have a very good army sergeant and some Korean agents at your disposal."

"I'm infantry. Not a bookkeeper and not a secret agent."

"Indeed, sir. That's the beauty of it."

Strickland pushed away from the table again. He bounced up to his feet. He wanted to leave. "I need to get away from this," he said bitterness ringing in his voice. Without looking back, he left Horace Taylor. He headed straight out of the famous hotel at 1-Chome Uchisaiwai cho Chiyoda-ku, where he grabbed a passing cab and sent the driver speeding toward the Ginza. It was time to get drunk again.

Before he was out of the hotel, Taylor motioned the waiter over to him. "Get the car."

CHAPTER 13

TAYLOR WAS PRETTY sure he knew where Frank Strickland would land for his drunken spree.

It was always the same routine, too. These guys would bolt on him after he explained their new job, get drunk in some bar along the Ginza, then think about his offer with their brains pretty well scrambled and then, without fail, he'd have another volunteer. He was also pretty sure, too, that this Marine might not behave like the others. Most were happy to get out of close up combat after that first six months in this absurd war. But this guy was different. He turned down his right to return stateside, was already anxious to get back into the fight and more than anything, he seemed pretty damned crazy. It was that last part that intrigued Taylor. It would be like caging a tiger possibly, but oh what that tiger could do if they channeled its energy.

Hans Tofte, his boss, wanted him as well. He'd never met the guy, but he had heard about him from other Marines and from Bradford. "He knows Korea from Inchon to the border and back," Hans had said. "He also hates the communists, and that, my friend, will make him a good agent for us." Taylor wondered though. There had been that question from Strickland about the materiel being be better off with the Marines. Now. And not with the French. He quickly put that concern behind him. This Marine was tough as nails and that's what they needed at The Hut. Keep others out. He smiled inwardly. Taylor and Tommy Makimoto, moved erratically along the Ginza. Makimoto was as foreign to this country as Taylor was, but he could speak their language. Learned not in Japan, but at USC.

Makimoto wasn't the biggest guy in town either, and would

probably get hurt if a tough Marine like Strickland wanted to beat up on him. But Makimoto did have some strength if not by muscle then by technique. The youngster had taken Judo and Karate from instructors in the states. And, he'd done very well with them. Taylor always figured he might need that talent someday. He hoped today wasn't that time.

What he had not counted on was Tokyo's completely insane traffic and the maze created by omni-directional driving. Anyone could get lost in the Tokyo mess, or totally bummed out. Unfortunately, that made it nearly impossible to tail someone. And Makimoto, in that regard, was not unusual.

"We lost him fifteen minutes ago," Makimoto said as he pulled up to the Bar New York per Taylor's directions.

"Go in. Check it out."

Makimoto headed straight into the joint.

Taylor got out of their staff car and walked around to the rear of it. He waved down a taxi driver.

"Ohio," he said meekly. He still wasn't comfortable even with the few Japanese words he knew. He handed the driver a ten dollar bill. In Tokyo an American dollar was worth three hundred and sixty yen and that could buy a lot of food or gasoline or clothing. So a ten dollar bill was big money.

"You speak English?"

"Hi, hi. Scoshi bit."

So Taylor explained who he was looking for. In Tokyo that's pretty much all you had to do. Taxi drivers had developed an extensive communications system. Without using radios, yet within minutes, nearly every cab driver in the city would know who Goichi was searching for. And, better yet, Goichi would share his wealth with those responsible for finding the American Marine.

Goichi left him. Taylor returned to his Chevy and waited for Makimoto.

After a few more minutes Makimoto returned. "Geez," he muttered. "Talk about the code of silence."

"Not in there?"

"No. But the lady finally remembered him from before."

Taylor glanced over to Makimoto. "Do I guess how you got that information?"

Before Makimoto could respond, Goichi returned. He pulled up alongside the Chevy and honked his horn. "You come with me. We find together." He jumped out and pulled open the back door of his very small car. He waved the two to get into the cab. "Hi, hi," he said, meaning "Yes, yes."

"Apparently he doesn't want to share his wealth."

"When in Rome," Makimoto said.

Goichi's car was terribly tight for the two Americans. But Goichi was a master at weaving through the dangerous Tokyo traffic. It was a period when there didn't seem to be any lanes or direction for anyone. You just got into your car and drove wherever you wanted to drive.

"Like bumper cars," Makimoto said. "My folks used to take me to the amusement park in Venice. There was a permanent carnival of rides and Ferris wheels there. Oh, my, I remember. A giant roller coaster, too. Huge. A big pier. But my favorite was the bumper cars. We used to get into small cars in this building and try to knock each other around by driving straight into them."

Taylor seemed a bit stiff at the moment. "Is that right?" he said. "Well, let's hope Goichi here doesn't try the same thing."

"They shut it all down about four or five years ago. Too bad. It was a fun place for kids."

After about ten minutes or was it more, Goichi hit the brakes. Taylor and Makimoto were nearly thrown into the back of Goichi's seat. Goichi hailed down a taxi coming from the opposite direction. Speaking Japanese only, he asked if the other driver had seen the Marine officer "in civilian suit."

During the animated conversation Taylor shifted uncomfortably in his seat. What the hell is this? A Datsun? Too damned small for Americans. That didn't matter. It was quick and Goichi proved it by hurtling the car forward with enough energy to force Taylor and Makimoto back into their seat.

"I think I'm getting seasick," Makimoto groaned.

"Here, honcho-san," Goichi called out. They were on the Ginza. "We stop here."

"You know for sure."

"Hi, hi. That my friend. He knows." He tapped his meter and pointed to the numbers. 720 yen. "Two dollars, American," the driver said. "He up there," he pointed halfway up the block. "Bar Cah-yeefornee."

Taylor paid the tab and got out. Makimoto was already waiting at the curb.

"Arrigato Goichi san," Makimoto said.

The cab drove off, inserting itself expertly into the never ending wild traffic.

"If he's really in this place," Taylor said to Makimoto, Then, I might consider hiring a bunch of these cab drivers to spy for us."

"Hmm. Have you noticed anything different here?"

Taylor glanced around. "More servicemen. More prostitutes."

"And more Chinese." He darted his eyes to a section across the road. "Sinister types at that."

Taylor spotted a threesome of obvious Chinese agents across the Ginza. He realized too, that they had made him. "Ah, yes. So it would seem."

Strickland was indeed in the Bar California. But it was more than a bar. It was one of those bar, hot tub, steam bath, whorehouses that many servicemen frequented during their liberty time.

Strickland had downed three quick beers and then, without much caring about what happened, he passed out in the steam box before Kazuko had finished pouring the hot water into the steam unit.

After a while she decided to let him stay that way until he woke. This was not going to be a calm American. He was in a hurry to self destruct as far as she could figure out. So be it. She needed the rest, and she desperately thirsted for a sip of tea. Besides, it was time for Imiko to come in and find out what she could about the war in Korea. After all, the American was going to pay only a few yen for their services, while Chang-san would pay hundreds of yen to learn what he could from the Marine officer.

Imiko had been just outside the room, rummaging through Strickland's pants and wallet—a small folded leather pouch with his military ID and some money. Only twenty American dollars were in the wallet. She let it be. She transcribed his name and serial number and returned the pouch to his pants.

Imiko could get away with her stealing ways because she was stunning. None of the servicemen who had caught her really got mad at her. She'd just shrug and say, "Clean pants for you?" Her good looks got her out of a lot of trouble.

She'd worked hard at her appearance, too. She studied pictures of beautiful women in American magazines. She understood what turned the American servicemen on. It wasn't just a need for sex. She had to look beautiful from head to toe and that didn't mean in the same fashion the Japanese men preferred. She had to have her hair a certain way, and put makeup on in a way the Geisha never accepted. She must at once appear innocent and seductive, and most importantly, her legs must show.

When Imiko entered the steam room, Strickland was snoring lightly. She unsnapped the latch and gently pulled the shell apart. The steamer looked like an egg sliced in half sideways and set with the tip up. The heads of her customers would appear to have been detached from their bodies that way. It always made her giggle a little.

When the clam shell popped open, Strickland fell forward into her arms. He was sweating, and Imiko knew, a bit dehydrated.

Perfect'o, she thought.

He awakened, but was too weak to do much about it.

"Okay, Marine-san. Okay."

She led him to the hot bath in the same room. Usually there would be other customers in the large sunken pool of water, but not when their customer was an American officer. These men knew more than the enlisted. Get them drunk and many of them babbled on forever. She led him to the pool of water. "Name-o Marine-san?"

"Frank," he muttered, still out of control.

"Ahh. Frank-san." They entered the water together where Imiko immediately began massaging Strickland's arms. He plunked down into the tepid water. It was only chest deep. The water revived him some, but not completely.

"Mizu," he said, pointing to his mouth. "Water. Drink."

She smiled and turned to the closed door. "Dozo, Kazuko."

When the door opened, Kazuko entered with a tray. The tray held two glasses and two bottles. One bottle was Akadama wine, the other Satori sake.

Strickland shook his head. "No. Water. Mizu."

Imiko nodded. When Kazuko set the tray down, she told her in her native tongue to get some drinking water or she may lose his cooperation. Kazuko rushed off in a shuffle.

When Taylor entered the Bar California with Makimoto at his side, he quickly noted the fear plastered on the woman who greeted him. They always spotted him and he could never figure out why. It was as though he was walking around with paste boards strapped on like those "Eat at Joe's" signs in the states during the Depression. Only his said, "CIA."

He stepped in front of the shoji screen that was being used as a partition and demanded, "Frank-san. Tall. Honcho!"

She shuffled around him to the door that would lead Taylor into the steam room and bowing said, "Frank-san okay. He in bath now. You wait here."

Taylor didn't trust Japanese whorehouses. More than once they'd proved to be hangouts for Chinese, Korean, and Soviet spies. More than once whole regiments had met up with Chinese divisions after some jerk on R and R blabbed what was happening. And lately U.N. ammo dumps had become targets for the Chinese MiGs. He headed to the shoji screen that made up the door to the steam room but the Geisha stood in front of it. She waved her hands meaning, no. Taylor pushed her aside and jerked the shoji screen open.

He was momentarily startled when he saw Strickland. The Marine lay writhing with ecstasy on the tatami mat with both naked women working his semi-conscious body over. Imiko was next to him, whispering into his ear, her fingers running up and down his front, while the other Geisha was unbelievably massaging his thighs at the same time.

"Captain!" Taylor said with a demanding tone.

Strickland moaned loudly.

"Amazing, you're already drunk."

"Get out of here, Taylor," Strickland said.

"No. You're coming with me."

Strickland's abrupt awareness of what and who Taylor was and where they were hit him like a mortar round smashing into his head. He bolted up as though NKs had just broken through the line. All the relaxation the two women had provided him disappeared. He tensed like a cougar ready to pounce on his prey. His body boasted its unique strength when his muscles hardened and his mind recaptured every bad image he'd worked so hard to rid himself of. "Dammit Taylor! Go away."

Taylor pulled the shoji closed behind him when he entered the room. He looked searchingly into the eyes of the two Geisha girls.

"You," he said pointing to Imiko. "What have you asked him?" When she shook her head he turned to Strickland, "Frank, what's happened here?"

Strickland scrambled across the small room for his clothes. "Not much. Now, get out of my life."

Imiko recognized Taylor immediately. He was one of the American agents who constantly combed the whorehouses looking for communist agents. Looking, sometimes she knew, for Geishas who worked with them.

Taylor moved to her. She was still down on the tatami and still naked. "You! Answer me."

She shook her head again and moved her arms back and forth meaning no English, even though she understood every word he spoke. Makimoto stepped up and in her language ordered her to tell Taylor what information they'd extracted from the Marine.

Kazuko crawled away from Strickland and worked her way toward the shoji screen exit. When Taylor caught sight of her, he pointed to her and demanded, "Stop her, Mac," he said to Makimoto.

Strickland sobered enough to catch on to Taylor's meaning. These ladies were spies for the North Koreans and Chinese. He responded by limping over to the door and putting his foot on Kazuko's back before Makimoto got there. He pressed her to the deck. He had one leg in his pants and one out. "Stay put," he said.

Taylor nearly lost concentration. Strickland did exactly what he would have wanted and he did it on his own. Imiko brought his attention back to her. Imiko was spread-eagle on her back on the tatami in front of Taylor. She pushed up on her elbows, and threw her right leg up with her foot hitting Taylor right in his nuts. Taylor went down momentarily, caught himself although his kidneys hurt like hell. He jumped on Imiko and yelled, "You fucking bitch. Tell me what the hell's gone on here."

Strickland was surprised at Taylor's action and language. The refined gentleman had turned into a primitive animal. "Well, I guess you got balls after all," he said with a light laugh. Then he answered for Imiko. "She was making small talk about the war."

Taylor didn't take his eyes off the girl. His right knee was planted in her abdomen with all his weight. She could barely breathe. "Frank, if she asked you about where you were, or what your job was, or how many of you died, then she's a commie spy and you should have killed her."

"Crap. You read too many Mickey Spillane novels."

"This is real life, Frank. How would you like to learn that possibly this whore caused you to lose your platoon? She may be the very spy who passed MacArthur's plans to the Chinese. Goddamn it, Frank, wake up."

Strickland let go of the shoji screen. He slammed his foot down on Kazuko's head so hard that he knocked her unconscious. Showing no remorse or reaction to her, he walked directly to Taylor.

"Spies? Yeah, they're spies. But we don't just kill them. Can you imagine what the news guys would do to us if we went around killing every whore our guys screwed?"

"The Communists, the Soviets, the Chinese in particular have thousands of agents in Japan and Korea, Frank. The Chinese and North Koreans have agents right here, working next door to EUSAK's main headquarters. Tokyo is crawling with them. Every American out there on the Ginza has spoken to at least one of them." Pointing to Imiko he said threateningly, "She's one of them. And nobody's going do anything to you for acing them."

Strickland finished dressing. He looked around for his shoes, then remembered they were at the entrance to the place. "These are Japanese ladies, Taylor, not Koreans. Not Chinese. You telling me the Japanese government will just let us kill them at will? I don't think so."

"These two are whores. Ever figure out what that means? They could care less where they make their money. And they make a lot of money telling the Chinese what they learn from guys like you. Their government doesn't care about them because they're screwing Americans. They are tainted Geishas, and that's death in this country." He turned away from the girl a moment to look into Strickland's eyes. "Frank, I told you the agency screwed up before this war. We thought we knew what we were doing. Big time spies without much history is what we were. Well, we were babes in the woods, pal. The commies were feeding us their misinformation right here in Tokyo, and in Korea. Lin Piao's own people were working with our journalists, while some were actually on MacArthur's staff. Syngman Rhee's people were duped as badly as we were. But no more. We've caught on."

Strickland thought of Max Store and Scoop Clifford. They'd said the same thing. "I've heard," he said simply.

While they spoke, Imiko tried to crawl out from under Taylor. But Taylor was aware of her efforts. Surprising Strickland with his ability to react menacingly, Taylor drove his knee deeper into her abdomen so hard that it appeared it might burst. "Tell me who you're working for, bitch!"

Makimoto translated, then turned to Taylor and said, "I left out bitch." Taylor didn't see the humor.

Kazuko regained consciousness, making it to the shoji screen on her knees. When Makimoto saw her trying to shove it away, he dove on her, and wrestled her back to the sunken tub's edge. She scratched at his face, and tried to kick him in the balls at the same time. But Makimoto turned out to be incredibly strong. His Judo also came into play. With one quick pinch of her neck with a Gyaku-juji-jime or adverse cross choke, he knocked her out again.

Imiko cried, "No spy. No spy."

Taylor glanced to Strickland. "She's lying Frank. They use the word spy only when they are spies. We've learned that much. What did you tell her?"

The booze was wearing off quickly. "These ladies have been milking our boys for info?"

"Every whore on the Ginza takes money for information they glean from our guys."

Strickland was surprised that it seemed so clear and so easy now. "Get out of here Taylor," he said with his eyes burning like fiery pools of napalm. "Tell the people out front the ladies are still doing their thing with me."

Taylor looked at him curiously a moment, then lifting his knee off Imiko when he stood he motioned to Makimoto to follow him and they left the room.

When the shoji closed, Strickland walked over to Imiko and helped her up. She was trying to catch her breath, breathing in and out as though she were about to deliver a baby. Once breathing, she bowed. "Arrigato, Frank-san." She was in obvious pain.

When she straightened, Strickland gazed into her eyes for a second. It was not Imiko he saw. It was Shipley, Blade and the others. All hauntingly dead. He should kill them, but something was racing wildly through his mind. Yes, he should kill them, but killing women wasn't what he'd been trained to do. Or did it matter?

Taylor heard only a few thumps, then silence.

For Strickland it was time to help his boys. To get help for his men who were still fighting. He straightened his clothes and walked as erectly as he thought he should through the shoji that he only partially opened. He moved through the reception area with Taylor trying to grab at him, but the Marine was too quick.

Out on the Ginza Taylor quickly shoved him into a cab.

"Got to get you out of here, now," Taylor said.

Makimoto was absent. Strickland glanced back to see the man who had been their waiter at the restaurant return to the Bar California. Taylor tugged at his sleeve.

"We've got to get you out of Tokyo quickly, Frank," Taylor said. "You're in it now, pal. Whether you want it or not."

"I'm in," Strickland said. "But it's my decision. Not yours."

Taylor smiled imperceptibly. "To kill commies."

"To kill commies."

CHAPTER 14

TWO DAYS AFTER THE START of the Korean War, President Truman directed the CIA to expand its operation in the Far East. On that same date, June 27, 1950, Hans V. Tofte was hired with an agency rank of major general and put on a plane to Tokyo. At that point, the CIA had only six agents working out of a hotel room in Tokyo. Tofte had orders to build CIA covert operations in Japan, Korea and China.

When he arrived in Tokyo, Tofte wasted no time. Even though MacArthur had been more than overt about not wanting the CIA anywhere near him, Tofte was able to build a spy empire in Korea. It was code named The Joint Advisory Commission, Korea, or JACK. His second in command of JACK was a man named Colwell Biers, who was himself a former OSS (Detachment 101) agent in Burma.

With an open-ended budget, Tofte was able to build a complex of impressive buildings at the Atsugi Air Force Base. Right under MacArthur's nose.

Tofte immediately conscripted the services of U.S. Marine Colonel "Dutch" Kramer, and placef him in charge of CIA JACK stations in Korea. Kramer also had an ultra top secret mission assigned to him by Tofte.

Meanwhile, Tofte requested and received the USS Bass for covert operations. The Bass had served as a US Navy destroyer. He then obtained the USS Perch, a former submarine tender.

The Bass was used to deploy underwater demolition teams and to insert agents into North Korea.

Tofte was a mid-sized blonde, about fifty-years of age when assigned his new job. He was considered a bold man, one with plenty of chutzpah. It was to his favor alone that his personality fit right in with his clandestine assignments.

He spoke with short sentences. Always. Some thought he was abrupt, while his personal assistant, Horace Taylor, understood it was because his mind was always translating different languages while he spoke. Rather than grasp the need for such work with long sentences, Tofte chose the shorter route.

Korea was a serious challenge for Tofte. The war had produced so many different spy agencies that communications with other units and the military itself would at times, completely break down.

That had its ups and its downs. For Tofte, the downside often proved to be an upside. He could hide more information, or simply not release it if he so chose. If later challenged, he'd simply state that the message was sent and that it was the intended receiver's problem.

The fact that there were so many quasi-independent spy operations literally competing with each other gave the military brass excuses for their tactical or strategic failures. Finger-pointing became a classic art, developed to the max by such luminaries as Generals Almond and MacArthur.

To confuse matters even more, the South Koreans ran their own spy operations. So, they had US Army, The Far East Air Force, MacArthur's own and an Army Translation and Interpretation Service (ATIS) and the South Koreans. All this plus a deeper threat. Lin Piao's own spy network, which was mostly headquartered right next door to MacArthur's headquarters.

It was a network of thieves and victims built for someone like Hans Tofte to cash in on.

Tofte had few friends among his associates, and as men like him knew, few in the world whom he could trust. Although he was referred to as a beanpole or "old scarecrow," he instinctively used his broad shoulders and sometimes slight and sometimes stocky build to form the image of an important man. When it came to appearance, his aides referred to him as "Plastic Man."

No matter. All along it was Tofte's intention to intimidate everyone he dealt with—especially those he ruled over in what he called his Far East CIA empire. He was empirical, powerful in his world, and possessed just the right mix of genes to have developed the instincts of a jackal.

Officially, Tofte was known in Washington as the director of the new Office of Policy Coordination in Korea (OPC), which was headquartered at his Atsugi Air Force Base, 47 miles south of Tokyo. OPC was his own creation, a cover for his spy unit which was designed exclusively for 'covert activity' in Korea. Tofte, known as "the Dane," became larger than life within the whole of the CIA. JACK was the official acronym for the entire group, but Tofte was the king. For Tofte, he didn't care what they called the organizations. Not as long as everyone understood that he was in command of all covert actions. Period!

So, it was only natural that when Taylor entered his office Tofte unnecessarily waved him in. He wasn't inviting Taylor in more than he was controlling him. The snap of his wrist was a command, not a friendly gesture.

"Horace! Quickly."

"I got him," Taylor said quietly and slowly. Taylor always wanted to make sure that Tofte processed his words correctly. He sat in the unscratched and perfectly varnished wood chair opposite Tofte's desk. "The tough guy came apart on me. He went over the edge, just as you predicted."

"Good! And his sergeant?"

Tofte had been recruiting men from the military for his clandestine operations since the beginning of the war. The military had the only pool of sufficiently trained personnel within his immediate reach, and they were all in Korea. They were restricted from doing what their government asked because of MacArthur's anti-CIA mandate.

"The man they call Snake," Taylor said. "Sergeant Fraker. Yes."

"And the other?"

"Lieutenant Drier is still in the hospital but with a good prognosis for returning to the front lines. I met him, but didn't present him with our offer. He's still a bit too drugged."

"What else?"

"Not sure the sergeant would ever sign with us. He's very Marine Corps. Devoted, you might say. I didn't pitch him."

"Dogs are devoted. But they can change."

"The lieutenant turned down rotation to the states. Gung-ho type. I was able to get his orders changed. He will report to Panmunjom."

Tofte eyed his army colonel. After considering what he'd heard he said flatly, "He won't sign."

"Their knowledge of the captain?" He wanted to know if the

lieutenant and the sergeant understood what Strickland had signed on for.

"Nothing. They know not of Strickland's role and nothing of ours."

Tofte nodded, but continued only to eyeball Taylor. For Taylor that meant he should explain more.

"I think that once at Bradford's our onsite agent can begin to work on Lieutenant Drier. But I hold little hope for his signing on."

"And Bradford?"

"He knows we are speaking with Strickland but not Fraker or Drier. He believes we are asking Strickland to keep an eye out for saboteurs and that's it."

"He worked counter-intel in the Corps."

"Yes. He knows the game well."

"How about a replacement for Fraker and Drier? If they become a hazard?"

"You wanted someone loyal to Strickland. I couldn't find any others. Most of his men were killed or wounded badly. Drier was wounded but as I said, he volunteered to stay after they release him."

"Hmm."

"Doc said nothing vital was damaged. And that the guy heels quickly. He's straight. All Corps. Same as Fraker."

"Over the edge?" Tofte was asking what Taylor meant when he'd said that Strickland had gone over the edge.

"Strickland flipped out. He was drunk. The last thing he wants is for the Corps to figure out what he did. We own him."

Tofte eyed his pipsqueak colonel and smiled tightly. This Horace guy was tiny for a soldier, but as nuts as any of them. He cocked an eye at Taylor, which clearly meant he wanted him to explain further.

"Okay. Is he here?"

Taylor nodded. "I sent him for a cup of coffee. "

"Colwell will make all the arrangements," Tofte said.

Colwell Biers was Tofte's deputy at the Atsugi operation. He was a former Panzer commander in the German Army during WW II, now a naturalized American citizen.

"The perfect bureaucrat," he muttered.

"A bit regimented one might say."

"And Strickland?"

"He knows how to kill. Our way." Taylor flashed a quick smile hoping that Tofte bought his line. Changing course he said, "Juliana came through again."

"A good agent."

Taylor glanced up from his note pad and then back to his writing. Tofte had no soul, why should any of his agents?

"Does he know? About any of this? I mean your recruiting style and all?"

"No, sir."

"Hmm. Juliana has a wonderful way about her."

"She had a tough go of it for a few days she tells me. Weird stuff on Mount Fuji." He wanted to add that he'd caught Strickland in the buff more than once, but then he remembered that Hans Tofte didn't give a damn about things like that.

"Everything's right on schedule," Tofte said. Then uncharacteristically he added, "We bought the civilian air transport outfit Claire Chennault cranked up. You can refer to it in the future as CAT. So, now we have our own navy, and our own air force. And oh yes, my new C-47. You must fly with me, Horace. Soon. It's like a Mercedes of the air."

"Yes, of course." Taylor wasn't fond of flying.

Everyone in Tofte's world knew of his XT-854 plane except for the American press. When the CIA took over Clair Chennault's old Flying Tiger air force, Tofte commandeered Chennault's personal C-47 known as the XT-854 for his own, then outfitted it for luxurious comfort. He used it to fly to Korea, Okinawa, Formosa, and around Japan. His new CAT fleet (later named Air America), was a collection of other "surplus" aircraft that included DC-2s and C-47s as well as a few fighter planes.

Taylor glanced away for a moment. He wanted to get his point across to the loghead who was his leader. "Strickland is different than the others we've recruited, Hans," he said. Then looking directly into Tofte's eyes, he added, "He may be a bit difficult to control."

Hans smiled. "Schizoid, maybe? How wonderful for us." He meant it.

Taylor bristled visibly, a signal for Tofte to stay on the subject. Hans was Taylor's boss, but Taylor was the one with the stronger links to the White House through an old buddy of his at Yale, who was working directly for Truman. All Tofte had going for his presidential connection was his position and his former record with the OSS. Of course, they both knew that if Ike won the election, neither Taylor nor Tofte would have trouble walking into the Oval office. It was Ike after all, who created the OSS.

"Tell me more," he said.

"He's strung like a top, as they say. He's up one minute and then he drops down to a common drunk. Manic I guess is a good word. He's a bright guy though. Gutsy as well. He Survived some horrific battles. Shoots very well." Taylor fumbled through papers, trying to find the rundown on Strickland sent to him by special ops.

"What's a top?"

Taylor smiled tightly. Tofte was from Denmark, not the U.S. where tops were the spinning wind-up toy his generation played with while in grammar school. Somehow Tofte seemed to have missed all that even though he had lived in New York and Mason, Iowa for a while.

"Allow me to change that. He's wound up like a coiled rattler. A huge spring ready to release all his tension at one moment and god help anyone in his path. I believe right now that he's torn between honor and," he hesitated while trying to find the right word. He thought about Tofte's choice of schizoid, but he couldn't use that since in his own opinion, Hans Tofte was probably the leading schizophrenic in Korea.

Hans Tofte was the one who came through China in the thirties, worked closely with the Marines in Shanghai, then helped facilitate the European underground during World War II. He'd joined Wild Bill Donovan at the OSS and continued doing his damndest to kill as many Germans as possible. He'd created a legend for himself that claimed he'd been a terror in hand-to-hand battles with German soldiers. Squinting at his boss, he remembered with some concern that Hans Tofte would just as soon kill you as invite you to lunch, and that included any agents who got in the way of his personally defined mission. Taylor sighed, finished with a simple, "and duty."

"An interesting concept, Horace. Honor among spies. It's a thing for novels."

"Clearly he could pose problems for us." Taylor was laying out the bureaucrat's ultimate need to cover his own ass. If the Marine failed for them, then it would be Tofte's fault, not his own.

But Tofte didn't give a damn about blame and guilt. He was

convinced that he understood Tofte best and what others thought of him either made no sense or he figured, they were nuts. He'd learned in Manchuria and Yugoslavia, that if someone screwed up, you just aced them and that was that. "You're walking on hallowed ground, Horace. I'm surprised by you." He paused, collected his thoughts and then said, "I chose this man. So, you're telling me he might be a poor choice?"

"Just cautious, Hans. Nothing more."

It was a rare speech from the Dane, but it was time for him to nail the coffin shut. "You are intimately aware that our fresh out of the box military agents have been, shall I say, trepiditious in the beginning. Each was honorable. Each was devoted to duty. Nevertheless, each ended up justifying their tour of duty with us after their first Agency assignment. Look at Colonel Singlaub. He thought we were crazy. Now he's one of us and doing a damned good job."

"Jack Singlaub," Horace said almost sounding reverent. For army colonel Horace Taylor, Singlaub was a hero. He'd served as a devoted paratrooper, then a duty bound Ranger. He'd accepted the job as the CIA's station chief. "He'd rather be fighting with his men."

Tofte shook his head. "Don't worry about this man. We've got plenty of experience with Marines now. Army and Navy, too. We've even got some Brits with us. There is nobody nuttier, more bound to their patriotic duty than a British commando or Ulster rifleman. He will do our job."

"I hope you're right."

"You will make me right."

Taylor's eyes fell to his hands and the papers he was holding. He'd just been put into one of Tofte's boxes and he didn't like it. Before he could look up and respond, Tofte continued.

"So, it's settled. We will insert him into the Panmunjom area as planned. He will serve as the Marine PMO. He will be assigned to Bradford. And he will guarantee our shipments."

Taylor looked up into Tofte's eyes. "To the French."

"All shipments."

That was a tall order for a straight shooting Marine. Taylor recognized that his job was going to get a lot tougher. He wondered if their sergeant, Stanley Delaplane was up to dealing with the arrogant Marine.

"From there Strickland can protect Pyongchee from prying eyes and oversee the shipments," Tofte said.

"And Sergeant Delaplane?"

Tofte ignored the question. Delaplane was in position and working out. He was army and a sergeant. The fact that he obeyed orders was good enough for him. If a new captain showed up then he'd have to obey that man's orders. Tofte hesitated in his thinking. It was that last bit that Taylor was probably concerned about. He rolled his lips one on the other, scrunching them down a bit with his teeth. Then he blew a breath of air out and said, "When it comes to policing themselves, Marines are kind of dumb, Horace. Nobody challenges a Marine PMO. They make him the top cop, and often as not, he's a, ah, what's that gent's name? The famous American criminal-hero during your prohibition period?"

"Capone?" Taylor had heard all this from Tofte before, so he knew his boss was reaching for Al Capone's name.

Hans allowed himself to laugh a little. "Yes. Capone. It's like putting him in charge of the security of a local bank. Only our guy will be a gangster in a Marine uniform and he won't even know it. Best part, neither will anyone else."

Taylor sighed audibly. He wanted away from Tofte at this point. But Tofte continued on. It was blabber time as far as Horace was concerned. And all if it came at him with a thick Danish accent, one Taylor could barely stand.

"First, Strickland will go on a secret mission we've been ordered on. From Washington, Horace. Directly from Truman himself. It will help us grow. It's that big." He leaned back into his chair again, stuck a Camel into his mouth and quickly lighted it with a Zippo and then said through a cloud of smoke, "Good opportunity for you to indoctrinate him."

"Your expectations are high for a TDA." TDA meant temporary duty agent.

Tofte made small ringlets with his cigarette smoke. He thought about his response to Taylor for a while. Taylor figured he was translating it all in his mind before speaking. He spoke slowly, with purpose but in short sentences. "This special mission? You can take charge of it right away. I'm going along as well. Just to observe. It's away from here. Formosa. Our success will impress Washington enough for them to lavish more money on us. Give me the funds for the air boat. Horace, this war is going to put the CIA on the map. We'll fly to Formosa. In my plane. That'll get you on board, eh? You'll see how big we're getting. Sometimes I think if they'd give it all to us, we could wrap this war up in a week."

Taylor blinked slowly. "Like you did in the commando film you made for them."

Tofte fired a glance back at Taylor. "Now, your a critic?" He crushed his Camel out in the ashtray as though he were killing a giant spider.

"The mission, Hans?"

"It's a Norwegian freighter. Loaded it with medical supplies in Bombay. All donated by that goddamned crazy Nehru. He's working with the commies."

"He denies that."

Tofte blew off Taylor's denial. "Right now, the Navy's got the ship on radar the whole way. We thought they might go into Hong Kong. Washington says we can't do anything if they do. The Brits and all. D. C. boys don't want to lose Hong Kong. Too strategic."

Taylor sat back in his chair so hard that it stopped Tofte from speaking for a moment. When Taylor appeared to be okay, Tofte said, "Washington wants the ship pirated. Seems they intercepted a message out of North Korea. Chinese troops took a bad hit during the last big campaign. They need those medical supplies. Can you believe it? There's enough penicillin aboard to give each soldier in the whole damned Chinese army three shots."

"Why us? Why not the Navy?"

"The Navy has agreed to keep us posted where the ship is at all times. That's it." He said, "It's Norwegian. Anyone but us would create all kinds of political problems. In other words, keeping it covert keeps the whodunit a mystery to the Norwegians."

Tofte was unable to hold back a grin. It had the makings of the top secret clandestine stuff that turned him on. Because his intelligence unit was in theory top secret, he could do whatever he pleased, and do it without having to answer for it. For him, that was one of the most important aphrodisiacs of unlimited power. For him, being in command of shadow people was the ultimate life experience.

"The mission?" Taylor wasn't as turned on by surreptitious matters. He was army. He followed orders, but sometimes he had to challenge those orders, if not aloud, then in his mind. This mission sounded strange, probably illegal, yet his boss was calling it necessary.

"The ship will pass near Formosa in two days. I've arranged for a flotilla of Nationalist Coast Guard gunboats."

"Hans! The president was specific about not drawing in Chiang's army. For any affairs of this war." He had placed emphasis on the word "any."

Tofte leaped up from his desk and paced away from Taylor. He went to the east side window and looked out over the airfield. "We have absolute unrestricted power to do this. Washington told me, 'at any cost.' Horace, they sent me one million bucks to pull this one off. That's big money. That means this is a big time mission. It will serve as a warning to other countries friendly to the Chinese and NKs to stay out of this war." He was breathless. But his speech had been easier since he'd practiced it somewhat in his mind. He knew he'd be challenged by Taylor, the man always did that. Tofte was a Major General in the CIA, but only to increase his personal income. His army rank was lieutenant colonel while Taylor's was full colonel. And oak leaf commanding an eagle. Didn't matter. Both were now CIA and Tofte was in charge. He went to Taylor and stood within inches of him when Taylor rose from his chair. Peering straight into his eyes, he said, "After the mission's a success, Truman will love us. Guarantee it."

"And if it's not? A success, that is."

"We can't miss. It's ultra-top-secret. If we fail nobody will know that we tried. Does anyone really understand what happened to the USS Indianapolis?"

Taylor shook his head. "Different baby."

"No. It's not. Look, Chiang's army will keep the medical supplies. They need them, too. If for some stupid reason it goes down the commode, our story will be that they did it on their own. At any rate, we aren't going to fail and the mission will turn out to be a feather in our cap. Also important to us is that you'll be able to watch Strickland in action."

Taylor grimaced. "I've already seen him in action."

"What's that mean?" Tofte snapped.

"Two nights ago, in Tokyo. He ditched me when I first pitched him and ended up in a Geisha whorehouse. I found him. The Geisha were spies."

Tofte rubbed his chin. "You did them in, right?"

"No, sir. I didn't." He had to fight off letting his eyes rove when he tried to push Tofte's buttons.

Hans shook his head displaying his dislike for Taylor's answer. He returned to his chair and sat. "Dammit Horace, you know the rules."

"Strickland did it for us."

The smile that creased Tofte's face came slowly. His eyes watered. Where do they find these great men? he asked himself. He reached for another Camel. Lighting it, he said, "Well I'll be go to hell. And you call him nuts?"

The Marine appeared lean enough to Tofte, kind of like himself, except for the little pot Tofte had developed around his abdomen. The Marine was also more muscled and lithe. It bothered Tofte some that the Marine was taller. Still, the Marine had an envious record in combat and obvious potential as an agent.

"Welcome," Tofte greeted. "Please, Captain, sit. Cigarette?" He held out a pack of Camels.

"No, thanks," Strickland said.

"In his notes to me, Colonel Taylor said you had doubts about the CIA's role over here. Before we continue with this meeting I would very much like to clear up something for you."

"Yes, sir," Strickland said.

Tofte went into a practiced spiel. "We aren't the military. I am personally responsible for setting up behind-the-lines covert activities such as rescuing downed pilots, which we do well. We also train North Korean friendlies in our own form of resistance fighting, much of which I learned in Europe during the war. They are then reinserted into North Korea where they do our bidding." He didn't explain that most of the NK footers they'd inserted into North Korea didn't make it alive for even one full day. After pausing a bit he continued. "We are also set up to move war materiel to the French in Indochina. The authority to do that is due any day now."

He paused, saw no reaction from the Marine officer. What he'd just said would have rocked most people out of their minds. Shuttling weapons through Korea to Vietnam was not known anywhere except with a few CIA agents, the president and those Frenchmen who had signed on with a desperation known only to those who faced death by defeat or survival by triumph. This Marine was different. Stoic, it seemed, even in the face of what Taylor had told him about the man. Poker faced if not stoic, meaning he was reacting within himself but would not show his hand, at least not now. He continued.

"I was involved in Yugoslavia with the same sort of mission, one the Brits dreamed up. And before that war, I was in Britain and managed weapons and armament supplied by F.D.R. and ah, that's the way it is with this program. At any rate, all of these seem to go hand in hand and certainly serve as precedent. Our operation is designed to fight and defeat communism and nothing else."

Strickland wasn't without a knowledge of military history. "Weapons to China and Britain were with the grace of Congress."

Tofte blew smoke upwards. He would not lower himself to argue with a mere captain. The man knew something of previous intrigue, but not much. It didn't matter.

"We operate only under the president's direction. One of the CIA's official roles in this theater is to supply Korean guerrillas with enough arms to keep them going."

"There aren't any guerrillas," Strickland said, interrupting him.

Tofte exhibited his smirk of confidence. "Let's assume there are. Many of the weapons we send to the French that are openly marked as armament are designated for the Korean guerrillas. I tell you this because you have been cleared for top-secret information. So, all this is official and I trust Captain, you'll keep your lips zipped."

Strickland stood as though to leave. "Maybe I shouldn't hear anymore of this Mr. Tofte. Thanks for the history lesson." He turned to leave and when he got to the door, Tofte called him back.

"Sit. Sir. It's necessary that you hear me out."

Strickland stood his ground at the door. "I don't think this is for me."

"From what I hear, it sounds as though it was designed just for you."

Strickland let go of the doorknob. He found himself curious now. He returned to the chair and sat. "Please be quick."

"What is bothering you, Captain?"

"I may be cleared for top secret sir, but I cannot accept illegal behavior. Yours sounds illegal."

"The war is illegal, Captain. Yet, here you are fighting in it and as I understand you've killed quite a few of our enemy."

"Commies. I was sent here to defend our country by killing commies."

"Good. So was I." Tofte leaned on his desk with both elbows. He took a cigarette from his pack and tapped one end on the desk. Then he realized he'd already lit one up and it was burning in the ashtray. He reached for it and squashed it out. Then, without lighting the fresh one, he put it into his mouth and continued speaking. "We have a hundred and fifty-two million dollar budget assigned to us for the weapons we are to shuttle to the French. We are awaiting the word to get a move on with that project. The budget has been authorized by the president himself. We have been stockpiling munitions for a few months now. I confess that we've already sent one load to them. A load consists of about ten to twenty truckloads, placed into the hold of a small cargo ship. Now, Captain. It seems to me that if those are our orders, then we are not behaving illegally. Does that help you?"

Strickland stole a look at Taylor who had seemed deathly motionless, then looked back to Tofte. "Keep talking."

"About the guerillas. You are basically correct in your assessment. Except for about eighteen hundred CIA trained NKs, the guerrillas in North Korea are non-existent. A Marine named Dutch Kramer is training them."

Strickland's warning flags went up. Something was amiss here. "You make it sound as though we're playing with the enemy. Like it's a high school intramural event?"

"Not quite."

"And it's all sheltered since it's top secret? You can do anything you want and tell me anything you want." The tone of his voice upset Taylor. The Marine was obviously charging them with not ever being held responsible for their actions, whether good or bad.

"It's not that primitive, Captain Strickland."

Tofte jumped back in before Strickland could react to Taylor's statement. "One of our roles in Korea is to fight the NKs with NKs. Like indicated before. The program is headed up by Marine Colonel 'Dutch' Kramer. He's currently training NKs. We screen them first. They must want to defeat the communists in their homeland. We teach them to infiltrate North Korea as NKs where they then fight the commies. Dutch's operation is on the island of Yong-do. We have been forced into doing this because at the beginning of this war we allowed all North Korean refugees to come south. Thousands of them. It was a mistake that I hope we never repeat. It stripped the north of pro-Western sympathizers. We have no friends left in the North. Nobody to help us." He paused to light his Camel. When he got hold of his first drag, he said, "At any rate, those are my primary missions and pretty much the CIA's total role."

"What's the shuttling of weapons got to do with that?"

"It's a side show. Let the French kill commies down there. We don't have the manpower or the national will to do it on our own right now."

"And my part?"

Taylor smiled. "I hope it proves no more dangerous than what you have already been through."

They flew in Tofte's C-47 from Atsugi to the Hsin-Hsiang airport in Taipai. They were greeted by a Nationalist Chinese Coast Guard commander who drove them quickly to the harbor northeast of the Formosa capital.

"We have little time left," Commander Wong told them. "The ship is about forty miles southeast of us right now. Your American destroyer is ten miles behind it, but insists on breaking off soon."

They climbed aboard an old American PT boat and before they could drop their bags, the lines were cast off and the boat headed out of the harbor at full speed.

"We must be careful," Wong said. He was referring to the Americans being seen when they approached the Norwegian ship. "We have our flotilla of gunboats waiting for the ship and we have our own cargo ship. Our men will board her first. You must wait below."

"We will board the freighter as well," Taylor stressed. "After you commandeer her."

Wong appeared confused. He looked straight into Tofte's eyes when he said, "My orders Mr. Tofte, were that you remain below. It would not serve your purpose well to have the American CIA director spotted on this mission."

Tofte nodded. In Chinese he said, "Agreed. I will remain below. However," he added, indicating toward Strickland and Taylor, "they will board after you have succeeded taking her."

The freighter showed up right on schedule. Strickland and Taylor watched from the PT boat's bridge while the flotilla of gunboats surrounded the ship. When the captain of the freighter realized his predicament, he lowered his ensign and raised a white flag. The Chinese swarmed aboard the ship while the Nationalist cargo ship pulled alongside the Norwegians to accept the transferred medical supplies.

Strickland watched through field glasses.

"They're boarding," he said.

Taylor nodded to Wong. "Let's move in, Commander."

When the helmsman pushed the throttles forward the PT boat's three 1350 horsepower Packard engines purred loudly like well oiled race car engines. When they got to the freighter, they lashed their lines to the gunship on the starboard side. Then they crossed the Chinese boat to get to the rope ladder that seemed to sway in opposition to the swells of the sea.

Once aboard, Taylor and Strickland headed for the bridge of the freighter where they ran into the ship's captain and two Nationalist Coast Guardsmen. Wong spoke first.

"This ship and its cargo is now in the possession of the people of the Nationalist Republic of China, Captain. These men will transfer your cargo to our boats."

"This is piracy," the captain exclaimed angrily. "American government piracy. My radioman has been instructed to signal that Americans have taken over our ship. You'll all hang for this."

"Your radioman was the first crewman we silenced, Captain. Please to sit in your captain's chair sir, while we transfer the goods of your ship to our own."

"I protest, sir. I am in command of this ship and I order you all off of her."

Taylor's attention swung rapidly to Strickland. He was surprised and pleased. The Marine seemed unusually detached when his deep voice penetrated the cabin like a warning from a hissing serpent.

"You are taking medical supplies to the North Koreans, Captain. That is an act of war against the United Nations and against the United States government. As such, you have elected to join the war and therefore you and your nation have become subject to the rules of war. You can complain all you want, but it will do you no good."

The captain flinched. He looked nervously around him. "You are taking me prisoner?"

"Something like that," Taylor said. He indicated with a nod for the Chinese to take the captain away.

Strickland waited until they'd cleared the bridge.

"Why are we here? You, me? These Chinese guys don't need us."

"Like Hans said, Frank, if it's a success, we'll be praised with higher budgets. And as far as I can tell, it's a hell of a success."

"Makes no sense. After we release them they'll scream to high hell to the United Nations."

"Mr. Taylor?" a voice interrupted. They turned to see a dark-skin man dressed in white clothes at the entrance to the bridge. "I am doctor Singh."

Strickland's expression changed. He'd thought only medical supplies were aboard the freighter. "Doctor?"

"I am in charge of the medical staff on board. We have a full complement of three field hospitals including surgeons, physicians, nurses and other medical personnel aboard."

Taylor looked as though he'd just been kicked in the gut. Catching his breath he said simply, "Doctor, you better tell your people that you are all now prisoners of war."

"But we are from India, and not a part of your war."

"You are now, sir."

It took the Chinese four hours to transfer all the medical supplies to their cargo ship. When they completed the job, the Nationalist Chinese cargo ship cast off and sailed back toward Taipai. Wong came to Taylor.

"We are ready to depart, Mr. Taylor."

Strickland's voice-of-the-captain returned when he asked, "What about the crew; the medical personnel?"

Wong stared sternly into the American's eyes. "My orders are to set the freighter adrift, Captain. They may sail when we depart."

"And the medical staff?"

Wong smiled tightly. "They have been well provided for, sir. Now, if you will please board my boat."

Taylor led Strickland to the main deck where they descended over the side to the all wood, 55 ton PT boat. Before climbing over the gunwale, Strickland took one last glance around the ship. He saw well armed, uniformed Chinese soldiers he hadn't noticed before, and three Americans. He assumed they were CIA agents who came aboard from another gunship. They had just come up from below decks where the crew quarters were located. They walked quickly to the gunwale to lower themselves to the gun ships on the port side.

"Come on, Frank," Taylor shouted from below. "We can't hang around here."

The PT boat's engines roared to life. With all the power the commander could get from his World War II craft, they sped back toward the island of Formosa at the boat's top speed of about 48 knots. Hans Tofte beamed. The mission had been a complete success. Well, almost, he thought. He came topside and stood alongside Strickland and Taylor.

When they were about halfway to the horizon, Strickland looked back at the freighter for a last glimpse. From behind him, Taylor said, "Frank, it's got to be this way. The war against communism is brutal at times. We just don't have a choice."

Strickland turned back to look into Taylor's eyes, to say something maybe, or to simply stare, he couldn't remember because he was interrupted by a thunderous explosion that split the Norwegian freighter in half. When he whirled around to see it, a huge fireball from the ship's fuel supply burst next. They watched quietly while the stern separated, and then with the bow appearing alongside it, they descended rapidly into the sea.

It all happened so quickly, that the hissing noise created by the fast sinking sections seemed to be God's response to the evil of the war Taylor was trying to justify.

Strickland heard only Tofte speak.

"Mission accomplished."

Tofte tucked his brand new subminiature Minox spy camera back into his pocket and allowed a broad grin to escape his usually placid demeanor.

After the war, Hans Tofte, the Far East CIA chief, would be brought before an investigative committee of Congress, where he would deny any knowledge of the disappearance of the Norwegian ship.

CHAPTER 15

"**THOSE BASTARDS!** They've damned near lost their entire army and this whole goddamned war," O.P. said into the phone with a bit too much juice to his tone.

Hawk and the rest of Smith's staff reacted to his anger by stepping backwards a few paces. The old man hardly ever blew his top like he was doing now.

"What the hell do you mean they've got control of my troops?" He winked at his staff who quickly relaxed. O.P. was operating at his best with the higher-ups and they were safe from his anger.

The communication line in his hand went dead. As far as the voice at EUSAK was concerned the order had been passed down; it didn't have to be explained. Smith's First Marine Division had been placed under the control of the Eighth Army. The proud, arrogant Marines would have to obey orders from slosh-minded doggies who were not doing well.

It didn't matter that Smith had miraculously saved his Division from hordes of Chinese, that he had held his losses out of a total 20,000 Marines to the same number the Army's 7th had lost with just one eleven-hundred man regiment. For Smith, this loss of command was a slap in the face he'd never forget. Smith jammed the receiver into its holder.

"Well," he cried out to his staff, "what the hell are you waiting for? Someone get that dogface general on the horn."

First Lieutenant Devonshire, short, taut, and erect leaped for the phone. While he tried to raise the Eighth army headquarters, Smith paced with such energy the others thought he'd burn a hole in the ancient wood deck.

Hawk watched him curiously. General Smith had become a good friend, a mentor to learn from although always a bit of a paradox. The man had all the bravado, guts and courage of a buck sergeant manning a machine gun in battle. He also carried a calm with him that belied his powerful energy as well as his anger. Outwardly, he appeared to be a refined gentlemen, one who hated war and its violent deaths. But inside that wiry body there raged a man with such fighting instincts that any enemy dealing with the general had better be prepared for the worst. Even if it was the U.S. Army.

"On the line, sir," Devonshire said.

Smith grabbed up the phone. "This is General Smith, First Marine Division."

Hawk couldn't hear the other end, but he could read Smith's changed expression. The army commander obviously outranked the Marine.

"Thank you General," Smith said crisply. "For your information, sir, I expressed that opinion before Thanksgiving last." Another quiet period. "Of course. Yes, sir. I have one of the best right here, General. I'd be happy to loan him to you." Smith turned to face Hawk. Placing his hand over the mouthpiece he asked, "Are you current in an AT-6?"

Hawk smiled. The Marines and Navy had their own version of the "AT-6 Texan." It was designated with the letters: SNJ. It was also known as a Harvard, but only in Great Britain. "Yes, sir."

Smith spoke into the phone. "He's available when you need him, General. Yes, sir. Absolutely!" Smith's eyes flared when he spoke. "The First Marine Division, General Ridgway, is always prepared to fight, sir. And I'm prepared to lead them into that fight. Again!" Smith actually held Ridgway in high regard.

Hawk smiled inwardly. There it was. Gentleman Smith, the balls out fighting Marine had just delivered his punch line to the man who replaced MacArthur as commander of all forces in Korea. You had to enjoy it while it happened, because life in Korea was just too tough otherwise.

Ridgway had been in Korea from the get go. But he served under MacArthur. Things would change now. Mac himself had handed the responsibility of Korea to Ridgway with a curt, "It's yours now, Mat."

Matthew Bunker Ridgway proved to be one of the greats of the American army. When he took over an outfit, morale shot skyward. When he went into battle, he did so knowing where the enemy was and how many there were. He never operated the way Mac did. Dreams and ego were not part of a successful battle plan for Mat Ridgway. He was also known to go into the field for a day or more at a time with his troops. Hike with them. Enter battle with them. Then he would return to his headquarters and debrief his commanders.

Upon his official return from Tokyo to Korea, Ridgway grabbed a young pilot named Mike Lynch and together they flew Lynch's small observation plane to all of the American forward areas. Ridgway found a disheveled army, one in chaos and one that hadn't attacked or engaged the enemy sometimes for weeks.

He changed that, and he changed it quickly. Now, he wanted to fly up the center of Korea, but Lynch was either in sickbay or out on a mission elsewhere, Hawk never learned. So, he turned to the Marines for an experienced combat pilot who could fly him into enemy territory in a larger and more powerful plane.

Smith handed the receiver back to his aid and said, "Trev, I'm gonna hate to lose you."

"Your not transferring me, General," Hawk said, stepping closer to Smith. "You're loaning me out for a few days."

"You're going to fly Ridgway up and down this country in his AT-6. He wants to go into enemy territory and see how many divisions of Chinese are out there. Apparently army intelligence has it at 27." Smith chuckled lightly, "Which, we have learned, can mean any goddamned thing they want it to mean."

"Yes, sir."

Smith glanced at his watch. "Ridgway is a calm man, Hawk. Most of the time. Keep that in mind when I tell you he wants you at the airfield right now. And Hawk," Smith said, continuing without waiting for an answer, "you are aware that you are eligible for rotation stateside." He meant Hawk could back out of the unarmed flight that was headed into enemy territory.

"Not in this lifetime," Hawk said. "I'm staying until we win."

Smith smiled while his staff stiffened. Smith understood what was running through their minds: Stay? they asked themselves. In Korea?

"Are you nuts, Hawk?" Smith asked, still smiling.

"Yes, sir.

"What about your family?" Smith cared about his men. Each of them, and he knew their names. If he met you once, he'd remember you years later. But he wanted his staff to hear this answer.

"The general forgets?"

"You still have a son."

"He's a plebe at the Academy. Otherwise the Marines are my family."

Smith glanced around to the others, fully expecting to hear them hum the Marine Corps Hymn. Why not? he thought. He'd heard Marines singing it during the march down from the Chosin.

"Well I'll be damned," he muttered instead.

When Hawk arrived, Ridgway already had his flight gear on. The ubiquitous grenade and first-aid pack he suspended around his neck over his chest caused the troops to nickname him, "Iron tits." Many thought both items were grenades, but they weren't.

The grimy, camo-painted army AT-6 was ready and so was he.

"Well, let's get aboard Colonel," Ridgway said.

Not yet, Hawk thought. He'd never flown a machine without a complete preflight check. He was under the left wing. "A few more minutes, General."

When he finished his inspection, he motioned to the crew chief to help the general up. Ridgway would sit in the front seat.

"We've got a demoralized army in disarray, Colonel," Ridgway began to explain while climbing up to the cockpit. "It's completely down. Well what the hell, its got a defeatist attitude. Our boys honestly feel they can't win a battle, and with your Marines cleaning house, even when they're trapped, my guys feel like hell."

"Yes, sir," Hawk said. He climbed into the rear cockpit smiling inwardly only.

"You see, the same's happening at home. The press is down on the army and the soldiers and the war. That kind of thing compounds into trouble. The troops read that, see what they experience here, and then feel worse. When that happens, we lose more of them in battle than we should."

Hawk snapped his safety belts together. He could see that the crew chief was finishing doing the same with Ridgway.

"So," Ridgway shouted over his shoulder, "I want to get a close look at just what old Lin Piao is doing up there. See if we can lick 'em when they're least expecting it. Drive the Chinese back to China and the NKs to the bargaining table."

"Yes, sir. Clear!" Hawk yelled to the ground crew.

But before he could fire the engine into action, Ridgway got in one last sentence. "And if that doesn't raise the country's morale, nothing will."

The engine exploded to life. White smoke billowed back past the cockpit, rolling along the fuselage as though a giant ring blown out by a cigar smoker.

Hawk taxied out to the runway where he quickly received instructions to take off. How about that, he laughed to himself. All you gotta do to get immediate clearance around here is put the Eighth Army commander aboard.

They flew up and down the imaginary MLR. "Deeper, Colonel," Ridgway demanded through the intercom. "Fly this SOB right up their ass."

Hawk banked the North American aircraft and headed deeper into Chinese Communist territory.

Ridgway kept his gaze glued to the snow below. He could not see any smoke, nor signs of wheel or foot traffic. "Nothing," he called out after they'd penetrated the lines fifty miles. "I don't see one single Goddamned enemy soldier anywhere."

Neither could Hawk. "Same here, General."

Ridgway nodded. He knew what he had to do. If there were Chinese up here, he was going to have to dig them out. The only way to find them was to launch another attack. It would be a whole new war.

"Take me back. I've seen enough."

The following day Ridgway ordered the 27th Infantry into battle in what he dubbed, "Operation Wolfhound." They launched their attack along the right flank, using a battalion from the 3rd Division. They moved quickly up the main highway toward Osnan, meeting only light resistance.

At the entrance to the town they had a short firefight, then the enemy retreated. The Americans entered town and occupied it with few losses. They were ecstatic. It was the first sign of life the Eighth Army had seen since their disastrous defeat at the Chongchon River battle line.

The following day the same task force swooped down on Suwon

in two columns. After meeting with hardly any resistance, they returned to their original positions.

Then the 8th Cavalry, supported by the 70th Tank Battalion, moved up along the Yoju road. Still, very little resistance.

At his headquarters, General Ridgway read the reports from his field commanders carefully. Truman wanted his answer and he wanted it today. The American press was demanding that the United States pull out of Korea because the "country is going to lose the war and thousands of American boys."

"According to these reports," Ridgway said to Oliver Smith over his phone line, "we can establish a new line, push the bastards out of the Hwachon Reservoir, free up the water and electricity for Seoul and get the enemy back to the bargaining table. The time for a new counteroffensive is now."

Smith agreed without hesitation. Maybe, he thought to himself, Hawk had been insightful when he'd asked for his extension. Maybe he wants to be a part of the victory, instead of a statistic of defeat.

"Thank you for your counsel," Ridgway said to Smith before disconnecting. "I am prepared to inform the president that we are going to remain and continue the fight."

He had no way of knowing whether his decision would turn away the tide of defeatism in America, but he was sure as hell willing to try.

In the White House, Harry Truman reacted with anger when he heard the latest response from the North Koreans and Chinese concerning the proposed peace talks. They refused to make any concessions on the prisoner-exchange program, which was Truman's secondary goal in the talks.

Truman had proposed that the United Nations would not force North Koreans nor Chinese prisoners to return to communist China if they didn't wish to. "Communism is a system that has no regard for human dignity nor human freedom," Truman said. "No right-thinking government can give its consent to the forcible return to such a system of men or women who would rather remain free."

The Chinese answer was to arrange for some of their soldiers to be captured so that they could gain control of the prisoner stockades and establish a reign of terror within the U.N. and U.S. guarded prisons. The riots that resulted from their actions created an additional burden on American commanders, who were stretched thin because of the continuing war.

At the Koje Island prison, the waffling American General in charge was kidnapped by communist prisoners. It was an act that stopped the peace negotiations for a day, until General Nam Il, the Red spokesman, insisted on the meetings continuing so that he could present his long propaganda denunciations—which, as if on cue, the total of the American press published as verbatim truth.

Syngman Rhee used the episode to declare martial law and thereafter had a number of his political opponents arrested.

The communists used the incident to increase the strength of the North Korean Army, which caused General Clark to request more troops for the pending offensive.

Chiang Kai-shek stepped forward to support Clark, suggesting that his Chinese Nationalist army was prepared to join in the fight. He was rebuked, because Truman openly believed that to add Chiang's gang would increase the chances of drawing in the Soviet Union and starting World War III.

"I have met with my generals and advisors," Truman declared, "and we stand fast in our demands. We will not buy an armistice by turning over human beings for slaughter or slavery."

After the flash bulbs and scribes left him, he turned to his VP, Alvin Barkly, and said, "We have no other course, Alvin. We can not stand idly by and allow the Communists to run free in Korea or anywhere else. We must meet this challenge here, and elsewhere, or we will be responsible for having plunged the world into a major war."

He then sat down and asked for his CIA director. He had some things to straighten out. Some other things to deal with. Maybe, he thought, just maybe, the French can stop those bastards in Indo China.

When CIA director Walter Bedell ("Beetle") Smith entered, Truman calmly asked him to get hold of Hans Tofte and congratulate him for his meritorious action and his solid leadership in the Far East. Beetle Smith was not related to O.P.

"And Beetle," he said to the man Ike had referred to as the greatest general manager of a war, "tell him it's a go for the French in Vietnam."

CHAPTER 16

THERE WERE NO SATELLITES back then, no cell phones, no telephones that could even reach from the mainland to Hawaii. Communication, when necessary, was accomplished by radio-telephone signals. The delay in voice transmission was always in the way of cohesion, creating a need for broken messages and the familiar, "Over," which often became redundant with hollow echoes.

Literally, one person would speak and wait for what seemed long minutes while his voice bounced across the ocean or under the clouds or however the damned signal went. After waiting for what seemed an interminably long time, Tofte heard a response from the other side of the world. At times the process had proved too laborious for him, but this time, he would have to endure. The man known as a Bulldog was at the other end.

Beetle Smith had also been known in the European Theater of World War II as "Ike's hatchet man."

"Good work, Hans," Beetle shouted through the static filled radiophone. "This will impress the boys in Congress. I'm confident now that we can speed up that hydrofoil project for you. Over."

Hans waited for the word "Over" to clear. The echoes would have to disappear first. Finally he was able to say, "We'll keep the pressure up Beetle. Over." He waited and wondered. Had Beetle disappeared, hung up or had the line simply gone dead? Of course not, it was that damned lag time.

"You're cleared for ops," Beetle said plainly. "It's a go. Over."

That's just what Hans wanted to hear. He thanked Smith and held on until the line went dead. When he clicked off his eyes glazed as they rested on Taylor and Strickland.

"Great work men. Terrific. Vietnam is a go."

But Strickland wasn't nearly as happy as Tofte. His thoughts hadn't left the Norwegian ship yet. Those people could simply have been captured and held until the end of the war. To murder innocents, pro commie or not, was simply not acceptable. "They weren't armed."

Tofte knew what he meant and who he was speaking about. He pointed his right forefinger at the Marine and said, "Neither were the whores."

Strickland shot a mean-assed look to Taylor then fired his anger back at Tofte. "What in the hell did that mean?"

Taylor's response was staccato, a style he used often to silence others or change the subject. "It's not new to you, Frank. War's hell. This one may be a step deeper than hell. The people on that ship were communists headed to North Korea to help the same people you were fighting, the same people who killed your friends."

Tofte rose from his chair and puffed rings of smoke from his Camel up toward the ceiling. He would not have Beetle's good news ruined by this nanny Marine. "The Norwegians and Indian government are playing around with our enemy as we speak. When you play dirty like that against us, you're going to get hurt." He stopped, puffed a few times against his Camel and blew smoke out as though he had just become a volcano. He looked down at Strickland after that and said, "You did well. You did what you had to do. Erase it from your mind. It was not unlike what you did at the reservoir."

Strickland stood. He understood why Tofte had taken to his feet. He wouldn't allow it to happen. He stood with his two feet separated and his toes pointed straight ahead. It was a classic aggressive football stance. He spoke with an intensity that surprised both Taylor and Tofte. "We could have taken them prisoner."

"Did you take prisoners when the Chinese were killing your boys?"

"They were armed. And they fought to the death."

"Would you have if they dropped their arms?"

Strickland hesitated. He had never taken any prisoners, not in Korea, not in the Pacific. "We'll never know."

Tofte sucked in on his cigarette, blew smoke out in one huge ball and said, "Frank, are you aware of H. L. Mencken? A writer; a good writer. Well, he wrote that, 'Every normal man must be tempted at times to spit on his hands, hoist the black flag, and begin slitting throats.' When I first read that, I wasn't sure what he meant. During the war in Europe, I came to understand. Now, right now, to save the world from those commie assholes in China and Russia, we are going to have to slit a few throats. If not to stop their aggression fully, then to warn them to cease where they are. I guarantee you, no more Indian or Norwegian ships will be seen sailing toward North Korea."

"You murdered unarmed doctors and nurses. Did it ever occur to you that we could have conscripted them to take care of our people or the South Koreans we've injured?"

Tofte waved the hand holding the cigarette around his head. "What the hell is this, Captain? You're a fucking Marine." His use of the vernacular sounded funny with his accent. He walked around his chair, demonstrating complete frustration with Strickland. Then he stopped, and sat down hard it. He leaned forward at his desk and firmly planted his elbows on the large green blotter where he worked. He stuck the Camel into his mouth and then folded his fists and rested his chin on them. With the Camel seeming to bounce up and down in his mouth while he spoke, he said, "They were armed with penicillin and many other weapons for the survival of communist soldiers. They would not have worked with us but instead would have reported our operation to the world. As you recall, it was a top secret event."

Strickland glanced to Taylor. "Do you agree with what happened?"

"Communist doctors repair communist soldiers to fight again and kill Americans. Marines. Therefore, they are also our enemy. If we had dragged them back to Formosa, news types would have gotten hold of the story and all hell would have broken loose. This is not an American war. It is a United Nations war."

"An oxymoron," Tofte threw in. "United Nations, indeed."

Taylor said, "Consequently, if we are to help hold up morale, we must do much of our fighting in a secret war. And we must keep it a secret at all costs. The Norwegian ship just happened to be part of that cost."

Hans sat back into his swivel chair and said, "I like to run a tight ship. One where there's faith and trust among all agents. I want to rely on you and I want you to rely on me. No other way will we succeed." He snuffed his Camel into his ashtray and asked, "Do we have you, Frank? Lock, stock and barrel?"

Strickland rose and paced between Tofte and Taylor, moving from bulkhead to bulkhead. "I'm a Marine officer," he said. "Not a spy."

"Yes, yes you are a Marine," Tofte answered. "You will remain an officer just like 'Dutch' Kramer is a Marine officer but he's also a CIA operative. Neither he nor you are spies. We aren't asking that of you."

"You are to be the Marine PMO at the new joint security area at Panmunjom. No matter what you decide," Taylor said.

Strickland stopped pacing. If the two CIA agents had known him well they would have seen an idea crease his expression as though he'd just been struck by a round from a heavy bore rifle. He'd just figured out what to do and it had nothing to do with what they were pitching. "How long? With you?"

"As long or as short as you want," Tofte answered. "However, I'd like to see you work with us for at least a year or until the war's over. After that, if you like the work, I'd be very amenable to adding you to our Intelligence roles. The CIA has many military personnel and they operate uniquely within each branch."

"Why Panmunjom?"

Tofte leaned back, "Pyongchee is just down the road from there. That's our location for storing the arms we are to ship to Indochina. It's crude, it's secret, it's guarded, and it works for us. EUSAK has assigned a Marine rifle company to Panmunjom for security purposes. Bradford is C.O."

"He's with the CIA?"

"No. He knows nothing of what's going on with this mission. I have spoken with him only to feel him out. You will have to operate, well, let's say, clandestinely. But you must remain within his reach. It's not going to be easy."

"You said you've already made shipments. So, why me?"

Tofte coughed lightly and thought perhaps he should quit smoking. His throat was beginning to feel harsh all the time. "Yes. We have. But that's our business, not yours. And we need you to keep the area swept of the curious or those who may wander by accident. It's a dead end road to it. Not much of a road, but good enough for what we're doing."

"Bradford knows me like a book. We were in the Pacific together. He was an officer, I was a sergeant. He's not going to like me ducking out to manage a hut full of your craziness."

"Okay. Let's get this straight. Bradford's unit will guard U.N. negotiators at the table, so to speak. I confess that that was not in our original plans."

"So, I fill the hole that's been created."

"Something like that. Basically, I don't want any Marines getting snoopy around our storage area. If one of them happened on to our cache, well, I don't know what we'd do about it. You'll also keep our sergeant in line."

"There's a small port just south of there," Taylor added. "It's not used by the military. It served as a fishing port before the war. Small dock. On the river. A building they used to use to store fishing equipment, some of their catch, that sort of thing. We will load there sometimes."

"And other times?"

"Trucks to port at Inchon or Pusan. At night. It's a tough call. A call you and Sergeant Delaplane will have to make."

"What does Bradford believe I'm doing here? With you?"

"Learning how to be an informed PMO in a country where our enemies are as conniving as any human on earth."

Taylor said, "You'll relieve Colonel Tilmon as PMO. You'll have absolute control over police matters in the area. All military and civilian police matters. You'll also have control over whether or not military personnel from any of the U.N. forces can travel down the road toward Pyongchee. Think about it Frank, you'll have more power at the peace talks than Ridgway will have."

"Bradford will not question your actions or absences. Your police area is huge. We've taken care of that."

Strickland sagged into his chair. "Your Mencken guy was prophetic. What we're doing is a form of piracy. But I tell you this now. If another Marine finds your location, I will not slit his throat."

Tofte smiled. "Then you'll join us? Fully. No regrets?"

Strickland nodded. "Yes."

Panmunjom Joint Security Area

Panmunjom was prepping for the arrival of the Peace-Talks from Kaesong later in the year. The new peace village was about 33 miles north-northwest of Seoul and six miles east of Kaesong. The meetings would take place in several large tents that were soon to be set up on the south side of the Kaesong-Seoul road on the west bank of the Sa'cheon stream. The new Peace Village would consist of a cluster of less than ten huts and sat opposite the negotiation site on the north side.

The Marines built a campsite just a half mile down the road. They would provide security forces until the United Nations arrived with an international team of guards and sentries for the talks. Since Panmunjom had also been the center of fierce fighting earlier, the Marines felt obligated to make sure North Koreans or Chinese didn't use the Kaesong Panmunjom road as a way to slip back into South Korea.

The Village was in effect, where the Military Demarcation Line (MDL) would later be drawn.

Colonel Harrison Bradford was in charge of the Marine unit. Bradford was well-known in the Corps as a straight-shooter and a damned good leader.

After Ridgway was through with the services of Trevor Hawk, he released him directly to Bradford's unit at Panmunjom. Ridgway explained that later, when a small airfield was cut into the area, he would need to visit the talks now and then and at that time Hawk would be assigned a new aircraft. In the meantime, Hawk would serve as liaison in the area for security personnel from both the Marines and the Army and of course keep Ridgway abreast of all news concerning progress.

Bradford welcomed the man he'd known for what seemed like many years, into his unit. To have a private session with him, he led Hawk immediately away from the conglomeration of military tents and plywood buildings that had been put into place for the upcoming arrival of the negotiators.

They drove up the short hill just south of the encampment in Bradford's jeep, crossed the ridge and dropped down into a stunted valley and headed for the palisades across the river that overlooked both valleys—the one they were driving through and the one where the world's foremost enemies would try to hammer out an impossible agreement.

"This valley is clean, Trev," Bradford said. "We've swept it over and over. There are no armed communist soldiers on this side of the line. Not here and not anywhere close to the village."

Hawk's eyes scanned the spacious arena of grass and broken trees. Jagged slopes of bare rocky hillsides swept northward as far as the eye could see. The valley floor was pockmarked with craters that he figured had either been driven into the ground by long range artillery or the new B-47s. He guessed it was the bombers. He was a pilot, not a ground-pounder. Everything down here looked so different, that the next time he flew ground support he'd have a much better idea of what the grunts were going through.

They stopped close to the edge of the palisade and sat in the jeep while they spoke. They overlooked the tent village below.

"We can speak up here without being overheard."

"What's bothering you?"

"Trevor, we've been in this man's Corps for a few years now. Our government has taken us from a position of knocking the piss out of the enemy in the Pacific to achieve total victory, to chitchatting with him in Korea about where we can draw lines and lay down our arms."

"Puller and Smith aren't happy about it. Neither, for that matter, is Ridgway."

"The change in our resolve has created other problems. Other things are going on that I don't like. Neither will the Commandant when he learns of them."

"Such as?"

Bradford thought a moment. He would get to that answer in due time. First, he'd make sure he could enlist Hawk's help.

"This battalion I command consists of sentries for the peace talks, a rifle company, and the usual array of support units. We guard the mud hut village even though we seem to be guarding it from ourselves at this point."

"And the problem is?"

"CID, mostly army types, who are, in my opinion, uncouth bastards."

"They're here to check out what, exactly?"

"Not the Chinese. But that's not all. A few French military are here, yet they aren't really part of the combat element in Korea. Dutch, Norwegians, and others as well. It makes life a bit tough when trying to keep things secure."

"Any other U. S. types here?"

"A couple of special navy investigation teams as well as a provo. The provost marshal right now is Lieutenant Colonel Tilmon. You know him?"

Hawk shook his head. "No, sir."

"Do you happen to know Frank Strickland? Captain Frank Strickland?"

Hawk shook his head again. "No, sir. Should I?"

"He's to replace Tilmon. Hot youngster. Well, he's not a youngster anymore. He was with us in the Pacific. A sergeant then. After the war he went to college and is now a captain. He's already garnered a Navy Cross and a second Silver Star over here. Picked up his first Silver on Okinawa. He's got three Purple Hearts, two Bronze Stars and a few others, plus he's been in all the big battles from Inchon to the Chosin."

Hawk stared into Bradford's eyes. The man was up to something. "He's the new Provo. That should work out for you."

"Maybe. Funny thing. I sent him on R and R because he'd had a pretty rough time of it. Chosin Reservoir, Hagaru, Hudong-ni. He was with the Faith group that took that awful beating and later with the Damnation Battalion. The guy got around. He's aggressive, a hustler."

Hawk whistled softly while Bradford continued.

"He was wounded before they got to Hungnam. But the Navy docs in Japan fixed him up very nicely. Nothing serious I was told. He recovered and then volunteered for more duty in Korea. He nearly lost a youngster he seemed to like a great deal. A former buck sergeant. Name is Drier. I know him well. He received a field commission over here and was wounded in the same battle with Strickland. He was shipped to Yokosuko hospital. It drove Strickland nuts. Thus, the R and R. I told him via courier that when he was finished with that, he was welcome to come up here and work for me, but urged that he return to the states."

"He reupped?"

"Yes. Thus the softer job as PMO. I figured the pressure would be off him. Once the negotiators move to this encampment, we're out of here. Shouldn't be too difficult for him."

"Is that what we came out here to chat about?"

"Partly. I want him to work directly for you."

"Shouldn't be a problem."

"There's this other matter."

Hawk turned to face Bradford. His friend had wrangled him into this one. He knew better than to let Bradford do this to him, but here he was asking the colonel a dumb question again,

"Other matter?"

Bradford smiled one of those thin-lip grins he'd give you when he thought he'd trapped you. "Uh, huh. I'm asking you to investigate a matter of grave concern. The one I alluded to early on."

"Time to come clean."

"Theft of government property, meaning weapons, and black-marketing to the NKs."

"Not our guys."

"We have both North and South Koreans working for us. Could be a gang of banditos in the mix. Haven't been able to put a handle on it yet."

"That's Naval Intelligence stuff."

"I think that's why we have some prowling around here but they are tight lipped with me. When I reported my suspicions to HQ they passed the buck back to us. If we find substantial evidence, then they'll send someone up here other than the crowd that's here."

"Makes it sound like the guys who are here are here for a totally different reason."

"Uh, huh. Colonel Tilmon has been working on this for a few weeks now. I don't want Strickland getting into something that might send him over the edge. Not yet. I'm afraid if he found anyone stealing our supplies and selling them to the NKs or Chinese he'd, well, I think he'd go nuts and just kill them."

"So, you want me to look into it."

"Yes. I've also got a good man coming to help you. Name's Fraker. He's a gunny with guts. Also knows Strickland and Drier."

"I don't know how to thank you, Colonel," Hawk said. He was jesting of course.

"I'm leaving tomorrow for Tokyo. Back in a few days. Keep your eyes and ears open while I'm gone."

He cranked over the jeep's engine and darted back onto the dusty road.

Drier stood at the window of his hospital room and wondered why he couldn't be on one of the warships anchored in the harbor. He'd been on a destroyer for just a week during the Pacific war and had loved every minute of it. He glanced to the dark clouds then back to the water. It was raining as hard as he'd ever seen in the Far East and yet sailors were working aboard each ship within his view as though it were a sunny day.

"Quite a sight, eh?" a brusque voice said behind him.

He turned expecting to see a doctor but instead it was a short, familiar face in a Marine uniform with birds on his epaulets. The Marine held a large manila-color envelope in his left hand. A red string seemed to tie the top closed.

"Sir. You've been promoted!" Drier smiled broadly.

Colonel Bradford returned the grin, came up to Drier. He plunked the envelope down on the small table next to Drier's bed. "Good to see you, David. They tell me you've made a remarkable recovery." He stuck his hand out to shake Drier's hand.

Drier took it firmly. "Anything to get out of here, sir."

"Hospitals have a way of doing that to us." Bradford pulled a set of papers out of the envelope. "I'd like you to read these over and let me know what you think."

"Yes, sir."

"Since you've refused a stateside transfer, I'm asking that you join me at Panmunjom. I need an experienced Marine officer at my side. and, well, now that you're an officer, as my aide. But it's a volunteer job. Read the papers if you will. I'll check back with you tomorrow." He headed for the door, glanced back once and said, "I believe you'll like what you read. And by the way, our new PMO is Frank Strickland."

CHAPTER 17

"IT'S STRAIGHT FORWARD, Cap'n," Army Sergeant Stanley Delaplane explained. They were headed toward the docks at Pusan in Delaplane's six-by, a standard military three axle all wheel drive truck. Six-bys were also known as multi-fuel vehicles. They could run on gasoline, diesel or jet fuel. Delaplane was a big oversized oaf of a grunt whose twang and slang along with a guttural voice worked against Strickland's composure.

Delaplane was an army sergeant with one rocker, one bald head and a huge Yosemite Sam cartoon character mustache of about the same color as Sam's. He was older than Strickland, old enough Strickland figured to be a master sergeant. That brought him to a conclusion. Sergeant Delaplane had spent his career getting busted a lot. He also chewed Copenhagen tobacco, which forced him to spit through the open window of the truck a lot. The window mechanism was conveniently broken so it was always open. Okay for today, but not when the weather turned bad.

"I get a call or message informin' when a shipment is due. We pick up the stuff, usin' these here forms," he slapped the clipboard next to him, "and then we take it to the hut. At's when the we divvy with the Frogs." He put a singular emphasis on "the hut."

Strickland felt agonizingly bored with Delaplane. He hated the odor that chewing tobacco produced for its users and he found himself not taking to the army guy. He had listened to the spiel and now he had questions beginning with Delaplane's own attitude about what seemed obviously illegitimate. When Delaplane shrugged his shoulders and said, "I jest take orders," Strickland jumped on him about other military personnel. Didn't anyone ever challenge them?

"Not yet, Cap'n. Maybe 'cause we just cranked up on this 'un. S'pose to be a big secret. Guess secret is that we ain't supposed to be doin' it, I guess."

"How long have you known Tofte and Taylor?"

"Cap'n, let's not use their names no where, sir. Makes a guy a bit jumpy. Them two, well, they's not to be fooled with. Sides, things are so screwed up over here, 'specially the fugging supply system, that most of the brass prob'ly figure we know what we're doin'." He slammed on the brakes and the truck skidded to a stop, barely missing hitting a jeep that had just cut across their path while coming out of what appeared to Strickland to be an area of native buildings. "Shit," he shouted out the window. "Where the fuck you creeps come from?" He flipped a finger at the jeep that sped away from them. "Fuggers," he yelled. Then, starting up the truck again he said to Strickland, "Mother fugging fuggers. Figure they can just do that and never get caught."

Strickland wasn't interested in what it was they did. He just wanted to know about what he and the sergeant were about to do. "If the brass aren't aware of this CIA business, how could they figure anything was wrong?"

"I figured it out first week I signed on. In the eyes of the honchos, we just don't exist. "

So, there it was, Strickland decided. Another one of those look-the-other-way missions. The kind that you could get away with, or if things collapsed, hang by.

When Delaplane realized Strickland hadn't responded to his statement, he said, "Hell, sometimes we could run off with the whole shipment ourselves. They ain't no accounting for it. Other than the Frogs. Already dealt with them once't. Mean son of a bitch name DuPre. You'll get to meet im, I'm sure of that."

Strickland's mind darted back to the Chosin, then returned quickly. A whole new attitude was enveloping him. It was like a bed sheet spreading out over his mind and tucking in tightly.

Damn, he thought. I'm now in charge of armament, ammo, munitions and anyone could just run off with them? Where the hell were these guys when he was losing men? If this stuff is available for a bunch of Frogs, where was ours? He considered what Delaplane had just said and asked, "Have you?"

"What?"

"Run off with some of the supplies?"

"Ahh, shit, sir. You know I wouldn't do that."

"What about Tofte and Taylor?"

Delaplane freaked out. He slammed the truck to a stop again pulling it to the side of the road. "Shit, Cap'n. You ever use their names with anyone else and we'll both be hangin' from a rope. Or have our throats slit. Don't do that." After a short pause, he added, "Sir."

Strickland motioned for him to drive again. After the truck was back on the road he said, "So, I'm going to assume that your two buddies whose names I can't mention, could steal all of this stuff, sell it to someone in the world, keep the money and no one would ever know it."

Delaplane could only gulp hard. He reached to the pouch built into his truck's door and pulled up a flask of his favorite I. W. Harper and bolted down a swig of it. He said nothing. He was in a trap with this Marine. And he thought he knew what the jarhead was up to.

Strickland pressed on. "We could just take it to our troops. And no one would be the wiser." His voice trailed off as though he was speaking to himself only.

Delaplane started to sweat. It wasn't from the weather, but from the tension building up in him. To release some of that stress he said, "I 'spose. But they catch us doin' that and we're dead. Like in dead dead."

He drew his right forefinger across his throat when he spoke, meaning clearly that Tofte and Taylor would see them dead should they deviate from the plan. He spit out the window. He was a muscular type more than a brain, a man who'd lifted more than a few bales of hay into his father's loft in southern Georgia. He was the kind of guy you'd rather have fight for you than against you, but you might also be wary about making him your 'best' friend. Strickland knew enlisted men. He'd been one. He'd commanded them. And what he figured about Delaplane was that he was the type who would protect Delaplane, before he'd protect a brother.

"Who handles all the material after you get it?" Strickland asked.

Delaplane coughed lightly, and spit chew on to the dusty road. "Well sir, if'n you mean who stocks it, loads it, inventories it then the best I can tell you is, you ain't gonna like 'em. Seems like our spy guys recruited a few NKs who came down as refugees. Turncoats."

"You're working with commies?"

"'Tween you and me, Cap'n, I bet all them turncoats they say their rehabbing, or retraining ain't changin' their ways at' tall. I bet they's just a bunch of commie spies suckin' up what they can. You can usually tell the good ones from the bad, though."

"And yours are good ones? No way, Sergeant. A commie is a commie is a commie."

Delaplane spit out the window again, then hid the chaw between his cheek and teeth and said with a defensive tone, "No way would I let the bad'ns work with us. My guys are good'ns. Bet on it." He snickered with a sound that Strickland never wanted to hear again. "I give 'em all a test. My guys passed."

Strickland took his eyes off the road and looked at Delaplane a moment. He didn't have to ask. Delaplane was already on the way to telling him.

"See, I get them to strip down. Then I make 'im walk into the Han River. They have to face away from me. Then when they're up to their hips in water I start shooting right over their heads." He laughed so hard at his vision of what he'd done that he couldn't finish right away.

Strickland shot him a look that said more than Delaplane wanted to hear or probably understand. Strickland was, Delaplane knew, demanding the complete story.

After the sarge settled down he spit out the whole wad of chew and then finished his tale. "Well, sir. those who are commies take off swimming into the river to save themselves. Those who aren't stop cold and turn back to face me. They have utter fear in their eyes. The same look real refugees have. So I figure those guys are probably either the people who wanted out of that commie stuff or they might actually be South Koreans who got mixed up with the others when we bombed the piss out of 'em."

Strickland's eyes rolled around in their sockets. Delaplane was as insane as he thought he'd become or else he was doing the enlisted thing of pulling a new officer's leg. "And I fell off the pumpkin truck just yesterday, right, Sarge?"

Delaplane glanced to the Marine and grinned. "Don't think so, sir. 'Sides, you didn't ask what happened to the ones that swam for it. I'll tell you anyways. They drowned. River ate them up. It's powerful swift and got an undertow like nothing you ever seen."

Just then he grabbed hold of the steering wheel and grabbed a turn to a different road. The action caused the truck to skid to the right in a fishtail motion. When the truck righted itself Strickland found himself jammed against the right door. "What the hell are you doing, Sergeant?" He pushed himself back on to the Naugahyde seat and straightened his cover.

The truck rolled on with its two occupants silent for a while. Delaplane was the first to break the quiet. "Not much further," he said.

Strickland nodded. He'd been thinking about his first idea and now it came out again. "You're not pissed off that our war materiel isn't going to our boys?"

It was like a shot out of a crowd for Delaplane. He hadn't expected to return to the same conversation. In fact he figured the Marine had accepted it all and that now they were done with that part. He thought a moment, wondering if the Marine captain was playing a game of chess with him. After drawing down his options he said, "Noncoms can't afford to get pissed off, Cap'n. Least ways can't show it to ossifers." He laughed lightly and added, "One reason I lost two rockers."

Strickland nodded. He clearly meant he understood. Delaplane accepted that, wondering why he felt appreciation for the understanding.

"Don't do me a world of good at' tall to get pissed off."

Strickland squinted through the spotty dirt-glazed windshield. "You ever fight in this war, Sergeant? Ever face the enemy one on one?"

It was the number one question Delaplane dreaded. To serve and not fight. How could you ever explain that? "No, sir. J'est been with them two."

The truck hit a bump and found itself on hardpan. Strickland could see that they were finally moving along a wharf. Glancing out to sea, he saw a dozen ships waiting at anchor in the bay for their berth. Others at dockside were unloading cargo. Without much fanfare or notice, they had arrived.

Delaplane pointed. "That one," he said. "The rusty bucket with the Panamanian flag on the mast. That's our baby."

Strickland saw a ship with patches of rust throughout her. It wasn't an especially large boat, but it would hold ten trucks worth of materiel, maybe a bit more. He found it amazing that the boat was afloat. It was also as far down to its waterline that it could go. "It's fully loaded," he said.

"Most of the time."

Strickland recalled his conversation with Taylor and Tofte. "Why doesn't it just take the stuff to the port south of your hut?"

"Sometimes he can, but most of the time he won't. He don't like gettin' close to the war."

They pulled up next to the ship and got out. Delaplane brought his clipboard with him. Pausing for a moment, he searched the dock for the loadmaster, but there was none in sight. That was good. It was pay-off time and the guy apparently had gotten what he wanted. He'd look the other way—Delaplane knew—until they got out of there.

"Up the gangway," Delaplane said motioning to Strickland to be first.

They headed up the long walkway toward the ship's deck where they stepped gingerly aboard the boat while side stepping some foul smelling crud.

"These ain't what you call your regular sailors," Delaplane said, as though he had to excuse the rust-bucket's crew.

"Let's get this over quickly Sergeant," Strickland said. He looked to the lifeless stern, then the bow. "Where's the crew?"

"Not many of 'em aboard. Don't need a large crew. Probably watchin' us through peepholes. Act like you own the damned wharf. They have orders to turn the goods over to the army if they's inspected by the military boys. Otherwise, they's just waitin' for us and that's a nervous moment for 'em."

"This one of Tofte's boats?"

"Pleeeeezzzzz, sir. Don't do that."

A voice pounded into their world. "Who ye two?"

A scruffy pirate look-alike came down from the bridge and headed straight at them. His hat looked like it was right out of a Daniel Defoe pirate tale. His hair came out from under the hat in all directions. He bore a large black mustache and apparently hadn't shaved or trimmed his beard ever. Strickland noted with some controlled humor that the man's beard was tucked into his Pea coat pocket. His clothes, a tattered black shirt and blood splattered sea pants hadn't been washed for a long time. He had a strong stench of tobacco mixed with unbathed body odor that he telegraphed a few meters ahead of him. His right eye was aimed off to starboard and wide opened without the ability to never blink, while his left eye returned Strickland's gaze. His nose was ruddy with pockmarks and dirty scabs, probably from years at the helm and at the bottle. No one knew where he'd come from and neither did they care. And then Strickland saw it. A highly colorful parrot, perched at the end of Black's left shoulder with it's head up proud and its claws dug deeply into Black's epaulet. It looked like a Macaw or one of those South American jungle birds with reds and yellows and glossy black, and this one with a Kelly green crown. He had been warned by Delaplane that Black's pirate chatter had a bit of a British or Welsh accent to it. Now, he wondered if the bird also spoke that way.

"The only thing he's missing is a peg leg," Strickland breathed to Delaplane.

Delaplane held out his forms to the boat captain. "Pickin' up the shipment, Mr. Black."

The bird squawked a repeat. "Pickin' up the shipment. Aww, go to hell."

"Quiet ye old scallywag," Black ordered the parrot.

"Yeah, quiet scallywag," the bird cawed back.

Black shook his head. "This here's Admiral Bird. Don't pay th' lad's heed." He settled his gaze on Strickland. "What ye got? An' be quick about it, I be shippin' out soon!" He squinted his good eye nearly shut and leaning to Delaplane said in a deeper voice, "We be sailin' at high tide, loaded or unloaded ya horn swollgin' swabbie!" With that, he headed back up the stairway to the bridge.

"Cap'n," Delaplane called to Black. "This is blood for the vampire."

The pirate-like figure-straightened up and turned back to them, slowly at first as though he did have a peg leg, then abruptly faced them square on. The parrot jumped to his right shoulder and squawked, "Vampire. Vampire." As though he was yelling a command to abandon ship.

Black's eyes seemed brighter, more alive to Strickland than before, although still aimed in different directions.

"Whyn't ye say so in th' first place ye scurvy dog?" He came back down the stairway. "Damn nuts I say. What's all th' sneakin' 'round fer. Fur chrissakes th' hold's full o' yer bilge. Nobody else's. Don't need nay loadmaster fer that. Get 't th' hell off me boat. Me hands'll swin' 't ou' an' lay 't down fer ya."

Delaplane had learned to be wary of Black. The man had

proved himself capable of using the dagger that hung freely from his blackened belt that seemed as wide as Delaplane's hand. When this guy said to get off his boat he meant it, but behind Delaplane stood the phantom pirates of Tofte and Taylor and they also could be severe. He felt as though he was in a vise made of knives and guns. With a voice recognized by Strickland as one from a man full of fear, Delaplane said, "We won't have to off load it, Cap'n." Delaplane would see if the man would sail north. It was always Taylor's desire, since loading and unloading in this port had way too many variables, meaning potential witnesses.

"Scum bucket bilge water says ye won't," Black replied. He wasn't stupid. He knew where the army guy was headed. His blackened teeth made his mouth seem empty of choppers. "Got me a set of fancy orders in me jacket here, fur chrissakes.' He yanked a folded piece of brown paper from his jacket pocket. "Cargo's gotta touch South Korean soil a-fore I leave." He spit on the deck, hacked out a deep rasping cough and said with a voice that sounded like something from a Hollywood B movie, "Would' a been better off scuttln' 't all on th' yardarm o' th' forkin' ocean, I would be havin'. Ye start forkin' wi' me an' that's ware 't will go."

Admiral Bird continually cocked his head, moving one way and then another. The motion bothered Delaplane, but not enough to make him give up with his effort.

"Pyongchee is South Korean soil," Delaplane said, responding to a language that sometimes made no sense to him at all.

"No bullshit. I didn't know that, ye scurvy bilge rat," Black roared with a guffaw. Admiral Bird joined him. When Black finished with his little joke he leaned forward right into Delaplane's space, the parrot joining him, and said, "They also got a bunch o' idiots up thar blowin' boats ou' 'a th' water. Ain't nay way we're goin' up thar less'n ye pay me triple. Ye take 't here, or we deli'er 't t' Davey Jones." He snickered with menacing intent. "You be seein', dummy, if this be so fuggin' secret, then nobody will come after me if I sink 't, steal 't or what th' hell, sell 't t' someone else." He let out a witch's cackle and added, "Like maybe th' Chinese? Now, what 'cha waitin' fur?"

Delaplane locked his eyes to the dagger when he said, "We prefer Pyongchee, Cap'n."

"Fug off, mate." Black turned to leave. The parrot repositioned itself to face Delaplane and squawked out, Fug off mate."

But Black stopped walking away when Strickland spoke.

"Mr. Black," he commanded.

Black turned back to him and glared straight at the Marine as though he'd just been kicked in the nuts.

"Mr. Black, I'd appreciate it if you'd speak English and explain to us what in the hell is going on here."

Black hunched up hius shoulders more like he was lifting his pants than shifting gears. He walked back to Strickland slowly, purposefully and when he got to the Marine he rolled his lips around in a pucker, then a grin, then a scowl. He leaned right into Strickland's face and said, "I be speakin' english, what be you usin'?"

Strickland raised his right hand, put it flat on Black's chest and pushed it back, although gently. "Okay, have it your way. Now answer me this: Isn't this a Company boat? The bill of lading says you're carrying a bunch of bananas, and other fresh fruit. The port up north is safe for that."

"You kiddin' me, dog'face? I mean don't play me fer a dumb bilge water swabbie. Ye know this old tub ain't ereseen a piece 'o fruit, 'cept maybe that queer we threw overboard last moon. Nay, sir, what ye got down in th' hold's 'eggsactly what ye came fer. Best I know be ye're gonna use 't t' blow them scurvy commie lads off th' planet. Either way, at high tide I'm t' proceed straight t' Guam. high tide. Ye hear? Now get yer lubber asses movin'."

"Mr. Strickland here is new with us Cap'n. But you ain't. And you are goin' to Pyongchee. And why do you give me so much shit every time. You know me. I know you." And, he wanted to say, get rid of the goddamned bird.

The old man pulled the cap from his head and scratched his itchy scalp while the parrot distanced himself from the cooties. "I don't know ye or ere no o'thr else an' 't will always be like that." He walked back to the stairwell again. Delaplane called after him.

"You cut a deal, Cap'n Black. You know that we're in charge here."

Black stopped as though he were about to turn and pull two six-shooters out to drop the scallywag who just insulted him. When he turned back to them he said, "Well Mr. In Charge O' Nothin', self-respect keeps me from shootin' ya fer tryin' t' hijack me boat." He pointed to Strickland, and with a surprising change of pace and tone he said, "Whatere'tis they expect from ye, 's gotta be scum dirty an' 't'll steal yer pride soon's ye look th' other way. Ats w'hen ye learn 't 'ruth. Ye can't return. Aye. Ye be r' ight. This be part o' that Company bilge water. Ah, ye say bullshit." He chuckled, which showed his teeth again and that was never a pleasant sight. For him the words bullshit and shit and so on were always translated to bilge water. "Big bullshit CIA stuff. What a horkin' navy they got, eh? This sumabitch would sink at th' drop o' a hint. But she's me boat, ya hear? I jes' lease time t' 'em. Fur th' duration. When they ain't nay war, I usually haul things like rice or lumber or th' whole scallywaggin' tree sometimes all th' way up this godforsaken river. I also pick up sticks in 'Frisco or Seattle. We haul arse 'cross th' 'cific fer fourteen days o'er an' thirteen aft. Twelve trips a voyage." He took a breath adding, "Ortin' ta nerehave gotten close t' these CIA forkers."

"But you are. For the same reasons I suspect."

"Ye be onboard lad. Th' booty. U.S. forkin' government spends 't like 't's water. I get more doin' this than haulin' them boards an' I be havin' shorter runs t' boot. An' I don't need but half th' crew." He grinned when he added, "Makes fer better profits. An' I like havin' ye lads by th' balls." When he turned to head up the stairwell Delaplane stopped him again even though he'd become very tired of listening to the ear-grating pirate's dialect.

"Cap'n here's sworn to secrecy. And, may I remind you, sir, so are you."

Admiral Bird cawed, "Oh, oh."

Black turned back, removed his hat with his left hand and wiped his brow with the other. He was very tired of these two. "You lubbers must be nervous as a keelhauled scallywag. Ye 're always remindin' me how secret ye be. Eresince I dropped off that shipment t' Saigon." He glanced to Strickland. "That load be legal." He went back to Delaplane. "You think I'm gonna cut me own throat? Nuts on ye." He returned to his deeper voice. "Truth be, I been lookin' o'er me shoulder since th' last voyage wi' yer secret bilge water. Don't trust ye mother'n sons o' bitches one inch. Now get that junk off me boat or lose it."

Strickland sat on a canvas stool in the shade of Delaplane's six-by. He sipped a mixture of VAT 69 and coffee from a military-green Thermos. He watched curiously while the Korean longshoremen unloaded the boat. His eyes hardly wandered from the Koreans, wondering which were from North Korea, which from the south.

Delaplane remained busy directing the unloading. The crates would swing out in huge nets hung from the ship's own crane, then drop down alongside one of nine waiting trucks. After the netting was released, Delaplane directed a forklift driver to load the pallets aboard the truck.

Another truck, one not with Delaplane's group, pulled up alongside Strickland.

"Hey Mac," the driver yelled, "Where you guys want this shit?" The driver saw Strickland's bars. "Jesus, Captain, sorry. Thought you were just another army dude."

"Where are you supposed to be?"

"Lookin' for a sergeant named Delaplane. Got a full load."

Strickland pointed to Delaplane. "That's him."

The driver faked a salute and chugged across the dock to Delaplane while Strickland watched. He saw Delaplane glance to him, then point the driver to the growing convoy. The truck rolled into last position and the driver jumped out. He immediately headed back toward Strickland.

"You're leaving?" Strickland asked.

"Yes, sir. Man has his own drivers." A jeep braked and the army driver boarded it. They sped off toward the main gate.

Strickland returned to his coffee. He watched the activity, especially around the new truck. Delaplane had gone to it when the driver came out, handed him some papers and then headed to Strickland. Delaplane went to the back of the truck and disappeared there for a while. Strickland could see his legs through the space between the truck's rear wheels. Then Delaplane walked around the other side of the truck back up the gangway. Strickland thought that was that. Another truckload of gear he guessed.

Then Delaplane was finished. There were now ten cargo trucks in their convoy. While the last truck, with a new driver, lined up with the others, Delaplane came over to him. "Mission accomplished."

"What's aboard?" Strickland asked. He nodded toward the trucks. "Especially that last one."

Delaplane looked back at the trucks as though it was his first time to see them. He thought a moment on how he was going to answer the Marine. "They tell me it's not a need-to-know. We'll find out when we get it to the hut."

"Sergeant. The last truck. What is in that truck?"

Delaplane exhausted air noisily, as though he was perturbed to the maximum and said, "You don't really want to know, Cap'n. And we don't want to display the stuff out here in the yard. Trust me. We'll see it all when we get to the hut."

The hut. Strickland still had more to learn about this operation. The hut was the CIA's storage building where Delaplane had already set up the operation for transfer to the French. It was alongside the Han River, north of Seoul. The river was used as a trade route to China through the Yellow Sea. But now the CIA and French were using it to haul munitions from Pyongchee to Vietnam, through the China Sea.

"I need to know," Strickland said. He headed off toward the last truck in the convoy but continued to speak while he walked. "I'm also confused as to why you pick it up here, drive it north, then ship it south again."

Delaplane chased after him. "Ahh, Cap'n, I don't think that there's a good idea."

Strickland didn't give a damn what Delaplane thought. He kept on walking to the last truck.

"Who are these drivers, Sergeant?" He pointed to two Koreans who waited by the third truck in line. "Where'd you get them?"

"NKs." Delaplane rushed to keep up with Strickland. "I already told you 'bout them."

"Commies. All commies?"

"Jesus, Cap'n," Delaplane said while trying to keep up with the Marine. "You're actin' paranoid. Not everyone in America's a danged Democrat, either."

Strickland wheeled on him. "What's that mean?"

"Means not everyone in the north is a commie. I mean, Cap'n, these guys been retrained by the Agency. They're on our side now. Good men."

"Good men? The Agency, Sergeant Delaplane, is an offshoot of the OSS. The OSS Sergeant Delaplane, was one big fucked up bureaucracy of lousy spies trying to play soldier-sailor. From what I've seen thus far, nothing's changed. Now, let's pretend I'm a captain and you're a sergeant and that I just asked you a question."

"We need 'em Cap'n, sir. We use turncoat NKs in Pyongchee, too. They know the ropes of gettin' things out of Korea without bein' strafed by MiGs, specially in the Yellow Sea."

"You mean they're still in contact with their commie bosses." Strickland went directly to the last truck. Turning back to an exhausted Delaplane he ordered, "Open the crates, Sergeant. Right here. Right now."

Delaplane climbed into the truck. "Them two ain't gonna like this, Cap'n. And 'sides, this'll bring attention to us and the MPs might come down on us."

"Do it. Your fearsome twosome will never know."

Delaplane angrily reached into a metal sleeve in the truck and yanked out a crowbar. He began prying the lid off the first box. While he was doing this the Korean driver jumped down from his cab and came back to see what was happening. He stood back a few feet and watched. When Delaplane spotted him, he said, "Back into the truck, Kim."

Kim's eyes darted from Strickland to Delaplane, then back to Strickland. When Strickland's eyes caught his, the Korean seemed to react as though he'd just been struck by lightning. He bolted away and headed toward the front of the convoy, running past his own truck as though he intended to never return.

"Dammit, Cap'n. The man thought you were going to kill him."

"Then he's smarter than I thought."

Delaplane's sudden apprehension showed. "He's okay. He's a former lieutenant for the NKs. Speaks a little English when he wants to. Our guys figured he run away from the commies. You gotta 'cept that. Sir."

"Commies are never okay, Sergeant," he said with his gaze locked to the lead truck. He turned back to Delaplane. "What's in the crate."

Delaplane peeled back the top of the crate he was working on. It was stenciled, "Rico Bananas." When the lid came up, Strickland climbed into the truck. When he looked into the crate, he let out a low whistle. "Mr. Delaplane," he said, "I know an entire Marine Corps regiment that could use these bananas. And by God, they're going to get 'em."

The crate contained 3.5 rockets. "No way, Cap'n. The Agency and the Corps would hang us for sure."

"Let's refer to it as cumshawing, Sergeant. It's an acceptable practice in our money-strapped Corps. Ever hear of it? The Fifth and the Seventh need these badly." He jumped from the truck back to the dock.

Delaplane pounded the crate back together with the crowbar.

"This program don't work that way, Cap'n. You ain't borrowin' from the Army or Air Force to give to the Corps. That's what cumshaw is, Cap'n, sir. Steal from Peter to pay Paul or trade somethin'. This is different. These rockets don't belong here. They's no record of 'em, no serial numbers writ down anywhere. You show up with 'em and some horny goddamned supply major or officer lookin' for a great fitness report's gonna have your ass hangin' from a flagpole."

"Fighting men don't give a crap about serial numbers or reports. Only that we have the firepower to kill the enemy. We're takin' 'em up. And no supply pogue ever cared to be out there with us before just to figure out where we got them."

"Someone in the Corps knows you're assigned to this project Cap'n. Same eyeballs on you that's on me."

Strickland grabbed the crowbar from Delaplane and opened another crate. This time the box was full of frags. Hand grenades. He reached in and pulled three of them out. He hung them to his field jacket pockets using the grenade spoons as hooks.

"I'm a Marine first, and always, Delaplane. We've got Marines up there on the lines getting their asses killed because they don't get supplied. This shipment's going there."

Delaplane wanted to argue with the man's statement about him bein' a 'rine and all, but held it in. Once't you join the CIA, he thought, you can't ever get back what you had. He jumped down from the truck. "It's for the Frogs, sir. I can't stop you without shootin' you, Cap'n. So, I suggest you follow us all the way through with this here shipment. You'll get your eyes open. And maybe you'll change your mind 'bout my drivers here and 'bout what we do."

"Where are we headed?"

"Pyongchee. A long way north of here by Korean standards. Might take us two days. Sumtimes, less. Roads are the shits. Roadblocks are worse."

"Why move this north if it's destined to be shipped to the south?"

"You won't find a Frenchy ship in this harbor loading crates to take away, Cap'n. Not now, not never. Not even our ships do that 'cept to evacuate wounded. Frenchies load up on the Han River, out of sight of other U.N. types, and of course our own."

Strickland kicked the ground lightly with the toe of his boot. When did all this start? Didn't he hear Tofte read a note from old

Beetle eyes that this was only now authorized. How long has it been going on? Or, is there something else here? No matter, he decided he'd move on his plan.

"You said it yourself. There are no records of this stuff anywhere. So we'll split the shipments. We send half to the French. Half to the Marines."

"Disobey orders?"

"We aren't under military orders, Sergeant."

"This is worse. This is like them Chicago crime bosses." The days of prohibition and the Chicago gangs were still fresh in their memories.

For a few moments neither man spoke. Finally, Strickland said, "Sergeant, have you ever seen miles and miles of American troops lying along the road? Dead. Have you ever watched while scores of wounded die because you couldn't help them or get them to safety? And all because they ran out of firepower?"

"I heard 'bout it. Ain't seen it. Don't want to."

"Well now. Maybe we can arrange that."

Delaplane's body stiffened and Strickland noted it. He'd seen men like this before. Play soldier-sailor but somehow avoid the fight. "You'll change your mind after we get into a firefight. And you will get some fighting along the route we're taking."

"It's clear from here to Taegu," Delaplane said with a display of false courage. "That's at the north end of the Perimeter. We pick up a truckload of soldiers there. Agency contract types. They ride shotgun from there to Seoul. Out of Seoul we're on our own. Maybe thirty miles. Last trip was clean. Things have changed, sir. Not like it was before."

Strickland looked toward the column head, then back to Delaplane. "You in or out?"

Delaplane closed his eyes and dropped his chin toward his chest. "For exactly what?"

"This shipment. Half to the 7th Marines. Half to the Frogs."

CHAPTER 18

A SIX-BY LOADED with shoulder to shoulder armed Korean soldiers joined them a mile south of Taegu. Taegu represented the northern most point of the original Pusan Perimeter, that area the Americans first opened upon their arrival into the first time ever that the free world openly fought the communist world. When the cold war turned hot Taegu became the new symbol of possible American combat efficiency.

But Strickland's trucks would have to journey farther north. Fortunately, the area had been opened most of the way to Pyongchee. Still, he knew that the Chinese and NKs didn't give a damn about what Americans thought was clear. It didn't work out that way. And good people died because they had thought it would.

Ahead of them, Kumch'on and Naktong-ni for instance, had become names indelible in the minds of the army, except for a few like Delaplane who simply were never even close to battle. Strickland understood though. He unconsciously tapped each of his two pistols, felt his ammo pouch to make sure he was well armed and only then did he relax some.

Delaplane had caught Strickland's moves and knew what was in the officer's mind. "Ours," Delaplane said "They'll ride shotgun."

Strickland eyed the troops warily. "Look like NKs to me."

"Now Cap'n, you know the story on that. They's along to make sure we don't get stopped by roadblocks or some such thing." What Delaplane didn't say was that he didn't believe his own words. If they got stopped by a roadblock, his first thinking was to run like hell the other way.

Strickland spoke quietly, but with a firmness that Delaplane found unsettling. "Your boys back there won't hold up five seconds against the Chinese."

They made it safely out of Taegu without incident. At Taejoo after driving east by northeast, they turned due north for Seoul. When they came to the flatlands they made a pee stop.

Strickland watched while the Agency soldiers got down from their six-by and crowded together for relief. He noted their rifles were U.S. Army issue Garands. Their utilities were also army and their boots as well. "You guys worked hard to make these people look like us," Strickland said.

"They's from that Marine colonel's training outfit. They come that way."

Strickland glanced to the sky, then the horizon up north. He decided the weather might hold, but this was Korea and sure as hell, the weather could change without notice.

"How far to Seoul?"

"'Bout a hunderd miles."

"Who's boss over there?"

Delaplane looked at the group of NK soldiers. He had no idea. "I'll check," he said. But before he could head over to them, Kim, the lead truck driver interrupted them.

"I am," he said. Kim was a good foot shorter than Strickland, lean as any Korean he'd seen, clean shaven and he stood erect, much like a trained military man would.

"This here's Kim," Delaplane said. He said nothing more.

Strickland gave Kim a once over and said, "Are your drivers armed as well?"

Kim nodded. "Yes. We are all soldiers. I am a second lieutenant."

"North Korean soldiers?"

Kim was already concerned about the American Marine. Marines had already developed a reputation in Korea and the rap from the Chinese stuck like super glue in his mind. Kim was originally from a coastal village called Chohgiu. It wasn't too far from where they were headed with the trucks. Life there had been peaceful until the communists took over. "We were not a part of the North Korean army. We do not like the communists. But yes, we come from North

Korea. Now, we are ready to fight them." He looked to Delaplane and then back to Strickland. "With your help, that is."

"Your English is quite good," Strickland said, making it sound more like a question of "how come" than a statement.

"Thank you. Many of us have learned English. When communists took over, my family moved to Seoul. American school there was open for us."

Strickland nodded as though he accepted the answer as something normal in his life. He checked his watch and said, "Okay, let's roll."

Somewhere not too far south of Seoul, he didn't give a damn at the moment, Strickland rested his head against the steel door jamb and closed his eyes. They had been lucky thus far. No roadblocks, not much traffic. But the roads were in very bad shape and the trucks had spent too much time dodging obstacles including large shell holes, fallen trees and a few oversized boulders.

It was also about to get dark. Dusk was approaching them like a huge unstoppable bank of fog.

Before passing out, he brought back his memories and reminded himself that night patrols and probes were costing both sides hundreds of lives a week. Hell, maybe hundreds a day. The First Marines were taking it in the shorts and nobody seemed to care. And now, loaded with what he believed to be contraband, they were headed right into the middle of it. He hoped that Delaplane and his band of greenhorns would be of some help if they met the enemy head on. He drifted off.

Bodies over trucks. Dead on the road. Shipley, MacLean, the kid with the hot cookies, Blade, for god sakes all the others. And Drier? How was he doing? Where the hell was Drier when he needed him the most. Finally he passed out.

He had no idea when it was, but the truck lurched and pitched him forward, nearly throwing him from his seat.

"We wait here," Delaplane said, his voice cutting through Strickland's grogginess. "Our people'll show up. Soon. If things is good up ahead, we continue on."

Strickland had not been warned of this stop. Nothing Delaplane had said before had even suggested it.

"Where the hell is this?"

"Jes't north of Seoul. Cross'd the Han River a few miles back."

He pointed to his right. "See that road yonder. You go down that road and you'd be right into the war. Last I heard it was your old outfit, the Marines." Then he pointed north. "We go up that road to get to our storage hut, but, and this is where we have a problem, that's also where we can run into the bad guys."

"And who the hell are we waiting for?"

"One of our guys. He scouts south of the hut to this point. If he shows by midnight we move on up. If he don't, we whip a U to Taegu."

Strickland shook his head. "Straight ahead, Sergeant. You got your alleged soldiers here. Armed. Keep on moving."

"No can do, Cap'n. Come midnight we might'n change plans. Right now we got a guy up there stickin' his neck out fer us. It's private here. Nobody'll bother us. No traffic ever. People 'round here don't move 'round much at night. We'll be okay."

The armed Koreans set up a perimeter around the trucks. The drivers huddled together near the lead truck, where they ate kimchi and smoked some American Lucky Strikes they'd gotten from C-rations. Strickland and Delaplane stayed in their truck. Strickland was able to return to his sleep while Delaplane waited nervously for word that it was safe to proceed to the hut.

At 2400 hours Delaplane's heart nearly stopped when he heard shots from automatic weapons. Bullets shattered his windshield splattering through his cab.

Strickland exploded into action. He rolled out of the truck before Delaplane even understood what was happening.

"Get your ass outta there, Sergeant," Strickland yelled with the old sergeant in him coming to the surface. He ran to the Korean guards who had gathered earlier to socialize, and jerked them back into action one at a time.

Turning back to Delaplane he yelled, "Break out one of those 3.5s and some rockets. Take one of these men with you." He noticed that the drivers had ducked under their trucks. "And get those assholes up here to fight."

"Captain," Kim shouted, "it is only a patrol." Kim was with his eight soldiers who'd pulled in from their perimeter watch roles.

"Patrol? Don't get dumb on me. Kill 'em all. Don't let one single son of a bitch get away alive or you'll have an entire Chinese battalion here."

Delaplane landed next to him. "Here," he said breathing heavily. "The launcher."

Strickland picked it up. "Welcome to combat, Sergeant. Where in the hell's your rifle?"

"Don't got one."

"Well get one. Everyone fights or we all die. That patrol's already radioed for help."

Pulling the 3.5 up to check it, Strickland shouted over the gunfire, "Where'd this come from?"

"The truck."

"Which truck, man?"

"The last one. From the crate we opened."

"It's been used. Look at it. It's all fucked up. Shit, it's from one of our outfits. You're shipping off our guy's weapons."

Delaplane shrugged. "Hey, Cap'n. I'm just a sergeant in charge of a bunch of trucks. Those two guys you met run this show. Where they get the shit ain't my problem."

Kim plopped down alongside them holding two rockets. Strickland grinned. "Great. A real soldier."

Kim smiled back. "I get more." He took off.

"Load it, Delaplane," Strickland ordered, placing the launcher on his shoulder. But Delaplane had no idea how to load it. Strickland flared. "Shit. What in hell did the army teach you?"

"Truck drivin'."

Strickland pulled the launcher down and loaded it himself.

"Do they teach you how to shoot rifles in the army?"

Delaplane was flat on his gut now. There was no longer any mystery about what combat was. It was noisy as hell, scary as shit, and not his cup of tea. He was amazed to see the Marine still sitting up, his upper body completely exposed to the enemy. Marines, he thought, are indeed very crazy.

"In boot camp," he answered meekly, "we all shot. I didn't get no medal to wear. Didn't qualify."

Strickland armed the rocket, which was not a safe procedure when off his shoulder. He lifted the launcher to his shoulder, pulled the sight to his right eye. "I'm going to fire this son of a bitch into the middle of 'em, Delaplane. Don't get behind me or you'll die."

Delaplane flattened on the ground and covered his head with his hands. "How'n hell do ya know where the middle is?"

"Crap, you really don't know anything about fighting, do you?

"No, sir."

Strickland found himself getting annoyed with the man. "Get your butt in gear sergeant, and tell your men to keep firing at them."

"Yes, sir," Delaplane answered, not aware of just what it was he should do. Kneeling up as far as he dared, he yelled, "Keep firing men." He dropped back down when a bullet grazed off his helmet. "Shit!" he yelled.

Strickland fired off the first rocket.

Whoosh! The high explosive anti-tank rocket (H.E.A.T.) disappeared into the darkness. It wasn't designed for this kind of work, but it might scare off the Chinese, or convince them that the American convoy had a lot of power.

Before the explosion could be heard, Strickland quickly had the launcher down and loaded again. He raised it up to his shoulder and kneeling on his left knee, he fired a second round. The first explosion came by the time the second rocket was out of the tube.

"More," he shouted. "Get more rockets."

Kim was already back with two more. Strickland eyed him quickly, understanding he had a man here who'd fought before. Maybe even against him. When he motioned to Kim to load the launcher, the Korean did it exactly right. He fired the missile and it exploded right where he thought they had a machine gun. The gun went silent.

Around him his convoy's Korean soldiers fired their rifles into the night where they could see only occasional flashes from enemy guns. Soon they heard no return fire. One by one they stopped, until the night was quiet once more.

Delaplane was sprawled out on his belly. "God," he moaned, "how do you do it?" He was exhausted.

"Sergeant," Strickland said, standing, "you got a long way to come before you can play soldier-Marine." With that he turned back toward the truck. "Mount up Delaplane. We're taking your load down the road to the Seventh Marines. Right now."

"In the dark?" his voice cracked.

"Poetic, isn't it?"

"Don't see no poems here."

"Let's get moving, now."

"This stuff has to go to Pyongchee. Or my ass is mud."

Strickland jerked Delaplane to him with a tight grab of the man's field jacket. "Stop whining, god damn it. If you don't do what I order you to do, your ass will be more than mud. You just got a whiff of what war's about and now you're arguing with me? It doesn't work that way. You sergeant. Me Captain. Get a move on."

Strickland was forced to look up. It was another one of those damned Korean rainfalls. Damn it, he thought. Now we gotta fight muddy roads?

The trucks roared to life and followed Delaplane out of the area, up the long road northward. And it had indeed turned muddy, just as Strickland knew it would. The roads were dusty or a loose dirt mixed with some gravel and in places solid hardpan. But the soft soil always converted to mud within minutes of even the lightest rainfall, and that was going to make the balance of the trip really crappy.

Delaplane was scared now, terribly scared. This Marine was nuts. The war was nuts. He was nuts. Crap, all he wanted to do now was get away from these people. The truck bounced along causing crates in the back to jump around and sound like they were tearing the truck-bed apart. He was doomed. There would be no tomorrow. God, how do I get out of this now?

"They ain't gonna do nobody no good if we keep jostling them like that," he said about their cargo, hoping Strickland would order him to slow down.

"You're a lucky son of a bitch, Delaplane. If we didn't have the launcher we'd be lying back there dead. Add that together son. Two and two always makes four."

"Four what?"

"You're a slow one, Figure it out. If my boys in the Seventh don't get these weapons, then they stand the same chance we stood before Kim brought the rockets up. Got it?"

Delaplane considered that for a moment then said, "They ain't our rockets."

"They are now. And we're taking them to the Marines. And by the way, that Korean back there who helped with the rockets. He's been in combat before. And I suspect for the other side. You really think they've been converted?"

"He helped us didn't he?"

"To save his own skin. That's the first order of humanity. Save your own butt first."

The ensuing silence got on Delaplane's nerves. He needed some chatter, anything, just to calm himself down. After a few moments he brought the conversation back to his own skin. "Them two will kill us. I mean it. They'll either kill us or have us kilt."

"They better be good if they try."

Delaplane almost sounded like he wanted to cry. "Stuff's scheduled to leave soon's we get to Pyongchee. A Frog's waitin' there. C'mon Cap'n. You signed on to do this job."

"A Frenchman. You want to hand all this over to the Frogs and not to our own people. Do you smell something wrong with that?"

It seemed that Delaplane didn't hear a word from the Marine. "He'll report the stuff's missing Cap'n. He'll go straight to them two guys."

"Say it Delaplane. Tofte. Taylor. Tofte, Taylor."

"Oh god. I can't man, I mean Cap'n. That pirate back there was right. Those guys play tough. Agents just disappear, never hear of 'em again. Those two ain't like you and me. They got their own rules and nobody stops 'em."

Strickland thought a moment. He grabbed the crook-neck flashlight off the truck's dash where it was mounted and aimed the beam at the chart they'd brought with them.

Delaplane kept driving even though he felt like peeing in his utility trousers. His eyes watered now, his face itched like hell from dirt and sweat and fear. What was next?

Strickland looked up. "Fork in the road up ahead a few miles. You take the first five trucks to your Frogs, I'll take the five with weapons and C-rations to the Marines. That's my best offer, Sergeant."

Delaplane's fear showed in his voice. To head up the road in the dark knowing that Chinese and NKs were out there and without more protection than a half dozen Korean kids as guards would be suicide.

"I can't sir. Crap Cap'n. It just ain't gonna happen."

"Okay," Strickland said in what Delaplane first thought a change of attitude. "You stay here. But I'm taking the rockets, the ammo trucks, the C-rations. If Tofte wants to start a war with the Marines, good luck to him."

"No war," Delaplane said. His voice was so weak now he wasn't sure Strickland could hear him. "They'll just kill us and bury us and no one'll ever know the diff'rence."

"I don't think so. There's not one goddamned record of what the Frog's are supposed to get. You said so yourself."

Delaplane shook his head. "The drivers will rat on you Cap'n! So will that truck full of soldiers."

"I doubt that. We split up for protection! Got it? Your men will never know. Mine won't talk. Guaranteed. Stop here. We'll make the switch now. I'll see you back at Pyongchee in the morning," Strickland said brusquely. Five trucks eased northward through the darkness toward the Seventh Marine position. They turned eastward at the fork in the road Strickland had spotted on the chart and headed toward the extreme western side of the Jamestown line, a defensive MLR position southeast of Panmunjom, an imaginary line established by the UN command. A line where too many were still dying.

The Chinese and North Koreans never stopped trying to push the UN line farther south. They had used the peace talks effectively to rearm, regroup and set another offensive into place. But after the rains had made all the roads muddy, the Americans assumed that both sides would suspend action beyond patrol encounters.

The American commanders had misjudged their enemy.

So, the 7th Marines were ordered to establish a secondary defense to the right of the First Marine division, which required they cross the rain swollen Imjin River. They were lucky. The rains had stopped for a while, which allowed the crest of the river to drop enough to expose the flooded bridges. Not long after, they ran into the Chinese and North Koreans who had been inching their way toward them during the heavy storms. A violent confrontation between the two erupted into a bloody battle.

While this was going on, Strickland's trucks continued along a road that nearly paralleled the existing MLR. He would drive on he decided, until he ran into a Marine outpost. They ran with their lights off. Only a wisp of the moon gave them the illumination they needed. It was enough.

"Lights ahead," Kim signaled. Strickland felt some awful twist in all this. He would have thought Kim a good Marine the way he fearlessly fed him 3.5s. But he was a North Korean and was not convinced that he had not been a communist. North Korea had no other kind of army. Kim had to have learned his lessons from the Chinese.

"Stop the truck."

He got out and walked up the road ahead of the eyeless six-by, his right hand fingering a hand grenade that rested in his jacket pocket. The night shadows caused by the brightness of the moon seemed to make the bushes around him jump and run as though they were really humans. Really the enemy. But he had grown accustomed to that visual hoax years ago.

He knew that the flashes in the distance were not the bobbing headlights of vehicles. "The Seventh," he said aloud. For a few moments he stood motionless while searching for sounds or a nearby Marine. No one. He returned to the truck. "Let me have the radio," he said to Kim.

Kim handed him the PRC-6 that he used to stay in touch with the other drivers.

Strickland walked back up the road to high ground so the PRC-6 could pull in the distant battle. When he got there, he clicked on the radio and listened. First came a hissing sound, then garbled voices that he assumed were from the battle that raged across the valley.

"Fox company is running out of ammo."

"Charlie company needs," but the voice dropped out.

"Corpsman. Goddamn it we need a corpsman down here!"

Glancing back to the trucks, Strickland made a quick decision.

The NK drivers who now realized that Strickland wasn't headed to their assigned port were not happy. "No can do, Captain," Kim argued. "We go to Pyongchee. Orders." He was appealing more than demanding. He knew it would do no good to demand anything from the Marine.

When Kim turned to get back into his truck and motioned the other drivers to follow, Strickland pulled his pistol out, the one with its distinctive hand carved ivory grip, and aimed it at Kim.

"Stop," he ordered.

Kim turned back. When he saw the pistol, his arms went quickly into the air. "No shoot, Captain. No shoot. Me good guy. Good guy."

"Drive these trucks down this road," Strickland commanded, "or kiss your ass goodbye."

Kim's head bobbed frantically. He looked around for his own men. They were armed but they'd ducked into their trucks very quickly. The dilemma Kim found himself in had become overwhelming. First it was the communists he couldn't trust. So, he turned to the Americans. Now, they don't trust him and his life was in immediate danger. "Okay. Okay, Captain. Will do."

Inside the truck, Strickland kept his pistol on Kim while he pulled his map up and checked their location. "Hill 229, Paekhak Hill is where they're located. It's only a mile from here." They were at an intersection turning onto the road from Panmunjom to Kaesong. "One more mile. After that, you can bug out and join your commie buddies," he said.

Kim was adamant. "Captain. I am not a communist. I hate communists. Why can't you believe that? Communists are bad. Very bad. I fight them like you do. You see."

Strickland pointed through the windshield. "Drive, Mr. Good Guy." He sat back in the seat and glanced to the Korean. Maybe the guy was right. Maybe he was with the Americans. No, he decided. Tofte and Taylor had explained it all. They got these guys from the north, retrained them and then inserted most back into North Korea. What a joke. If he were captured, wouldn't he do the same thing. Play along until his enemy inserted him back into America. To do what? Spy on his own people. No way.

The trucks coughed, jumped back to life and headed down the road slowly. Sooner than they expected they could see the prominent flashes of gunfire and artillery explosions. Strickland listened on his PRC-6 to the shouting from platoon commanders and others pleading for more ammunition, more supplies. When they got to within a quarter mile of what he considered the hot spot he held his hand up for Kim to stop.

"Here," he said. "We'll leave the trucks here." He pointed to his target area. "That's got to be an outpost of Marines. In that area right there. See the glow from a burning cigarette?" Inwardly, Strickland swore at the young Marine for smoking at night in a combat zone.

Kim tried to see through the blackness that reminded him of emptiness his heart now felt for life. "Not see," he said.

"Trust me," Strickland said. "You take one of your men and go there. Get the Marines to come to this convoy and find the supplies."

The Korean lieutenant's eyes flashed. "That's nuts."

Strickland thought Kim was right. It was nuts, but then hadn't he accepted nuttiness as a common combat virtue. "Decoy them here." He looked back to Kim. "You can do that. Easily."

Kim shook his head. "Tell me exactly what you want."

Strickland got out of the truck and walked around to Kim's door. He opened it and motioned Kim to get out. He led him to the last truck in the line. The one with the squad of soldiers still sitting obediently inside. "I want the driver of this truck to take this truck a half mile farther up the road. And wait there. Keep these guys away from here. We don't need witnesses. I will meet them there later."

Kim frowned. He didn't like this.

"Do it for me, Lieutenant," Strickland said as though they'd been friends for a lifetime. "It's for your country as well as mine."

Kim's shoulders sagged with defeat. He would have to go along with the Marine's crazy plan. He saw no other choice. He went to the driver of the truck. His name was Ji and Kim ordered him to pull out of the convoy and head up the road about a half a mile and park and wait. Ji cranked the engine to life and slowly pulled away and around the other trucks.

When the truck had moved out of sight, Kim turned back to Strickland.

Strickland pointed up the side road and said, "Walk up that road. When you hear Marines call to you, raise your arms in the air and stand still. They won't shoot you. They will order you to walk toward them slowly. Surrender to them. Do you understand?"

Kim nodded anxiously. "Yes. I go alone?"

Strickland nodded. "Say only that your trucks are broken."

The Korean lieutenant frowned. "They'll shoot me."

"No. They won't. I know my people. You will lead them here. They'll check out the trucks. You will be taken as a POW and be treated better than your own government treats you. By that time we'll be far away. Nobody will suspect that all this came from us." Strickland thought that he'd considered all angles and he figured that since the equipment was contraband, who in the hell would ever be able to trace it? "You tell them you stole the trucks. That you want to trade for your life."

"Why did you chose me?"

Strickland thought a moment. It was a damned good question. "I think," he began slowly, "that you have told me the truth. I believe that you are what you say you are. And I was impressed with your courage back there during that firefight."

Kim nodded. At last someone trusted him, he decided. "Okay. I'll do this. But I don't like it."

Strickland found himself putting his hand on the Korean's shoulder. "You will do well," he said. "You will be okay."

Kim moved way slowly at first. Then, after encouraging himself to move on up the road more quickly, he stepped out like a true infantryman. He soon disappeared into the darkness.

Strickland went to the three remaining drivers and took them to the rear of the column. Each man had a rifle slung over his shoulder and each rifle appeared to Strickland to be longer than the men were tall. He also didn't recognize the make of the odd guns. For one thing, they were bolt action rifles, ancient weapons for warfare, used last by the Poles and other small european countries during World War II. The soldiers in the truck had M-1s. But the drivers were outfitted completely differently.

"Your rifles," he said to the lead man. "What kind."

"French," the man replied, with an Asian accent Strickland was not familiar with. "Old. Not very good. Frenchman give us."

Strickland knew of German weapons the French had gotten hold of, but these weren't German. He instructed them to walk up the slope of the sage covered hillside and sit in an open space they found. It was surrounded by brush but they couldn't see it, so they felt their way to an open space.

Strickland noticed that the man who seemed to be in charge of the three didn't look like the others. He nodded to the leader and asked where he was from.

"Saigon. Vietnam."

Strickland recalled that Max Store had mentioned Saigon in one of his conversations. He motioned all three to sit. "And these two?"

"North Koreans. They help us now."

"Your name?"

"I named Quan. Means soldier in my language. French call me Pierre. Sergeant Deecall me GI Joe." He meant Delaplane.

The young man shook his head. "I came with French officer. Trucks for French."

"Maybe."

"No. We come to get American weapons."

Strickland let that go by for a moment.

"How did you learn English? Ah, wait, you have a French accent."

"Oui. French teach in our schools. They say English needed."

"Are you working for Tofte?"

Quan shook his head as though to indicate he didn't understand the question. "I work for French soldier. His name is DuPre. He brought me here from Saigon."

Strickland pondered that a moment then said, "Stay here. Someone will find you before daylight."

"Kim come back?" Strickland understood why the young soldier was concerned about Kim. He was afraid that he might return with a bunch of pissed off American Marines.

"Someone will come for the trucks. You can drive them then."

He glanced to the two Koreans. They had been staring at him during the entire conversation. They had not moved. He was satisfied that they'd behave after he left, but something inside him kept his warning flags up.

He turned away from the three and headed up the road to the truck Ji had taken earlier. After about ten paces he heard the distinct slide of a bolt action rifle slip a round into a chamber. He whirled around on his heels and saw one of the NKs raising his rifle directly at him with the other encouraging him to shoot. The Korean pulled his trigger and the sound of war returned to Strickland.

With a burst of Bat Masterson's best, Strickland's two pistols were out of their holsters and each fired a single round, one into each of the two armed Koreans.

The noise and smoke that his homemade rounds generated cleared quickly. But by the time he could see by moonlight only, Quan had ducked out of sight, making his way somehow into the night and probably, he figured, right into the arms of the Marines. One dead Korean couldn't shoot straight, the other never got a chance and the Vietnamese guy took the smart way out. Good for him, he thought.

"Joe," he called out to Quan. "It's okay. I won't shoot you."

No response, which is exactly what Strickland thought he'd get.

He moved closer to the two Koreans. He pulled out a C-ration match and struck it across his butt, the canvas like utilities offering enough roughness for the match to ignite.

He held it down near the two Koreans. One round had gone through the gunman's forehead and burst out the back of his head ripping it apart as though a baseball had passed through. The other round, from the pistol in his left hand, had entered the other NK's right eye. His brains had been scrambled and more than likely exploded within his skull. The eyes were missing from the man, probably splintered into slime and droppings now splattered across the ground he was lying on.

The rounds were Strickland's own handmade lead bullets with crosses cut into them. You could always trust them to kill your target instantly.

He went back to where he fired his weapons and found the brass, which he pocketed.

He paused, closed his eyes. Was this his mission? He shook it off, he hadn't been wrong about these guys. They were going to kill him and this was self-defense. Then he looked up in the direction of where his truck was. If these men were going to shoot him, what did the soldiers in the truck have planned for him?

He headed up the road. There was only one way to find out.

When he got to a crest in the road, he clicked on the PRC-6. After about twenty minutes he heard the message he wanted to hear.

"This is outpost Baker. Captain, we got us a very strange situation here, sir. Four army trucks loaded with ammo, rockets, damn, sir. C-rations. And sir, one gook prisoner."

CHAPTER 19

IT TOOK LONGER to move north than he first thought. The road was broken everywhere. War had practically destroyed every village and town along the way. The road had not been repaired except for occasional evidence of a bulldozer having pushed burned out trucks and tanks and other debris aside. And then there was the off and on rain. The road was muddy in some places and dry as a desert in others. But always the road was rough, and sometimes barely drivable.

When he first got to the truck, Ji had asked what the gunshots were. He was afraid for his drivers, and his lieutenant Kim.

Strickland told him that his drivers tried to kill him. He didn't need to tell Ji that he shot them. Ji's expression told him that he'd figured that out instantly.

Ji popped open his door and tried to jump ship, but Strickland grabbed him by his arm and strongly drew him back into the truck. "If you're thinking of trying to kill me, then forget it. You're driving. North. To the hut. We'll let Sergeant Delaplane deal with this."

But Ji was scared. His teeth chattered from fear and his body developed a shaking not unlike someone with palsy. Strickland offered him his canteen. Ji waved it off until he got a whiff of the Scotch in it. Then he looked at the Marine and nodded okay. He took a deep swig of the whiskey, wiped his mouth and seemed to settle down a bit. He handed the canteen back and said, "No way, American. No way I try to kill you."

Strickland looked hard into his eyes and nodded. He was only affirming to Ji that should the man try, it would be him who died and not Strickland. He slipped his canteen back into its pouch and opened his door. He would check the men in the back. After he ensured the eight soldiers had ejected the live rounds from their chambers and locked their bolts back with safeties on, he moved Ji into the passenger seat and he did the driving himself.

Four hours later and just a few miles short of their destination, and just before dawn, Strickland pulled off the road and stopped the truck in an open area that was surrounded by steep walls of boulders and crag rocks. He felt like he was in an upside down pyramid. "Everybody pee," he said. "And you Ji, will drive us to the hut."

Ji's inherent fear of the Marine sent up a warning signal. Something unnatural sounded clearly in the American's voice. Strickland stared straight ahead through the windshield, which had seen too much war and eaten too much gravel. "You, too. Get out and pee."

"You tell me." he said, referring to the shots he'd heard.

Strickland knew what was going through the Korean's mind. "They tried to kill me, Ji. They lost."

Ji had heard three shots. One was definitely from a rifle and two were from a pistol. The sounds were unique to each weapon. The Marine was telling the truth. Maybe. Two pistol shots but three drivers. Something wrong. He peeled the door to the truck open as though strippings a banana, and jumped down to the ground. He turned back, "You kill them? All?"

Strickland sniffed while cocking his head upward a bit. "I had to." He saw no need to explain Quan's escape.

Ji eyed him for a moment, then headed into the night. One must have gotten away. One would be his witness concerning the goddamned stupid American.

Ten minutes later the eight Korean soldiers returned to the truck and settled into place. Ji climbed into the driver's seat as ordered and waited for the Marine captain who was standing alone about fifteen feet in front of his truck. He was in the middle of the road, sipping Scotch from his canteen. Ji eyed him with renewed fear and a sudden desire to start the truck and run the damned American down.

For Ji, Americans had all been different, yet the same. But this one, he decided, was dangerous to him personally, and the others as well. He looked behind him at the soldiers. His truck had a good sized window made out of plastic and stitched into the canvas cover of the shell. He caught the eye of their leader, a corporal and nodded that maybe they should arm themselves with live rifles. In just a few seconds, each soldier raised his rifle and as quietly as they could, they loaded their empty chambers with a round from their seated clips. Garands were hard to keep quiet during the loading procedure, so the men had leaned forward over their rifles to help shield the recognizable sounds of the bolt driving a round home, from the Marine.

Ji then reached down and started the truck. The diesel rumbled to life causing the truck to shake, but it settled into the rhythm of the engine quickly. The Marine didn't even turn around to note the engine's spark to life.

Ji paused to give more thought to his plan. If he ran the Marine down, Mr. Tofte would kill him. Maybe. Maybe not. If he didn't run down the Marine, he'd have to get through the rest of the trip and then report what happened later. Maybe. Maybe the Marine would not let him live, too. He pressed on the pedal and listened while the engine's cylinders revved up a bit.

Strickland capped his canteen and slammed it into its pouch that hung over his right rear pocket. He'd heard something familiar just before the truck fired up. Something so familiar that while he pouched his canteen, he also released the snaps on his two pistols.

When Ji pressed on the pedal to rev the engine up, Strickland instantly understood the Korean's intentions. He felt his two Colts weighing heavily against his hips. He could get them out in a flash if he had to.

He licked his lips once, then turned back to the truck. No lights were on. Ji wasn't even using the night lights. He could make out the silhouette of the vehicle against the backdrop of a weak moon illuminating the shale that rose behind it. The truck suddenly fascinated him. The sound of its engine with its evenly paced rumbling and the nine living souls waiting for him to return. He took two steps toward the truck and that's when he realized the truck was beginning to roll toward him with its speed increasing. Kim was not at idle, and he was not moving slowly as though coming to pick him up. Strickland jumped to the side of the road and yanked a hand grenade from his belt where he had two of them hanging.

The truck picked up speed, and inside the cabin Ji was now tensed for death. He could barely make out Strickland's figure. The

American had moved to the side of the road. He would pretend he was staying on the road and at the last moment he would jerk the wheel over and run the treacherous Marine down. He would need his headlights. He reached for the switch, but held off for a moment.

Strickland thought he had it figured. Ji had to kill him or he'd suffer at the hands of Tofte and Taylor for allowing him to send trucks up to the Marines. If Ji and his soldiers got him out of the way, he could return to his trucks, assign men in the back to drive them and that would be that.

The truck picked up speed, just enough to convince driver and victim that this was indeed a death run.

Strickland pulled the pin off the grenade but held tightly to the spoon. He knew where the gas cap was and he knew how to get it off in a flash. He would jump aside, grab the rear view mirror brace, swing up on the running board and stick the grenade into the tube that jutted out from the fuel tank. He could quickly remove the cap, set the grenade and then roll off the truck, releasing the spoon at the same time. It was a plan, and the only one he could come up with on such a short notice.

Ji snapped on the headlights and jerked the truck to his right, and waited for the thud of a human body. But none came. Instead the American was at the window, moving at the same speed, facing backwards and holding on to the mirror bracket. Ji jammed the accelerator to the floor of the truck and pulled back on to the road. He would get rid of the Marine with swerving motions and then come back and finish him off.

But the American seemed to fall off the truck with the first swerve and Ji straightened out on the road. He took his foot off the pedal and tapped the brake pedal to slow down.

Meanwhile, Strickland dove for cover off to the side of the road, landing in brush that didn't make his life pleasant but at least he was behind one of the oversized boulders.

At the moment Ji was able to come to a stop the grenade went off and the truck exploded into a fireball of hell. A second explosion followed when the left side fuel tank post-detonated.

After the shrapnel from the explosion had settled, Strickland pushed himself up from the ground and came around the huge rock that had protected him.

"Another one for you gents," Strickland shouted skyward toward all the men he'd lost in battle. He turned to where the truck frame was smoldering with flames and smoke and some popping of shells, probably from ammo belts worn by the soldiers. He was convinced that Ji had just tried to kill him and he'd reacted with the only defense he had. And there was that sound before. Rounds being seated by M-1 bolts.

He slapped his hands together to kick off the dirt, and backed away from the heat. Then he turned and headed up the road toward the hut.

A few hours later, about an hour after sunrise, a tired Strickland arrived at Tofte's covert Quonset Hut outside of Pyongchee, where he found Delaplane's four trucks parked in front. An empty jeep stood silently at the head of the convoy. He found only silence. No movement, no bodies, nothing but the sounds of crickets.

The hut was backed up to a hill with enough open space at the rear to park one truck or two jeeps. A clump of trees seemed to thrive behind the hut, offering some shade but not enough for the building. A dirt road was the only access to the hut and he was on it. The road went no farther, although he could see a foot path continuing on toward the north. A dirty kind of brush, not the same as the lavender bushes he'd seen earlier, surrounded the hut but stopped at the road. They were strictly a native brush and looked dirty even after a heavy rain. The hut faced the Han River, which flowed from north to south providing the Koreans a waterway for traveling or shipping goods and of course the ubiquitous fleet of fishing boats. An old dock, so old it looked unusable, ran about one hundred feet along the river bank. The wood had turned black from weathered age and there were no signs that it had ever been painted.

Three gangways stretched from the shore to the dock, which paralleled the river. Of course he thought, a boat would have to tie to bow to stern upriver or be swept away. He noted however, that no boat would ever lash to this dock anymore, since it appeared that any stress on the pilings would more than likely collapse it.

From the river, he figured the hut looked like another fisherman's storage building thrown up by locals who'd stolen or inherited some American parts and supplies to build it. Quonset huts like this one had sprung up all over Korea until they became so normal that no one questioned their business or reason for being where they were. How convenient for Tofte, Strickland thought.

When he entered the hut he found Delaplane with a tall slender man who was dressed militarily neatly in khaki trousers, and a khaki blouse that held three rows of ribbons pinned to his left breast pocket. His military green beret style cover told him this must be the Frenchman who was shuttling arms to Vietnam.

Delaplane did not appear happy.

A small light, kind of like the ones he'd seen in Western Union telegraph offices in old westerns, hung from the overhead by a wire that powered it, thereby providing all the light at this end of the hut. There was of course, some light provided by the fore hatch he'd just passed through. The overhead light had swung slightly when Strickland opened the door, causing shadows to sway as though they were ghosts moving about. The Frenchman grabbed the wire to steady the light.

Delaplane didn't take the time to greet Strickland. He simply nodded to the Frenchman and said, "This here is Major DuPre of the French Union Army Cap'n," Delaplane said.

The Frenchman had red puffy cheeks but a firm chin. The whites of his eyes were road mapped with visible vessels, while his pupils glowed like the tail end of tracer bullets headed out of his own rifle. He was the same height as Strickland, but about fifteen pounds heavier. He stood slouched, not as erect. Strickland noted that his ears seemed pinned to his head, and somewhat pointed at the tops. The man's nose was as red as his cheeks, either from anger or some form of genetic disposition. The Frenchman's legs were shorter and his torso longer than Strickland's, and his legs were braced as though the man was ready for a fight.

Strickland immediately sized him up as a very capable combatant, and more importantly, one who would not signal when he was about to launch an attack—either against the gooks or against Strickland.

"Good morning," DuPre said in English laced comfortably with a French accent. His lips were pursed when he spoke. He stuck his hand out tenuously to shake Strickland's.

Strickland shook the hand, felt the man's anger vibrate through his grip. "Major," he said.

"We were expecting more, Captain," DuPre said. "Launchers and rockets especially. Some rations."

"We had 'em."

"Explain." DuPre said with an abrupt tone.

"We were ambushed on the road last night."

"Ambushed? Your route was clear."

"Someone should have told the Chinese. We lost four trucks," he looked to Delaplane and added, "and the guard."

"All of 'em?" Delaplane gasped.

Strickland continued speaking, cutting Delaplane off. "Lieutenant Kim may have made it out of there safely."

"Mon Dieu, I don't believe this. And Quan. What of him? My man."

Strickland moved away from the light to a stack of crates that were stenciled "Thermite Grenades." He leaned back against the deadly crates. "I really don't know. I suppose he's been captured, killed or he's out there trying to find his way to safety. It happens."

The Frenchman's genetic arrogance rose to the surface. "M'sieur, I am most aware of the war here. We are involved in this war just as you. We are also trapped in a war against Communist Viet Minh soldiers in Vietnam. You are most certainly aware of that," he said. "That is where your supplies were headed. All of them, sir. And now, this. You have taken our chances for survival away from us."

Strickland found that he had little sympathy for the Frenchman. "Be happy with what you get, DuPre." He turned to Delaplane. "Any coffee around here, Sergeant?"

"Capitaine Strickland!" DuPre commanded firmly. He seemed to launch his words with the same hissing sound a missile made when leaving a 3.5 launcher. "There is such a thing as military rank. I am a major. You are a captain. Please to answer me. Now."

Strickland's disdain for the Frenchman bubbled up like lava from Vesuvius. "You, DuPre are a French soldier. I am a United States Marine. Rank doesn't have much to do between us. You happen to be a CIA agent, and not, I suggest, a soldier anymore. And apparently, they believe I am one also. Top Secret stuff here, DuPre. So, there's nobody around to enforce your rank for you. And frankly, I don't give a rat's ass about your whining. Take what you got and get back to your own war."

DuPre recognized only that he was in trouble. He had his own people to answer to. He had to deliver the goods, that was his assignment. He would have to calm down he told himself. This

American was an asshole, but hadn't he dealt with this before, with other arrogant American assholes? He said with a much calmer voice, "I am not an agent."

"Then there's nothing to discuss, is there? That coffee, Delaplane?"

Delaplane jumped up from the crates he was sitting on and headed to the back of the building. The hut was jammed with wooden crates of weapons, ammo, parts for guns and jeeps and other military gear. It also had C-rations, some of which Delaplane had ripped into. He was munching on a John Wayne cracker and smoking a Lucky Strike when Strickland entered. To get from one end of the hut to the other he had to weave through the stacked crates like he would in a Coney Island maze. "Comin' up Cap'n," he said with resignation.

DuPre continued with Strickland. "You are arrogant, Captain. A soldier must always be careful to, ah, that is we should be careful about becoming arrogant among our own."

"The irony DuPre is obvious," Strickland said. Why argue that point he wondered. "What I mean is that neither you nor I are standing here. The weapons are unknown and not recorded as supply items. None of this exists. It's a phantom world we work in right now."

"Meaning."

"Meaning you've got what you need right here and in those trucks out there. Four trucks of missing equipment isn't going to make a dent in your effort." Strickland had waved his right arm around the hut, which seemed to be stuffed to the gills with materiel.

"M'sieur Capitain Strickland! My men will die in Vietnam without everything we came for." DuPre glanced around the hut. It did contain a lot of materiel, he concluded.

"And my men died here without them. So why are we sending materiel to you in Vietnam when we could have used it right here?" Strickland pointed to the crates in the hut. "Are you taking all of these crates?"

"Oui."

Strickland tried to take in the scope of the hut's contents. "So, what's missing?"

"Launchers. We need them desperately. They were on your trucks."

"Uh, hmm. Your launchers saved us last night. Guess I should thank you for that." As soon as he finished he remembered the launcher he had used had come from the battlefield. He turned his attention to Delaplane, but DuPre cut him off before he could speak.

"Sarcasm is unnecessary. You must understand, Capitain. For the past year we have suffered many losses caused by communist guerrilla attacks in an area called Hoa Binh Basin. They have depleted our forces and our supplies. We have stopped the Viet Minh communists there, but we are barely holding on. We have suffered great disruptions in Saigon and we have lost Annam, our very first protectorate. And our colony at Cochin China. Our only remaining protectorate, the Tonkin Delta, is right now falling to the communists because my army is out of ammunition and losing the will to fight when they have only bayonets." He hesitated for a moment, then continued. "We have been fortunate for the past few months because of the monsoon season. But now the dry season is upon us soon and we are told that we must launch a major offensive to push through Viet Minh territory. North of Hanoi to the Chinese border."

Strickland understood the problems DuPre faced but still had no sympathy for the man. "Yes and MacArthur wanted us to push all the way through Manchuria. Cost us a lot of lives with that failed effort and forced us to regroup. Sounds like the same problem. Guess that's the name of the game these days."

"I am just a major, Capitain. I do as ordered. Our immediate problem is that we are not fully prepared for the planned offensive against General Giap's Communist army." Sighing heavily he added, "Neither are we properly prepared for an assault by Giap at our Red River Delta fortress and that seems to be in the offing. M'Sieur, without the supplies my paratroopers will suffer a worse bloodbath than your Seventh division did at Chosin."

Strickland eased off a little.

"Major," he said, finally acknowledging DuPre's position, "I could sympathize with you if I chose to. I understand what losing troops means. I have lost more than my share. But no matter your arguments, I cannot undo what is done. I have helped my people, which is my duty. So, now we have to deal with things as they stand."

DuPre paced. "Capitain, France may have made a mistake when we failed to understand Vietnam's president Ho Chi-Minh by not allowing them to claim Annam in '46, and we may have exacerbated that by allowing the civil war to escalate, but we have politicians at home, and our president De Gaulle, telling us to prevail in Vietnam nevertheless. Politicians you see, cannot admit policy errors. So, we die or live based on what we have to fight with."

"I'm not going to whine, DuPre. None of my men knew why they died or for what. But they fought with great pride, valor and just goddamned plain guts. If I dropped to my knees and whined about it, then all their courage will have been for nothing."

DuPre shifted his body weight by taking a few steps toward Strickland. He lowered his voice a notch with a more serious and confiding tone. "We volunteer. And then we follow orders. Now, in France we have the press stirring up the people, Mostly Le Monde. For what? Who knows. They say it's because of that price that you and I pay. They know not about us since they have never fought for their country. They say they believe we should back out of the fight to save our lives. They have very short memories of the Nazis. We didn't fight well then and look, they still don't want to fight." He took a deep breath, "I'd rather live a useful life, than one of a coward." He sighed heavily. "Are you not made of the same stock?"

Strickland found himself recalling Max Store and Scoop Clifford again. Same theories, same conversation, only with them it was about his Marines, his country, his efforts. He nodded without thinking about it. "We're hearing the same thing. Kind of like jumping out of the boxing ring before your opponent administers a knock out punch."

The Frenchman was going on now. He'd gotten himself wound up and couldn't stop. He was angry, but Strickland finally figured out that he wasn't really angry at him, instead he was angry at his own countrymen. "They want to extract us. Let the communists win. If that happens, a few million innocent people in Vietnam will die." He paused to catch his breath, and continued his appeal for more weapons. "But alas, you, me, we are fighting communism sir, and we cannot give up. It is an outrage to all of humanity that we must fight such criminals. Each one of us." He puffed loudly, exhausting breath as though he were blowing up a balloon and said, "The alternative however, is much worse. Sir, we need all the supplies we can get."

Strickland's thoughts flashed on his actions just a few hours before. He found no guilt. He had helped his own men who needed weapons just as badly. "We do what we must do."

"That is one reason I have volunteered for this mission."

"Worldwide cumshaw. That's what this is," Strickland said as though rationalizing his new role.

"Right Cap'n" Delaplane appeared around the stack of grenades. He handed Strickland his coffee. "You finally got it right."

"So, what is it you want from me?" Strickland asked DuPre, letting Delaplane's words fall unheralded to the deck. "I have told you what happened. We have only the three-fives that are already in this hut." He looked to Delaplane for confirmation.

"Yes, sir. A few." Delaplane was obviously not happy with Strickland.

Han Kyoo and Choi Kim Chong were North Korean refugees, or in Strickland's mind, turncoats who worked for Delaplane at the Hut as laborers. They maintained the materiel, and then loaded trucks or ships or cargo barges for what they knew to be a secretive supply line. The two men lived in a small village north of the hut and always entered through the back door although they loaded merchandise into the hut through a side door and later transported the same supplies out the same door, back on the trucks and then off to the boats that would dock at the small port a mile south of them. Only Han Kyoo drove the forklift. Choi Kim Chong seemed a bit dumber if not totally stupid to Strickland. He'd have to keep an eye on the smart one.

They were innocuously standard size, and very stoic North Koreans. Shorter than most average size Americans they wore greenish gray Mongolian pisscutters on their heads, which gave them the appearance of being a few inches taller. They were pleased to have confiscated thick gray quilt stitched Chinese overcoats along with American thermal boots. The combination gave them needed warmth for the long cold winter.

As soon as they entered the hut, Delaplane called to them. "Kyoo! Chong!" Delaplane had tried giving them names like Manny and Moe, but they had refused to respond to them. "Load this list of stuff quickly." He handed them a piece of paper, "The boat is leaving at high tide, tonight."

Kyoo glanced at the paper. He could read the military designations for the supplies in English because he'd become accustomed to them. He could not read English otherwise, but he was familiar enough with the language to understand Delaplane's time of departure. He nodded and without speaking he walked to his forklift parked in the corner of the hut. Chong stayed. He asked, "Who they?"

Without looking behind him, Delaplane said simply, "The Frog, and a new very dangerous Marine. The one I told you about. So watch out. Marines are crazy and as deadly as a haboo," he said. "Choo. Do you understand what I'm sayin'?"

Choo nodded. He didn't understand exactly, but Delaplane's tone and his demeanor added up to danger.

Delaplane said, "I think this guy'd kill us in a breath."

"You change our deal?" Chong asked with obvious fear in his voice. "Marine Megook not good."

Delaplane shook his head. He held his finger to his lips. "Later," he said. "For now, we are loading optionals."

Back in Yokosuko, Drier was wheeled out of the hospital by what he referred to as a "damned good lookin'" nurse. Once outside he took hold of his two crutches and waited for the official driver Colonel Bradford had promised him. In just a few short days he'd be back in Korea where a "good goddamned Marine belonged." The documents Bradford had handed him were more than interesting. He would be joining Bradford's unit at Panmunjom as the colonel's aide de camp. Strickland would be there as well. And Fraker, too. Fraker was now a master sergeant. He'd serve as the unit's top sergeant, and would be known as "Top." Funny, Drier thought, he might have a problem switching from Gunny to Top when speaking to Fraker. He smiled. Hell, he was a full fledged officer. He'd just call him by his real name. Snake.

He climbed into the Chevy staff car when it arrived and set his crutches on the floor. He no longer owned a duffle bag or a Dopp kit. He'd have to get all that again at supply. He smiled inwardly. Things were looking up. He was headed back to Korea where they were holding peace talks. Not bad duty. A great future. Not much could go wrong now.

DuPre was happier. The two Americans had acquiesced by loading his boat with materiel the sergeant had referred to as optionals. The American had said they were for his troops in Vietnam later on, but he had his doubts. He had suspected the American group of double-dealing. He'd witnessed the same things happen in France while holding the line in Algiers. He personally had become afraid that Algiers would be the next to fall. Algerians were getting better at guerilla warfare, and soon they would be able to overpower his own army. And arms dealers, Germans and French, were sucking his own country dry and dealing with the enemy.

He'd already concluded that the American sergeant and the two Koreans were dealing with someone else and collecting money for it. But not the Marine. That man, he finally accepted, was a straight shooter, although pretty much unbearable.

He had shook Strickland's hand and thanked him, "Merci, Capitain. I am happy we were able to work this out."

The American had said simply, "Kill them all for me. That's thanks enough."

Strange people, he decided. But not his problem. With his shipment complete, and with the others that were scheduled for the coming months, he felt assured that his paratroopers could survive and maybe achieve victory.

It didn't take long to load the boat DuPre had arranged for. The small port was a real hideaway, a port no longer used by locals since the war had either driven them off or killed most of them. The dock was strong enough to tie to, and the road to the port was poor enough to discourage traffic. He would sail on schedule.

A tired Strickland spotted Delaplane's cot, an army retread tucked alongside the bulkhead between crates of grenades. "I'm putting it down for a few hours," he said. He walked to the cot and curled up on a poncho where he quickly passed out.

Around 1900 hours, Strickland's eyes snapped open when the front door that he generally referred to as a hatch, banged against a stack of ammunition crates.

Footsteps from someone who wore leather heels and didn't mind letting you know about it came toward him. Before he could sit up the angry voice of Horace Taylor came at him.

"You son of a bitch" Taylor growled with the most menacing voice Strickland had heard since his boot camp days. Taylor tugged at Strickland to get him out of the cot. He was stronger than he appeared to be, well-muscled as a matter of fact. "You goddamned asshole. Get up here and tell me why the Seventh Marines found four trucks loaded with my supplies. And dead Korean drivers and soldiers in my trucks. Goddamn you, what the hell did you do?"

Strickland grabbed Taylor's arm and yanked it away from his utility blouse. He rose slowly, unwinding a bit like a snake might just before a strike.

"They needed them."

"You admit doing it?"

"The Frenchman got his goods."

"He got optionals. Do you read me? You gave your Marines equipment designated for the French. The fucking commandant of the United States fucking Marines wants an answer." Taylor had clearly lost control of his bearing. His language had fallen to the gutter and for an educated officer, that was a sure signal to anyone he addressed that he was now controlled by over the top anger.

"Stop swearing Taylor. It doesn't fit you."

"Answer me. Now! That's an order," Taylor said with a high pitch to his rage infected voice.

Strickland scratched at his three day-old stubble. He'd have to shave he decided. Soon. He didn't like the itch that came with too much hair on his face. He looked around the hut and then into Taylor's reddened eyes. He knew that if he kept his demeanor, that he would probably drive Taylor even crazier. "What does optionals mean?"

Taylor flayed his arms about and walked in a circle like a rabid animal might. "Christ, Frank. Do you have any idea what you've done?"

Strickland shrugged. "I helped the Seventh win a battle they would have otherwise lost. What are optionals?"

Taylor's anger had nearly shut off his senses including his hearing. The hissing in his ears had returned and he tried now to calm himself. The medic had explained to him only a month ago that he was getting some form of disease, the name of which he couldn't remember. But the hissing would only get worse, especially if he got angry or let his blood pressure climb. He walked to the door and then back, more to work off his anger than for anything else. He let out a huge sigh and said, "Discretionary." He had to sit, he thought. He looked around but all he saw were dirty crates.

"Meaning?" Strickland felt a sudden need to dig into Taylor's secrets. And an angry man might let go of some of them. And DuPre. He'd said something on the side that bothered him. He wasn't about to answer Taylor's first questions without a good trade for them. And what he wanted to trade was knowledge about why Delaplane,

DuPre and Taylor had each used the same word to describe phantom weapons and other supplies.

"They can't be traced. You did a dumb shit thing. You probably sealed your own coffin."

Strickland considered Taylor's answer for a few moments. Something was wrong here. Never before in his career had Marines argued with equipment that fell into their laps. It was the Marines who were always shortchanged in military budgets. It was the Marines who operated with hand me downs from the army and the navy. And Clifford Cates was well aware of that. So this army guy, Horace Taylor, was lying to him about something and probably it was the tale about the commandant wanting answers. After a moment he said, "Who in the hell is going to stop in the middle of a battle and yell out, hey, trace these goddamned serial numbers?"

"Answers, Captain. I do not want your questions. I want your answers."

A tidbit was in order. "I opened some of your crates. You're dumping old equipment—that we've already used—on the French. Which, brings up a question you may have to answer. Where's all that new stuff you and Tofte talked about? It doesn't appear to be going to the French."

Taylor backed away from what he now considered a lunatic Marine. He began to pace, slowly at first and then with a quicker beat.

For Strickland, the man's silence was worse than his diatribe. Strickland thought he might have just tripped the man up. Maybe touched a nerve concerning ulterior missions.

Taylor came back to him. He stood within a foot of Strickland and in a more controlled voice he said, "Okay. You want it, you got it. The powers that be will trace the untraceable to us. Once it lands at our feet, it goes straight to the news boys because even the Agency can't keep secrets. Truth is, we have moles like all other intel orgs. Those traitors will have a heyday and play lynch mob with the president. And you'll dangle heavily from Tofte's hanging tree." He backed away from Strickland a few steps. "There will be a price to pay for this, Frank."

"What price costs too much to save American lives?"

Taylor glanced away. He wanted to avoid eye contact with the arrogant Marine. Both of them were angry. He'd been with the OSS and CIA too long to forget that angry men often did crazy things. Taylor was tough, he knew that, but the Marine was probably capable of killing him instantly. The NKs in the truck. The drivers of the supplies. This man had killed them. He'd already said too much when he'd used the word discretionary. His thoughts drifted a moment to Tofte. Tofte would expend both of them if he couldn't get this incident silenced. Still looking away from Strickland he responded to his challenge. "Possibly your own life."

"You said those weapons were not traceable."

Taylor turned back to Strickland and looked straight into his eyes. "There was a mix in those trucks. You know that since you broke into a few crates. Numbers on the traceable, the field weapons, will go straight to our source. Our source will cop a plea and bingo, the Agency becomes the culprit. Some were brand new shipments from Guam, those, only those, were not traceable. All records of those weapons were struck from the books before they ever left the states. We alone control those weapons."

"So, if they search for the numbers and don't find them, then they know they were yours?"

"Probabilities. Yes. The other material, recovered from battlefields, was registered by the supply types. Those are directly traceable to the recover unit in Pusan."

Strickland's curiosity increased. "How'd you get them?"

Taylor looked away then back. "I've told you too much already. You don't want to know."

But Strickland guessed and he was probably right. The CIA had most likely performed what was known as a "midnight requisition." They'd stolen them.

Taylor continued. "Your actions could expose the Operation."

"What's discretionary mean?" Strickland still hadn't gotten an answer to his satisfaction. Taylor had only converted optionals to the word discretionary.

Taylor regretted having opened up. "Poor choice of words. Forget it."

Strickland studied Taylor for a moment. The man wasn't as sure of himself as he thought. He was backing down. Something else was going on maybe? Discretionary meant what? Were these guys black-marketing these supplies? Using them for their covert army?

Before he could respond to Taylor the colonel turned back to him and said, "They found the Koreans you murdered. Not just the drivers. A whole truck load. All agents of ours. All indoctrinated. All trained by Dutch Kramer. That was a very stupid thing to do. Those were our people," he added with emphasis. "You killed allies. You murdered Tofte's own men."

"Men using discretionary weapons?"

Taylor waved him off while shaking his head.

Strickland thought correctly that Taylor wouldn't believe the truth if he told him. So instead he sang the song of Korea. "They were commie soldiers. The headlines would've been pretty bad— Intel Falls Prey to Enemy."

"Where's the Vietnamese kid? You kill him, too?"

"The Marines probably have him."

"No. No one reported him. Just deaths of our Korean friends and one POW."

"Do you guys actually believe that those commies came over to our side and believe in us just because you say so?" He thought a moment then said, "Only one of them was brave during a firefight we ran into. But he was a South Korean."

Taylor looked around to Delaplane who stood only a few feet away. "That true, Sergeant Delaplane?"

"Yes, sir. The cap'n there, sir, put an end to the enemy in short time. One of 'em was good. The others not so good."

"And how was that?"

"Our guys 'cept'n for one, pretty much ducked down. Cap'n here pulled out some three-fives and did a number on the gooks."

Taylor motioned for Delaplane to leave the hut. "And take your men with you." Regaining his composure he said to Strickland, "Sit down, Frank."

"I'll stand."

Taylor was too frustrated with Strickland to argue. "Okay. It's simple. Even you can understand this: If you aren't willing to play along with our president's wishes, then you can damn well be sure you'll see duty at some remote outpost right on the goddamned China border. You can vent your anger at the communists there."

Strickland headed for the coffeepot. "You guys drop HST's name a lot. What? You old pals or something?" The sarcasm returned with a bite that Taylor didn't like.

"Listen carefully, Frank, before it's too late." He came alongside Strickland. Words came difficultly from him now since he'd rather be a few thousand miles away from Strickland. "Your actions last night jeopardized the entire war effort here in Korea and the French effort in Indochina. The United States has been involved in Indochina with advisors and military support for the French since '45, Frank. We have been helping the French with their protectorate of Annam and Tonkin since before that. First President Roosevelt, then Truman. But you, you believe you can change all that. You, Frank Strickland, a captain in the Marines believe you know more about international duty than your presidents do. You're wrong. Dead wrong."

Strickland lifted his fresh cup of coffee and turned to Taylor. "Sounds pretty foolhardy to me. If all our presidents want to play war games, why don't they come over here and play? Let Truman himself tell me to steal shit from my troops and send it to the Frogs."

"He has. Tofte's voice is Truman's. As long as the president is Tofte's immediate boss, then you can figure it's Truman you're dealing with."

Strickland snorted lightly and then took a swig of his coffee. He said nothing.

Settling down a bit Taylor explained it one more time. "Hans works directly for Truman—your commander in chief. No middlemen, no interlopers. There's Harry, and there's Hans. Beetle might be considered a co-partner, but he isn't really Tofte's boss although that's how the world believes it is. And then, so you don't get too screwed up, after Tofte, there's me."

Strickland ran the chain through his mind quickly, then said, "So, this is Harry's dirty little war and we are his dirty little soldiers? So, according to you I've played dirty, and now you and Hans and Harry don't like it. Well, Colonel, you aren't clean, and that's going to make it very difficult for you to deal with me. Guess what? We're just alike. I've come to a conclusion during this war. Whoever said war is hell was on the money. But it's more than that. War condemns each of us for life. We no longer own our own souls."

Taylor waved off Strickland's rant. The Marine was getting melancholy on him as far as he was concerned. "You must work this out, Frank. You have to play the role that you volunteered for. You signed on to the CIA. You must work the way we work. There is no time left to screw around anymore. One more violation of Tofte's wishes and you'll get hammered hard."

"I saved Marines last night. I killed commies. That's my contract over here. You want to run me up for that? I don't think so." He put his coffee down and rested his hands on his hips, just above his pistols. "You guys have gotten yourself into a pickle here. I can do whatever I want. And what I want is to help my comrades and to kill commies. Last I heard, that's what Truman wanted. And guess what? You can't do a damned thing about it. See, you don't' exist, the weapons don't exist and I don't exist."

With a cold frost hanging from his words Taylor said, "You finally got it right. But for one thing," Taylor added. He paused long enough to force Strickland's eyes to return to his own. "We can kill you. You'd be listed with the Marines as a KIA, but sadly, no CIA records would ever surface with your name on them. As to your death, who cares? You have no family, no heirs, no relatives. You're a loner, Frank. Our favorite kind of agent. When that kind of agent turns on us, then they become our favorite kind of target. Now, you listen, and listen carefully. You have two options. Our way, or our way."

Strickland's face flushed with anger. But he was able to hold it in. "You better be good at killing Marines, Colonel. Because I'm very good at staying alive. And one more thing. I don't take to threats well. So, back off."

Taylor poured his coffee out and then refreshed the cup. Strickland noticed Taylor's hands shake while he did.

"Touché. Threatening each other doesn't get us anywhere."

"Tells me what you think of me." He didn't add his thought that it also told him what the agency had planned for him after his mission. How could they let him walk out alive after this kind of assignment. He glanced around the hut. They were still alone. But he knew at that moment that they probably had planned the demise of Delaplane and the two NKs as well.

Taylor's frustration showed. "Let's reviw this one more time. The president has directed Hans Tofte to build the CIA here, in Korea, to build a third fighting force to conquer communism in Asia." He turned to face Strickland. "I thought you'd like that. I guess you don't. You, on your own, have now threatened to undo all the work that has been successfully completed before your magnificent fucking arrival. You have unalterably endangered the position of the President of the United States and his foreign policy and this operation."

"If one act can put an end to your total efforts then your foundation is too weak for your program to survive anyway."

"When the First Marine Division commander received word of

the trucks, he figured they were from a lost convoy caught up in the firefight. Then, when the word came to him that two North Koreans, assumed to be at least two of the truck drivers had been killed only a few yards from the six-bys, and with another captured, he asked for a full report. He's a smart general, Frank. He suspected right away that either the NKs wiped out a supply line, or someone, somewhere is dealing in stolen government materiel and selling it to the communists and maybe they got caught."

"So, tell him he's right."

"It doesn't work that way. General Puller has demanded an investigation. Right now orders are being cut for the Marine provost marshal at Panmunjom to investigate the incident." It was like dropping a mortar shell into Strickland's brain.

Taylor had fully backed off from his aggressive behavior and now Strickland felt suddenly in command. They were setting him up to make a phony investigation and the bastards had planned that right from the beginning. It wasn't his trucks they were worried about. It was the earlier incident that they themselves had generated through carelessness. The investigation that Colonel Tilmon had begun before he got there. Sure the diverted trucks had caused alarm and questions, but something deeper was happening. He caught himself getting angry again. Had Taylor dragged him thorugh all this crap just to give him a slap on the wrist?

"This isn't about me is it?" he demanded.

Taylor feigned surprise "Of course it is. But now you can investigate the incident and come to a conclusion that the weapons were stolen by NKs and they got caught."

"I'm going to investigate me? And Puller's going to tug on my chain?"

Taylor allowedt his shoulders droop. He decided on his only remaining tact. He'd all but given up. "If Colonel Bradford discovers the truth, the Agency network designed to route materiel to the French will collapse. Truman will be publicly embarrassed. You are here to keep up the smokescreen until all the weapons get out of Korea to Vietnam. After that, you go back to the Marines."

Strickland moved to a stack of crates and pulled himself up to sit on them. He kept his eyes on Taylor and waited for him to finish.

"You will have to fix it so that you are not discovered to be the culprit here."

"You mean fix it so that the CIA won't be the culprits."

Taylor shook his head, but not to say more, instead as a sign that he'd resigned to Strickland's inflexible behavior. "It comes down to that. You want to save our efforts or let the commies win? It's your choice. But no matter, you will follow our orders, or I repeat, you will suffer the consequences. That is not an idle threat. Is that understood?"

Strickland's eyes glazed over while he sipped coffee and stared over the brim of the cup into Taylor's dancing pupils. "Yeah, Horace," he said, completely disregarding the man's rank. Then with a bodiless tone he added, "I understand."

CHAPTER 20

A FEW DAYS LATER, sometime just before sunset, someone in the Marine camp at Peace Village dropped a needle on a 78 RPM vinyl and the voice of Kitty Wells filled the tent camp with her happy new tune, "It Wasn't God Who Made Honky Tonk Angels." Country music was always popular in the military, but nobody loved it more than the Marines. Ass-kicking cowboy juice from the Victrola was enough to set a man off for the day.

Strickland paused at the entrance to Colonel Bradford's command tent and listened to the music for a moment. It took him back to his home, to his youth and even to a few of his problems with the sisters at the orphanage. They hated cowboy songs, which of course was one reason all the kids loved Hank and Lefty and the others including Kitty Wells. He shook off the past and entered through the pyramidal's overlapping flaps.

"Reporting late for duty, sir," he said when Bradford motioned him in.

Bradford came to his feet, a huge grin cutting across his face. He went to Strickland and enthusiastically shook his hand.

"My God, man, good to see you." He looked at his watch and then back to Strickland. "Just in time for evening chow."

"Sorry for the delay, Colonel. They had me running around Tokyo and then Pusan. Army snafu type in charge."

Bradford motioned him to sit in the collapsible metal chair in front of his desk. In upper Manhattan the desk would have looked like a construction crew had left it behind, but for Bradford, who was working in a worn out canvas tent, it looked like something out of Architectural Digest.

"Want to thank you Colonel for the R&R and for The Barracks."

"Wasn't me. R&R yes. The Barracks? Someone else must be on your side. You met with those G.S. types in Tokyo? Bet they did that."

Strickland caught the end of Kitty Wells in the background. He even heard the needle scrape across the tail end of the 78 when the man playing it lifted the arm off the record.

"Yes, sir. They were a strange bunch." He'd keep his trap shut about the results of the meeting, unless Bradford asked directly. He was no longer so sure that he'd made the right choices at Atsugi. And there was Hill 229 to be concerned about as well. Already he'd gotten in so deeply with the CIA that he felt like he was no longer his own man. Worse, he was beginning to wonder if he'd betrayed his Corps. He considered telling Bradford all of it, but then wondered if dragging his friend into the mess would only cause the colonel to become another statistic. He'd wait. Hopefully he could get through it all without disrupting other good careers.

"Direct. I like that. Don't know what the hell those people are doing over here, but it can't be good. They were CIA types, correct?"

"Yes, sir."

Bradford reflected on Strickland's brief replies. Bradford had served between wars at Headquarters Marine Corps in the counter-intelligence section. Such replies became a necessity due to military secrets and of course top level discretion. He wondered now if his PMO had been taken in or had become a part of the CIA. As a former CI officer in the Marines, he'd keep his trap shut. He trusted Frank Strickland and that would be that.

He rocked back on the two rear legs of his wooden chair and said, "It's good to have you here, Frank. We've known each other for a long time. I need someone I can trust. So, you're relieving Colonel Tilmon right away. Not much to do, but you will have to ensure the Guard Company stays alert. Full time."

"Yes, sir."

"And you might find yourself helping an old friend who was transferred up here a few days ago. Colonel Hawk. Know him?"

Strickland shook his head. "No, sir."

The needle dropped on a new vinyl and it was heard by both men. It was Slim Whitman singing his new hit, "Love Song of the Waterfall."

"I've got to get that boy to change his tastes in music," Bradford quipped. "I'm a jazz man."

Strickland had to grin at his new C.O. "Won't happen, Colonel. Not even if we ordered it."

Early mornings in Korea just weren't the same as mornings in the usually excellent climate of northern Arizona.

Harrison "Harry" Bradford spent his youth on a ranch in Arizona. He always considered himself lucky because his parents had settled halfway up the mountain to Flagstaff, just on the other side of Sedona. Cow horses were their product. They were the kind a cowboy could trust. He helped train them to herd and rope cattle, and then to carry the cowboy home or hide out with him on the open ranges of the wide-open west if they had to lay over.

It seemed so long ago. First the ranch, then college and now this. He'd just gotten out of Arizona State when the big war broke out. The Zeroes had bombed Pearl Harbor and he hadn't even found a job yet. He'd majored in ranch management, a relatively new field but one that had a lot of potential.

Like a lot of youngsters back then, he'd signed on to the army reserves to help pick up some money when he was a freshman. It wasn't a big deal back then. No wars, no big budgets, very little threat of interrupting school and an exceptionally small military. And, back in '37, the Depression was very much a challenge. The army paid just a few bucks, but in those days a few bucks went a long way.

Lucky him, too. Since he'd already entered college the army guys gave him a test and he'd scored so high they put him into a 90-day wonder school that first summer. He came out the other end a reserve second lieutenant.

So it was, upon graduation. The war started and the army gave him a choice. They actually let him choose which service to go to war with. That was easy. Any good shit-kicking cowboy would join the Marines.

Every time he thought about his decision it forced a chuckle from him as though he'd just been tickled over his Philco by Bob Hope. In what seemed like a flash of time, he'd gone from hot Arizona, to very hot and dangerous Guadalcanal. After the war he'd decided to stay with the Corps for a few years until the country got itself together again. From his viewpoint, ranch management jobs still weren't available. And besides, he'd come to love the Corps.

The war had taken a lot of lives and a lot of his friends as well. The ranks had thinned out and attrition moved him up the ladder. Pay was good and, better yet, the girl he'd met at Camp Pendleton, the one who was now his wife, liked the Marine Corps and was willing to go the distance with him. So, moving up the ladder was important. Each grade brought more pay.

What his marriage hadn't planned on was Korea. It all happened so suddenly, too. One day they were swimming at the San Onofre beach and the next he was packing his duffel bag for shipping out. He glanced toward his desk. His latest letter to Roberta, or as he liked to call her, Bobby, would have to be mailed this afternoon.

He grunted a little while he tugged at his boot. Damn he was getting old, he thought. A Lieutenant Colonel at the ripe old age of thirty-two and he was an old man. What the hell happened? Ah, well, he thought, pretty soon full bird and Bobby can decorate the house like she wants to.

He tugged again and the boot finally slipped into place. It felt like he was trying to pull on his favorite but very tight Tony Lama boots. Now, those were boots, he chortled. But his light hearted feeling didn't last long.

What wasn't funny for him right now was waking in the early morning on a crappy cot, in a dusty tent and with a message he found disturbing. It made him feel old, tiresome and worse, irritable. Once his boots were in place he spotted his fancy variegated hardwood pipe, the one he hadn't smoked in a week. He stuck it into his mouth like a fireman would jam a hose into a hydrant, clenched it tight with his teeth and fired it up with his Zippo. The Zippo had been given to him by an old classmate who had served on the U.S.S. Cunningham, a destroyer now in the Atlantic fleet. A hand carved picture of the ship was on the front of the lighter and a note to Bradford on the back. The note read simply, "For Brad, a great friend." The giver's name was inscribed in his own handwriting. Terry Coates. The tobacco in the pipe was a cheap Prince Albert's out of a thin can, the only kind that had been available at the PX in Yokosuka, where he'd bought it. It flamed instantly.

He sucked on it hard until he got the smoke he wanted, exhaled and with his mind captured on the current challenges facing him he muttered, "Shit. Sure don't need this problem in my lap right now." He went to his desk with the pipe bouncing up and down to the rhythm of his walk.

His morning habits struck him as quirky. He had behaved like this ever since his first frightening night on Guadalcanal. God that was a lifetime ago, he thought. He groaned. Back then he was a newly appointed captain, only because they didn't have any other captains in the outfit, and he found himself leading a bunch of very young hungry-for-battle Marines into a steamy, malaria infested jungle, and he couldn't remember ever sleeping.

But he would always remember that he found it, well shit, say it Harry: exciting.

He wondered often if others felt the same way. He thought that his new aide might. His new gutsy aide, First Lieutenant David Drier had already arrived in camp. Amazing kid this one he thought. He had first known Drier in the Pacific as a young corporal who still had a few pimples and a shiny outlook on life even though his pals were getting killed or wounded or just scared out of their wits. Drier had remained cool and collected during the entire campaign.

Bradford had been the commanding officer of a rifle company and Private Drier had been one of the stalwarts in the machine gun platoon. After their first battle together Bradford had moved the kid up to squad leader and then the battles for the Canal ended and he'd not seen him again until Tokyo. When Bradford had learned that Drier had been commissioned he found himself "tickled pink." He would hire this kid anytime.

Just when he'd gotten fully dressed, Drier entered his command tent without knocking. Drier needed two crutches but he wouldn't admit or accept that. He arrived with only one and it wasn't government issue. The youngster had taken a hardwood branch from a local tree and carved it down to a great looking long swagger stick that served as his cane.

"Coffee, Colonel?" Drier set a canteen cup full of steamy brew on Bradford's desk, which the colonel had constructed out of empty ammo crates and a smooth plywood door blown out of a Quonset hut just a few weeks ago. Thank God it didn't have a window.

"Young man, you don't have to wait on me like I'm some old fart," Bradford said, meaning thank you.

Drier found himself smiling at the bouncing pipe that moved with each word Bradford spoke. The flame had already died out.

Bradford kept his eyes on his heroic aide. He marveled at

how hairless Drier's face looked, an appearance that offered up an innocence that camouflaged the man behind the smooth cheeks. "Sit down, son, please," the gentleman Bradford said. He pulled the pipe out and set it back into it's hand carved cradle. Probably for another week he mused.

Drier sat. He laid his stick across his lap.

"You're young David, but already you're old corps."

"Beginning to feel like it, sir."

Bradford held his words for a moment then decided he'd made the right decision. "Look, I've a mystery to solve. And it's not a fun whodunit." Bradford quite suddenly sprang out of his chair landing on his feet with a thud. Drier likened it to a dog taking off after a nearby cat His eyes followed the colonel while the man paced. "David. I hope you've read a bunch of whodunits."

Drier felt perplexed. Actually, he admitted to himself, he found the colonel behaving a bit strange this morning. "Spillane, Gardner and oh, Sherlock Holmes, my favorite," he said almost sounding like he was apologizing. He didn't think it necessary to explain that the books had belonged to bunkmates or other Marines in the field.

"Good. Have you seen Captain Strickland yet?"

Drier shook his head. "No, sir. Didn't know he'd reported in."

"Last night. By the way. When you're outside around here, don't salute, and be cautious about displaying your gold bar. There have been reports of snipers in the area."

Drier nodded without speaking. He knew that snipers searched out officers and that they were very patient about it. A salute was like giving them a signal.

Bradford took to his chair again. "A few days ago, David," he paused and looked down at his calendar. "Three to be exact. Yes. Anyway, someone dropped four truck loads of munitions and other gear off near an outpost of the Seventh Marines. And two Koreans were found dead on the site. They'd been shot in the head." He looked up. "Four trucks. Two men." He said as though he was expecting a question, but the one he got wasn't what he thought he'd hear. "And one POW," he added.

"Our trucks or theirs?"

Bradford nodded. He hadn't made it clear. "Ours. The Koreans turned out to be from the North, but suited up in U. S. Army fatigues. They had French rifles. All very strange. The POW was brought here."

Drier wasn't sure what to make of Bradford's effort here, so he didn't react but instead kept his attention glued to the colonel as though every word the man said counted.

"This is just one mystery for us. Colonel Hawk arrived here a few days ago looking into another question about missing materiel. Have you met Hawk yet?"

Drier shook his head. He'd only been here thirty six hours. He'd spent half of that in the sack recuperating from the trip and the other half setting up his quarters.

"You'll like him. Hawk's a pilot by trade. He's been flying General Smith around and then was assigned to Ridgway. He's been assigned his new mission by someone at EUSAK. Might even have been Ridgway himself. He won't clue me in even though we've known each other for years."

"I understand."

Bradford leaned over his desk toward Drier and lowered his voice. "He's a good man. Straightforward sort and all that."

Drier nodded. He knew why Bradford was speaking in a lower tone. Canvas tents offered no protection. Speaking in one was like speaking out in the open.

"Hawk's involved in an investigation that I want you to work on as well. I hope he finds nothing, but, unfortunately, something stinks in Denmark."

"Denmark, sir?"

"An old saying. I guess I'm older than I thought," Bradford said with a voice as light as the smoke he exhaled earlier. Sherlock Holmes might have said it differently, but the meaning was the same when Bradford continued, "The crimes and the investigation may indicate that we have some scoundrels among us."

"Marines?"

Bradford barely nodded. "Possibly. Remember though. The camp is also staffed with army, navy and foreign personnel. He pulled up a piece of paper and read the message on it. "From: blah, To: blah blah and all that. Here's the message. About six days ago four trucks loaded with C-rations, 3.5s, .30 caliber AP, mortar rounds, and some 782 gear showed up at a perimeter outpost for the Seventh Marines on or near Hill 229. The trucks appeared to be US Army, but no records of their existence can be found. Two North Koreans were found shot to death nearby. No other personnel were in the area. One

North Korean ventured into outpost area. He was transported to PV Marine Detachment for confinement." He looked up to Drier. "That's us." He pushed back in his chair again and said, "Well, what do you make of that?"

Drier was mulling the note over. This was over his head he figured, but he'd give it a shot. "What are NKs doing down here driving around in our trucks?"

"We don't know that they were driving them. But you're right. They could have been. So, what does it all mean?" Then he remembered something and waved the message and then read the last part of it. "Prisoner speaks Korean." He looked up.

Drier had to stand for a moment and stretch out his leg. It was beginning to hurt a lot again. He disdained the pain pills offered him since they made him dizzy and also constipated to such a degree that the pain they caused his abdomen was often worse than the pain in his leg. He used his stick to stand and then bent forward on his toes to stretch out the backs of his knees. "I think, Colonel," he began slowly, "that there are a lot of questions here. First someone has to figure out where all that material came from. Then who was it who had it. Where was it headed. Why did it end up there, and—" He stopped. He sat back down. "And who killed the Koreans."

Bradford felt elated and redeemed all at the same moment. The kid was good. He had a head on his shoulders. He would indeed make a good detective for him. Now Hawk and Strickland had the kind of help they would need. "Good questions. Very good." He crashed his chair forward, banging on the wood deck and said, "Is Sergeant Fraker ready to work with you?"

Drier smiled. "Yes, sir. Always."

"Well, son, Hawk has been on this case now for a few days and I think possibly the four of you can solve this mystery, such as it is." He paused to sip coffee from the canteen cup. "We've asked for a translator but none has shown up yet."

"We've killed a lot of NKs so far. What's the difference here? I mean a couple of NKs are killed and, well, what's the real problem? The materiel? Didn't it help the Seventh?"

"Go back to your question. Why were they driving U.S. trucks? And how did they come to have U.S. military supplies?"

"And the POW is one of them."

"Probably speaks some English but not much. You know, things like hello, water. pee. That sort of thing." He glanced to the note again. "Refused to say anything further. He's under guard in the tank compound. Hawk has tried to get info out of him, but no luck."

Drier wished for a moment that he was back in the Navy hospital. He wasn't a detective, heck, he had never even suspected anyone of doing anything wrong. But, he thought, he did enjoy those novels he read. And, he reminded himself, Sherlock would have asked those questions for foundation. All he needed now was help clear things up was his own Dr. Watson.

"The trucks?" he said.

"This message came in late last night. Hawk is on it with the First Cav right now. So far, trucks remain a mystery."

Drier let out a low whistle. "What about the skipper? He know about this?"

"Not yet. Now, usually the PMO would direct the investigation of this sort of thing if it happened in his territory or on his watch. But Hawk arrived with higher orders and so, you and Fraker and Strickland will be working for him on this case. Officially you're my aide, but you'll spend some time helping him until you have solved this thing, or, at least come up enough to get command off my back." He stood. "Is your leg up to it?"

"Yes, sir."

"Ever done anything like this before?"

"No, sir. Question though. The weapons you mentioned. What happened to them?"

"First report was that they were shipped back to Pusan. But that was not accurate. In fact the Seventh used all of it. In fact they might have been in big trouble had they not gotten them. They had to drive the Chinese off Hill 229 but only when the weapons showed up did they succeed. They were especially happy to get a large supply of AP rounds and three-fives."

"So, what's wrong here?" Drier still wasn't clear why there was an investigation for something that he sure could have used at the reservoir.

"G-4 is unforgiving. Might be as simple as wounded egos. Actually I think someone at EUSAK has a crawdad prowling around in his pants. But, the fact that the trucks, more than the weapons, might be contraband has other implications. The assumption that a bunch of drivers from North Korea put them there, makes for a giant mystery, especially when found in the Seventh's sector. They were, by the way, on a road that intersected with the main north south route. So, we have unmarked trucks, U. S. weapons and we assume NK drivers, and all near the Peace Talks."

Drier was well aware of what G-4 or S-4 was and he had become more than aware of the internal bickering among the supply types, usually caused by exactly what Bradford had referred to. Bruised egos.

The "4" stood for the supply and logistics sector in every outfit that boasted one. The supply types at all levels guarded their power with zest. Unfortunately, sometimes their mission seemed to become confused with their endemic need to protect their bureaucratic status.

"Why is an American suspected?"

"No Korean, or other indigenous commander in the area. Just dead NKs and one who won't speak. It's just one of those everyone's-a-suspect things." He smiled and added, "You're going to be busy."

Drier looked straight at Bradford. "Colonel, you know that we needed supplies like that in every battle we fought here." He remembered Almond and the Chinese and Shipley and Blade again. "I mean, sir, it sounds like the Seventh made out here. A few NKs were killed." He looked away for a moment and shifted his weight against his stick a bit. Looking back at Bradford he said, "Isn't that what we wanted?"

Bradford's nod signaled agreement. He sat back into his chair, knowing that Drier would follow his motion. The kid was having a tough time on his leg, but he hadn't complained or even made a facial expression for the pain that he knew was there. Drier did sit. Bradford said, "Yes. You'd figure we'd all be happy about that. But this war is not like what you and I saw in the Pacific. We've got politicians now. And battles going on at home in the press and in Congress. No Ernie Pyles here. No Kilroys. Some of our own countrymen are turning out to be unfriendly to our side and God knows why. I sure don't. And we have one more thing happening over here that I'm sure as hell not accustomed to." He checked Drier's curiosity, then said, "It's the CIA. I believe they are trying to fight this war alongside us. It's nuts. Stupid, but here they are. Hawk has promised to look into that, too." He didn't say it would surprise him if he learned anything, but that's what he believed. "Maybe those trucks belonged to them and maybe they didn't. No matter. Whoever they belonged to will have to answer to the top."

"Why not just call in the CIA and ask them straight out?"

"Still my level-headed Mr. Drier, aren't you? Well maybe we can. Colonel Tilmon learned something the other day about that before he left here." He ruffled through some papers then pulled a sheet of Thermo fax up. "Ahh, here. It seems that nobody including the powers that be in the CIA knows where this stuff came from." He set the paper down. "And nobody is laying claim to the trucks."

"No records?"

"None yet."

"Serial numbers?" He knew he was being redundant, but he had to get things clear in his head before he moved on. The colonel was asking a lot from him. He didn't want to let him down.

"Nothing valid." Without thinking about it, he grabbed up his pipe, shoved it into his mouth and rocked back in his chair. "So, you see why I need you to work with Hawk?"

"Why does the army command suspect they were First Cav trucks?"

"You can start with that question. You and Hawk."

Drier nodded.

"Now, for the meat. There are no records for munitions and other materiel on the trucks, as I said. What we do know is that it's all legitimate U.S. of A. materiel. And that may be the mystery we have to solve. It may be the materiel that EUSAK wants to know about. The trucks would be a lead. The dead Koreans a sideshow. But those supplies? Someone's going to have to answer up to those."

Drier suddenly felt himself elevated to heights way over his head. "No records anywhere?"

"Not in Korea."

"They have serial numbers on them?"

"Yes. But it's going to take time to see if anyone stateside has a record of them."

"New stuff?"

"Yes. Except for one truck. It seemed to have supplies that were taken right off the battlefield. Some from Seventh and Fifth Marines at the Chosin. It proved to be the exception to the problem of unrecorded weapons. Some of that materiel has been traced to the reconstitution battalion in Pusan. Of course, they know nothing of their disappearance."

Drier remained silent. He was trying to think of avenues or

paths for his mind to wander along, something to grab hold of here, something that he thought maybe he could help with.

Bradford decided to think aloud. "Stick with me on this one. We know the launchers found in that one truck belonged to Marine units at the Chosin. So now we assume few NKs show up with them in army trucks that aren't army—according to the army. And three trucks full of new supplies including enough rockets to help the Seventh get past Russky tanks on 229. Some equipment was still in cosmoline. Yet no registration of lot, or serial numbers anywhere in our supply system." He shook his head. "It is fathomable that, well, that this is where we will find the CIA involvement."

"You sound convinced."

"Process of elimination." He pulled the flamed out pipe from his mouth and slurped lukewarm coffee from the time-blackened canteen cup. Drier watched the pipe as Bradford waved around while he spoke. "There have been other unexplained incidents involving munitions and weapons that might provide us further leads. Colonel Hawk is up to date with that info."

"Yes, sir."

"And one more thing, David. Keep Sergeant Fraker busy. He'll drive me nuts if you don't."

"Hot damn, he hasn't changed." Drier sat straight up as though to say he was sorry for the outburst.

Bradford noted the reaction and allowed a friendly smile.

"Where you from, Lieutenant?" Hawk asked. They were in Hawk's pyramidal tent. The tent had more than likely seen its best days somewhere in the Pacific. Hawk looked worn out and probably was. He moved slowly, not like most of the cocksure pilots did. Drier figured he was just getting tired of being in Korea, and probably never getting any sleep.

"Sallisaw, Oklahoma, sir."

"Welcome aboard." Hawk also seemed to be a bit abrupt, something like a school teacher back home when the class misbehaved. Maybe that's what the colonel meant when he said Hawk was straightforward. Drier watched while the colonel walked to a .50 caliber ammo can sitting on a stack of crates. Opening it he asked, "Had breakfast?"

"No sir."

Hawk tossed him a fresh apple. "Catch. Colonel Bradford gave you a synopsis of what I'm looking into. Any thoughts after reading that folder?" He nodded to a manila folder Drier had returned to his desktop.

"I wondered why someone would want to kill two North Korean truck drivers and not take the goods in the truck? Or did they? And the drivers who got away, well, I guess two got away. I'm guessing the two KIAs were drivers. But why did one approach the Marine outpost so directly on his own. He didn't seem to have been forced to do that. Unless the Seventh made up that tale."

"Ahh, yes. Well, I suspect he wanted to get away from whoever shot the others. I suspect driver number four did the same but he didn't run into the Marines or else he did on the wrong hill and was killed. We'll probably never know. As to the troops. I don't believe anyone from the Seventh had time to look for wayward trucks that far from Hill 229. I believe the outpost told us the truth."

Drier thought for a few moments, then said, "The driver was a Korean. We aren't completely sure if he was north or south. No papers. The deceased were NKs. At least their papers showed that. Maybe the Chinese caught them working for Americans and killed them."

"Americans like the CIA? That's not impossible. Neither we, nor the army, have records for those trucks. And those wannabes in the CIA claim to have no record."

"The new materiel was U.S. How would NKs get their hands on them? And the battlefield equipment? Doesn't make sense to me, Colonel."

"That's our mission. To learn the truth."

"Maybe someone in command doesn't want us to find out."

Hawk eyed his new young officer. The kid had a point, one he'd not thought of before. "Interesting."

"Do you think someone here killed them? I mean in this camp?"

Hawk swallowed his chewed apple down. "Lots of different souls here. That's possible. Everyone here has a gun and a few may have a motive."

Hawk bit off another chunk and chewed quietly before speaking again. "They're crawling all over Korea."

Drier tilted his head as though it was hanging from his rearview mirror in Sallisaw. "Sir?"

"CIA. Colonel Bradford's met some of 'em. He suggested we see if they might be involved. It's a long shot. And by the way. Your friend Captain Strickland? Bradford is aware that he met with them in Atsugi I believe. They're recruiting military types for some of their work. Maybe he can clue us in."

"Skipper's a good man."

"Skipper?"

"He was in command of our unit at the Chosin."

"Oh." Hawk tossed his well chewed apple core into the circular file and said, "Military lawyers at EUSAK think the two drivers were murdered. Cold blood."

"Lawyers?"

"Yeah. One of the great new combat units of this war. Spoke with one late last night. Crappy com here." He referred to the communications system. "By the way, who carved the top of that stick you carry?"

"I did, sir."

"Good job," Hawk said. "Depressing, isn't it? The murders I mean. We have a Marine officer among us who was a lawyer in civilian life. I spoke with him. He brought up a legal term called the "but for" rule. But for the fact and so forth. Now, apply that to this case and we ask why were the trucks there? But for the fact they were there the Chinese may have pushed the Seventh off that mountain. That's a stretch, of course, but it sets up an assumed scenario that asks an important question."

"Like maybe a Marine realized that without those supplies the Seventh could lose that battle."

"Or a CIA operative who had access to them."

"Colonel, if I'd been there, and knew about the Seventh and saw those trucks I probably would have done the same thing."

"Would you have stayed to help in the fight?"

Without hesitation Drier said, "Yes, sir."

"Whoever sent the NK up there didn't stay."

"Then he probably wasn't a Marine."

"Talk it through."

Drier considered what he'd heard so far this morning and then said, "Where did the supplies come from? Who was moving them up the road? How did they get through Chinese or NK patrols? All that doesn't make sense. NK drivers? No Americans in sight. Trucks left behind." Drier shook his head. "It's out of my league to make a guess, but someone liked those Marines up there and helped them out of a tough spot."

Hawk gulped down the last of his very black coffee. "You'd look the other way then?"

Drier reflected on that a moment before answering. "Yes, sir, I guess that's what I'm saying."

Hawk displayed his days-as-a-flight-instructor expression when a student finally figured out how to land the damned plane. "Thanks for being honest. So would I."

"The trucks could have been on their way to help the Chinese, sir, and just got messed up. No, wait. What if there were more trucks than those four? What if some did make it to the Chinese?"

"Keep going."

"I remember a crime at Pendleton, Colonel. Never really got the full scoop but all units had to report who was AWOL the week it happened. They found the culprits that way."

Hawk's eyes brightened. "We've gone through that. Nobody was missing from this camp. But, you make a good point. We'll have to check all units in Korea."

"Your files said the two NKs were found together as though they had been sitting, having a smoke or waiting for someone."

Hawk nodded. "That's right."

"Were they armed?"

Hawk glanced to his notepad, then into Drier's eyes. "Yes." He thought his answer through for a moment then added, "Okay. I want you and Sergeant Fraker to check out the site where they died. See if you can find the brass and anything that might help. Look for brass from a rifle as well as from a pistol. If you do find brass, then bring it back for EUSAK to check finger prints or anything material about them. In other words, pick them up with gloves on. And, oh, don't know if this is possible, but see if you can find the expended rounds."

Drier understood what Hawk was looking for. "If it was a Marine?"

"If it was, then that will narrow our search. If it wasn't," Hawk paused, "well, if it wasn't we'll have to take the challenge up a notch to Colonel Bradford and possibly Division G-1."

Drier stood to leave.

"Mr. Drier, I know about your relationship with our new PMO and Sergeant Fraker. Don't let that get in your way during this investigation. You are working for me."

Drier leaned on his crutches while staring at the tent flap that would get him outside and into fresh air. "Yes, sir," he said.

They bounced along the dirt road with dust flying behind them like a rooster tail that eventually spread out like a peacock's fan. There was enough daylight left for them to get to the spot where the NKs had been killed, and back to camp before nightfall. The challenge as far as Fraker could see was that they had been issued an older battle weary jeep that wasn't exactly a confidence builder for keeping to their schedule.

"What the hell did he mean by that?" Fraker shouted over the grating sounds of the irritated engine.

"I don't know. I guess maybe he thinks we got too close to each other during our last tours." Or, Drier didn't say out loud, maybe he thinks it's one of us.

"Too close for what?" Fraker's cigar appeared to be new although the fire had gone out.

Drier shrugged. "Dunno. He's probably stricter than he appears. You know that officer-enlisted man thing."

"The man's a pilot, right? Never met a strict Marine pilot. They's more like docs. They got rank, but mostly for the extra pay."

"Yeah."

Fraker knew about the officer-enlisted thing all right. They had all been enlisted men before Strickland and Drier had been promoted. Since the pilot hadn't been there, he'd never know why they were so close. But he decided he'd better play the game when in the presence of the other officers. "Okay, Lieutenant," he said with a straight face. "I'll stand my distance when it matters."

"That's bullshit Snake. You saved my life. Hell, you saved the skipper's life. I'll not let them change that."

"Yes, sir," Snake said with a slight grin.

Drier pulled his green canvas map case up. "I saw an X marked on the chart found in one of the trucks."

"What's that tell us?"

"Not sure. But seems like it might be where they were headed, since the X wasn't where they were found."

Fraker wasn't good at detective work but he did know how to hunt down snakes. "Meaning they weren't headed to the Seventh."

"Right."

"I remember finding charts like that in the 'cific. Never figured out what some of 'em meant."

"The X was marked along the coast just north west of our camp."

"Drier, I mean, Lieutenant. What's that up ahead?" Snake pointed as though it would help his friend to see what he was looking at.

Drier pulled the field glasses off the jeep's stanchion where they'd been hanging. The stanchion had been used to mount a thirty-caliber light machine gun before they became the jeep's owners. He focused the glasses on the road ahead while Fraker braked to a stop.

"Holy smokes," Drier muttered. He handed the glasses to Fraker. "Take a look for yourself, Snake."

Fraker squinted through the lenses. He never cared for the Corps's choice in binoculars. "Holy Jesus. Parts of a truck." He moved the glasses around a bit and then stopped. "Uh, oh."

CHAPTER 21

IT WAS LATE EVENING when Bradford found himself with his aromatic pipe. He packed a fresh bowl of Prince Albert until he thought it was perfect. Then he flamed his Zippo and sucked the fire into the tobacco. He puffed on it as though he were sucking up a malted through a thin straw. When the Prince Albert took hold, he snapped the lighter's lid shut and returned it to his desk. His eyes went to Strickland at that point.

"Colonel Hawk would like to meet with you, Frank."

Strickland's vision sharpened, Slim Whitman's voice drifting through camp again. His song became clearer, smoother, a bit like well defined water scrambling over polished rocks and landing in the pool below with a slippery-smooth sound. Strickland let it pass. Maybe he would visit the Marine playing those records and put a stop to it. But for now, he was curious about more serious things. He needed to know if they were on to his CIA activity. "What's he investigating?" he asked.

Bradford eased the pipe from between his teeth and said, "Hawk. Well, strange but not unfamiliar territory. It seems quite a bit of military materiel is disappearing, some of it apparently falling into the hands of North Koreans. You're aware of this aren't you?"

"North Koreans are getting hold of our arms?"

"Army CID has recovered a bunch of Corps equipment left behind at the Chosin in the hands of North Korean agents. Matter of fact, a great deal of it. Mostly C-rations, 782 gear. Some has also made its way into the civilian black-market in Seoul and Pusan." 782-gear was a Gyrene-only term for equipment and clothing usually carried by each Marine.

"Any munitions?" Strickland asked. "I mean in North Korean hands?"

"Not sure. Hawk's on top of that." He tapped ashes from his pipe into his ashtray. "Strangely enough, just three nights ago unregistered arms showed up at the Seventh Marines. Nobody knows where they came from. Can't seem to trace the serial numbers except for some launchers that may have come from the Fifth at the reservoir. Hawk can brief you on that."

"Yes, sir."

Bradford continued. "I suspect some indigenous types are doing some field picking and putting it out there for the highest bidders. That would be the NKs or the Chinese. Nothing else makes sense. Anyway," he flamed his pipe again and the spoke between puffs. "Hawk is looking into that as well. You can help him if he needs it. Man is quite capable."

Strickland remained outwardly stoic even though his heart beat as though pounded on by a drummer's sticks. Slow, fast, faster, harder, louder.

"Sounds intriguing," he said. He had to catch his breath.

Bradford's eyes brightened like crystals under a light beam. A new thought, a new approach. "Say, Frank, you don't speak Korean, do you?"

Strickland nodded once. "A few words."

"Uh, probably doesn't matter. Here's one for you. Maybe your experience with these people will help you interrogate the prisoner in the tank compound better than we can. Hawk's waiting for an interpreter but we've not seen one yet. Like I told Lieutenant Drier, we aren't exactly a priority outfit here."

The tent flap parted and Hawk appeared. Bradford wasn't surprised. After setting his pipe into its cradle he quickly introduced them to each other.

After his greeting, Hawk said, "Colonel Bradford has painted an impressive picture of you."

"I hope he didn't oversell me."

"I don't think he oversells anybody," Hawk said with a grin. He motioned Strickland to sit down where he had been sitting. "At any rate, it's good to have you aboard. I guess we'll be working together."

Strickland only nodded.

"Your experience with Koreans is what we need right now."

"Whatever I can do," Strickland said. He wasn't sure what they thought his experience consisted of since all he'd done before was kill North Koreans.

"The NK in the tank compound speaks a few words of English, yes, no, that sort of thing."

"Would you like me to try and interrogate the prisoner now?"

"You bet," Hawk said. "It's getting late, but anything you can do. By the way, I sent Lieutenant Drier and Sergeant Fraker out to search the site for evidence. I understand you know them well."

The military compound didn't have a brig as such, so the Marines confined Kim in the fenced off motor pool area where they'd anchored the North Korean to a broken World War Two model Sherman tank.

When Strickland found him, two sentries were sitting on empty ammo cans facing the Korean who squatted on the icy ground in front of the tank. Kim had freedom of movement for about a ten foot area.

Strickland noted that Kim was dressed warmly and didn't appear to be uncomfortable. When Kim saw Strickland, he stood quickly and flashed a smile of recognition.

"That's enough, prisoner," Strickland said. Turning to the two sentries who had already stood at attention, he said, "I'm Captain Strickland. Your new PMO."

"Yes, sir," Corporal Donovan said.

The word was already out about Strickland, and about his recent action in Korea. Private First Class Winfield remained quiet. Both Marines were eighteen years old. Neither had yet seen combat. Donovan was lean and about six feet tall. He had country high-school-kid written all over him. He was from just west of Wichita, Kansas, a farm boy who lifted bales of hay so much his biceps still bulged out a bit like Popeye's, at least that's how Strickland pictured them.

Winfield was clearly from another world. Strickland could see by the shadowy fuzz on his face that the boy hadn't shaved since boot and wasn't about to. He had a knife scar that ran from the lower edge of his right eye to the corner of his mouth. Despite his youthful complexion, his countenance was that of a man who would kill on command and not think much about it. Strickland thought he liked

Winfield. He would remember this kid in case he had to get back into the fight.

"Leave us for a few moments, gents, get a cup at the mess hall," he said. After the two sentries moved out, Strickland turned to Kim.

"Play along with me Kim, and I'll get you out of here."

Kim nodded. He understood. He was smarter and spoke more English than he'd let on to his captors.

"What have you told them?"

"Nothing. I speak only Korean with them. They say they want to hang me. As spy."

Strickland gave off a grunt indicating that the comments were bullshit. "Not going to happen. They were just trying to get you to talk." He scanned the compound to see if anyone else was nearby. Turning back to Kim he said, "Has anyone from Taylor's group tried to contact you? Delaplane? Anyone?"

"No. What happened to my men? To Ji. To his men? And Quan. He missing?"

Strickland glanced up at the darkening sky. Clouds had moved in. Another storm was due. Damn Korea. Rain or snow. Mud, ice. What in the hell were they fighting over? He looked back to Kim. "One of your drivers took a shot at me. I killed him and his friend who was urging him on. Quan got away. Don't know where he went."

"Ji? His men?"

It would be too difficult to explain what really happened to Kim. Strickland considered the truth for a moment, then decided he would make up a story so that he could use the tale to help him learn more about what his CIA connections might be doing other than what they said they doing. "Ji and others are dead. Sergeant killed them."

Kim looked confused.

Strickland sighed, bowed his head as though he felt sympathy. "I'm sorry, Kim. I'm telling you the truth. No one else here knows about this."

"Why you not dead?"

Strickland's eyes narrowed. Kim was not a dumb soldier. He weighed Kim's question and thought that he might possibly be able to use this man if things got out of control and they sure as hell always did. A North Korean on his team might just do the trick.

"I was scouting up ahead, on foot. I heard a commotion. By the time I got back, Ji and his truck had exploded and I saw Sergeant

Delaplane speeding off in his truck. Remember? They went ahead of us. But he must have come back for something."

"Oh." He looked away. "I worried about him. Maybe he not such a good man."

"Translators. Coming, you know that."

"They say so. I will tell them nothing, only that I tried to escape."

"From?"

"Bad soldiers. I tell them soldiers bad. All communists."

"Tell them the truth. Tell them that you came under fire and were trying to escape and thought your friends were going to hightail it as well."

"Hi tale?"

"Run for cover." Strickland wanted Kim to believe that he was figuring a way for him to get out of his imprisonment.

"Okay. I tell them. Sergeant. He is here too?" He was asking about Delaplane.

"He's in the camp. This camp. You see, the problem is," he paused. He was talking too fast for the NK to translate in his own mind. With a slower pace he said, "The sergeant works for the CIA."

"Yes. I know. Me, too. He say CIA not good. Bad."

"Yes. Well the sergeant's not such a good man, either. So, we're going to fix that. We might have to hang him." Strickland kept his eyes glued to Kim to see if the man would offer up any reaction at all to the suggestion. But Kim seemed to accept his thought of Americans hanging another American. Why not? In his own country men were severely punished for doing much less. After a few seconds Kim brightened.

"I help you."

"And who was in charge of the convoy?"

"Convoy?"

"Trucks."

"Ahh," Kim was confused. The man asking him the question was the one in charge. "Not you?"

"No. Sergeant and I in charge of cargo."

"Ah. Then I was in charge."

"Tell them another man was in charge. Use Ji if you have to."

"I will try."

Strickland saw the flash in Kim's eyes when the man's mind changed from accepting everything he'd suggested as truth to that of doubt. Could he afford doubt if he was going to use him later? Could he trust a man who was still considered an enemy?

"Where do they want you to sleep tonight?"

Kim nodded to the tank. "In there. I sleep okay before. Good place. They give me pad, blankets. A little cold, but soon I fall asleep. Not matter."

The tank was made of steel. Steel transmitted cold and heat quickly like water running through cracks. Strickland thought about that for a moment before responding. "I'll be back later. I promise you I'll get you out of here before tomorrow morning. Meanwhile, we have to keep you warm in there."

Kim grinned. "Okay. You boss man now. I do what you want."

When the two sentries returned, Strickland said, "Keep a close watch on him."

"Yes, sir."

Nodding up to the clouds he said, "It's going to get cold tonight. Make sure he has a way to keep warm."

Donovan nodded. "We have a hibachi for him."

Strickland headed back to his new billet. Colonel Tilmon's records concerning Colonel Hawk's investigation would need a good going over.

On their return trip, Fraker and Drier ran into a new challenge. A cold front had moved through the area and now it was bringing fresh snow.

"Crap, does this country ever have good weather?" Fraker said. "Ain't supposed to snow now."

They pulled their field jackets up over their necks and pulled down on their pith helmets. They'd left the steel pots behind in the camp, assuming they wouldn't need them.

It was later in the day than they had planned. The sun would drop out of sight shortly and things could get a bit sticky wicket.

"We'll make it," Drier said.

Clank! "Aww, shit," Fraker muttered. The jeep stopped even though the engine was still running. "That Mr. Drier, sir, was the tranny."

Drier reacted quickly. Back at the reservoir Snake gave the orders, now it was Drier's turn and he played his role well.

"Let's go, Snake. Hoof it back before it gets too deep."

Fraker watched his friend grab his stick from the back of the jeep and start down the road, hobbled, limping, yet full of the strength that made him such a great Marine. He shook his head, switched off the useless engine and caught up with his new skipper.

While Strickland read through the documents the snow outside began to pile up silently against his military olive colored canvas tent. Cold air slipped through the double flap entry, causing him to stoke his hibachi to increase the heat. The hibachi was relatively safe in his tent. He knew that. The carbon monoxide would escape through the leaky entry as well as through the smoke hole built into the top of the pyramidal. He would be safe and warm on this night.

Halfway through the records he recognized that Colonel Hawk was an amateur investigator, but when he got to the page concerning the trucks that had appeared for the Seventh Marines, he tensed up. Right there in the second paragraph of Hawk's analysis, he read, ". . . although no evidence yet exists, nor do we have any viable witnesses, it appears from our initial investigation of Marine and Army records, that the trucks may have been under the control of a member of the United States military or an American from another agency (CIA). This agent could be responsible for the deaths of the two North Koreans found at the outpost. A check of Marine and Army records in the peace camp showed no AWOL personnel at the time in question." The paragraph ended with, "The only potential witness we have is currently incarcerated in the tank compound."

There was more. "There has been one other similar incident approximately six months previous where discovery of stolen materiel prompted a major investigation. I have attached a one page report from EUSAK of that incident. You will note that the report offers no resolution to the investigating officer's findings. Also, when I questioned EUSAK I learned that the initial investigating officer was transferred back to the States immediately after his report was submitted."

The implications of that statement were obvious and they struck Strickland straight on. Tofte and Taylor had power over the military. Nobody was going to screw with them and get away with it. And, more importantly, it seemed that their operation had been working longer than they'd led him to believe. Or, were they dealing with the Chinese or NKs on the QT? And that brought up another question.

Were they really authorized by HST to shuttle arms?

He whipped through the report to the last page. There it was. A fading Thermofax copy of the original report from EUSAK. He read it quickly, his eyes stumbling over the words like a drunk trying to walk home. His heart nearly stopped when he saw the signature of the investigating officer. Colonel H. Taylor, USA.

He fell back into his chair and stared at the hibachi with its red and yellow burning coals glowing in the barely lit tent. H. Taylor was not transferred back to the States. Why would they write that he had been? Who in EUSAK is part of their team?

Damn. Someone down there knows about me. He asked the damning question again. Who in EUSAK knows about me?

He jumped up and began pacing around the hibachi. EUSAK's report was about two trucks of goods stopped near the port where he'd been with Delaplane. Army personnel inspected the trucks and found the written records to be "out of order." The report clearly stated that after two days of checking serial numbers the officer in charge of the cargo was transferred stateside.

No.

No god damn it, he wasn't.

He's in Korea right now.

Wait. Was there another officer? Are there other officer's and noncoms involved? What's going on here? Do we really have Americans dealing arms with the Chinese? Are they selling them to the French?

He brought the papers up closer to his eyes as he stopped pacing. The tent was dark, but the light provided by the hibachi and his Coleman lantern were enough to keep reading.

The report continued: No further investigation is pending. Looking up, he asked himself the important question again, Which officer in charge? He closed his eyes. My God, there's someone missing here. They killed the guy. Isn't that what Taylor said would happen if I fucked up?

No. There was no officer in charge. It was probably a noncom in charge. Yes, that's it. They put enlisted in charge of these shipments. Delaplane? Did he replace the guy who was killed. Did he know him? Or was that a hoax?

Or am I the replacement?

A chill ran up his backside like someone had poured ice water over him. Who killed the guy? Delaplane? Taylor?

Yes, that was it. One of them. Sergeant Delaplane was in charge while he watched the shipment he traveled with. They don't endanger officers with this stuff. Taylor is top level. That Marine, what's his name? Kramer? Dutch, yes, Dutch Kramer. He's top level. But me? No way. Okay, so why am I suddenly wrapped up in this crap. And who put me into this PMO spot?

Bradford. Bradford? I've lied to him and he knows what the hell I've been up to?

No. He would have told me from the get go. He doesn't play games.

Shit. Taylor set me up. They own me. They took me out to that ship and blew the son of a bitch up. The Geisha? Makimoto killed them, not me. But Taylor told Tofte that I had. And Juliana! Who the hell is she?

CIA!

He paced again, continuing his circle around his hibachi. He had to work through this.

"Drier? Fraker? Why are they here? Now? Damn. Got to get them out of here. Two good men could be wasted. Can't let that happen."

He sat back into his camp chair and leaned toward the hibachi. He stoked the coals while he put his mind in gear. The officer thing. If they didn't have an officer, then why all of a sudden do they need one? Why me?

They don't endanger officers rang in his head over and over until he finally got it. It wasn't a noncom. A noncom couldn't get someone transferred for hiding an investigation. It was Taylor. Taylor was the officer in charge. But he's a colonel and that, hell, that would really bring the world down on the army if a colonel was caught dealing in arms with an enemy or an ally, no matter who authorized it.

His attitude brightened. An army colonel. It was him after all. Taylor signed on with the CIA before they even got here. He was caught on a mission like I was on. He was still active army so instead of having his career chopped off the CIA steps in and bingo. A PR nightmare handled swiftly.

He shook his head.

It's all so clear now.

Nearly everyone in the CIA over here is military or former military. Tofte was an army colonel. Goddamn it. Taylor was doing what he was hired to do. He was investigating himself. He was always in the CIA. He came out of the Deuce. He was probably with the OSS. Holy Jesus Christ.

His brain nearly froze.

He had been assigned this job so that he would be in charge of investigating himself if something happened. But Bradford or someone at EUSAK threw a monkey wrench into the deal. This guy, Hawk, was in charge of investigation instead of Strickland.

I'm shit for Shinola.

Or am I? Bradford said EUSAK sent this guy up here.

And someone in EUSAK fixed Taylor? Or did they?

He glanced into the small metal mirror that hung on the canvas near the entry. He picked at his chin while the thoughts continued to race through his mind. What's happened since Taylor's event? Delaplane, he remembered abruptly, said nobody hassled them. That's the talk of a criminal.

Maybe he's not really in the army. Didn't know much about shooting a rifle. Never had seen combat and he's a four stripe sergeant.

He's pure CIA? He has no military assignment even though he's over here as a soldier.

"It's as though none of us exist," he said aloud. "The CIA will dispose of us, the Marines will either court martial me or hang me without a trial. Or, he said aloud, "They kill me and that'll be that. I'm fucked and I haven't done a damned thing but follow orders."

He walked slowly to the hibachi and squinted into the whimpering but colorful coals. Delaplane said something else didn't he? Yes, he said, . . .sometimes we could run off with the whole shipment ourselves. We could make a lot of money.

He looked up with a totally new thought.

"So, that's it," he blurted. "That's the discretionary stuff. The optionals. Tofte's got his own goods coming in, plus they're confiscating materiel from the field. And Sergeant Delaplane's most likely making deals of his own." he stopped. "He as much as said so. He was trying to tell me something. Test me? Was I in or out?"

Hold it Frank, slow down. He said Truman had authorized the weapons for the Frenchies. Something about millions of dollars. He had authority to spend over a hundred fifty million dollars.

Spend it or steal it?

"Those bastards! They're taking weapons and ammo from our fresh supplies. That goddamned pirate captain probably had contraband from Guam. And from the battlefield. He's handing all of that to the French and keeping the goddamned Truman money."

He shook his head almost violently. No, he shouted inwardly. The weapons are coming here on that pig of a boat but that captain's not smart enough to steal it. So, let's assume Truman did authorize weapons for the French to be passed through Korea. If so, why are these guys shipping them materiel off the field?

So, partial loads of new stuff but not all the new stuff, and partial loads of recovered materiel. How do they accomplish this? Switch trucks. The trucks are unregistered.

They're selling the new arms?

To the Chinese? The NKs?

His mind raced back to the Chosin. The Chinese were using Russian weapons.

He plunked down into his camp chair again. He realized just then that he had no idea what the hell was going on other than Tofte and Taylor and everyone else involved in this arms transfer was probably making a profit off government materiel and costing Americans their lives.

The French?

He looked up. We know about their brutality against the natives in Vietnam. Why would we help them with that war? No! They're trading these to the NKs for what? Good God! Instead of handing over the gold bars Tofte mentioned he used for downed pilots, they're handing over weapons and keeping the gold.

It came together solidly for him. Gold and new weapons and our lost weapons, and sinking hospital ships, and I'm in the middle of it.

He felt his forehead. It was wet. His neck was drenched. He was sweating and it had nothing to do with the hibachi. For the first time in his life, he was afraid for his life. This was the kind of stuff you couldn't fight, could not defend against.

And might never figure out.

He glanced around his tent as though there might be some help available, but instead his mind once again froze on a name.

Kim. He must know more than he's told me.

The shimmering glow from the hibachi finally caught Strickland's attention as though it had been trying to all evening. "Kim," he said aloud.

His whole being exploded with new fear.

He tore out of the tent and ran as fast as he could through a foot deep of new snow to the motor pool. Kim would have the answers, if Kim was alive, Aww Dammit! If Kim is alive.

A single sentry, a relief for Donovan and Winfield greeted him at the compound.

"PFC Jack Delgado, sir," he replied when Strickland demanded his name.

"The prisoner. Where is he?"

"Tucked away, Captain. He's in the tank."

Strickland shoved the sentry aside and went straight to the tank. He leaped up to the tank's deck. All the hatches were battened down. Delgado came up alongside, out of breath and confused.

"Something wrong, Captain?"

"Dammit!" Strickland yelled. He yanked open the top hatch. "Open the driver's hatch, Marine. Quickly!"

Delgado jumped down and popped open the hatch. It was dark inside the tank except for the dying glow of the hibachi coals. Then his field flashlight caught sight of Kim. "Shit," Delgado blurted. "Fuck, fuck, fuck."

Strickland jumped down alongside him. "Get him out of there," Strickland ordered. "Now!"

"Damn it Captain. Damn it, damn it. They're gonna blame me for this, sir."

He climbed up to the top hatch of the tank hoping he could get into the vehicle and pull the NK out that way, possibly save him. But he was too late. They spread Kim out on the snow. He was as dead as you can get.

"Aww, shit, Captain. I'm shit for brains, ain't I?"

Strickland placed his hand on Delgado's shoulder. In a soothing, calm voice he said, "No son. It's not your fault. It's mine."

The two men stared at Kim for a few moments, then Strickland said in a matter of fact voice, "You won't be held responsible for this, private. It was just a dumb mistake on the prisoner's part, one I could have stopped earlier."

He ordered the sentry to find the O.D.

While the sentry went off for the officer of the day, Strickland stared at Kim who had asphyxiated from the carbon monoxide created by the burning coals of the hibachi.

Dammit, goddammit, Strickland swore to himself. He would have to think things through more carefully in the future. The man he could have obtained some answers from was dead and he had set him up for it and all without intending any harm come to the man. Abruptly, he felt the biting cold of the Korean wind that slipped inexorably across the ice-crusted ground. He kicked at the snow a few times, then turned and headed back toward his tent. One thought stuck in his mind now. He was convinced that Tofte and Taylor had seduced him into the scheme of arms for the Frogs for a reason he never before considered.

Tofte and Taylor were ripping off the U. S. Government. And I'm the only officer they can tag. I'm going to take the fall if their goddamned scam doesn't work, he said to himself.

Drier was tiring. Limping was bad enough, but sloshing through a few feet of a lousy mixture of dry and wet snow with his bad leg was even worse. So, Fraker had become his crutch for a while. His arm was over Fraker's shoulders while the two forged straight ahead. What seemed more serious to Drier was that he actually considered throwing away his walking stick, but in the end he had decided not to.

Just when things were looking bleak the sound of a six-by's engine reached their ears.

"Truck coming," Snake said.

He stopped walking and looked behind them to search for the vehicle. Blackout lights could be seen while the truck pushed through the snow. Drier was relieved to see that it was a U.S. Army truck. It pulled up to a brake-squealing stop.

"You fellas need'n a lift?" the driver called out while he kicked the passenger side door open.

They climbed in and sat tightly together on the bench seat of the large truck.

"Thanks," Snake said. He reached his hand over to shake the driver's hand. "Sergeant Fraker. This here's Lieutenant Drier."

"Nice to meecha. Sergeant Delaplane. Stanley to you."

"There goes our only link with the materiel found by the Seventh Marines," Hawk groaned.

"It's my fault," Strickland said. "I don't feel a bit good about this. I told the sentries to make sure he was kept warm and they did."

Hawk put his hand on Strickland's shoulder as though he were laying it on his own son. "Take it easy on yourself Frank. The hibachi is new to our troops."

"It was my job to warn them."

Hawk shook his head. "No. It was just another snafu." He gazed around then brought his attention back to Strickland. "We'll have to put a warning out so that our men don't kill themselves trying to keep warm with the damned things."

They walked together through the white powder to the mess tent where they sat at the end of a plywood table.

"What this country doesn't need," Hawk complained, "is more snow."

Strickland just nodded his agreement. For the first time in his life he was upset that he'd caused the death of an enemy soldier. Especially since the man might very well have had the answers to his questions. He was also quiet because he figured he was being tested now by the colonel. For what, he wasn't sure, but the man seemed a bit too keenly interested in chatting.

They drank their coffee, passed on the meal the cook said was reconstituted powdered eggs, powdered milk and John Wayne biscuits, made with something that looked like flour but he wasn't sure.

Strickland decided to alter the course of the conversation. "Colonel Bradford told me that the commies are locating our supply depots for their MiG attacks from someone but we don't know who. I also read Tilmon's reports last night. He had tried to figure it out before he left here."

Hawk rubbed his stubble with his right hand. He looked into Strickland's eyes with his own head bent down, his attention seemingly drawn by the warm coffee. "That's one of my assignments. We aren't sure. Some say spies. Others think the boys who visit the bars are spilling the beans."

"Whores?"

"Yes. Those kinds of bars. Prostitutes," Hawk said, more gentleman like. "We don't have the resources to put men on that.

We've spoken with the Koreans, but they aren't exactly keen on the idea of cleaning up prostitution."

Strickland bit into one of the biscuits. "What the hell is this?"

Hawk laughed and downed some coffee. "That'll teach you, Frank. Pay attention to the cook next time. C-rations are almost better than what you'll get in this mess." He looked at his watch. "Reveille in a few hours. Better get some shut eye."

"I'm up for the day, sir. Not been a good night."

Hawk stood but then seemed to remember something. "I haven't seen Drier or Fraker since I sent them out. Could you look into that for me? Make sure they got back safely. And oh, one other thing. If you want to work on the MiG thing, it's okay with me. I think you'd have to visit Seoul for that, though."

Strickland nodded.

CHAPTER 22

STRICKLAND'S JEEP SKIDDED to a stop at the rear of the CIA Quonset known as "The Hut." He paused a few seconds to reflect on his own history with similar huts. The CIA building was straight out of the Big Deuce, where it had been used as a "pisser" for Marines on an airfield at Espiritu Santo in the New Hebrides. The main hatch, as Marines referred to doorways, had seen better days. The hinges had corroded but like an old bricklayer's knees, they still worked, even though they squeaked a lot. The hatch cover, in this case a lightweight plywood door, had been slammed, jammed, kicked, slugged and darned near bombed out during its life and it still survived. So, what did one more pissed off Marine pushing through it mean?

He angrily, and with purpose, slammed the door against the ammo crates that were used sometimes as a door jam, with a sound that jarred Delaplane out of his inventory effort with Chong and Kyoo. Strickland had announced his entry and capped it off with a loud statement that surprised even the Koreans, who were now used to the American's anger.

"Those goddamned whores are why the MiGs are blasting our supply depots." For Delaplane the declaration was out of the blue.

He set his clipboard down, nodded to the two Koreans to keep on working. He went to the coffeepot to pour Strickland a cup.

"What are you talkin' 'bout, Cap'n?" He kept his eyes on the Marine. As far as he was concerned, Strickland was a bit possessed by demons if not simply insane. He was also ranting about something Delaplane had not heard of before and did not care about.

Strickland thrust a piece of paper into Delaplane's space. "We're losing fuel, tons of munitions and food to commie air attacks. The Chinese are using our loses to strengthen their position at the talks. And nobody's doing a thing about it including this goddamned Third Army of yours."

Delaplane glanced at the report, handed it back.

"What the hell's that got to do with us, Cap'n? Let the flyboys worry 'bout it." Before Strickland could respond, Delaplane added, "Ya know, Cap'n, you just can't win this war all by yourself. I know you've tried, but I learnt in this man's outfit that one job at a time is 'bout all we're good for."

Strickland's voice rose higher. He was truly angry now and he needed to vent. "I'll draw it out for you. When we lose supplies, we lose men. That's what this war's *about*, Sergeant."

"We can't do a danged thing 'bout that, Cap'n." Delaplane shoved a pea green Melmac cup into Strickland's hand. Anything to calm the bastard down, he thought. "Look, sir, you already got us into a heap of dung. Stick with the mission. We'll all be better off."

"Not likely as long as my guys are getting killed."

Delaplane threw his arms in the air and headed back to his two Koreans. "I can't help."

"Yes. You can."

Delaplane stopped. He looked at Kyoo and Chong and then slowly turned back to Strickland. "How's that?"

"You know where the prostitutes are."

"You're takin' this cop thing a bit too serious, sir. I told you that I knew where some of the them are. Crap Cap'n, maybe a dozen of 'em. Can you imagine how many whores there are in this country? In Tokyo? C'mon Cap'n. Get real."

Strickland set his coffee on a dark wooden crate that was stenciled in bold black military type fonts: "30.06 - AP."

"Take me to them."

"What good is that going to do? You gonna kill a few hookers in Seoul?"

Seoul was the location of the Korean command's information center. It was also just a few miles east of Inchon where MacArthur had shelled, bombed, and practically destroyed everything in his path in order to make a landing that would cut the enemy in the south from the enemy in the north. More civilians than military died in that assault.

"Why would I be takin' you there, sir?" Delaplane had already heard from Taylor about Strickland at the Tokyo bathhouse. He wasn't aware that it was Makimoto who did in the prostitutes, but instead believed the tale from Taylor. He glanced to Chong and Kyoo. They were still working, but Delaplane knew they had heard them and that wasn't a good thing. Turning back to Strickland he said, "Let's talk outside, Cap'n."

The sky had swung from dark storm clouds to severe clear with fresh sunlight washing the sky to a pale cobalt. The glistening but melting ice and snow forced them to put their sunglasses on. They stood next to Strickland's jeep.

"Cap'n," Delaplane said with resignation, "I gotta tell you sumthin'. We're s'pose to stay low profile on this job. You are my boss. You are s'pose to sign off on transfers. You, sir, are s'pose to protect this area from buttinskies." Delaplane stopped. He glanced to the broken down dock and the racing river and then back to Strickland. With more calm to his voice he said, "I met your friends, sir. Sergeant Fraker and Lieutenant Drier. Nice men. Good men. I gave 'em a hitch. They was in trouble on the road last night. Walkin'. I mean the lieutenant had a crutch with him and he was pushing through that damned storm last night. Gutsy."

"Get to the point, sergeant."

"They had found the truck you blew up."

Strickland flinched visibly. Delaplane was testing him, pushing on him. He was instantly pissed at himself for allowing his expression to change, even though it was so little a change.

"They went out to inspect the area where you left our cargo."

Strickland already knew that, but he contemplated Delaplane's statement and his reason for jumping to this info. He paced a few steps then turned back. In his mind he'd done nothing wrong. Except maybe the part where he didn't report his actions.

"Did they know who you were?"

"Sergeant Stanley Delaplane, U. S. Army. And nothin' more. But they's keepin' their eyes on you. You aware of that?"

Strickland scoffed audibly. "I doubt those two would tell you that sergeant. So what's this crap all about?"

"I got a crypto from Taylor. More 'n you is investigatin' those supplies you dumped on the Seventh. Seems like all of Korea wants to know what the hell happened. Good goin'. Sir."

Strickland pondered Delaplane's words. Others were investigating his actions? So, this wasn't to be exactly like Taylor's own experience. And why are so many people looking into this? Simple answer, Frank, he said to himself. Because this isn't the first time it's happened. But this time they want answers.

"Did they learn anything out there?" he asked.

"Jesus. You listenin' to me, Cap'n. Taylor knows about them two goin' there and he's madder'n shit. You done it. Sir. You fixed us a good one."

Strickland decided that Delaplane was not being straight with him. Why would he be? The man had proved he was a one concept jerk, and that concept was to save only his own hide.

"How did they learn that, Sergeant?" His voice became menacing. It was enough to back Delaplane off a bit.

"I told 'em."

Strickland's gaze bore through Delaplane's veneer. "Finish your inventory, Sergeant and then turn it over to me. And then be ready to travel to Seoul."

Delaplane now feared for his life. "Cap'n, you ain't getting' it. Where ever we go, those two are gonna know 'bout it. We go see them whores and they'll know. We do anything, and they's gonna be on our ass." He meant the two of them would become targets.

"Someone's got to send a message to those hookers. And your the one who's going to help deliver it."

Delaplane froze for a second or two. It was enough time for Strickland to see his expression and the fear that blocked out his earlier cockiness.

While Delaplane spoke, Strickland took the driver's seat in the jeep.

"Look, Cap'n, sir, let's get somethin' straight 'tween us. We're the same age. Served the same number of years. Sorry I ain't seen no combat, but I have seen the political side of what's goin' on here. You, me, we're just pawns. So, we do what we're told. Now, sir, if you want some advice, I'd stick with the program and forget this whore stuff and the depot stuff and all that and help me cover our asses with this shit we ship to the French."

"Get into the jeep."

Delaplane's chin fell to his chest as though he'd just visited a French guillotine. "You out rank me. But we can't leave these guys alone." He pointed back to the two Koreans.

"Then get rid of them."

Delaplane shook his head. "Can't. Taylor would kill me. And that ain't no figure of speech."

"You're driving."

Delaplane shook his head while he tried to figure a way out of Strickland's plan. "Look, I got a good idea. Maybe we can work this out."

"You've got thirty seconds to tell me."

"I know the area where the whores are. They move around a bit to keep from gettin' kilt by their own police. Mean shits, those ones. I'll go to Seoul for you right now. I'll find the broads, many's I can. But you gotta stay here for me and make sure these two do the inventory without takin' half of it home with 'em. That's why we inventory. After I locate the ladies, I'll come back and take you to Seoul tonight. Best I can do. This shipment's due out of here day after tomorrow."

Strickland gave thought to Delaplane's idea. It wasn't bad. If he went cold turkey to Seoul it might take him days to find what he was searching for. He grabbed the top of the windshield frame in the roofless jeep and pulled himself up and out of the vehicle.

"Don't take too long." He reached down with his left hand and pulled out his standard issue Colt, which left him with only his ivory handled special on his right hip.

"Here. Take this with you. You shouldn't wander around Seoul unarmed."

Delaplane accepted the pistol. "I'll be quick." Then he added, "We've got an incoming due tomorrow. I'm told its a special for the Frogs." He smirked slightly and added, "It's a make-good 'cause of your nice gift to the Seventh." Then with a wink that bothered the living hell out of Strickland, he added, "Load's comin' in ten trucks. That's gonna create a traffic jam. Can you keep your pals from wanderin' the road?"

After Delaplane left, Strickland sat near the coffeepot where he could watch the two North Koreans. He poured a few hits of VAT 69 into his coffee and proceeded to drink the black stuff. At least the Scotch made downing the bitter coffee easier.

When the two Koreans were finished for the day, Chong approached him.

"All done," he said. He handed Strickland the clipboard with the inventory forms.

Strickland took it. "Bring your pal here."

Chong paused a moment, he became instantly fearful because of the sound in the Marine's voice. He'd heard that same inflection before from another American. A mean geseki, a word familiar to many of the American military. He called back in his native tongue for Kyoo to come up. When Kyoo arrived, Strickland stood from his seat and ordered them to sit.

They squatted on the deck of the hut, which was the ground itself. Strickland paced around them in a circle of sorts.

"You two are North Koreans?"

They nodded, although Kyoo waited for Chong to nod first. "We South Koreans now. North Korea Bad," Chong said, displaying a stutter that was caused mostly by his weak translations to English. "Very bad. Here better."

Strickland cocked his head back. "Why's that?"

"Communists take over country. Bad. Very bad. Kill old people. Kill babies. Kill everyone. Seki rule now. Bad."

"Yeah?" Strickland knelt down and looked straight into Chong's eyes. "Tell me something, pal. Where do we get these supplies? From our people or from yours?" He meant North Koreans.

Chong glanced to Kyoo then back to Strickland. He shrugged. "They come. We not know."

Strickland withdrew his ivory Colt from its holster. He played with it for a moment before speaking again.

"Now, tell me again. Where do we get these supplies? The used weapons, the crates all marked with the red dots?"

Chong's expression changed. He held his hands and arms up in a gesture of confusion. "Not know," he said. "Tell megook the truth. They come, we count, Sergeant Dee ship out."

"Duk-cho shibaalnom," Kyoo seemed to order Chong. They were the first words Kyoo had spoken since Strickland's arrival, and they surprised the Marine. Chong waved him off as if he wanted him to shut up. He returned his attention to Strickland.

"We not know. No more. We not know."

Strickland cocked his pistol. He aimed it directly at Chong's forehead.

"Where?"

Kyoo's eyes bulged out like a ballooning bubble on an old bicycle innertube.

"Battlefield," he blurted. "Some come from battlefield. That all I know."

Keeping the pistol to Chong's head, Strickland squinted at Kyoo and asked, "What battlefields? Where?"

Chong rolled his eyes over to Kyoo, then back to Strickland.

"He not speak English." He nearly smiled, recognizing that his own translations were slow to come.

Strickland turned to Chong and said, "Then, you tell me."

"From everywhere," he said pointing all around. "Sergeant get them. Pay sometime. Trade sometime. We stay here. Always."

Strickland rocked back. These guys knew more than they were alluding to. "Trade with who? Trade what?" He rattled the pistol at Chong as though he were about to lose control.

"My friends. A few. They get American weapons lost in the war. They bring here. Trade for food, clothes. Tents. Sergeant call them brass pickers."

"You're lying."

"No. True. Chong not want shoot. We not lie, 'rine."

Strickland's mind careened around a race track of questions. He was sure that someone was double-dealing. If it wasn't Delaplane, or Tofte or Taylor, then who? "You lie."

Chong thought he saw the end of his life coming. "No. No, Capt'n. Not lie. Can prove."

That's what Strickland was looking for. He motioned them to stand. They did. "Okay, prove."

Chong nodded to crates stacked along the west bulkhead. Strickland motioned for them to go there. At the crates, Chong opened the top box. When the lid came off, Strickland's eyes fell on the contents.

"Dammit! God damn them."

The crate held used army and Marine utility uniforms, jackets with names stitched over the left breast pocket. Some were stained with blood, some had holes in them from frags or bullets. He pulled them out until he came to one with an emblem of the 7th Army Division. The Faith RCT.

"Son of a bitch," he groaned. His anger meter climbed and so did the pitch of his voice. "Son of a bitch!"

Chong and Kyoo stepped back, moving stiffly toward the rear exit. The captain had been drinking, they could smell that, but his demeanor was more than a man with alcohol in him. A volcano would be a safer place to hang out.

Chong spoke softly while continuing to take one step at a time away from Strickland. His gaze was glued to Strickland's expressions with some wonderment of how many times the man's features changed as he rifled through the large crate.

"Sergeant use these to trade. He give that to people and get back weapons."

Strickland reached into the crate and pulled out a short piece of green ripstop nylon from one of the jacket tops. It was in the form of a scarf. His heart nearly stopped.

"Damnation Battalion!" His voice sounded disembodied, as though it gurgled up from an empty grave. Chong and Kyoo saw the fierce anger in the Marine's eyes. Just when they decided to run for it, Strickland spun around, raised his pistol and aimed directly at them. "You grave robbing assholes, stop!"

Chong and Kyoo froze. Chong looked back, "No, Cap'n Megook," he pleaded. "Not like you think. We not do this. Sergeant D has people. He trade."

"E kago shipsumnida," Kyoo muttered.

Chong spoke for him. "He need take piss."

Strickland went to them and pushed the pistol against Kyoo's forehead. "Then piss."

Chong shook his head. "Cap'n. We not steal. We work. We feed family. This only money we can make. We not do bad. Sergeant pay us. Not know what he do. Please. Don't kill. We can help," he said in desperation. "We help you."

"You're working for the communists."

Kyoo glanced to Chong, pleadingly, wanting the pistol taken away from his forehead. Chong's body sagged when he sighed, "No. We not communist. We hate communists. They kill our families. My father. My brother. Kyoo's mother and his brother. You not know how bad. Very bad. You good Megook. You kill communists. Make you good. We like that. We not communists."

A tear rolled down the usually unexpressive face of the speaker. Strickland wasn't so cold that he hadn't noticed the sincerity in the man's statements.

"How bad? The communists?"

"Burn our houses. Take our food. Take our babies. They kill our animals and then torture us." He whirled around and pulled up the back side of his shirt. "See."

Strickland's eyes fell on long scars that creased across Chong's back from his neck to his buttocks. Chong then whirled around and pulled up the front side. They whip me here, too."

"Your own people did that?"

Chong nodded only. "They join communists. Become very bad."

Strickland released the pistol from Kyoo's forehead. "How can you help me?" Strickland's voice had returned to a normal tone and both Kyoo and Chong relaxed a bit, although not completely.

Chong nodded wildly. "First. Let him piss. We wait. He will come back."

Strickland eyed Kyoo suspiciously, then waved him out of the hut.

"He good man, 'rine. We not do this."

After a few moments, Kyoo returned, sheepishly but better off.

Chong pointed across the hut to a stack of boxes. "Those. Come from your country," he said. "They all new." Pointing to another stack, closer to them, he said, "Those, come from war."

Strickland appeared confused. "My country? They all come from my country."

"No. They come by ship to here. Not in battlefield. That come from battlefield. French not get all. Some go to north." He pointed to the battlefield goods.

"To the fucking commies?"

"Ssibural?" Kyoo actually chuckled. "Ssibural?"

Chong jumped in quickly. "He know one word, 'rine. That word you used. It's ssibural in Korean." He smiled. "We think it funny."

Strickland loosened his grip on the pistol. He was beginning to believe the two NKs.

Chong nodded. "Trade. Sergeant trade. For money. Not all go to Frenchman."

Strickland ripped open a crate while Chong and Kyoo held their position. When the lid came up, he staggered back a few feet. The stench from inside was awful. "Damn," he muttered. He glanced to Kyoo and Chong, decided they weren't going to run for it. "Pull that stuff out of there, Chong," he ordered.

Chong reached into the crate and slowly pulled up a Marine Corps field jacket. It had a huge hole and a blood stain on the front where the Marine had probably had his abdomen ripped open. He let it drop to the deck. Then he pulled out blood stained caps, trousers and socks. He stopped and peered down into the crate.

"Captain."

Strickland came up cautiously. He looked into the crate.

"Syringes? Plasma bottles?" He reached down and pulled up a used syringe. The first plasma bottle was empty. "Son of a bitch," he swore, "these are straight out of a MASH unit." A lightning sharp pain ran along his temple. Stepping back, he reached down to the deck and pulled up the field jacket. He read the name plate, a cloth patch stitched into the jacket over the left breast pocket.

And then he roared with such anger that the Quonset Hut seemed to shake. Kyoo and Chong ran from him when he raised his pistol and started firing shots through the roof. He then aimed at them and fired, but they ducked down behind crates. Bullets ripped through the crates, sending splinters off into all directions.

The roar of the gun was so loud that the ricocheting sounds bounded from bulkhead to bulkhead until the front door banged open and Delaplane appeared.

"What the goddamned hell's goin' on?" Delaplane yelled from the front hatch. "Don't shoot in here! You'll blow us all up."

Strickland spun around to face the sergeant.

"You mother'n assholes. You are going to hang."

Delaplane walked bravely into the hut. He approached Strickland until the Marine waved his Colt directly at him.

"Stop, Sergeant. That's close enough."

"I don't know what's sparked you, but I ain't gonna hang, and you ain't gonna get away with anythin' that Tofte or Taylor don't want."

Strickland threw the field jacket at him. Delaplane caught it, held it up, lowered it. "What's this?"

"It's from one of your crates. You going to sell it or donate it to the commies?" His voice still rang with anger while blazing fire poured violently from his eyes. "Read it, asshole. Read the name."

Delaplane held the jacket up, turned it around to find the name. Out loud he read, "Gibson." He looked to Strickland for an explanation. But what he found was a Marine Captain with free flowing tears streaming down his face. "Jesus. You knew him?"

Strickland turned away. He couldn't speak. Delaplane glanced to Kyoo and Chong, nodded for them to sit. They did. He pulled the hatch cover and closed the hatch. He walked to Strickland. Strickland took in a deep breath and turned back to Delaplane.

"This is my war, Sergeant. These uniforms were taken off my Marines, men I trained and fought with."

"We can't separate 'em—"

"Shut up! You're trading with the goddamned commies." He wiped the involuntary tears away. He waved the Colt wildly while he spoke, forcing Delaplane to nervously duck away from the dangerous weapon.

"Taylor says—"

"Taylor?" Strickland yelled. He stepped to Delaplane and demanded, "Just what do you know about Taylor's doings, Delaplane? Tell me!"

Delaplane looked away. It seemed to the three men in the hut that he was silent for a very long time. When he turned back and spoke, his words flowed smoothly with a different pace than he usually used.

"It ain't Taylor the one's in charge. It's Tofte. Taylor's just a goddamned hack like you and me." He turned back to look Strickland in the eyes. "And Tofte answers to the president. Swear to God. Whatever happens here, happens 'cause of Tofte and his boss. I'm just a truck loader. No less, no more." He stepped away from Strickland, bumping into the crates behind him. "I'm sorry if this has touched your nerves," he said with his voice quivering. "But maybe you'll help me soon's I 'splain some things."

Strickland glanced back to Chong and Kyoo, saw them edging their way to the back hatchway. "Stop!" he shouted. He raised his pistol toward them.

"No, Cap'n. Don't do that. Let 'em go."

Strickland turned back to Delaplane. "There's no excuse for all this, Sergeant. Naval Intelligence and your goddamned CID will be very interested to learn about this op."

"Cap'n, sir. You made a deal. You can't report any of this 'cause they'd slam you in the stockade. Or the nut house. And you can't bug out 'cause the long arm of the agency will squash you like a bug." Delaplane paused long enough to make Strickland believe he was done, but he wasn't.

"Tofte will have us both kilt prob'ly by someone nearby. And sir, someone in your Corps knows you are doing this. Your job was authorized by someone higher up. Probly higher than Bradford."

Strickland waved his pistol at Delaplane as though it were a baton. "Keep talking."

"You fucked up this job, sir, and you might's well figure on gettin' a ticket to hell." Delaplane came away from the crates, moved closer to Strickland. "Cap'n, when I first learned of this, I became so pissed I got drunker'n hell and then pistol whipped to death the first two Koreans I ran into. Lucky for me, Mr. Taylor understood."

"Wake up Delaplane. What he understood was that he suckered you into it. That's how they get you. That's how they own you. They killed those two Koreans, not you."

Delaplane considered that for a moment. "Maybe."

Strickland's voice changed again. Anger was reappearing. "Lieutenant Gibson's jacket. The others. You paid for them. With what? Why? Do you trade them for gold? Favors? What?"

Delaplane was clearly frustrated. His mind was tiring and his spirit had died a lot earlier in the day. He wanted to change the subject, get back on course, but the Marine in front of him wasn't about to let that happen.

"Taylor explained to me that these uniforms and stuff we get? Well, we trade 'em for these weapons and munitions that the Koreans pick up from the battlefield. Sometimes they shred them so that the north can make paper or other goods. If the uniforms are in good condition, they told me they sell them to their citizens who have money and who are in need of the cloth."

"Your friends here say you trade them for money."

Delaplane ran his forefinger around the collar of his utility shirt. "They don't know jack 'bout nothin' here. Like I said, the Korean citizens accept everything, even the shot up jackets and utilities. They make somethin' out of 'em. Our KIAs will get their revenge, is what Taylor said mostly 'cause we get munitions for them. Yes, sir. The Frogs will use the weapons we get in trade," he nodded to Gibson's jacket, "to kill more commies. Cap'n, does it really matter who fights on our side or where? Or with what?"

Strickland returned his pistol to its leather home. "What about the materiel that's supposedly from the states? Was that all a lie?"

"That's straight as hell the truth, Cap'n. Tofte hisself told me that Truman authorized over a hunderd million for that. But like that three-five you used that first night when the Chinks attacked us? The used stuff is mixed in sometimes with the new stuff. Don't know where that happens or why. Taylor and Tofte are the ones who handle that. The Agency's got sumthin' goin', a deal of some kind. I don't know what. But it works. The commies don't shoot at me and for that I'm grateful. All's I know, is that when I get back from a tradin' mission, or when we get here with the trucks, I got to get the stuff 'board the Frenchie boats and out of here."

Strickland ran the words through his mind again. The Agency's got something going? With commies? And this Sergeant? Didn't he have something going, too? Wasn't that what he figured out earlier? Didn't the two Koreans tell him that?

Delaplane stepped back a few feet. "Cap'n," he said, "it's okay. You've got to look at it like it's just another part of the war effort."

"Do you ever meet with them?" Strickland asked. His voice seemed calm again like the serene back flush of an ocean's wave on a shining surface of sand.

"A few. The ones who bring the stuff here. Sometimes we meet them up north on the road. We exchange the goods there." After a few moments he added, "Never liked that part. Scares the bejesus out of me."

Strickland chewed on Delaplane's words. He would be here next time materiel arrived. Abruptly changing the subject, he asked, "The whores? Were you able to locate them?"

Delaplane sounded relieved.

"Some that I believe our military guys are blabbin' to. Yes, sir. Had to bribe a Seoul cop for the info. Cost me a case of forty-five ammo."

Strickland glanced around the hut. He stared hard at Chong and Kyoo for a few beats, then turned back to Delaplane.

"Okay," he said fingering his pistol, "Let's go."

CHAPTER 23

DELAPLANE CAREFULLY WEAVED the jeep through the broken streets of Seoul right up to the nose of an alley in the western outskirts of the city. He wanted to penetrate deeper into the narrow street, but rubble and chunks of buildings had not been removed since the invasion at Inchon, which had included massive bombardments of Seoul. He parked the jeep in an open space surrounded by concrete, rebars and one unidentifiable overturned and burned out car.

Without speaking, Delaplane pointed down the alley, got out of the jeep and after a moment of waiting for Strickland to come alongside they headed toward the area where he'd promised the Marine his whores.

Delaplane started humming, something Strickland had not heard from the man before. He was walking and humming a familiar tune.

"You going to break out in song next?" Strickland said.

Delaplane pulled up to a stop. "Uh, sorry, Cap'n. Just comes outta me at times. Don't know why I do it. I heard this one in camp last night, over and over. Some nut with a Victrola."

"Mills Brothers." Strickland had to smile to himself. He'd found the nut with the record player and told him to stop playing country songs. So the guy must have switched to the Mills Brothers.

"Across the Alley From the Alamo. Dang. We're in an alley and I start humming an alley tune. Weird."

Strickland agreed without saying so. Instead he motioned him to move on.

Concrete, clay and dried mud lay gray in the light. Bent metal and broken vehicles became accents to what Strickland visualized as war time art.

Fire had gutted most of the surrounding buildings, which were than assaulted by flowing mud caused by heavy rains after American generals had destroyed the city. Nature had finished off what MacArthur couldn't.

Delaplane led him around a huge chunk of concrete and broken glass to the only doorway still standing. He'd been here earlier. Nothing had changed. Even the sounds were the same, or he thought, the lack of sound.

Strickland stopped. The door was gone but someone had built a shield against weather or to keep people or unwanted guests out. It was more a psychological shield than one of iron or steel. Cloth and beads and strings of sewn poncho material hung from an overhead pipe that more than likely was a water line before the Americans altered the area. Delaplane pointed. "You'll find what you're lookin' for in there."

Strickland brushed past the sergeant. Delaplane followed him in.

Getting up before reveille was rubbing thin on Drier. Especially after spending a long day chasing after mysterious ghosts that he figured were already vaporized. He reached down and rubbed his legs. The walk through the snow hadn't helped. Bullshit bravado, he thought. Never again. Besides things seeming to have been fruitless, they had never been able to get with the skipper to make their report. 2300 hours was a bit too late to awaken anyone like that man. And of course he remembered Snake's attitude after that jaunt in the snow wasn't very pleasant.

The bravado had gone only so far to conceal his own pains, which still haunted him without relief. Pains from his wounds that now made him wonder why he turned down the offer to return to the states.

Dumb shit.

He limped off his cot, stumbled across the complaining wooden deck and picked up his Dopp kit. He would have to put a rush on things. The Colonel, he knew, was already up and at them. He would be looking for his aide.

With only his olive colored skivvies in place he rolled back the tent flaps to head to the shower. Korean snow had turned into Korean rain, which had settled into the pocket of canvas above the flap, giving Drier an earlier than planned shower when he pushed the flaps aside. "Aww, Christ. Is it going to be that kind of day?"

"Morning, Lieutenant," Hawk greeted when Drier entered the officer head.

"Morning, Colonel."

"Still getting a grip on this bivouac life, eh?" Hawk teased.

Drier mumbled something about it being too early for any living breathing thing and plopped his Dopp kit down on the unpainted plywood table near the shower.

Hawk zipped his kit closed, a military-clone of the green canvas bag like Drier's. "I've received an interesting report from the Koreans out of Seoul, Lieutenant. Came in by pony express around 0330. Orderly woke me with it." He picked up his towel, slung it over his shoulder and headed out.

"Sir?"

"Soon as you're ready, I'll brief you. And I would like to be with you and Colonel Bradford when you brief us on your investigation last night. Get some breakfast first."

Drier nodded with a weak, "Yes, sir."

"And Lieutenant, I want you to go to Seoul for me today. Going to be a busy day for you. Are you up to that?"

Drier peered into the mirror that hung over the plywood then turned and smiled tightly at Hawk. "Yes, sir." After Hawk left he turned back to the mirror and said, "I guess this beats getting kicked around by gooks."

"You bet your sweet ass it does," a chuckling Strickland greeted.

Drier whirled around to find Frank Strickland entering the head. "Skipper. Didn't see you. I mean, great to see you."

Strickland grinned. He set his Dopp kit down and after checking the mirror to make sure he could see himself, he turned back to Drier. He reached out to shake Drier's hand.

"It's truly good to see you, David. My god, look how healthy you are." He glanced to Drier's leg. "Amazing recovery."

"Good to see you, too, Skipper. They let me out of the hospital because I was causing too much trouble." He smiled broadly. "That was my plan. And sir, thanks for visiting me. I swear that kept me going."

"No sweat. The trouble you caused was mentioned by that doctor of yours. I think he found it humorous. The nurses disagreed."

"I believe that." Drier lowered the razor from his face and asked, "Did you know that Snake and I were looking for you yesterday?"

"No. In camp?"

"Yes, sir. But we had to head out to check out the location where the Seventh found those trucks. Going to brief the colonels after chow. You going to be there?"

Strickland's mind froze for a moment. His kid, the man he thought of as a son, was investigating his actions. He caught his breath, held his composure. "Yes. I'll make sure I'm there." Then with a weak effort at acting as though he wasn't interested he asked, "Did you find anything important?"

Drier shook his head. "Nothing I consider helpful. I think the army guys who looked into it the next day pretty much swept the area. Did find a piece of lead, looks like it might have been involved, but no way of telling. The lead looked like it had been a bullet." He turned to Strickland, "Like the kind you use."

"Lot of NKs and Chinese used lead."

"That's what Snake said. After that, nothing. Guess we weren't a big help. And, oh, sorry. My groggy mind is sort of screwed up this morning. We found what looked like a truck that had been blown up. Farther up the road from the truck site. Looked like a bunch of NKs took an arty or something. Spooky area. In a hole sort of. The round had to come at them practically vertically. Maybe one of our flyboys got 'em."

Strickland felt some relief. "We know about that one," he said. "How are you doing all this with that leg? It's gotta hurt a lot."

"Yes. I braved it for a while but last night did me in. Hate to sound un-Marine like, but I ducked the pain with pain pills. Hate those. They plug me up badly." Drier picked up his worn out toothbrush and sprayed tooth powder on it from a military green tin.

"You expect me to buy into that, David? You ducking pain, I mean." Strickland slapped his cheeks a couple of times to wake up. He then lathered up some shaving cream in a small metal container and brushed it across his face. While he went to work with a straight razor he broke the momentary silence with a question. "Do you remember the three rules of being a fighter that we learned at the reservoir?"

Drier slowed his toothbrush. "Sir?"

"Ruthlessness, mostly. Then courage, and lastly, brains. Or was it the other way round?"

Drier stopped brushing. He stared into the mirror at his own eyes wondering where this was going.

"The ability to make a decision at the flash of an artillery round and live with it. To decide whether to kill or be killed, or send other men to their death."

"That would be judgment, wouldn't it?"

"No, David. I mean hero stuff. You, more than most of the others know there's no time allotted in this man's corps for perfect judgment. We are taught that, but we never are given time to practice it. It has to be a natural act, a reaction we live through many times instead of an action only once." He paused, held his razor motionless while he finished. "Judgment. Like it's out of a book or something. Written down neatly, succinctly and defined so well you don't ever have to think at times of action. You do everything by the book."

Drier turned to Strickland. "We rewrote the book at the Chosin. So, what's this about, Skipper?"

"You weren't in pain yesterday. You know that?"

Drier shook his head, meaning he didn't know what Strickland was getting at.

"You were ducking the job not the leg. You were built to fight, David. Built for combat and now you're in an admin job and it is that, that hurts. No place for you to fight, no place here to make snap decisions or let that testosterone run rampant. That's what you were both missing. So, son, get off the kick that you were hiding from pain in your leg. You don't have pain in your leg. Got it?"

Drier seemed surprised and excited at the same moment. "Goddamn, Skipper. You nailed it."

"You bet your sweet ass I did. Listen up. We have admin jobs here. The rules don't change like they do on the battlefield. We are supposed to be cops or something like that and neither one of us knows how to do that well, or has had any experience with it."

"Agreed."

"So, we can't be Mike Hammer here. I figure we do our best and let the admins figure things out."

Mike Hammer was Mickey Spillane's fictional detective.

The ammo storage unit at the Marine encampment was a medium sized metal unit that looked like a former shortened railroad freight car without windows. In fact, it had been a cargo box aboard an AKA. AKA was the navy's designation for "attack cargo ships." Originally commissioned as AK, the ships discharged cargo and equipment on beachheads.

It was inside this unit that the officers met to discuss Drier's findings as well as plans for how to push ahead with an investigation that no one of them felt comfortable with. The ammo dump, as it was referred to, would help keep their conversation private. They could no longer discuss the case in Bradford's canvas pyramidal.

The unit was no larger than the tents. It was fairly empty of ammo, too. Only about ten crates of 30.06 were stacked at the back of the space. One crate of .45 ammo, the full metal jacket type, was available. The rest of the unit's ammo was stored in a similar unit at a location they referred to as "the range," although the range needed more work before it could be considered complete.

Folding chairs had been brought to the unit and the five men sat in those, around a table that Corpsman Dobbins had provided from the med tent. It was actually a metal tray table used for the doctors at sick call. It held things like swabs, tweezers, gloves, etc.

Since Fraker was a top sergeant and was considered part of the investigation, he sat with them. Present were Bradford, Hawk, Drier, Strickland and Fraker.

Since the box had no ventilation, the door was left open about a foot. Outside the sentry assigned to keep others away was Private Winfield, who was now known throughout camp as Scar face.

Bradford, out of regard for the others, kept his pipe quiet. Fraker's cigar was absent, and each of the others appreciated him for it. None of the others smoked. Bradford began the meeting.

"Lieutenant Drier and Sergeant Fraker had a tough night of it last night." He smiled at Drier. "Hope you're doing well now. You want to tell us what you found." It wasn't a question but instead a directive.

Drier outlined pretty much what he'd already told Strickland. When he finished he looked to Fraker and asked him if he'd left anything out. That's when Strickland tensed up. He knew Snake well. Snake might have seen signs that Drier missed. Snake was a scout, a man with experience in running down clues left on the ground and even in the air.

"You purty much covered it, Lieutenant." He coughed lightly to clear his throat. When he spoke his words came out slowly, his mind capturing the previous evening as though he was playing back a slo-mo movie. "Did see somethin' though. Might be of interest. That truck we found. When I was lookin' at it I thought to myself that it purty much looked like the hit was fresh. Maybe a few days old. Tire tracks undisturbed. Bodies still there like the Lieutenant said. Some bloated like I seen before. I'm thinkin' that maybe it was part of the four trucks found by the Seventh. And oh, the men were wearing USA army fatigues. One had a 'Merican name plate still showin. Name was O'Neal."

Hawk was sitting back in his chair holding his chin with his right hand, moving his thumb back and forth under his jaw. His attention was glued to the sergeant who he decided was one hell of a good observer. "What's your feeling for why it blew up, Top?"

Fraker shrugged a little and said, "Like maybe the lieutenant said. A stray arty or an air strike."

"But you don't believe that, do you?" Hawk said.

Fraker glanced to Drier more in defense than anything and said, "Not really. The danged truck was in a hell hole. It might have hit a mine or just been hit by something from one of the ledges above. I mean it was in an area that reminded me of being in the bottom of a funnel. That'd be a tough hit for an arty or a plane. Real tough."

"How about if someone on board blew it up intentionally?"

Both Drier and Fraker looked at Hawk with surprise registered in their eyes. So did Strickland. They said nothing.

"The report said the trucks had three-fives aboard. Could one of those have done the damage you saw?" Bradford asked.

Snake took the question. "Colonel, a whole lot of things could have blown up that truck. I think it would take a witness in order to learn the truth."

Strickland said, "Were there any witnesses?"

Fraker looked straight at his friend. "Not that we know of." But Strickland thought the look in his eyes contradicted his statement. He'd have to chat with Snake later.

Bradford stood. "It's getting a big stuffy in here gents. Let's take ten. Get some fresh air. And oh, Top, get a detail together to bury those NKs."

* * * *

"Apparently it was as nasty as the St. Valentine's Day massacre," Hawk said as he handed a report to Drier and a copy to Strickland. "Late last night. Local cops reported to the army CID types that there were witnesses who said more than one American soldier was involved. CID sent this info to all units."

Bradford said, "We'd like you to check it out, David."

Drier was surprised. "What can I do there? I mean, what am I to look for?"

Bradford stood. The damned ammo dump was already getting stuffy again. He moved to the hatch and pushed it all the way open. "Private Winfield," he called out. "We'll leave this open." Winfield nodded. He'd been instructed to not salute any of the officers when they arrived or when they left. It was still a case of not being sure if all snipers had been cleared from the area.

Turning back to Drier, Bradford said, "This is not a normal assignment, David. In other words, I'm not sure what you can do there or learn there. I am sure that this war is big enough without this sort of thing. But, that report indicates that the ladies were killed with lead bullets."

Hawk finished for Bradford. "And you found what appears to have been a lead bullet at the site last night."

"Which means something or means nothing," Bradford said. He then turned to Strickland. "Frank, you know more about ammo than we do. You shot at Perry didn't you?"

"Yes, sir. For the Corps."

"And you made your own ammo. Did you ever make lead bullets?"

Strickland nodded. "Yes, sir. We all do. Practice with lead. Shooters that is. Much cheaper. The Corps supplies us with the raw material."

Bradford returned to his chair. "So, there you have it. It's down to ballistics. If you can find or obtain a piece of lead from the events in Seoul last night, possibly we can send the two down to navy forensics and get a reading."

"What will that show, sir?" Drier felt suddenly dumb.

"I should think that it would show we are looking for one person. One American military type, or if possibly we're barking up the wrong tree." He glanced at his watch, which was not military style but instead an expensive Bulova that had been given to him by his wife. "Time to get on the road, David. I think you can do all the above in one day."

Drier felt like he'd just swallowed a wild gooseberry with the thorns now stuck in his throat. This was not going to be a fun day. "Are they expecting me?" he asked.

Hawk answered. "We tried to contact army CID. It seems they aren't exactly cooperative. Maybe it's our com system or theirs, but no replies. That's the good news. The bad news? Koreans don't care much about what happens with this case. Prostitutes aren't high on their list of priorities. And something else. Take Fraker along. Their cops don't like being questioned by Americans. You might need back up."

"Yes, sir." He gulped and wet his lips and hoped his desire to avoid this trip didn't show too much.

"Your mission is the ammo. It's not solving the local problem. If you can find shells or lead, then we might be able to link the killer to our case."

Drier's throat parched even more. He couldn't even speak. Hawk saw his problem. "You need some water?"

Drier shook his head, coughed a little. "No, sir."

Snake spoke up. "I think the Lieutenant would like to know why we are interested in them women." Drier grinned at him and relaxed a whole lot. Thanks, Snake, he said to himself only.

Strickland surprised them by answering the question. "Prostitutes are suspected of working as spies. They sell the info they get from our men. To the NKs and Chinese."

Hawk added, "So, you might run into a two-pronged crime here. We just don't know yet."

Bradford pulled the unlit pipe from his mouth and said, "Just be damned careful gents. Consider yourselves still in enemy territory."

"Shouldn't the army CID guys be doing this?" Drier asked.

"Yes," Hawk said. "That was my thought."

Bradford cleared his throat and said, "Lot of crap going on over here. Lots of crap."

Drier thought through his assignment and what he already knew. Then without realizing it, he started thinking out loud. "Did the army report what kind of rounds killed the NKs? At the truck site?"

Bradford nodded. "They found one round. Lead, like the one you brought back. That makes two shots. Two victims, two shots."

Strickland's gaze fell to his hands that he had unconsciously cupped together on his lap.

The sharp sound of a Colt ricocheted through the narrow valley where Strickland had set up his own impromptu practice bench at what was supposed to be the camp's range. The range was to be run by the army, but the army was very slow at getting things down. At least at making the range right.

United States Army Corporal Anthony Bowers, the village's armorer who was responsible for all UN weapons repairs in the area watched while Strickland plugged away at paper targets with his ivory-handled .45. They'd made the targets out of old C-ration cartons by drawing black circles with a black grease pencil on the brown cardboard. The ten targets were then tacked to sticks they'd driven into the ground.

Bowers had already been ordered by the new PMO to construct a better range, but he'd not gotten around to it. He would have to take care of it this afternoon. Wouldn't take much, just some wood from supply and a few friends with hammers and nails. The target area would be a backhoe job. The target racks easier still.

And Bowers knew how to do it, too. He'd done it in his home town a few years ago. He'd been told by the judge who could have sent him to the county jail for six months, to rebuild the local school's playground equipment and do it quickly. That included three sheds for storing ball equipment and other stuff and a teeter totter for the younger ones. He was able to do it because his dad owned the local lumber yard, but, shit, even his old man charged money for the supplies. At least here, all he had to do was call down to the construction people who were preparing to build a village into a town and bingo, he'd have what he needed.

He recalled the assault charge against him for knocking another student around, a bully who had instigated the fight. The fight. That's what it had become known as. Big old Jeff Blast-in-the-Ass came at him again. He'd been the school bully only this time Bowers was ready. He whipped out the butt end of one of his dad's old wooden golf clubs and beat the "living shit" out of Jeff. He smiled inwardly.

For him, it had all been worth it. Old Blast-in-the-ass never bothered him or anyone else again. He heard another shot. He looked up from his reverie. Strickland was shooting again. Each round passed straight through the heart of each separate bulls-eye. Bowers wasn't overly impressed but this was an officer and so he did his thing and kissed ass.

"That's damned good shooting sir," Bowers said. Bowers was young although he appeared older. He was short, muscular and pink chinked. He was strong enough to press three ammo crates stacked one on the other. He'd also been with the army at the Chosin.

Strickland knew the man's short combat history and respected him for it. The kid was lucky, he thought. His unit was still in the thick of things and this youngster gets a transfer to the Village. His MOS was that of an armorer and God knew you needed a great armorer backing up your men after firefights. But men on the line needed him more than the admin types here. He considered it a wonder that the boy was now ensconced in a non-combat area. He wondered what kind of pull the kid had. "Want to try?"

"Yes sir," Bowers ran the two words together as though they were a compound word, as in yessir. "But I ain't that good with a pistol, sir. Just know how to fix them."

"I've read your jacket, Corporal. You're an expert with the M-1."

"Yes. Yes sir. Done a lot of shooting at varmints and all. Just not expert with the forty-five."

"Chinese? Get any of those?"

Bowers nodded. "A few. With my rifle."

Strickland nodded. He understood. "Here, try with this." He handed him his Colt.

"Mighty fine looking grip."

"Hand-carved. Cost me a bundle but it was worth it."

Bowers stepped up to the line that had been cut into the ground with the heel of Strickland's boot. They were approximately twenty five yards from the targets. He raised the pistol in the official one-arm stance and pulled the trigger. He missed the first target in the line of ten. The bullet landed higher in the pits, right where Bowers had had new dirt piled a few days before with the backhoe. He grinned. The bullet had kicked up a cloud of fresh dry dust.

"Keep your wrist locked," Strickland instructed. He grabbed Bowers' shooting hand and showed him. "Now, hold the pistol out like this. That's it. Now, your arm."

Bowers followed each instruction directly.

"Lock your elbow and your wrist. Spread your legs more. That's it. Straighten up your back, put your free arm out like this, and rest your other hand on your hip like this." He moved Bowers around as though he were a rag doll. "Shoot at my target this time. Let's see how close you can come to my holes."

Bowers nodded okay.

"Now, son! Now, you'll do well."

Bowers fired. The bullet passed through the target two inches from Strickland's hole. "Crap, sir. Look at that. I ain't ever shot like that." Bowers lowered the pistol and looked at it exhibiting what appeared to Strickland to be a look of mystery.

Strickland smiled. "You ain't ever been instructed by the best. Now, do it again. Only this time, start high and bring the pistol down through the target and squeeze slowly. Like it's your girl friend you're feeling for, huh? Time the move so that the trigger fires when you're passing through the black."

Bowers raised the pistol high and then let if float down. When he was near the target he began to squeeze the trigger. As the sights passed through the black, he finished the squeeze. Bang! "No hole. Damn, I missed."

Strickland laughed heartily. "Come with me," he said. He headed off toward the target with Bowers stringing along behind him. This kind of shooting was as curious to him as he was curious about the captain. Back home, most of the men shot pistols at cans and mostly from the hip. Who in the hell would stand up in combat and brace their legs and hold their arm straight out to kill a guy charging at you with bayonet or something. Not me.

Strickland picked the target up and showed it to Bowers. "See that?"

Bowers leaned closer. "Looks oval. How'd you do that? The hole's not round."

Strickland laughed again. "Your bullet grazed through my hole, Bowers. Your shot was almost perfect."

Bowers scratched at his head. "Well, I'll be damned," he said.

"Nice shooting," Hawk said from about ten feet behind them.

Strickland about faced. "Colonel?"

"Came to see what all the noise was about. I was impressed this morning to learn that you shot at Perry for the Corps."

Strickland nodded. "Yes, sir."

Hawk reached for the pistol. "Not a regulation grip, Captain. You know that?"

"I had the grip made in Thailand. Had it with me at the Chosin. Paid off. Try it, Colonel."

Bowers backed away a few steps. Best to leave two chatting officers to themselves.

"You're already a legend with a pistol in this war," Hawk said. "Is this the pistol of fame?"

Strickland pulled a fresh clip from his belt. "The only difference is the grip, and, of course, I keep it tight for match shooting."

From the firing line Hawk fired seven rounds, one after the other with the rhythm of a trained match shooter. When he finished, Strickland let out a low whistle. Hawk had cut a circle with his first six shots and then blasted open the target by putting the seventh through the middle of the circle.

"Easy to tell you've done a lot of shooting yourself, Colonel."

"I shot for three years at El Toro and a couple at Cherry Point. I was on the team. Never made it to Perry."

"It's overblown."

"Where's your issue pistol? "

Strickland looked over to Bowers. "Corporal, will you get my issue out of my shooting box?"

A moment later Bowers had Strickland's box and set it down on the temporary shooting bench. He left them. Strickland opened the box and pulled the pistol out. "Been fired. Need to clean it."

Hawk accepted it. "Does it shoot as well?"

Strickland allowed the sign of a smile. "Yes, sir. If the shooter's good, the pistol is good." He handed Hawk another clip.

Hawk inserted the clip neatly, and then turned to the blank target next to the one they'd been shooting at and fired the full clip at the target. He cut a perfect circle with the rounds. When he finished, he handed the pistol back to Strickland. "It's in excellent condition." With just a breath for a pause he added, "You have any lead bullets out here? The kind you said you make?"

Strickland's sense of self defense went into automatic. Everything about him steadied. He handled pressure better than he dealt with boredom. Hawk wasn't here to chit chat. He was digging for info, investigating everyone. Strickland understand that at least for the moment he was a suspect. He reloaded Hawk's emptied clip with lead rounds, slipped the clip into his pistol and turned to the target Hawk had fired into. Raising the pistol up he said, "Just like you and your team, Colonel. I made these. Watch how they shoot as accurately as the more expensive copper rounds."

He fired all nine rounds. He duplicated the circle Hawk had made but he placed each hole inside Hawk's ring, making the target appear to have two circles of holes. The target barely made it though. The paper gave in and folded over. It had only been stapled to the quickly produced wooden frame.

"Impressive. Ever make any dum-dums?" Hawk said.

Strickland lowered his Colt. "I've made lead bullets. And sure, we've all made dum dums out of some of them. You know how to do that."

Hawk nodded. He knew that just cutting a cross into the lead at the tip of the bullet made it a dum dum. But he had personally not made them. "The armorer did that for us. We were too busy looking for flight pay." He smiled at the memory of the extra pay he was no longer receiving.

"Putting that cross into the lead doesn't make them any more accurate. Actually, they can fly out and go wherever they want if they're cut badly."

"After twenty five yards or so, correct?"

Strickland shrugged. No one had ever measured the response range of such bullets that he knew of. "Don't know about that. We could test that if you'd like."

Hawk shook his head. "Thanks, but not necessary. Someday though we might meet competitively on a range. I think I should enjoy that."

"Yes, sir. I think I'd like that. How about tomorrow?"

Hawk shook his head. "Too busy."

Strickland smiled. "It would be a fun match."

Hawk pressed on with his business. "We need to know who uses lead bullets around here. Maybe the corporal can keep an eye on those who shoot out here. I understand competitive shooters, but if he sees standard issue shooters, then maybe we should know about them."

"I'll take care of that," Strickland said. "Remember, the NKs use dum-dums. They don't accept the Geneva Convention so they use them in combat as well. Theirs are much better than the ones you and

I have fired. Manufactured it would seem, my guess is in China or Russia. They aren't forty-five caliber, but when one of those things tears apart it's often very difficult to tell which weapon they came from."

"After our meeting this morning, Navy forensics boys notified us that at least one of the Koreans was killed by a dum dum. They were not manufactured by Federal, Remington or any of the others. They were definitely homemade. We're going to send the lead Lieutenant Drier found down to them tomorrow on the courier run. See if it matches."

Strickland glanced to Bowers, then back to Hawk. "Like I said, the Chinese and Koreans used dum-dums at the reservoir. If the same lab has checked some of the lead found after those battles, their reports might be interesting."

"Already checked that angle. And, we'll wait for Drier to return from Seoul. Maybe he can come back with evidence."

Strickland stopped polishing his pistol with the rag he'd pulled out of his jacket pocket. "After this morning's meeting I wondered what possible connection the Seoul incident would have with the trucks."

"We were ordered by command to investigate that. It's probably not connected. But no harm in checking it out."

Strickland thought it a good idea to add more information. "Our forty-fives are standard issue pistol for Americans but a helluva lot of Koreans have gotten their hands on them."

"All we can do is work through this," Hawk said. He turned toward the area where his vehicle awaited him and said, "Got to go. See you later, Frank."

Strickland's gaze followed Hawk while he drove away until he rounded the knoll down the road. When he turned back to the range, Bowers was already packing up the ammo cases and pistol clips.

"Figured you'd want to get back right away," he said.

Without speaking, Strickland handed Bowers his issue weapon and asked him to clean it and have it for him later that afternoon. Then, he drove away in his Jeep, leaving the armorer corporal behind him to sweep the area as well as clean his standard weapon.

Bowers walked to his Jeep, pulled out his armorer's kit and returned to the roughed out range. He opened his kit box ran a swab through Strickland's pistol, then shoved a fresh clip of lead ammo from his own box into the handle, drew the slide back and let it ram forward, an act that loaded the chamber. He pushed the trigger lock forward with his thumb.

Then he faced the targets as though one of them was Randolph Scott coming at him down the center of main street and whipped the pistol up from the side of his hip as though he was the errant cowboy Scott was about to duel with.

He fired six shots in rapid succession.

Each shot went directly into the black ring of one of the unused targets.

He then went to the target area to collect his lead.

CHAPTER 24

FOR HANS TOFTE LIFE and history were changing fast. Someone had stepped up to the plate and challenged his activities. Truman was pissed.

The CIA was under the direct command of the President of the United States. Tofte often referred to the CIA as the president's private army. In Korea it was fortifying a tyrannical Syngman Rhee just as it had begun doing in other dictator states that pretended to the world they were democracies. Tofte's responsibilities however, lay only with two of those chaotic republics. Korea and Vietnam.

From the outset he recognized that the U.S. had entered muddy waters. He also recognized that the Frenchman might have been involved in his exposure. For their war in Vietnam the CIA was now mucking things up. No, not the CIA, he corrected himself. One son of a bitch of a Marine mucked things up.

Yes, yes, he counseled himself. I know they claim my guerilla flick brought me down, but I doubt that. They're just using the film to get rid of the guy who's screwing up Harry's arms deal. They think I made that mess.

He puffed on his Camel while he thought through the history of his being in Korea and what was about to happen. He was as aware as anyone that Korea was not now nor before this war a democracy. BFD he thought. "Big fucking deal," he said aloud.

For him Koreans were not humans. He wasn't really alone with that thinking, either. For the American press, Koreans weren't capable of defending themselves even though they had fought valiantly right from the get-go. Tofte always smiled at that irony. The Koreans he'd drafted had turned out to be goddamned good soldiers. It was a secret, however, that he would keep for a long time and one that the American press never caught on to. Just as well, he figured.

But, he was also aware, apparently more than Taylor was, that it was he, Tofte, and not HST, who was expendable.

Especially after screwing up badly. And the screw up was in conscripting the errant, radical Marine.

Even while Strickland was being hunted down by amateur investigators, men who had no idea it was their own friend who had been serving the errant CIA master, Tofte found himself under direct fire. Someone locally was out to get him before he was able to silence the Marine. Someone locally must have pointed out the discrepancies in the commando movie he made. Shit, how was he to know they'd start using that as a training aid. He had made it to prove that his "army" was working overtime and succeeding.

It backfired. Things were falling apart.

Tofte wasn't dumb. He understood the future simply because he understood history so well. The president would never reveal to the world, not even if he ever wrote his memoirs, who it was who threw stones at Tofte. No matter, Hans Tofte received a life changing message from CIA headquarters in Virginia. He was to relinquish his position and return to the states immediately.

He was fired.

And fired by the President of the United States.

Personally, he was told.

There was more in the note, but the finality of the firing was all he cared about. It was the end and it had only just begun. He looked up into Taylor's eyes and hesitated before he sailed the decoded message across his desk.

Horace and Stanley Delaplane were there. The Bobsy twins in his mind. Two robots. Mechanics who were supposed to carry out his plans. They had failed. And now he was going to have to trust them to one last mission.

"Is this your guy at work?" he demanded from Taylor. "That fucking Marine? He did this."

Taylor read the note. "Internal investigation? I doubt it. Like I said when you called me. The Frenchman is pissed. And in France, he has access to the top."

"DeGaulle?"

Taylor nodded. "You have access to Truman."

"He was really pissed, Mr. Tofte, sir," Delaplane said feeling as though he had to fill in a void. "DuPre was."

Taylor shot a hard look at Tofte. "The message doesn't mention anything about the arms package."

Tofte blew out smoke and waved his cigarette around as though a wand in the hands of a magician. "They aren't going to put that into writing anywhere, Horace. You think they're that stupid?"

Taylor backed off.

"They have intimated that things aren't going well here. They're using that goddamned movie as a decoy to get rid of me. They think I fucked up this deal." He jammed the Camel into his mouth and let it roll around as though it was a large cigar. "No way could they find anything out of order without being pointed to it by a birddog like your goddamned Marine," Tofte said. "The Frogs might not like what happened, but they aren't dumb enough to flush the whole thing down the binjo ditch. Yeah, it was Strickland. And you know what that means."

Taylor cleared his throat. His boss was off target but how did he tell him that? Nobody had yet really nailed them for their actions with the transference of weapons and supplies. It was indeed the film. That ignominious flick. He would hit it straight on. Get it over.

"They're accusing you of a hoax," Taylor said. He glanced to Tofte's current favorite photograph, a picture snapped by the Nationalist PT boat captain when the Norwegian ship blew up and sank. The captain had handed over the roll of film and thank heavens for that, he thought. "They still don't know about that or they'd hang us all." He turned back to Tofte. "But the film. That's bothering them. It was fake and you know it was. You just got caught."

Early in the war Tofte had sent Washington a movie clip he'd put together of what he referred to as a real guerilla operation in Korea. Unfortunately it was a staged hoax, but Bedell and the president had believed it and authorized it for training purposes. And that's when someone—who understood things like infiltrating on rubber boats didn't take place in broad daylight—exposed the film as a fake effort.

Two countries had extensive experience with such maneuvers, Great Britain, and France. The French underground during World War II and the British Commandoes. The Brits were good allies in Korea, but the French were in Korea only to get more arms for Vietnam and

Truman had willingly helped them. His only problem with the effort was that apparently he chose the wrong man to deal with it.

For Tofte, the French, who had actually been dumb enough to invade Korea with a failed effort in 1866, were too busy trying to survive in Vietnam to worry about his activities in Korea. And the Brits didn't give a damn about what he was doing. Tofte stared blankly at Taylor while he spoke. He replied to Taylor, "They needed something to jack up the country's spirit. How the hell was I to know they'd use the damned thing as a training film?"

Taylor thought it was time to broach the second charge in the message. Tofte had purposefully left it out of their discussion, he figured, but it had to be brought up.

"That's not the total of it Hans." He flicked the message with his fingers, "Money? Unaccounted for funds? They're accusing you of felonies here."

Tofte laughed. It was involuntary but it was still a roar. "Good for you, Horace. Such bullshit. Look. Someone's searching for reasons to get us out of here."

"Maybe Ridgway," Delaplane instantly regretted entering the conversation. Both Tofte and Taylor shot him a look that could kill. He seemed to withdraw into his shirt like a turtle might when ducking back into its shell.

"Money, Sergeant," Taylor said. "It's always money or government equipment. No proof required. Just a serious charge. And that's when you'll be hanged."

"We've got 'em then," Tofte said. "Figure it out. They can't mention the money they authorized for the weapons. They do and bingo! Everyone discovers the Vietnam connection and good old Harry is history. We like Ike takes hold and it's back to Hannibal for Truman."

Tofte had acquired a great base of power in Korea. He had been given the U. S. Navy destroyer Bass, which he was to use in infiltration missions, and the submarine Perch (SS-313), a well-known WW-II sub that had undergone modifications as an amphibious raiding sub. After he assigned Marine Colonel "Dutch" Kramer as C.O. of training North Korean partisans, Kramer moved them to Yong-do island. The Marine ejected all natives from the resort island and after that Tofte moved into one of the exclusive and established homes that overlooked the ocean. He would commute with his DC-3 to Pusan or Atsugi. In other words, he spent millions of American dollars on himself and accounted for none of them. But for him, using the money for such comforts wasn't the same as stealing it. He left out of the conversation his control over the gold bars. Delaplane already knew too much.

"They," Taylor began slowly, understanding the thin sheet of ice he stood on. "They won't tell the public. But they, Hans, will hang us all because of it. In this business, they don't even need a witness."

Delaplane shook his head. "I ain't gonna tell nobody," he said quickly.

No, you won't, Tofte thought.

"The Marine," Taylor said, "has been far more erratic than I would ever have thought. He turned on us."

"And the Frenchman?" Tofte asked with such a low tone that both men almost missed it.

"He's back tomorrow for another load," Delaplane said.

Like many in his predicament, paranoia had a right to establish itself but Tofte wasn't like other men. He recognized the defeat that paranoia brought most of its victims and rejected it outright. Retaliation was his goal, part of his new mission. Strike first and survive later. Strickland and the Frenchman would have to go.

"I want those sons a bitches on a platter."

Taylor still held the message Tofte had sailed to him. He looked up from into Tofte's eyes. "KIA?"

"Make sure Bradford understands that Strickland killed the prostitutes and the Koreans. And that he signed off on the last shipment of goods out of there. Then delete him."

"Our guy can handle that."

Delaplane glanced to Taylor and locked his eyes to the colonel's. "Our guy?"

"We have a few agents near you, Stanley. You'll be clean with this."

Tofte turned his attention to Delaplane. "Maybe not too clean." Tofte had always been quick to transfer guilt for his schemes to others.

"Sir?"

"What I want is that you get the skinny to this Colonel Hawk. You let him know that Strickland killed those ladies and that you witnessed it. They'll charge you with accessory and maybe you'll get off for exposing it. Or maybe get six months at the worst."

Delaplane's shoulders drooped. His paunch stuck out while he sat there as though a balloon had just been puffed up. "That ain't gonna work, Mr. Tofte."

"Why not? Remember. We have a deal. You and me. You understand that we put money in a Swiss account for you. You have the code and you know how to get it. Enough to live on forever. So, what's the problem here?"

"Colonel Hawk is the guy, Stanley. He'll believe you."

Delaplane shook his head slowly while he spoke. "Strickland's crazy as they come. If I rat him out, he'll kill me and then come after you. Both of you. He's nuts. Man's had too much war. He loves it. Guaran-damn-tee it. He's always pullin' that goddamned pistol out of his holster and threatening us with it. He'll kill me for sure."

For Tofte that wasn't exactly bad news. Tofte stared intensely at Taylor for a moment before he spoke. His signal concerning Delaplane came through his eyes. Taylor nodded imperceptivity.

"Tell you what, Horace. Get those weapons and supplies out of the hut, immediately. Sell 'em. You know where. We'll split the money. Do it before I have to leave here."

Taylor had already come to grips with his own fate. The communiqué hadn't mentioned it, but he was fully aware of how the government worked. With Tofte's firing, he would also be excommunicated from the CIA. And it would be under such a huge cloud that his career would end. His future was now scribed and unchangeable. Now, he knew. He too, would need money to survive on.

Delaplane responded to the order to get rid of the munitions at the hut. "Disposal might not be so simple by the time I return. Kyoo and Chong might be goners."

"You keep them alive," Taylor ordered.

"It's Strickland. He threatened to kill 'em. He hates North Koreans."

"Does he know their role?"

"Only that they inventory." He thought a moment and added, "And there's the forklift. He seen 'em work that. Gotta tell ya, also. He's threatened to kill me, too."

"Then why don't you kill him before he shoots you?"

Taylor glanced to Tofte, then back to Delaplane. Tofte had just opened the door and now they were all accomplices. It was a mistake that he hoped wouldn't backfire. "Stanley, we need you to do this. It'll be your last job. If you don't do it, none of that money will be there for any of us. We can't allow them to find that materiel."

Tofte leaned forward on his desk with his palms flat on the surface and his fingers looking white from gripping the old green blotter as though he wanted to roll it up. "Get your ass up there now," he said. "Get the word to Hawk that you are witness to what Strickland did. The drivers. The whores, Stanley. Can you picture what they'll do to him?"

Taylor took a shot. "Bradford may already know about all this. You going in as a witness could clinch it and draw attention away from the hut."

Delaplane jumped to his feet. He paced nervously between Tofte's desk and the closed doorway to freedom. Their eyes followed him since pacing was unusual for the sergeant. "Colonel, I ain't never spoke back to a officer yet. No, I ain't. But I'm doin' it now. I think you're lyin' to me. I think you want me to take the fall for this whole fuckin' mess so that you two can amscray out of here with the loot and go Scot free. That man, Bradford, he don't know shit about all this and you know it. And his boy Strickland? No way you going to kill him. I sure ain't going to. I know what you're plannin'. No way. Marines think that guy's a god. A legend. Uh, uh. No fuckin' way." Then an idea flashed across his burned out mind. "'Sides. if'n I go in there who moves the shit? Nobody but me knows how to get that done."

"No need to swear," Tofte said. It was as though none of what Delaplane has said mattered.

"Yeah, there is a need," Delaplane said. "It's cause I can't figure out what else to say to you two. I only know that I can't go up there and just dump weapons and ammo and kill off a Marine j'est 'cause you say I gotta. Just can't do all that. Man's gotta have a good reason to kill another man. I mean bad, mean, evil reason."

Tofte smiled. His phrase about wanting Strickland on a platter and his question to Delaplane about killing him had indeed sunk into the sergeant's mind. "You turning on us, Stanley?" Tofte said. He stood from his desk to face the sergeant. "We've treated you right. Kept you out of combat. Kept you alive. Now you listen to me you son of a bitch—"

"Hold it," Taylor shouted jumping up to intercept what looked like the beginnings of a wrestling match. "Settle down. Hans you sit back at the desk. For Christ sakes you two are going to blow up any chance we have for getting out of here alive and with our own futures secured."

Tofte looked at him as though he were an approaching typhoon.

Taylor pointed to Tofte's chair and firmly said, "Sit."

Tofte slowly returned to the chair and sat. Taylor turned back to Delaplane. "Stanley, you're going to go up there and arrange for getting all that materiel out of the hut. You don't have to kill Strickland. And that's an order."

"We have someone up there who can do that," Tofte said calmly.

Delaplane whirled around on his heels to look Tofte in the eyes. "You what?"

"Like I said before. You aren't alone up there."

"Yes. Experienced," Taylor said, stopping Tofte from continuing. "Now look, after you get rid of the supplies, tell Hawk you're a witness to the killings. Once you do that, you're clear on our side. They'll ship you back to the states and after you testify you'll be able to draw down on your account. It's all very simple."

"I don't have to kill the man?" It was a statement more than a question.

"No," Taylor said.

"Just the Frenchman," Tofte said.

Delaplane bolted out of his chair. "What?"

"Witnesses, Stanley. Those two know what you did."

Delaplane's entire system felt as though he'd just been hit in the gut with a baseball bat. His legs lost energy and his abdomen began to ache. Dizziness set in so quickly that he found himself plunking down hard into his chair. "Can't do it. Can't kill a man."

Taylor was about to admonish his sergeant when Tofte waved him off with a slight movement of his hand. He had only run the idea up the flag pole to see how Delaplane would react. He was fascinated that the idea hadn't bothered Taylor. "But you can get the goods out of there?"

Delaplane nodded yes.

"And you can tell them you were a witness to the dozen whores?"

Delaplane shook his head slowly at first in a clear response that meant, "No."

"Does that mean no?" Tofte asked.

Delaplane stood again. He inhaled a bunch of fresh air and said, "It means that I can't be a witness to that."

Tofte jumped up again but Taylor waved him back down. "What he means Hans, is that he killed them." Taylor shot a steadying look into Delaplane's eyes. "Sit down, Stanley."

Delaplane sat. His eyes were as red as a spring rose and sweat appeared on his face as though he'd just splashed it with water. For the first time since he'd signed on with these guys he was in serious trouble. He had not carried out his mission of seducing Strickland into killing the whores, yet Taylor had to come up with a tale that said he had.

Tofte leaped to his feet again only this time Taylor didn't try to stop him. He paced behind his desk like a coyote might when prepared to harvest a meal of a meek rabbit. Then he stopped and turned to Delaplane. "I don't believe it. You don't have it in you to kill men. I'm convinced therefore, that you don't have the will to kill women as well."

Taylor remained silent during their exchange.

"Them whores is dead. That's all that matters isn't it?"

Tofte was convinced that he understood the whole scenario before Delaplane did. But now his sergeant was showing signs of weakness. Bedell was recalling Tofte and Tofte's numero uno sergeant was falling apart. This was not good. "Witnesses?"

Delaplane shook his headf, "Negative on that."

"Strickland killed them, didn't he?" Tofte urged. "You're covering for him, right?"

Delaplane's demeanor changed. Something had just struck him square on. Tofte wasn't asking questions to learn answers. He was instead, making suggestions and they were clear. He thought he might want to get the hell away from these two guys. But his legs had become too weak to stand.

Delaplane glanced to Taylor hoping to get direction, but found only a blank expression. "I thought Strickland would do it, but he didn't. He just took one look at their pathetic asses and then took a hike."

"You're telling us a tough Marine backed down?"

"They were women."

"So, you shot them?"

Delaplane looked again to Taylor for help, but nothing changed. "Strickland left. He headed up the alley and disappeared into the night. Took me an hour to find him after."

Tofte wasn't satisfied with the army sergeant's denials or his story. He would need loyal witnesses. He would need Delaplane to get a story together and make sure the man told the same goddamned thing to whomever else might ask him. Grill him, as it were. "Why did you have Strickland's pistol?"

"He had given me his Colt and a few mags to go to Seoul before I took him there."

He reached into his canvas knapsack and pulled out a few rounds of lead bullets. He laid them on the desk.

"Dum-dums?" Tofte picked one of them up. He rolled the bullet around in his hand and said, "Sudden violent death." His eyes moved straight into Delaplane's.

"I don't like killin'. I ain't ever gonna sleep well after that. Not ever," Delaplane said.

"Those women knew all about our dealings, Sergeant," Tofte said. "You knew that, right? They had been told by one of your drivers that the American government was shuttling weapons to the French, right? They had to go? Isn't that the story?"

Delaplane was afraid that his expression gave way his reaction. He coughed, then figured out what Tofte wanted to hear. "They had to go, sir. That was my thinkin' at the time. Yes, sir."

"So, you did kill them, right? If Strickland didn't do it, then you did, right Stanley?"

He had come to learn that when they called him by his first name they wanted more than life could give. His fear now was that they wanted his life. His goal now was to get the hell away from them. "Strickland don't know nothin' about that."

"You will testify that Strickland did the killing, though, right?" Tofte leaned forward on his elbows and pointed his right index finger at Delaplane. "Do you understand what I mean?"

Delaplane understood but couldn't respond orally. He only nodded. Like a child though, he had crossed his fingers, which were hidden by Tofte's overlapping desk top.

"This could work for us," Taylor said.

"And get that crap out of the hut and up north. We don't want it discovered by anyone."

"I'll need twenty trucks."

"We have ten available. Make it in two loads. They're in the yard. I'll make the deal by wire. Head north with them. You'll be met." He dismissed Delaplane who held his elation at surviving the pair until after he'd left.

After a few minutes Tofte lit up a cigarette. He puffed on it a few times before speaking. "Take care of Strickland. Make sure he has the pistol on him after he's dead."

Taylor allowed a very tight grin.

"Working on that now."

"And then I want to read about Stanley's demise. Hero stuff."

Strickland waited for Delaplane's arrival. The sun was low on the horizon doing its usual art work, sketching playful clouds with a golden hue as though the scene had been set to canvas. It was quiet except for the putt-putt of the throaty diesel engines from two departing Korean fishing boats. He glanced to the antique dock alongside his piece of real estate and wondered if fishermen used it before the war.

Yes, he answered. The CIA had probably chased everyone out of here. He cocked his head and wondered how they got away with that. He returned his gaze to the river and watched while a small group of fishing boats headed north on the Han River. He contemplated firing off a few 3.5s, believing the boats were most likely operated by NK spies. He quickly vetoed that idea.

He wondered if he'd pretty much lost his sense of direction, and his sense of any civility. War does that to you, he thought. Too much killing and too many friends dying. Life becomes ghostly, you become a subject of your mind, another person you must deal with. He nodded and added, we all become schizoid.

He had startled himself last night as well. Looking down on those women and blaming them for the war finally got to him. Maybe they were spies, but mostly, he figured, they were just trying to survive. They operated in a bombed out building, on straw mattresses and they looked sick. Ill. Diseased probably. And they were unarmed. That got to him mostly. He could never shoot anyone who was unarmed and he wondered if he could shoot a woman under any conditions. He reflected back to the Pacific and one early morning when a Japanese soldier had staggered out of a tunnel and come face to face with him. The man was nearly naked. Obviously unarmed and he had overreacted. He'd fired at the soldier without thinking. When the man gasped and stared with utter surprise into his eyes, his whole world changed. He had just murdered someone he should have taken as a prisoner.

Heat of battle he'd called it.

It hadn't, however, stopped him from killing armed men who would otherwise have killed him. No remorse there. But unarmed women? Were they spies? Hell, he thought, no way. They could barely move or survive where they were. Delaplane had led him into a hovel, not a brothel.

So, he left the women and hiked nearly across town. He'd gone soul searching, he thought they called it. A weakness for a Marine. A stupid softening of the heart. It wasn't a good idea, but there it was. He'd lost his fire. Lost for that matter, his desire to continue on as a warrior. And Delaplane, who was with him the whole time, seemed so far out of it, that the two of them nearly bonded.

Weird experience he decided.

A familiar sound brought him back to reality. Trucks coming from his left. He pushed away from the hut where he'd sought the shade and stepped into the road. A convoy of what appeared to be U.S. army trucks came around the turn and headed toward him. One, two, more. He counted them. Ten, eleven, twelve and two behind that.

The first truck braked to a stop at the hut. Delaplane jumped out of the passenger side hitting the ground hard and nearly tumbling over. When he looked up he was staring straight into Strickland's eyes.

"Nice stunt," Strickland said.

Delaplane urged Strickland into the hut for a private confab, but Strickland rejected that with a growl. Delaplane felt the Korean driver approach from behind him. He motioned the man back to the truck. Then he headed for the hut.

"We need to talk. Serious shit."

"Out here."

"No, sir. Inside. Now, Cap'n."

Strickland was listening to a different Delaplane. A man with a surprisingly different energy. He wouldn't argue out here or reprimand the army sergeant for disobedience. Not in front of a bunch of NK drivers. He followed Delaplane into the hut.

The hut was dark inside. The small cut-out windows that allowed some light into the building were shut tight. The generator behind the hut was out of diesel and only a streak of light through the front entryway put a shine on a few of the first crates. Delaplane's features were shadowed, not discernable enough for Strickland to make out whether the man was lying or telling the truth.

"We're movin' the stuff out of here, Cap'n. All of it."

Delaplane's voice was speaking one set of words but his expression gave way to another meaning. "What the hell's going on? The Frenchman?"

Delaplane shook his head slightly. Strickland was his only stumbling block now. Somehow he had to convince the taut Marine to work with him even though he was sure the man could turn at the drop of the wrong word. "I wish. That mission may be over."

"So what's the problem?"

Delaplane stepped away from Strickland. His answer wasn't going to be happy news to the Marine and he didn't want the Colt shoved at his forehead. He spoke haltingly and in short brief sentences.

"We have guerrillas in the north. Trained by your Marine colonel on Yong Do. They also operate as spies. Even Ridgway says they's givin' us good info. They need these supplies. The ones in here. We gotta get 'em there."

From the sergeant's tone Strickland was sure that he had guessed right. These assholes were stealing from his Corps, the army, probably the navy, and selling materiel to the NKs. Without responding to Delaplane, he headed to the rear of the hut.

"There are no guerrillas, you idiot," he said loudly. "If there were they'd be in the news all the time."

He reached a stack of crates stenciled in capital letters: LAUNCHERS: 3.5.

Along with that were lot numbers, which were in Strickland's mind just bureaucratic bafflegab. He ripped the cover off the top crate and pulled out a launcher. It was broken down into two parts. He quickly jammed them together. "You're dealing with the goddamned Chinese," he shouted. "Commies! Doesn't that mean anything to you, Sergeant?" He then tore into a crate and pulled out a 3.5 round. He quickly loaded the launcher.

Delaplane freaked. "Cap'n. It means a lot to me. I ain't no stinkin' goddamned turncoat. You got to listen to me. I mean it. You can't fly off the handle this time. Cap'n. We got us a problem here. Bigger'n you s'pect, sir."

Strickland headed to the front hatchway. He had the launcher rested on his right shoulder. "I'm going to take your trucks after you load 'em Sergeant. I'm taking 'em to the Marines. They need this crap. Your drivers will either follow my orders, or they'll all meet their goddamned Buddha. Get ready to load them. And quickly."

"Cap'n. Sir, they want us dead. Both of us. Dead, do you hear me?"

Strickland wheeled on him. "Who wants us dead?"

"Tofte and Taylor, sir. They're history. They been fired by the president hisself."

Strickland froze in place. "Fired?"

"Fired. Kaput. That's what's going on. Don't you get it? The whole thing is down the tubes. You want to win this war on your own? Then we gotta get this shit up to the rebels. We got to get it outta here or else you and me gonna be the two they hang. You and me. We got our fingerprints all over this shit. I mean from Pusan to here it's us. And those two will make sure our commanders know about it."

Strickland looked from the hatchway to Delaplane and then back to the trucks just outside the hut. Delaplane continued.

"You got me wrong, Cap'n. I ain't dealin' with no commies. The NKs who get this are rebels in the north. They are trying to beat the commie regime. They've got ROKs with them to help them fight. Man, you saw them work. Those ROK guys are good fighters. But they need this shit."

Strickland lowered the launcher from his shoulder. He had to come to grips with all this. He had to control his anger and he knew it.

"You and me, sir. We've been hung out to dry. Only way we can come out of this alive is to get this crap outta here and into the right hands. Otherwise, those two want us to sell it to the NKs. They got agents up there."

"Who's going to kill us?" Strickland's memory of Taylor's earlier threat was still vivid.

Delaplane was trembling and it affected his speech. "They said they got someone up here, maybe more 'n one. They wanted me to kill you, but I said no way. I mean it, Cap'n. They wanted me to kill you." He suddenly found some humor in that and started to laugh even though it was a sick kind of laugh. "Shit, that's funny. Me kill you. Man, you're Wyatt Earp. You'd smell me comin' a mile away." His tongue got twisted and he knew it. He stopped laughing. He was weak now. He looked for a place to sit and found the ammo crates the easiest spot.

"Who is going to kill us?" Strickland repeated.

Delaplane looked up from his perch. He was exhausted physically and emotionally and Strickland could see that. "Taylor said a soldier. One of my kind. Army guy. But Tofte said there might be more 'n one. Hell, knowin' them two might even be a Marine or two up here gunnin' fer us."

"They told you this."

"They told me they were going to get you kilt. After I left I stayed at the closed door, mostly 'cause I know they talk to each other. That's when I learned they want us both out of the picture. Before they leave for the states."

"The Army is in charge of this one Herr Leutnant, and we are not telling you people anything," Army Major Jurgen Reineke said with a lightly influenced German accent that surprised Drier. Reineke spoke with a seesaw tone and he clipped his words. He had referred correctly to Drier's rank in German. Drier knew nothing of the language, but had heard reference before.

Reineke wore his Army gabardine uniform with a jacket and tie, which made him appear out of place in the city of destroyed dreams and buildings. His ribbons indicated to Drier that he hadn't seen action in Korea. The World War II ribbons spoke a different history. Then he remembered hearing about how some German soldiers had become American citizens and were allowed into the U.S. services. This guy, he figured, must be one of those.

Drier had come to Seoul alone. He'd dropped Fraker off at motor pool after agreeing with Snake that some research of the area around their camp was necessary. Fraker had asked where those trucks could possibly have been headed if not to the Seventh Marines. He made a strong enough case to turn him loose to search on his own.

Now Drier alone faced the head CID guy in his office. The room was small, even by a pyramidal tent's comparison. The walls were totally bare of any decorations or corkboard, the usual adornment for a bureaucrat's office. The man's desk had a few folders on it. Other than that, the place was sterile.

"Yes, sir. Can you give me any information, Major. I need to return with something. A witness maybe, or a record of a report of what happened here."

"These were prostitutes murdered by some pissed-off-private, Lieutenant. He probably got his dick stuck in the wrong hole, and now he's got holes of his own. The frauleins were prostitutes, not thieves. Es ist nicht ein Vorrang hier."

Drier cocked his head a bit and said, "Translated?"

Reineke appeared irritated. "They are not a priority." Reineke allowed a very tight grin, which was perceived by Drier as more of a smirk. The man probably felt some power in having two languages and knowing Drier had but one.

Drier needed more information. "I understood that two American soldiers were involved."

Reineke dropped his pencil on the desk from about a foot or more above the surface and leaned back. His wish right then was that this Marine would get out of his hair. "Two men? That's news to me, Mr. Drier."

"So, you do have a witness."

Reineke shook his head and then said, "Are you familiar with VD, Lieutenant? Do you know what it does to a man? It puts holes in his pecker. He pees through all of them, too. Little fissures that make his dick look like his mother's cooking sieve. That's enough to anger any man and this guy probably got so mean and angry with VD that he killed those women. Not the first time it's happened here, won't be the last. Are you going to hang a man for that?" He leaned forward and with a sharp tone of sarcasm added, "If you like, I'll translate that message so that you can understand it as well."

Drier let the sarcasm go. "I should think we would. Hang them, that is."

Reineke inhaled deeply and let the air out slowly as he spoke. He was both a bit impressed by the persistence of this young officer and pissed, that he was so persistent. "We'd never be able to prove one of our personnel did it, anyway. The Koreans would tell you—seen one GI, seen them all."

"Can you at least tell me how they were murdered?"

Reineke glanced around his tight office as though he was inspecting it. Fully exasperated he finally decided to let Drier read the report he had prepared. Just maybe he might be the right guy. He picked up a folder from his desk and pulled a piece of paper from it. "Here. Read it and then get the hell out of my hair."

Drier took the report.

Slowly and intentionally secretive, Reineke said, "And don't tell anyone I let you see this."

A surprised Drier scanned the sheet quickly, picking up key words and statements. .45 caliber. Apparently lead rounds; two males, Caucasian; drove off in jeep, military origin unknown; twelve local prostitutes; heads shattered by blasts; probable motive: alcohol or revenge. Bodies picked up by Korean authorities.

Drier looked up. "Were these ladies spies?"

Reineke reacted surprisingly. He stood from his seat and grabbed the paper back from Drier and with a hissing sound to his words he said, "Dismissed, Lieutenant Drier. Get yourself back to your outfit. Schnell." Drier understood what schnell meant, but he hesitated just long enough to completely piss off Reineke. "It's time for you to leave here, Lieutenant," Reineke ordered.

The Major was angry and Drier wasn't oblivious to the man's authority. The order he'd just given also had a meaning he understood, but he also had a mission and he'd do his damndest to accomplish it. "Major, I'm actually under orders to do this. Are you going to argue with General Ridgway?"

Reineke curled his brow. It was a look that told Drier the man had more experience with this sort of thing than Drier did and that he probably just screwed up. "Credentials, Lieutenant?"

"Call EUSAK headquarters, sir. Ask for General Oliver Smith." Drier's throat turned to sawdust. He wasn't good at lying but he had to do something to get this intimidating officer off his clerical ass and help him. "What's the army afraid of here, Major?"

Reineke's complexion turned crimson. With his most serious Teutonic inflection he said, "We are afraid of nothing." He went to his door, opened it and called down the hallway. "Lieutenant Brennan."

Brennan appeared at the door of the office across the hallway. "Sir!"

"Escort this Marine out of here. Straight to his jeep. If he gives you any trouble, shoot him." He looked back to Drier. "EUSAK, indeed. You insult me Lieutenant. Why would they bother with a bunch of whores?"

"Spies, Major. We're dealing with spies."

"Schnell, Brennan!"

Brennan glanced furtively to Drier. One just didn't easily arrest a Marine. Not usually, but Drier resigned himself to leaving.

After they left, Horace Taylor appeared at the door one office down from Brennan's. He looked to Reineke who barely acknowledged the CIA man's presence. Taylor turned back into his office and closed the door.

Outside, Drier asked Brennan, "You have any idea what's going on here?"

Brennan glanced back to the plywood building that housed the temporary CID offices. Did he dare explain the deep hell where he lived and worked? "I'm due for rotation Lieutenant. They put me here two weeks ago. They aren't my kind of people. They hate and suspect everyone of everything. They aren't our types."

"Figured as much."

Brennan led him away from the entryway down the street toward Drier's jeep.

"We've had naval intelligence, CIA and more army CID than any human can handle in here. We get Korean cops every day and Lieutenant, they are the worst. Everybody here is secretive, clandestine and very, very weird." He paused and then expressed a reflective thought. "I have no idea why I'm here. I'm infantry. I want out. But man, it's like I've sunk into a giant fire pit."

Drier only nodded. He was too taken back to respond.

Brennan went on as though he'd been waiting a long time to get a weight of fear off his shoulders. "Their operative word is 'discreet,' their operative manner spooky. Worse, they'd just as soon kill you as ask questions. Reineke meant it when he said I should shoot you. Never would I do that, but they might. You'd best move on and keep your lips zipped."

"Is he CIA?" Drier didn't show signs of leaving.

"Reineke? He repeated his boss's name as though it were the first time he heard it. "I doubt it."

Drier glanced to the building, then back to Brennan. The Army lieutenant wasn't being totally straight with him. He remembered something that Hawk had said and pressed the officer for more. "Did they know about the prostitutes? I mean was that why the CIA guys showed up?"

Brennan glanced to the watch on his left wrist. He shook his head. "Nobody showed up for them. Say, I've got to get back. He'll think I'm telling tales."

"Where's the Korean Police station located?"

Brennan cringed. "You really want to get yourself shot don't you?"

"Got to return with answers."

"I've not been around the city. Reineke keeps me pinned here doing his paperwork. Korean cops traipse in and out all day. They're probably in the area. They'll call, then show up in a minute or two. Most of them on foot."

"Thanks."

Drier stepped into his jeep and cranked over the lifeless engine. It coughed once then burst into action He let it rumble at gear speed by pressing the clutch down hard while Brennan continued speaking.

"Take care," Brennan said. Then he put his hand on the jeep windshield frame as though trying to stop the vehicle and said, "I mean it. Major Reineke is a former German Gestapo officer. No shit. He means business."

Drier's expression demanded an explanation.

"OSS types converted him in Europe after they captured him. At least that's the scuttlebutt. He helped with the French underground. He was a spy I guess. He's a mean son of a bitch who will do what it takes for him to get his job done. He's more than he appears to be. So, watch your ass."

"He's an Army officer," Drier said emphasizing the word Army.

"Don't get too close. Let your commanders do that. Otherwise, you'll vanish. Swear to God." He looked back over his shoulder then back to Drier. He raised his right arm just a little and said again, "Swear it, man. Be careful."

After Drier left, Brennan entered the tenuous building. Before he was able to get to his workstation though, Major Reineke motioned him into his office. He closed the door behind him. All he said to his aide was, "Put 'em together. Now." He then handed Brennan a tightly wrapped box. It was about ten-inches long by six-inches wide and nearly two-inches deep. The tape that wrapped held the old newspaper wrapping around the box seemed old and worn. "You know what to do with this."

Brennan accepted the package. They had discussed it a few days before. "That Marine was very curious about the ladies," Major.

Reineke nodded. "Yes. He was. And he was honest." He walked to the small window that gave him a look out at the devastated area surrounding them and held his stare on the broken street. Then he said it again, as though Drier had been a one of a kind. "And he is honest."

Drier found the Korean Police headquarters twenty minutes later. Brennan's guess had been correct. They were only two war shattered blocks away. One down, one over. Driving around the area searching for the station had proved more difficult than if he had walked. The old brick building that housed the station was barely standing. The police had obviously taken it for their own after the invasion.

He entered the building cautiously, remembering Brennan's warning. Inside, he stopped short of the desk that faced the entry. The place was a shambles, not yet cleaned up from the bombing that had taken place during the invasion. Only one Korean cop was around; the sergeant at the desk. He was wearing his helmet and dressed in a clean and starched blue cotton utility uniform. His night stick was intentionally visible, hanging boldly from its scabbard at his waist. He was writing into a notebook when he spotted Drier.

"Marine CP down the road. Two mile," he said.

When Drier approached him he noticed two more Korean cops step from a doorway a few feet to his right and pause in an 'at-ease' position with their arms folded across their chests. Their night sticks also appeared huge and obvious.

"I need to ask you a few questions," he said.

The sergeant sat straight up, glanced to his uniformed types and then back to Drier. "What?"

"We received a report that some women were murdered nearby last night. Possibly by an American."

"Yes. Every night women die. Men, too."

"I'm talking about twelve prostitutes."

"Prostitutes," he repeated as though attempting to make it clear in his own mind.

"Do you know who did it? Who killed them?"

The sergeant shook his head as though to say no but said, "American? Maybe."

Drier realized too late that he shouldn't have suggested an American might have killed them. "You tell me."

The sergeant got up and walked around his desk where he sat at the edge of it. "Why you ask?" For Drier, the cop seemed to struggle with his english with an overdone accent.

"My boss needs to know," he began. The two cops came closer to him, standing behind him now. Their hands rested on their night sticks. "I'm investigating a case that might have something to do with the women."

"We don't know anything," the cop said. "They prostitutes. They get killed. Maybe by American. Maybe by Frenchman. Maybe by British guy. All look alike."

"Frenchman?"

"Sometime."

Drier glanced back to the two cops. They stared at him with death in their eyes. Now there were three. He looked back to the sergeant. "Could you take me to the location where it happened?"

"No," the sergeant said dryly. He said nothing more.

Drier squinted. He was in trouble here. "Were there any witnesses?"

"No."

Two more cops came out of doorways and lined up behind Drier. That was it. He was pissed off now. He stepped up to the sergeant and said, "I don't know what's going on here, but I'm actively involved in an investigation for the United States Government. You are actively involved in trying to intimidate me. Now back these guys away and do it now." He hoped to god the guy would do what he wanted.

The sergeant cut a thin smile, nodded to the others. They backed away, but didn't leave. "Now, Lieutenant," the sergeant said in perfect English, "unless you have more legitimate questions, I have work to do."

Drier glanced back to the others, then to the sergeant. "You played with me. You speak perfect English. What's going on here?"

The cop smiled broadly. "We don't like you. My English. Yes. I graduated from Ohio State." He let a chuckle creep out and added, "You see. After college I returned to my country. The guys up north decided they wanted it and you came to kick them out. You're done. So go home and leave us alone."

"I would love to."

"Good bye."

"Expect to hear from my superiors," he said. He regretted it immediately. It was an idle threat and one this asshole probably heard all the time. Hadn't he learned with the CID guy?

The sergeant smiled again, nodded. "Ridgway or Smith?" he said. "Good bye, Lieutenant." When Drier got to the door the sergeant called to him, "And oh by the way. Go Buckeyes."

Drier left him. After he was outside, a lone non-Korean Asian man inside the police station, dressed in civilian clothes, stepped from the doorway where the first two cops had come from and nodded approval to the sergeant.

Back in his jeep, Drier paused to catch his breath and his thoughts. He accepted that thus far the trip had pretty much been a waste. He'd come, but he'd not succeeded in learning a damned thing.

"M'sieur?"

He looked up to find a young woman dressed in American military clothes except that her jacket was a worn out denim with some telltale signs of having had emroidery work at the ends of the sleeves. She had a light backpack with her, one of those green canvas bags he used to carry on his back during boot camp during the big war. He figured her to be about eighteen or maybe a couple years older, it was hard to tell. Any fool though could see that she was beautiful. Definitely Korean but tall with European features. "My name is Huenyrsook." She pronounced it honorsook.

Drier was confused. Was she hustling? "Yes?"

"I will take you and I will show you."

"Where?" he asked, glancing back to the police station.

"Soeur," she said in French. When Drier seemed confused she translated to English. "Sister."

He shook his head. A prostitute. "No thanks. Not interested."

"No. de No. Pas cela. Pas prostituée."

"Sorry. I don't speak French."

The girl tried a smile but it was a weak effort. In English with a French accent she said, "I said my sister is not a prostitute."

Drier felt completely out of place. All he could respond with was, "You speak English well."

"Oui, M'Sieur. Je parle le français et l'anglais et le Coréen." She had told him that she spoke French, English and Korean. But Drier remained in the dark. She smiled more strongly this time and said.

"You do not speak French or Korean?"

He shook his head. "Only English."

"I speak English with you then. Will you take me?"

"Yes," he said meekly, still not understanding where they'd be going. "Jump in."

Huenyrsook walked around the back of the jeep and climbed aboard sitting in the empty passenger seat in the front. Drier pulled out into the damaged street. "Where to?"

She pointed. "Cette voie," she said in French. Then with a lighter tone she said, "That way. Sorry. French is my primary language."

Drier felt inadequate with the girl. First she was very pretty and second, she'd obviously been educated by someone much smarter than he was. "You're Korean, right?"

She nodded. "Half."

Drier was curious. "The other half?"

"French. I went to Catholic school. They taught us a lot." She glanced to him and wondered if he was able to figure her out. She decided that he would never be able to understand her or any other woman. She smiled inwardly. He was as innocent as any man she'd ever expect to run into.

So that was it, Drier thought as he pushed the jeep along. He remembered hearing that lots of Korean children were cared for in mostly Catholic orphanages run by the sisters. The church had come to Korea nearly a century before and apparently had a strong influence. He laughed at his sudden clumsiness. At least he decided, she's not a prostitute. He stole a look at her again and still found her beautiful. It unnerved him a bit. He never found it easy to be around gorgeous women. Actually, he admitted to himself, they intimidated him.

"Turn here," she said. He dodged the bomb craters and turned left, happy to have something new to do. They headed down a narrow alley. The war had not been kind to Seoul. Everywhere he looked the buildings seemed to be piles of bricks and steel, stone, wood and stinking death. Then they had to stop. The alley was blocked by rubble and not even the agile jeep could pass through all that.

"Là," she said. "There. My sister is in there."

"Wait. Look, I know the bombing was horrible."

"Not bombing. M'sieur. An American killed her. Three days ago."

It sounded like a loud switch just went on in his mind, or was it his brain. Wait a minute. "Hold it. When?"

She didn't answer the question directly. "I watched. I hid in a large pile of laundry in the back corner. You will see it. I could not move or they would have killed me, too. I didn't have a gun or a knife to defend myself." Her voice faltered. It sounded to Drier like she was about to cry. Her speech slowed. "I went to police right away. The police refused to listen to me. They threw me out of the station." She pulled up the sleeve of her blue denim jacket and showed Drier the bruises on her arm. "Hit me here. The police hit me with a club and shoved me out the door."

Icy chills raced along Drier's spine, a speed demon of a cold front decimating all warmth engulfed him. Nets, thousands of them were falling from the sky to snare him and jerk him into oblivion. The trap had just been opened and he had fallen into it.

"Holy Jesus," he moaned.

"Venez avec moi," she said, meaning come with me. She was out of the jeep before he even thought about it, and heading toward the only open doorway remaining in the building. He noted the baubles and grass and cloth that hung down from the overhead to keep the weather or people out.

Drier looked around cautiously. God, what's this all about? Where's the punch line? Who's gonna shoot me now? The Korean cops? The killer? He slapped at the .45 at his hip. It offered him some comfort just knowing it was there.

"Okay. Hey!" he had to call after her, "Slow down."

The girl pushed aside the facade door. "Entre Ici," she said so naturally that Drier understood he was to enter.

He wondered if he was about to step right into a machine gun nest. Or step on a trip-wire and hear the boom of the booby trap. But the girl entered cleanly. Nothing happened to her. He grabbed his stick and headed for the entry. He probed ahead of himself with the stick as though searching for booby trap wires. When he got there, he paused. Captain Strickland's wrong, he told himself. Judgment is important because no book had been written about this.

He peered around the entryway to check the deck, the ceiling, or what was left of it, and then the room. He probed every corner and each space with his stick. No wires. No people. No machine gun nests. He stepped gingerly across the threshold and entered the room safely. He tried hard to not limp. There was just something unmanly about limping in front of civilians, especially female civilians.

The girl was already down the corridor which was more rubble than hallway. Half of one wall was gone, the other half seemed to teeter.

"Suivez-moi." She apologized again and translated her command to follow to her into English.

He followed, waiting for the explosion or gunfire or whatever plan there was to end his life. She stopped at the door at the end, and turned back to him. "Soeur," she said, pointing into the room.

Something queer here. Place stinks. Whorehouse odors he thought possibly, not really knowing, since he had never been in one. But no cops. No security. What kind of place is this? Something strange.

He got to the door. "Look, Honor sook," he said. But oh man, this place stinks worse than a battlefield. Rotten. Human waste in here and human flesh. Now he was worried about what he would find. Were there dead ladies in here and, if so, dead for how long? More than a day, two days? God, the horrendous odor was going to bring up his last meal.

"Peggy. Americans call me Peggy," Huenyrsook was saying.

He tried to smile but no way could he.

"Okay, Peggy. Look, there's nothing I can do here."

"Please go in. Help me, M'Sieur." Her accent seemed heavier, but Drier figured that was just his imagination or her excitement.

He shrugged. He knew he was committed.

She went in first. Drier followed and even though he was nervous about it, he couldn't help but see that she had a great figure, even in dungarees. Maybe, he thought, that's what is intimidating me right now.

But, when he got inside he quickly changed his mind. The gurgling came first. The taste of blood at the back of his mouth. The odor was worse than a collapsed septic tank. Oh God, I hate to throw up. Gluuummmp. Geez hold it back. Gluuuuummmmmmp. His mouth billowed, air puffed out, then last night's C-rations and this morning's coffee and horrible biscuits. Window. No glass. Open.

He stuck his head out and barfed everything up and out. He gasped for fresh air, sucking it in like a miner stuffing his bags full of new found nuggets. He wanted to crawl out the window and run to his jeep and drive all the way back to Sallisaw. Ride horses again. Hell, ride in the Sallisaw rodeo again, that's where life meant something. Plain, simple stuff. Get up on the rail, straddle your bronco and go for it. Breaking your leg is better than taking a hollow point or dum-dum in the ass and anything was better than this room.

"Please, help me," Peggy pleaded.

Drier braced himself. He'd been on the battlefield and seen carnage, but these were women. This could be worse. He turned back slowly to face the girl. "Why is she still here?" he asked. He looked around for the others. God, this woman had already started the process of decaying but the odors in the room were telling him yet another story. Others. There must be others here.

"My sister," Peggy repeated. "Can we give her a Christian burial?"

Drier choked down his sickness. "Why?"

"Police beat me when I asked them for help," she said.

He looked around the room. Everywhere except at Peggy's sister who was literally headless from the gunshot. She was also bloated, and purple or something, he wasn't sure because he hadn't looked at her very long before losing it. Then he wondered, is this what body snatchers go through after we die in a firefight?

"Bury her?" He asked, a bit astonished. "Where?"

Then he wondered. Are the other girls here, too? How many rooms are there? But Peggy broke into his questions.

"Please help me. She must be buried Marine. We are Catholic."

"Ahh, God." A Catholic prostitute? What's this world coming to? Wait! A bullet? A slug? His eyes caught something on the deck next to the bed. Next to the dead woman. I've got to get that. But it's so close to her.

The odor. She stinks so much. The whole place stinks. The whole place? My God, his mind raced back to the awful. All twelve of the dead women must still be here. His stomach rebelled again. He turned back to the window and coughed out dry air. His stomach sucked and compressed with painful spasms.

Peggy tugged at his belt.

"S'il vous plaît, M'sieur. Before they catch us."

"The Police?" he asked. He turned back into the room.

She nodded. "They will kill us. They do not want anyone to know this."

His gaze returned to the piece of lead on the floor. A spent dum-dum. That had to be it. How did the police miss it? He walked to it on shaky legs, keeping his eyes glued to the spent bullet to avoid the woman. He bent down and picked it up. It was lead. It was a bullet, or what was left of one. At least he thought it's large enough for ballistics tests. He pocketed it and prayed it had nothing to do with his skipper, the only Marine he'd known who used lead. Why am I thinking about him? he asked incredulously. Damn. Damn. The skipper wouldn't do this even in his angriest moments. His eyes caught hold of something. In the corner. A stack of sheets and blankets. Army blankets.

"Are there others here?"

Peggy glanced back down the narrow hallway they'd come through and then back to Drier. "What is your name?"

"David."

"You are a lieutenant, right?"

"Yes."

"If we don't get out of here quickly, Lieutenant David, we will be killed. I will answer questions later."

Drier let out a heavy sigh and said, "We can roll her up in those," He pointed at the blankets and the poncho. "Get them."

Peggy got the blankets and brought two back. They had been neatly folded. Drier spread one out, still refusing to look down at the corpse. Then he sailed it out over the bed and let if float down over the dead woman. When it covered her, he finally looked down. Good, can't see her. Then he remembered Blade for some reason. Blade hadn't looked nearly this shot up and yet he was dead, too.

"Tuck it under her on the other side," he said releasing his past for a few moments.

Peggy ran around the bed and did as told. Drier tucked his side in. Now what? Roll her over? Bag her with the other blanket. Fart sack. My God, those aren't sheets. Those are official military fart sacks and they're stamped U. S. Army. The off white cotton bags were designed to be used to slip over cot or bunk mattresses to help keep them clean. The men were expected to launder them once a week.

He went to the corner and picked one up. Holding on to one end, he flipped it out and the mattress sack billowed like a huge condom. Perfect, he thought. Stolen, maybe black-marketed, but perfect. We'll bag her.

He put the open end at her headless shoulders. His stomach complained violently again, but he held it back. Getting better at it, he decided. He pulled the bag down around the woman, tugging it under her as he went. When he finished, he tied it off.

Peggy had become sullen. Sad.

"What's the matter?" Drier asked.

"Gone. My sister is gone."

Drier went to her and put a hand on her shoulder to comfort her. "Where do you live?"

"No where now. My sister's place was bombed by the Americans when they attacked this city. My sister and I have lived here and other places for a while. Do you know the word nomads?"

Crap! It was true then. Women, children, orphanages. Indiscriminate bombings. We murdered these people to save them from murderers. No wonder that cop didn't like me. He shook off the thoughts to settle himself down and looked around. "Well, you can't live here any longer."

She nodded.

Damn, what to do. He couldn't just drive off and leave her here. And her sister. She'd been shot with a lead slug. The answer became a big bingo in his brain. "C'mon," he said. "Let's get your sister into the jeep." He would take her back. She might be the evidence they needed. He wasn't sure. He felt for the lead round again in his pocket and it was safe.

He lifted the dead woman with new found strength. "Get my stick, will you?" She did and he followed her to the Jeep. He set the corpse into the back and climbed in. Peggy sat next to him.

Firing the jeep engine to life, he drove away from the shattered house of nightmares and headed straight back to Freedom Village with the fragmented family of two ghostly sisters and a piece of lead in his pocket that he thought might be productive evidence.

CHAPTER 25

STRICKLAND LEFT THE HUT to get away from its objectionable stench. He thought that the odor of treason was overpowering him more than the stench from the crates of blood stained war that Tofte was selling to Koreans. The realization that he was hung up with an outfit that was as screwed up as the CIA was causing him to review his involvement and his immediate need to act.

He wanted to arrange everything into a mental file of sorts, something like the vision of his shooter's leather bound box. A competitive shooter at a rifle or pistol match always had a case that held his practice records as well as his ammo. Neat rows of holes in cherry wood along the inside front held twenty rounds of 30.06 for his M-1 and the interior backside held 15 rounds of .45 caliber for his pistol.

A notebook of sorts rested in the middle of the box along with his black-carbon smoker and field-cleaning equipment. The smoker was used to blacken his front sights with a matte finish of smoke so that the sight didn't glare from sunlight and throw off the shooter's otherwise accurate aim. Somehow, he decided, his moral compass had needed some of that black smoke and he'd not used it.

He glanced up from the ground in front of him to the river. No one was on the water today. No fishermen, no barges, nobody. He looked northward and wondered if fighting had increased. Usually when the war got hot near the river the water traffic stopped. But all he could hear was the hiss of a light breeze slipping past his ears. No birds, no animals, no people.

First things first. Who the hell got him into this trap and why? Bradford? He's the one who assigned him to R&R that led him to The Barracks, that led him to Juliana.

Juliana? Maybe if he could get back to Tokyo he could find her and understand what that was all about. He'd never before met a woman of her caliber who had pushed herself on him and then ended up in bed with him within a few hours. Hell, he'd never even gone that far on his own volition. She had to be one of them.

Taylor was next to enter his life. Taylor. How in the hell did Taylor find him? He pushed away from the hut and walked toward water's edge. He noticed that the closer he got to the river the faster it seemed to move. At least the river was behaving normally. He picked up a flat rock, one about the size of a silver dollar and skimmed it across the surface. It made four skips before sinking into oblivion.

Taylor!

The Barracks. He arranged for The Barracks. He left civvies there for me. He knew my clothing sizes. Shoes. Everything.

Drunk. I let myself get drunk and woke up in a different world. The Tokyo whorehouse. And then Taylor again. Taylor and Juliana. They worked together. Juliana said she was the daughter of the ambassador from the Netherlands?

Tofte was from Copenhagen. An OSS spy in the deuce. Speaks German well. Juliana speaks German. Maybe she lied. Or worse. Maybe the two of them worked for the OSS during the big one.

Taylor. He was OSS as well.

He picked up another rock. This one was rather large. He stepped back and then moved athletically forward pushing the rock out over the river like a shot putter would. It landed like a mortar shell might, causing a splash that sent water into a fountain like spray. He watched the results of his put until it completely dissipated.

Then he decided.

"She's a goddamned agent."

Delaplane was right. Tofte's only way out of a trial was for all the witnesses to his crimes be killed and that included himself.

He had become a target. Who, he wanted to know, was the shooter? "Nobody. I can't trust anyone over here." He shuddered, his shoulders shaking as though he were dumping weight off. "Drier. Snake. I have them. And right now I need them."

Fourteen trucks waited to be loaded. Fourteen trucks that were going to be easy for anyone to spot.

Delaplane came alongside him. "We gotta move, Cap'n."

Strickland's mission had changed. The roadmap was clear. In the distance, coming down from the north, he was surprised to see a boat that was about the same size as the pirate captain's boat had been. He jerked his thumb toward the boat and said, "Why not ship them out of here straight to Tofte on that boat?"

"Don't get crazy on me Cap'n. First off, you ain't gonna stop that junkie. Second we'd still be the one's caught. Do you see them two guy's fingerprints on this stuff anywhere? No, sir. It's you and me they'd hang. Fer sure. If'n that is, Tofte don't get us kilt first."

"Have you thought about walking away from here? Just leaving it here. Let the army intelligence guys find it. Turn yourself in, confess all."

Delaplane nearly laughed. So easy, he thought, but so impossible. "Now I know you're nuts. You ever work with CID?"

Strickland shook his head. "No need to."

"Well, it ain't gonna happen that way. Tofte and Taylor would make sure we were linked to all this crap and as far as the UCMJ goes, we're guilty unless we can prove us-selves innocent."

"That boat's ripe for the picking, Sarge. Be a touch of irony to send it to them."

Delaplane continued on as though Strickland hadn't spoken. "'member what I said b'fore? They's gonna kill us. Somebody out there's already got the job ta to do it. Why ain't you so bothered by that? After they deep six us they's gonna tell the world we done it all and they get the credit for catchin' us."

Strickland frowned. He turned back to the water. The boat was getting closer. "Why then are you so interested in finishing off this job?"

Delaplane bowed his head. He was not proud of the reason. "Them two scare the shit outta me. Maybe if'n this gets done they'll leave me alone. Don't care 'bout the Swiss account no more."

Strickland was stunned. It was the first admission of guilt he'd heard directly from any of them. Either Delaplane had lost his mind or he'd turned totally cowardly on him. He skipped another rock across the river's surface and noting the boat again he asked, "Is that damned thing our pirate friend, Mr. Black?" It was beginning to look like Black's boat, the JR.

Delaplane strained to ID the boat. Damn. It did look like Black's boat. "Why?" He was afraid of the answer.

"What Black said."

"What Black said?"

Strickland grinned. "Remember? He said we'd be better off if his cargo sank to the bottom of the ocean." He turned and headed back to the hut but before he got there he shouted, "Get those trucks loaded quickly. We've got a new plan. And what the hell, you can go along for the ride."

"No way, Cap'n. No new plans. We do what they want. I don't wantta get kilt, sir."

Strickland stopped at the entrance to the hut. He turned back to face Delaplane. With a taut expression he said, "You said it yourself, Sergeant. We're the ones who either die at Taylor's hands or take a dive with brig time. Well, if I'm going to be dumped on, it's going to be for helping the Marines, and not for selling our arms to the commies and being a goddamned traitor."

Delaplane knew he deserved the hit. But he was panicked. He'd seen what Tofte and Taylor would do. "Nobody wants this shit, Cap'n. It's hot. All of it. Straight to the top hot. It was meant for the Frogs. Now, we gonna take it to the rebels. That's the only plan I know and the one I'll obey."

"It's the Chinese paying for them, Delaplane. Rebels, there aren't any rebels. And if there were, they wouldn't have any money except for CIA money. And we aren't going to play that game. Now move your ass, sergeant, or you'll have a third problem. Me!"

Delaplane was clearly freaked out, nearly as badly as Strickland had seen some men when way too many Chinese had stormed down on them.

Strickland darted into the hut, leaving Delaplane outside.

The lead driver approached Delaplane. "We have to load now, Sergeant. Can't wait longer." He pointed to the sun. The drivers would not leave in the dark nor drive in the dark. Still too many Chinese roaming the country.

Delaplane recovered enough to answer him. "We got two guys inside to help. Use the forklift and hurry it along."

Strickland reappeared. He had a 3.5 launcher resting on his right shoulder with his right hand locked on the trigger guard and his finger on the trigger.

"Load the trucks and prepare to drive where I tell you," he said firmly with a voice that convinced the Korean driver but not

Delaplane. Then he headed for river's edge and aimed across the bow of the boat that looked like the Pirate's ship.

Delaplane's voice was clear when he cried out, "Damn, man. You've gone plumb loco."

Hans Tofte smashed his bony fist on the desk so hard the veneer split. "Goddamn it, Horace," he shouted. "Why can't you keep that son of a bitch leashed?" He plunked down into his chair. "Dutch Kramer's a Marine and we don't have problems with him."

Taylor found himself shrugging his shoulders out of frustration. He had no reasonable response.

"You're an experienced officer, dammit! What's going on with you Horace? You didn't have these problems in France. So, handle him!" Taylor, who had worked with Tofte during WW-II in France, nodded acknowledgement of Tofte's admonishment. But he said nothing.

"Your silence is deafening, Horace. So, what the hell are you going to do?"

Taylor spent a few more seconds contemplating the narrow paths he'd fallen upon as though he were being prodded like a steer heading to slaughter. When he spoke, he did so with caution. "I think we should let DuPre pick up the supplies. That might be the cleanest way out of this mess." Then, as if to cap off his new idea he added, "That's what Truman wanted us to do anyway, isn't it?"

Tofte had no love left for Truman. "Screw Truman. Is Black still in the area or did the Marine finish him off, too?"

Strickland had fired across Black's bow and had then directed the man to dock at the small port south of the hut, the port known by each of them as Port Salvation. But Taylor explained, it had gone no further. Strickland had not made a move yet to load the boat. The message had come to Taylor quite clearly though. And it had come directly from the pirate captain.

For the moment, Taylor's internal processor went blank. Where was Tofte going with this and more importantly where the hell was Strickland headed. Finally he said, "He's tied to. He's madder than hell at Strickland. Referred to him as a mad man."

Tofte cocked an eye, and then laughed. "I wish I'd seen that shot. Black's not exactly my favorite operative." He jumped up and paced behind his desk. "Your thought about the French. Yes. Possibly they could pick it up. Hell, you could put the stuff in Black's boat along with the asshole Frenchman who turned us in." He made a motion with his hands as though he were holding a giant ball in front of them. Then he shook them and pointed a finger at Taylor. "Possibly we could pass this whole thing off on the French." He stopped, turned to Taylor. "Forget what Truman wanted. What the fuck do we care? The bastard fired us. I'm more interested in seeing that a few of our loyal subjects disappear." He spoke with sarcasm ringing in his voice. But Taylor knew what he wanted. It was always the same thing. Clean house before the house cleans you.

Taylor's eyes were trapped by Tofte's. For him Tofte's motives were clear but his hang-up with the Frenchman was disturbing. Tofte was just not ready to accept the fact that it was he who had screwed up, not the French or any of his agents. Tofte himself had tied the rope around his own neck and therefore hung the two of them. Taylor would go down as hard as his boss. That's the way it always worked in The Company.

Tofte continued, "We have twenty-four hours before anyone chases us out of here. Wrap up business by then." Then, without any indication, he changed his tone to that of a friend in need and said, "The Chinese art work? What about that?"

"Delaplane was able to pull that truck out of the convoy on their way north. Feigned engine trouble. None of it was damaged."

Tofte ruminated a moment. He wondered whether he'd made a mistake trading off the Han dynasty paintings and the 4th century AD Chinese script work. Profitable, yes. Backfire? Possibly.

"Delivered?"

"Yes."

Tofte nodded. "Okay, you have a mission. Use the Cessna 195."

By the time Drier made it back to camp, he'd given his field jacket to Peggy to use as a pillow against the hard steel back rest. She'd fallen asleep. The corpse had shifted into the jeep's well between the rear side seats where he'd left it. He wondered the whole way back why in the hell he'd taken the girl's sister with him but finally settled on a thought that was lodged deeply within his mind: The Navy pathologists might be able to confirm the that dum-dums were really used to kill the prostitutes and Peggy's sister. Three days separated their deaths. Was it the same shooter? Maybe they could figure it out.

He pulled up in front of the sickbay and braked to a stop. Peggy remained asleep. He went into the pyramidal where he found the duty corpsman reading a Mickey Spillane paperback. "I've got a present for you out here, Dobbins," he said. "Need your help."

Red haired and intensely freckled corpsman Michael Dobbins jumped up and followed Drier to the jeep. Dobbins was shorter than Drier but a hell of a lot stronger. He had tried to grow a beard and a mustache, just to be different, but the effort had failed and now "baby face" Dobbins, as strong as he was, had subdued his conscious personality to all those around him. Whatever they wanted, they got.

"Another KIA?"

"Sort of. It's a woman. I want you to put her into the reefer for tonight."

"Man, Lieutenant. You shot a woman?"

Drier was quick to shake his head. "No, Doc. And don't ask any more questions. Better for you if you don't." Drier leaned closer to the corpsman and with a whisper of secrecy said, "It's about an investigation. Top secret. Okay?"

The corpsman liked Lieutenant Drier. He was a good officer, not one of those asshole Navy admin types. "Sure. I'll tag her KIA/ Unknown. I'll put your name on the tag for contact. That okay?"

Drier nodded. Together they carried her around the back of the pyramidal where the generator kept the reefer cold. Occasional KIAs passed through the area on their way to Pusan and then home. In the interim they were kept on ice where the fresh food for the galley was stored. Fortunately for Dobbins the fighting had kept its distance from Freedom Village, so he found himself handling very few dead soldiers and Marines.

Drier thanked him and then drove to Hawk's quarters where Hawk was catching up on his letter writing. When Drier entered his tent, Hawk glanced up with surprise. Drier explained what had happened to him in Seoul and then told Hawk about the two girls.

"You brought them here?" Hawk seemed startled but accepting.

"Dobbins has them." He pulled the shattered bullet from his pocket and handed it to Hawk. "That's the only evidence I found, Colonel."

Hawk rolled the spent round in his hand.

"Yes, yes. That's it. Just like the rounds found at the trucks. Good work, David. I'll courier this to Pusan."

Drier explained Peggy and then said with a weaker voice, "The Koreans beat her with night sticks, their own police, Colonel."

Hawk understood, he'd witnessed ROK officers beating their own troops if they didn't do exactly as told.

"It's a strange culture to us, David. Koreans are very good fighters. But for some reason they seem to beat on their own people for punishment or for training purposes. It's one of the discouraging things about fighting this war."

"The Army CID guy in Seoul threatened to have me shot if I didn't get out of his office. Doesn't sound like we're much better."

Hawk considered what Drier said. "They're tough, but that sounds like an ungrounded threat. One way to get you out of his hair I guess."

Drier understood Hawk's response to mean he didn't want to push the CID subject further.

"Tell Dobbins to quarter the girl in sickbay," Hawk said, side stepping Drier's comment. "A plan of sorts is mulling around in my mind right now. As to the corpse, maybe I can get a Naval coroner type up here to do an autopsy. Maybe they can figure out if these bullets were used on all the ladies or not." Hawk appeared as though he had just thought of something. "Our doctor might be able to do an autopsy."

"Yes, sir." Then he remembered, "Peggy would like us to provide her sister with a Catholic burial."

"Peggy? Ah, the girl. Check with the Chaplain on that. You said she speaks English."

"Yes, sir. French and Korean, too. I learned on the drive here that she grew up in Paris. Her old man was a Frenchman. He married a Korean woman in the late twenties when the French were monkeying around over here. She was born in thirty-one. He died just before the war in Europe ended."

Hawk flashed a smile. Women he thought. They can tell you their life story quicker than you can get a day's information from a man's life. He thought about the girl. A Korean girl born in Paris, speaking at least three languages and now involved with prostitutes in Korea. He'd have to return to that subject later. Maybe question the girl. He said, "Do you think she knows anything about what her sister may have been up to? A reason for her death?"

"Didn't get that far, sir."

"CID know about it?"

Drier shook his head. "Don't know, Colonel. The Major I mentioned refused to answer questions about the prostitutes so I didn't drop in on them with Peggy's sister. Oh, he did let me read a report. They were shot with lead slugs from a .45 caliber. Head shots, all of them." He paused and saw that Hawk was considering his report. He went on, "The Korean cops were also very unfriendly." He gulped down a mouthful of fresh air and added, "Maybe Captain Strickland can learn more from her."

Hawk looked hard into Drier's eyes and said, "Don't inform Captain Strickland about the girl just yet."

"Sir?"

"I'd like to think about this some more tonight before the word gets out. Dobbins good for silence?"

"His hatch is always closed. Good man, sir."

Drier left Hawk while his colonel continued to roll the lead around in his hand. For him it was a major piece of evidence. A clue to more than just one crime.

"All I've got to do," he mumbled aloud, "is figure it out."

CHAPTER 26

THERE WASN'T MUCH to Port Salvation. Not after the U.S. Navy's bombardment and then total abandonment by the locals. One long dock remained and it had a doubtful future. The river wasn't exactly the Mississippi, either. It seemed much narrower and a lot calmer although the port was in an area that could be marginally referred to as a bay. The river's narrowness was probably the reason the dock ran parallel to the river instead of jutting out into the water.

The area would probably later grow into a large suburb of the main city, but for now six truck drivers and two U.S. Army personnel didn't give a hoot about that. Four trucks had already unloaded and returned to the hut.

Neither did Captain Black, who watched with Admiral Bird from the starboard flying bridge in a silence surrounded by his own pleasure at what he considered the biggest boondoggle yet in this war. He was to take all the materiel that these trucks could load aboard and do with it what he wanted. More profit from a mindless government. It all suited him just fine.

This was the second loading the trucks had accomplished and the army sergeant, who was obviously one of those CIA types, was grousing that their fucking hut was still half loaded with shit. Too bad he couldn't take it all aboard. But fourteen truck loads had filled his hold.

He thought about contacting his old friend, another shipper with a boat his size who he'd known all his life, but putting news like this on the wire would have brought the entire U.S. fugging navy down on him.

Black walked to the port side of the JR to check on the river's flow. It rose and settled with the ocean tide exactly according to his tide tables. That was something you just couldn't change. His displacement would allow him to sail out at high tide. He sure as hell didn't want to run into old sunken ship masts, hulls or some of the other trash that had made small islands of potential disaster in the Han River. It was getting close to sailing time. And when it came, he'd cast off and get the hell out of there. Quickly. Forever as far as he was concerned. No way would he deal with these rotten bastards again.

He returned to the starboard bridge and called down through his megaphone to the stupid army sergeant in charge. "How th' hork much longer ye gonna take?"

Delaplane held up one finger. "One hour," he called back.

Another truck backed up to the boat and the large crane that worked from amidships swung around with it's net. The operator lowered it to the dock and the truckers started to moved crates to it immediately.

Delaplane worked his way up the gangplank. He headed past the crane house and up to the flying bridge. He needed to ensure that Black would allow him to travel out of there when he sailed.

"Ye surprise me dogface," Black said when he got there.

"How's that, Cap'n?"

"Didn't think ye liked me boat."

"Awk," Admiral Bird squawked. "Not good fer ye."

Delaplane stared at the parrot when he said, "Nothing 'gainst you or your boat, Cap'n Black."

Black looked out to the Koreans who seemed nervous with what he called a 'zooka and asked, "Why be they thar?" The parrot cocked his head and glared at Delaplane as though demanding an answer.

The Koreans were sitting by the storage building, an old metal affair that was pretty much shot up.

"Cap'n Strickland's doings. Guess he wants the area guarded."

Black didn't' believe him. "From what? Us?"

Delaplane didn't know where Black was going with the conversation. He looked to Black and said, "Don't' really know. He didn't tell me."

Black returned his attention to Delaplane. "So, what do ye want?"

"A ride out of here."

Admiral Bird squawked, "A ride out of here." The bird then

jumped from his left shoulder to the other and seemed to be going into convulsions with a high pitched laughing sound.

Black grinned. "The admiral be laughin' at ye, Sergeant. So, Ye want t' go AWOL?"

Delaplane nodded. "Forever."

"Ye won't like th' quarters."

"I'll get off in Formosa."

Black nodded. "Tell ye what. After Formosa I'm headed t' Australia. Ye can ride that far. I'll sell th' boat thar an' then I'm flyin' t' Cuba. Or maybe Jamaica. They tell me that's a really nice place t' retire."

"I be goin' wit ya," the parrot cried out. Then it laughed again.

Delaplane wasn't sure if he'd get along with the parrot on a trip that long but the alternative wasn't good looking either. "Agreed," he said. "Thank you."

"You might nay thank me half way ou' t' sea," he said with a deep chuckle that carried a negative message. "This old tub be a rough voyage sometimes."

Delaplane considered that and then said, "Not nearly as wild as the one I'm on."

CHAPTER 27

COLONEL HARRISON BRADFORD, Jr., son of the legendary Lieutenant General Harrison Bradford of World War I fame, decided it was time to come clean to his two investigators before they moved further ahead.

Harrison had been a good infantry officer according to his peers and his previous commanders, who included the current commandant, Clifford Cates. But after all his years of proving himself capable of earning stars, he had gotten himself hanged at the end of a political rope. When Harry S Truman had referred to the Marines in a letter to Congressman Gordon McDonough made public by the New York Times, as "the Navy's police force and nothing more," he'd screwed himself with his "big mouth," a phrase used in a follow-up story. Unfortunately, he'd voiced his opinion of HST's outlandish allegations loud enough to be heard by reporters who then published mostly accurate quotes.

In the same letter to the congressman, Truman had also accused the Corps of having a "propaganda machine almost equal to Stalin's." Bradford wasn't the only complaining Marine, but he found himself the most visible.

Bradford learned the hard way that his ultimate commander in chief was HST, not Clifford Cates. So, off he went from his counter-intelligence job at Headquarters Marine Corps to being the senior Marine in the heart of the enemy's territory, with the not so favorable job of trying to keep peace in Peace Village. At least he was no longer a news item.

He spent his first month in Korea in Pusan, then moved to Gijeong-dong, otherwise known as Peace Village. He reflected now on his month in Pusan, and decided it was time to reveal another secret of his existence. He was an 0302, but he also remained part of the Marine counter-intelligence office, a fact that his freshly minted nemesis HST wasn't aware of. When Truman had ordered Cates to "send that SOB" to Korea, the CIC thought that was that.

But CI needed someone in Korea as well. So, now, he had a challenge. Should he explain himself before Hawk, Strickland and Drier reported their findings to him, or afterwards? He stared at his pipe in its cradle. He thought a fresh bowl of tobacco might clear his mind. Then he changed his mind and decided against wasting it. If he was actually feeling pangs of guilt or stress, then he was sure that smoking a pipe would probably go unnoticed by his tastebuds. What a waste that would be, he thought. So instead, he jammed two pieces of Dentyne gum into his mouth and worked them over for a few minutes before removing them and dumping them into his waste basket. The gum always refreshed his mind, he'd tell you, but the chewing part was a pain in the ass and definitely un-officer like.

Hawk was first to arrive. After the nuances of brisk greetings he took a seat in front of Bradford's desk and spread open his manila folder. He wasn't sure at the moment what he was going to explain or detail to the boss man. He felt immensely out of place. He was a pilot, not a detective. He'd traveled from this end of Korea to Pusan and Seoul twice in two days on the ground. He was tired of jeeps, trucks, dust and bureaucrats. He wanted back into the air.

He looked into Bradford's eyes and said, "Lieutenant Drier is behind me by a few minutes. Haven't heard back from Frank. But, Brad, I'd like to offer an opinion and a suggestion about all this before they get here."

Bradford wanted to move the meeting to the bunker again. This stuff was too important to be overheard. However, for Hawk, he nodded his approval and impulsively reached for the pipe after all. He knew Hawk well enough to understand the tone in the man's voice. The aviator was probably as frustrated or nuts about all this as he was. So, what the hell? Smoke the damned thing. Out came the Zippo.

Hawk kept his voice low. "As I see it, we are in the middle of a war zone that is in itself a giant mesh of various conspiracies. I'm not talking about the politics of this war. But the war itself."

Bradford flashed his Zippo and sucked in on the stem. It tasted a ton better than the goddamned gum. "Go on."

"Right. First, let's erase the Navy from anything to do with what we're looking at. The only Navy types around here are three doctors and six corpsmen. Second, let's erase from the equation the non-American members of the U.N."

"All of them?" Brad blew smoke away from Hawk.

Hawk squinted for a moment, considered Bradford's meaning and then said, "Yes, sir. All of them. Except Koreans, of course."

Bradford rocked back on the hind legs of his chair and motioned Hawk to continue.

"Third. There is no Air Force involved here."

"Okay. Agreed."

"That leaves the Marines and the Army."

"And the Koreans."

Hawk nodded. "Yes. I want to push to the end of my opinion before Lieutenant Drier and Frank get here. For reasons that I believe you'll understand."

"Go."

Hawk took a deep breath and said, "I think that Captain Strickland may be guilty of treason. I believe he's guilty of murder in the first degree and that—"

Bradford rocked forward with a crash. He leaned across his desk as best his paunch would allow. Hawk had just made a decision for him. "For god's sake Hawk, we're in a tent. Let's lower our voices. You're charging a Marine Corps legend with high crimes here." He was sorry that he'd jumped on his friend and said so.

Hawk nodded in the affirmative. "That's okay. I forget about the canvas sometimes."

Bradford eased off.

"I also said that I have some suggestions."

Bradford held his right hand up. "Hold on. Just a moment." He stood from his desk and went to the adjoining tent that was stapled to his with a makeshift plywood doorway. He opened it to make sure his adjutant and clerk had taken their mess hall call. They were gone. He closed the door. "This hatch is useless," he said. He returned to his desk.

"Brad, I —"

Bradford held his hand up again. "I'm the one who has some

explaining to do, Hawk. Maybe I've let you go too far already. Apologies are in order here, but I think you'll understand."

Hawk's expression twisted the pilot's features as though he'd just broken the sound barrier. "Sir?"

Bradford knew that Hawk was cleared for top-secret information so he wasn't bothered by that. He cleared his mouth of smoke and then explained to Hawk that besides the Marines and the Army there was another organization involved. "The CIA," he told him.

Bradford explained that he was fully aware of what they were now referring to as the CIA's "third army" in Korea, and that there were other clearly illegal activities in the zone that made no sense even though he was aware of their existence and that, depressingly, they had been authorized by the U.S. government. Specifically, the commander in chief. Bradford paused when he suggested that. There he was again, ragging on the president. He moved forward explaining that, "These activities include money laundering by the Koreans and some military personnel, the involvement of all four military services in Korea in clandestine activities among others," and that their own Frank Strickland had probably become involved with the CIA. "I'm not sure how deep Frank has gotten into this CIA crap," he said, "but I think you've uncovered some of it."

Hawk fell back into his chair. It was though someone had just hit him alongside his head. "I think we better go to the bunker, sir."

After Winfield and Donovan took their posts in front of the bunker, the two colonels continued their meeting.

Bradford explained his own role in Korea to Hawk to get things back in order, and why he'd been sent there. He then explained how counter-intelligence operated differently than the CIA. When he finished he sat back in his chair hard, as though he'd just dumped a huge weight from his shoulders. He waited in silence until finally Hawk spoke.

"I never thought I'd want to retire, Brad. But this is a lot of heavy stuff here. Enough to make anyone want to retire."

Bradford agreed.

Hawk said, "However, none of this exonerates Frank, unless we can get him to come clean. Brad, if we let Marines kill or trade with the enemy just because the intel types tell them to, then we will have lost our most trusted men and women to an enemy within. We can't just sit on Frank Strickland's activities. They could prove disastrous to our Corps."

Bradford bent forward slightly and searched Hawk's eyes through the tops of his own. "Good points. Maybe more dramatic than real, however." He glanced to his watch. "He's due here."

Hawk pushed harder. "If we keep silent on this, then we too are guilty."

The fraternity of the Marine Corps was being threatened is how Bradford read Hawk's warning. And he was right. Loyalty to Corps and other Marines was far more important than the illicit behavior that had apparently overpowered one of the best fighting Marines Bradford had ever known. He spoke carefully and clearly. "Can you prove any of these allegations?"

Hawk was stuck. The word allegations seemed inflexible to him. He was a pilot, not a lawyer or cop or infantryman. He passed his findings through his mind for a minute and then went ahead. "Sergeant Fraker witnessed him loading munitions from a mysterious Quonset hut aboard unmarked trucks this morning. Actually," he glanced to his watch, "they're probably still at it. Up the road, not far from here. The Han River. Fraker claims they were North Koreans. When I put that together with the trucks left at the Seventh I concluded Strickland was involved with that as well."

"Anything else?"

"The lead bullets. Dum dums they're called. You know about them. I ran them down to Navy pathologists and the bullets found at the sight and in the whorehouse were identical."

Bradford thought a moment then said, "Ballistics tests?"

Hawk felt out of place. "I sent the round that Lieutenant Drier found at the truck site down. They sent a report back. The two rounds were different than the round found by the original site investigators. That's a bit of a hang up."

"Both were forty-fives?"

"Yes."

"Two different forty-fives?" Bradford asked.

"Apparently."

Bradford rocked back in his chair. "Dammit."

Hawk was instantly curious. "What?"

Bradford bit his lower lip for a moment then said, "I know of only one Marine who carries two pistols and can fire them together. Accurately."

Hawk caught on. "Strickland."

Bradford nodded.

Drier showed up. The silence that came over them was thunderous. Drier detected it immediately. "Would it be better if I came at another time?" he asked.

Bradford waved him in. "No, David. Pull up a chair. We have some things to talk about."

Captain Black adjusted his felt hat that had once been an off cream color, but was now black from diesel smoke and grease, and decided that it was time to go. Admiral Bird jumped into the air for a moment when the hat came off and then landed squarely on his left epaulet again. He screeched like an owl but squawked out no words.

It was time for Black to get his boat out of this dinky port and sail away from Korea. He'd already figured out who would pay for the American arms and munitions and they weren't too far away. No, he thought, not the Chinese in Korea. The man who would pay him was the Nationalist Chinese leader in Formosa. America had tightened the screws on them and refused them further arms. Political help, yes. But America had decided to restrict arms for the Nationalist government, hoping he guessed, that they'd figure out how to defend themselves when the mainland Chinese decided it was time to kill off their anti-communist offspring. Oh yeah, they'd been teased by the Americans with used weapons like a few fighter planes and tanks and some ground support. But not enough to hold back even a light wave of Chinese from the mainland. They were a ripe market ready for his new cargo.

He also figured that his boat load of new military goods was worth a few million American dollars from the Nationalists. That would be enough to get out of this business for good. Return to his choice of home port in Cuba or maybe Jamaica, and live the life of a good pirate until Davey Jones called for him.

Below him, toward the aft section, Delaplane directed the last of the cargo nets into the hold. Black marveled that American military types could be so dumb. Here they were in someone else's country, fighting North Koreans and Chinese, and yet they were using North

Koreans to smuggle their own arms to a bunch of Frenchies in yet another country where they didn't belong. Besides seeming terribly complex, something in America had gone terribly haywire.

He pushed himself up from the gunnel, cast his Camel butt over the side and muttered, "The horkin' war's made everyone nuts and a few of us rich."

"Man th' canon," Admiral Bird squawked.

Delaplane stumbled down the gangplank to the unstable dock. He was not a sailor and hated ships and boats and gangplanks. How in the hell, he wondered do they walk on those damned things when they keep rolling around like that? Even the dock moves. He went straight to Strickland. "Done," he said. "That's it."

"There's still more in the hut."

Delaplane threw his head toward Black and said, "His hold is full. Couldn't even get another round in there if we wanted to. Fourteen truck loads. *Big* truck loads."

Strickland had made up his mind about what to do. He walked to the edge of the dock directly under Black who leaned once again over the gunnel.

"I don't want you to depart until twenty-hundred."

Black was irritated. "Why th' hork nay? We're loaded. Tides up. I'm castin' off now."

"Avast ye scallywag," Admiral Bird called out.

"No," Strickland said firmly. "Twenty-hundred hours, maybe later."

Delaplane came close to Strickland and in a low voice said, "Let 'im go, Cap'n. Changed my mind. Ain't gonna go with 'im."

Strickland didn't react. "You want to get out of here alive, Black, do as I say."

He turned to his two Koreans with the launcher and said in a clear, sharp voice loud enough for Black to hear, "If he leaves this dock before I release him, I want a 3.5 sent up his ass." He glanced up to Black, held the pirate's blazing stare for a moment then headed back to his jeep. "Come with me, Delaplane. We're going back to camp for some chow. I was supposed to appear before the colonel as well." He glanced to his watch. Dammit, he probably missed the meeting.

Black's eyes followed them until his gaze fell on the two Korean soldiers. One man was sitting on a military stool holding a 3.5 launcher while the other stood behind him cradling a rocket. It was obvious to Black that they'd been sitting there for a while.

"Fuggers," he muttered. He glanced to his timepiece, which was mounted on the bulkhead aft of the wheel. It was Fourteen-hundred hours. Shit, six hours. Dusk. To his crew he called out, "Batten th' hatches. Prepare t' cast off at seventeen bucketfull o' hours." It would be low tide but he no longer cared about that. He went into the wheelhouse to check on his navigation radar. He'd be needing it soon.

Admiral Bird seemed to be applauding with his wings.

They were still in the bunker and Hawk was still pitching his investigation results. "We've linked him to the women, to the drivers, and I wonder at times about the POW we had in the tank farm."

Bradford had his own thoughts, however. "Something's fishy here, Hawk. I mean this smacks of tactics I learned about at Marine Barracks." He meant Headquarters Marine Corps. "OSS actions during the Deuce. And now we got the CIA. No," he repeated, "something's fishy here. I'm sure of it. There's another element. Missing. Something is missing."

Hawk respected Bradford and had to bend some. "I'd like to prove Strickland isn't the one responsible. But Brad, the evidence seems to be stacked against him."

Bradford took a deep puff of his pipe. After he blew out the smoke he said, "Have you presented all this to Frank?"

"No, sir."

"David?" Bradford said to Drier, stabbing the youngster in the heart with his abrupt attention. "Your thoughts."

Drier spoke slowly. "Skipper's a good man, Colonel. This is very difficult for me. I can't believe he's a criminal. No way." He had to take a deep breath. For some reason he could hardly breathe. "I think you're right, Colonel. Something's missing here."

Bradford thought about the girl in sickbay and Drier's trip to Seoul. Again he asked what Drier might have learned that he may not have reported.

Drier reached into his memory bank. So much had happened

in such a short period. "The girl. Her dead sister. Some threatening Koreans. An army CID major who I thought would like to see me dead. A lead slug where her sister was killed."

"It was a match to one of the slugs at the trucks," Hawk interjected.

"So, where do we stand now?" Bradford asked.

"I interviewed the girl," Hawk said. "She witnessed the shooting of her sister. Won't fess up about the prostitutes."

"Description?"

"She said her mind went blank.'"

Bradford mulled that over for a minute. He reached out for his counter intelligence schooling. It was rare when a witness couldn't remember something. "Anything at all?"

"Nothing."

Bradford played with that. The girl was probably lying. How did she happen to latch on to Drier of all people? He shut his eyes to try to envision the scene and what had happened. "Military or civilian?" he asked with his eyes still shut.

Drier remembered Peggy's conversation during their first meeting. "There were two of them. At first she said an American killed her sister, then she told me she hid in a pile of laundry and clearly said if she hadn't that they would have killed her."

"Why is she holding back?" Bradford asked.

Drier was at a loss. His beauty queen was becoming tarnished. She was holding back. "She told me to hustle out of there and that she'd answer questions later."

Bradford tapped his ashtray with his pipe. A fresh thought hit him square on. "Possibly another CIA type. Question is, why does she want up here?" He looked into their eyes one at a time. "Is she armed, gents?"

"Sir?"

Bradford was about to enter into foreign territory. He'd never been great at guessing, but this challenge demanded some. "I know a lot about the man Strickland met with in Pusan. It's a guess, but Frank may be in a lot of trouble. Let me explain. If Frank signed on with them, and then discovered what they were up to, and if he thought their activities smacked of treason, then I suspect," he paused, leaned back into his chair and held both hands up as though surrendering, "I suspect that he's fighting them from within and they know it."

"Which means?" Hawk said.

"Which could very well mean that his life is in danger. He's leading two lives and walking a thin line. He's what we used to call a free agent out. He's discovered some dirty business and can't really go anywhere with it so he's trying to square it away himself. A very, very thin layer of ice to walk on." He paused and bit his lower lip for a few seconds. His audience didn't interrupt since they recognized the habit and knew more was coming. After a few seconds Bradford said, "He could lose his life."

Hawk was trying to keep up. "And you think the girl might have something to do with that?"

Brad nodded slightly. "Anything is possible. What I do believe is that Frank very likely needs our help right now."

Drier gulped so hard he thought they could hear him. "He was the one who left the trucks for the Seventh to find, wasn't he?"

"Appears so." Bradford said. "I can't tell you where they were originally headed, but you can take a guess they weren't headed to us."

"You're not making this easy, Brad," Hawk said.

"Then move on what you have quickly. We can't drag this out. I suggest that there are probably other CIA agents in this camp. I should think that your Sergeant Delaplane may be one and that he too may be a target."

"Preposterous," Hawk muttered not really wanting to be heard. But Bradford picked it up.

"Not after two years at counter-intelligence. Trust me on this Hawk. These people are capable of anything. Including killing a few of their own."

Hawk sounded introspective when he asked, "Is it possible that Frank has just gone crazy? He's had a lot of war in a short period of time."

Bradford sucked on his pipe but got nothing more than the sound of whooshing air. That was okay since he was really only searching for a few moments to think about Hawk's suggestion. Yes, he said to himself only, I have thought about that. He reached into his field jacket pocket and pulled a .45 clip out and set it on the desk in front of the two Marines whose job was about to get tougher. "When I arrived at the range a while ago to speak with him, he was shooting. This was sitting on the seat of his jeep."

Hawk reached over and grabbed it up. "Damn."

Drier easily saw the bullets. "Dum dums."

Bradford said, "If he isn't working for the CIA then we have a challenge here. If he is working for the CIA then—"

"Then we still have a challenge," Hawk said.

"Right. Let's get through this quickly. Find a witness or be a witness. Otherwise everything you have is circumstantial."

Hawk leaned forward with clasped hands, his elbows on his knees and his eyes glued to the steel deck of the bunker. He let out a breath of air and said, "The girl claims to be a witness to the killings. Now, I'm not sure of her credibility."

"Maybe we could test her," Drier said, not fully understanding what kind of test would work.

Hawk said, "Okay. Let's go with that. We could arrange for her to I.D. Frank or hopefully tell us it wasn't him."

Bradford set his pipe back into its cradle. "Quickly."

The mess hall was made from four double length tents linked together into one facility. That didn't improve the look of the canvasback, but it did offer up more room inside for the troops to chow down.

Mess was served all day since the personnel at the camp were on so many various time schedules many couldn't eat in the typical shifts. Off-duty sentries, watches, and corpsmen ate generally during normal periods. Others came and went at odd hours including the middle of the night. They would then relieve their counterparts who would eat on their own schedule. The mess served breakfast from midnight to eleven hundred hours, lunch from midday through about sixteen hundred hours and dinner until midnight. Lunch on this day was not very edible anyway, so some on-duty personnel might not show, instead choosing to get a half-hour of shut-eye rather than feel crappy the rest of the day with the "puke" served in the giant tent with the misnomer of "meatloaf."

Peggy appeared in the mess just as Hawk wanted her to. She looked like a very young North Korean soldier on his way to the prisoner of war camp near Seoul. The two sentries, Winfield and Donovan, marched her into the mess hall during first chow call and sat her down at the table reserved for MPs and POWs. The sight of the POW with them was not unusual. Drier had explained earlier that if it worked out that way they would remain until everyone in camp had been served.

Winfield went to the chow line and picked up two trays for food. After they were filled, he took them to the table where he placed one in front of Donovan, and one in front of Peggy. Then he returned for his own.

While waiting in line, Corporal Bowers bumped Winfield's shoulder and asked, "Who's the newbie?"

"Came in this afternoon."

"Ought 'a shoot 'im."

Winfield eyed Bowers suspiciously. "Not on my watch, asshole" he said, clearly indicating with the tone of his voice and the fire in his eyes that if Bowers tried to do so he'd find himself dead first.

At the table, Peggy sat motionlessly just as she'd been instructed to do. POWs were not allowed to move, gesticulate or look around, but her eyes marched from one American to another, ostensibly searching for the man who murdered her sister. Abruptly, her gaze locked on someone. Her lips parted. She could hardly sit still.

"What is it?" Donovan asked between clenched teeth and unmoving lips.

"Him. His friend."

Donovan glanced to Peggy to check the trail of her stare. When he followed it his eyes settled on Sergeant Stanley Delaplane. He turned back to Peggy. "The Army guy?"

She nodded. "He came there."

Winfield returned with his food tray. He quickly caught the expressions on the two faces and knew something was up.

"Who?"

"Delaplane."

"Oh man. Not good. You don't mess with that bastard. He's the strangest dude I ever seen."

"Get the lieutenant."

Winfield left them. A few moments later he returned and sat down opposite Donovan. Donovan understood Winfield's expression. Lieutenant Drier couldn't be found.

"How's the meatloaf?" Winfield asked blankly while trying like hell to remain nonchalant.

"Don't even touch it. Try the potato. Not too bad if you smear it with butter."

"She's not eating," Winfield said.

"Neither are you."

"Smart ass. She's got to eat or someone's gonna spot her."

Peggy picked up a spoon.

"You need chopsticks?"

She shook her head nearly breaking out in laughter. At that same moment it seemed to them that she'd frozen up like an icicle. She'd become so rigid that they thought she'd turned into a statue. Her eyes frosted over with a look of terror. Her lips pursed tightly. She stopped breathing. She couldn't function further. All hell seemed to have broken loose in her mind with a fire so hot it seemed to Donovan that she'd totally melted down.

"Holy Jesus," Donovan said. "I seen this happen to my buddy on the line. She's freaked by our guy. Our fucking PMO, man."

Winfield, his back to the crowd, asked, "What?"

"He just walked in. She's lookin' straight at him man, and she's freaked out. I mean it's like she's saying he's the one who pulled the trigger." His voice cracked when he added hoarsely, "The PMO man, the fucking PMO is the fucking killer."

Winfield snuck a look. He saw Strickland standing with Delaplane. When he turned back he said, "I don't know what he done, but she's just singled out two guys I don't ever wantta fuck with. Which one did it? Both? Uh, man, let's get our asses out 'a here."

"We need the lieutenant."

"I couldn't find the lieutenant. Look, this thing he's got us into could come down hard on us. I'm for gettin' outta here, man. Look at her. She ain't moved. She's froze. They see that and we're good as dead."

They gulped down a blast of coffee and escorted Peggy out of the mess hall walking briskly past Strickland, who never gave them a glance.

Outside, after they'd walked nearly a hundred feet toward the sickbay, Drier came up to them. Both he and Hawk had stayed out of the mess hall for fear that Delaplane and Strickland might be distracted by their presence.

"Thanks gents. I watched through the tent flap on the east side. Job well done." Drier didn't tell them that Colonel Hawk had also watched.

"It's the PMO, sir. She came unglued when he walked in," Winfield said.

Donovan added, "Both of 'em, Lieutenant. She froze solid when she saw 'em both."

Drier looked into Peggy's reddened eyes and asked, "Peggy? Are you sure?"

She nodded, then ran to the sickbay where she disappeared behind the makeshift wooden hatch.

"Man, this is freaky, Lieutenant. We gonna get into trouble with this?" Winfield asked.

Drier turned his attention from sickbay to the two men. "Don't talk about this even if asked. Don't ever mention it. Your survival may depend upon that." Then he headed for sickbay to find Corpsman Dobbins.

Dobbins was in the fourth of a five tent sickbay. The fifth tent, separated by a solid plywood wall, was where the reefers were kept. He was at a stainless steel table that was long enough to hold a body, and usually did. Drier found him when Dobbins was cleaning up a mess from a surgical procedure that two of the medical officers had performed on a wounded Marine. The Marine had already been transported out of the area by a road-bound ambulance.

"Dobbins," Drier greeted.

"She just ran into her bunk area, Lieutenant" Dobbins said in a low voice.

"Not looking for her. Wanted to ask you a few questions."

Dobbins was enlisted. Drier was an officer. Even though Dobbins liked Drier, he went into immediate defense mode. Something was always up when an officer said he wanted to ask some questions. "What can I help with?"

Drier put his finger to his lips to indicate they should speak in low tones. Dobbins nodded that was okay.

Drier wanted to know how long the sister had been dead. He also wanted to know how she'd been killed or how she'd died. And what about bruises?

"Doctor McPherson looked at her. Said she'd been dead for about three or four days. Best he could tell, her head was pretty much blown away by a shotgun or a high impact round of ammo. Like maybe a forty-five shoved up her mouth or something. It wasn't pretty, Lieutenant."

Drier remembered his first moments with the corpse. Dobbins had got it right. She wasn't pretty. "Bruises?" he asked.

Dobbins shook his head. "Doc said he didn't think so. She was decomposing pretty fast, Lieutenant." He held up his hand and motioned that he was going to go to the files and get the report. When he returned he opened and then pointed to McPherson's notes.

"She was shot twice. Once in the head and once in the heart with a 7.62 round. Doc couldn't tell which one killed her. But he thinks it was the heart shot." He looked into Drier's eyes. "That's NATO ammo."

"NATO?"

"Yeah. NATO has a same caliber round. Works in all their weapons."

The time of death had stuck in Drier's mind as though it had been glued there. The prostitutes had been murdered three days later. Something was not right here. And a NATO weapon? Was he dealing with someone from Europe? He closed his eyes. The OSS was in Europe. The CIA is the old OSS. He didn't want to wander off into that headache and found himself glad that Dobbins interrupted his thoughts.

The corpsman handed his report to Drier and pointed to where he'd written the cause of death. "Here," he was pointing to another note McPherson had written. "Doc thinks the head wound was administered later to prevent anyone eye-deeing the lady." He looked up, "Doc says that happens 'round here. He was in Taegu before he got this wonderful job. Local cops did that. Especially if they killed someone they didn't want the blame for."

"M.P.s sometimes carry sawed off shotguns."

"Yes, sir. But everyone in this country also has a forty-five or something like it. And Lieutenant, the Koreans use them. Sometimes on drunken American personnel. I know. We've patched up a few of them and buried others."

Drier walked to the hatch between the tents trying to remember what the Korean cops in Seoul used as side arms. The nightsticks had been prominent, but what firepower had he noted? His eyes searched for Peggy's cubicle. It was closed up with surgical curtains. He turned back to Dobbins. "Have you had any conversations with her?"

"Yes. A few. They don't get very far though. She's pretty tight-lipped."

Drier nodded. "What do you think of her?"

"Foreign. Something missing there."

"She claims she witnessed twelve prostitutes die at the hands of Americans. In the location where her sister was."

Dobbins motioned Drier to come back into the surgical area. He lowered his voice. "She could have. But something else bothers me 'bout her. Not sure what it is. Just a feeling. She's more interested in that army sergeant who drives that six-by. And, the PMO. Him, too."

"Captain Strickland?"

"Yes, sir. And Lieutenant, I had to give Delaplane a penny shot in the ass yesterday. I think the guy was in Seoul screwing one o' them witches. Figured he dipped into the wrong one. He really didn't say why, just figured it. Peggy watched us and afterwards pulled him aside and probably tried to get him for some money. You know, typical refugee stuff."

Drier was stunned. Peggy had just identified Delaplane as though it was the first time she'd seen him. "Has he spoken to her before?"

Dobbins seemed confused. Why would the lieutenant ask that question? "No, sir. Not that I know of."

Drier glanced to his watch. He had to ask her some questions but Hawk would be waiting for him. He'd be quick.

"I need to speak to her. Now." He darted around the partition and headed straight for Peggy's area. When he got there he announced himself through the curtain.

"Venez," Peggy responded.

Drier parted the curtains and saw Peggy lying on the cot, covered up to her neck under a cream white Navy hospital blanket with solid blue stripes running along the width at each end and the medical symbol imprinted in the center of the blue areas.

"Hi. You doing okay?"

She nodded.

"You identified two men. Do you know either one of them?"

Her eyes darted away from Drier toward the curtains when she said, "No."

Drier found himself breathing heavily. "Your escorts said you identified the two as being at your place. As the killers."

She shook her head. "No."

Drier was confused. This was not the same woman he'd brought up with him. Something had changed her. "Peggy, what's going on? I thought we were friends."

She nodded but remained silent.

Drier recalled Delaplane's visit to Peggy after his penicillin shot. "Was it the husky sergeant?"

She looked from the overhead light to his eyes, exhibiting a startled reaction as though Drier had just hit the nail on the head. She said nothing.

Drier nodded but wasn't sure about his interpretation of her meaning. "I'll be back, Peggy. I have an errand to run." He figured she was in shock or near it from having to I.D. the two men. "We'll talk then."

Back with Dobbins he said, "Don't let her out of here."

Dobbins rolled his head on his neck as though it were a swivel and said, "That's up to your guys, Lieutenant."

Drier would speak to Donovan and Winfield.

Half way to Seoul the road dipped down into a valley where Delaplane pulled off the road into an excessively large level meadow. It stretched from where he was parked for about a mile south with nearly a half mile open area. A single road seemed to be cut into the meadow from north to south. It was getting late in the day. He figured he'd lose his daylight before he got back to the hut and the loaded trucks. He searched the sky. Storm clouds were building. It would definitely rain before the night was over.

Behind and above him, Hawk pulled his jeep into a large clump of brush on the ridge that overlooked the valley. He and Drier watched through field glasses. The sunlight caused a flare in the glasses to the extent that they had to tilt their binoculars to port a little to dump the glint. That put the scene off-center for a while, which also put Delaplane at the edge of the frame. "Maybe I should shift the jeep instead," Hawk chuckled.

"He's not moving, Colonel. Seems to be waiting for someone."

Drier was right. Delaplane remained still, almost as though snoozing. "We'll wait," Hawk said.

A six-by roared past them, coming from behind. It dove down into the valley, drowning them in a sea of dust that floated silently but inexorably toward them. "Dammit," Hawk moaned when the dust rolled over them. He started the jeep's engine and pulled farther up the ridge, to the upwind side of the road. Drier kept his eyes on Delaplane while Hawk found a spot where they could continue to observe. At least the flare from the sun that was getting closer to the horizon was gone from his glasses now.

The truck got to the bottom of the hill and kept on going.

"Maybe," Drier said after a few moments of silence, "whoever he's waiting for, saw us."

Hawk nodded acknowledgment of the thought, but said nothing.

"Why don't we just approach him, Colonel? Tell him we know everything. Scare the hell out of him. Get him to confess. Peggy did I.D. him."

"Yes. But from what you told me on the way here, she'd be thrown out of court in a flash. Matter of fact, when we get back to camp I want to question her motives. She may not be what she pretends to be."

At that moment they heard a small airplane approaching. It popped over the ridgeline and buzzed right over them and dove for the meadow. "Cessna 195," Hawk said. "What in the hell is one of those doing over here?" He knew the pilot of the plane would not have seen their jeep. Wrong angle, too fast and already dumping flaps.

They watched while the plane landed and taxied up to Delaplane.

"This is it. He's making a deal of some kind."

Below them, a man dressed in civilian clothes got out and went straight to Delaplane. Horace Taylor didn't offer to shake hands, however.

Drier and Hawk noticed that whoever the civilian was, he simply held his hand up in a gesture of hello to the sergeant then spoke first. They turned to face Taylor's jeep, which put their backsides to the idling prop wash and to Hawk and Drier.

"By tomorrow morning, Stanley," Taylor said against the sound of the engine. "It's a necessity if we're to survive with money in the bank. Hans is out of here tomorrow. That means you'll soon be receiving new orders for duty elsewhere. You've got to get this cleaned up before then."

"I can get most of the stuff out of there tonight. Then blow up the hut with what's left."

"No. Just leave the hut standing. Empty, but standing. Blowing it up might draw attention. What did you do with the merchandise you've moved out already?"

"Black. On his boat. He's taking it out of here. Right now Strickland has a hold on him. Won't let him go until twenty-hundred."

His meeting with Tofte flashed quickly through Taylor's mind. Strickland's actions with the boat had nearly driven Tofte over the edge. He thought for a few moments that maybe Tofte himself would come up to shoot the Marine. "Destination?"

"He's not saying. I 'spect he's got a buyer on his own."

Taylor had lost control of the materiel. That meant they'd lost a lot of money that otherwise would have been in their pockets. "The Bass could intercept him."

Delaplane allowed the same kind of grin he had when he found a good Almond Joy candy bar. "That tub? No way, sir. That there's a tender, not a fightin' ship. That pirate's got a canon on board and he'd use the danged thing."

Taylor considered that and then said, "We'll figure something out. What about the girl?" He never referred to her by name or agent number. Delaplane wondered if he had even met her. She'd come to them from a different source and possibly Taylor didn't know her personally. Tofte either, he figured.

"Ready to go. That damned needle hurt, though. I think the doc stuck me bad on purpose." Delaplane had faked his need for the penicillin. It was the only way Dobbins would allow him in the med tent and he needed to get close to the girl named Peggy. And by Taylor's orders, he had to speak with her or leave her a note. He got the job done and then got the hell out of there.

"That girl didn't like that note, Mr. Taylor."

Taylor looked away for a moment. The sun was dropping quickly. He'd have to get going if his mission was to be completed by night's end. "Yeah. I suspect." He turned back to Delaplane. "Hans still thinks you killed the whores."

"You know I didn't do that."

Now it was Taylor's turn for the sneer. "Not necessary for him to know. The job was clean and that crazy Marine will get the blame. We've already heard about the slugs. Good job, Stanley."

After a few moments of silence Taylor added, "Get the rest of the stuff up north. Before sunrise. I don't care how. Just do it."

"Yes, sir."

"And Stanley. Keep your eyes open. Hans wants you dead. He doesn't know about our deal. He believes I want you dead as well. No telling who he might have working for him on this."

* * * *

"Military officer," Hawk said with conviction.

"Dressed as a civilian?" Drier asked.

"You don't find ramrod civilians with close-cropped hair in the middle of a Korean field."

Drier considered that a moment then said, "The plane may belong to the CIA."

Hawk started his engine. "Exactly."

They would follow Delaplane.

A half-hour later, Drier and Hawk watched while Delaplane ordered goods from a Quonset Hut they figured was the same as Fraker reported, into the trucks that had returned from Port Salvation. Eight armed NK soldiers who also served as drivers were doing the loading. Their weapons had been stacked, which meant butts on the ground, barrels supporting each other forming something like an open-air teepee. The stacks, if read correctly, accounted for fourteen driver-soldiers.

"We're in trouble, David."

Just then a voice broke the silence behind them. Drier whirled around, ready to draw his .45. With a hoarse whisper he said, "Snake!"

They were concealed visually from Delaplane's position, but not audibly. Sounds in the area carried well. Snake motioned them to follow him. They hiked up the road around a bend and then knelt down behind a large boulder. "I been watching the place all day. Early this morning a load went out of here, then the trucks returned."

"Delaplane?"

"Sorry sir. It was the skipper and the sergeant. Captain Strickland, sir."

Hawk thought a moment then asked, "Where'd they take it this morning?"

Snake pointed south with his hand and thumb, as though he was giving a thumbs up. "A small port about a mile south of here. Not used much I figure. They loaded it aboard a rickety old boat. No name on it. Just the letters JR. Flying a Korea flag with of all things a Jolly Roger under it. Skull and crossbones. I figure the guy flies ensigns for wherever he is and that he might be a bit nuts. Who else would fly a pirate's ensign in these waters? Anyway, it's still there. Got a few NKs keeping it from leaving. Guys with a three-five."

Hawk contemplated that info for a few more moments then said, "We've got them cold-turkey."

Snake nodded. "Yes sir. But exactly what we got we don't know."

"We've got to arrest Sergeant Delaplane, and when we find him, the good captain."

Fraker shook his head. "Those are armed NK soldiers over there, Colonel. We got one rifle and your two pistols. How long you think we'd last?"

Hawk caught his breath and said, "Their arms are stacked."

But Fraker had been in the Marines long enough. This guy was a pilot, not a ground-pounder. He probably never saw a squad of Marines stack and unstack. "Sir. A good soldier can unstack those arms in less than a few seconds. We'd never get closer'n the other side of this rock." He then informed the colonel that there were fourteen rifles in those stacks and that he might want to take that into consideration.

"Take me a half-hour to get men here," Drier said.

Hawk nodded approval. "Go!"

CHAPTER 28

OUTSIDE BRADFORD'S pyramidal the wind kicked up. A new storm front from the north looked menacing. The temperature was also dropping. He knew that everyone in camp would soon be huddled around their hibachis wearing field jackets and those damned furry pisscutters pulled down over their ears. The seasons in Korea baffled him. Korea was either subject to odd weather patterns or he'd just forgotten what it was like in Connecticut. He smiled inwardly. New England colors came to mind and that settled his jangled nerves a bit.

He eyed his flamed out pipe, about half of which he'd smoked already. He yanked it out of his ashtray, which was his favorite. It had been a 3-inch-38 shell casing from the Cunningham that a navy chief had ground down for him. He flamed the pipe with his ubiquitous Zippo.

He was alone except for his new adjutant who was at work in the adjacent tent, the one separated by a piece of plywood that as far as Bradford was concerned was a joke. The canvas tents had been stapled to the door frame and that was all that separated him from his new adjutant, Captain William Karoly.

He'd been sent forward by General Smith to serve Brad. Smith had told him that Karoly had done a great job during the fight from the Chosin to Hagaru-ri. Good. The lieutenant who'd previously served as his adjutant was not an administrator but instead one hell of an infantry leader, so Bradford sent him back to the lines where the guy wanted to be and Karoly showed up within hours.

He wondered if Karoly was close enough to Smith to be slipping the general information from his meetings. There it was again. That stupid thing Bradford referred to as military paranoia. He blocked it out. He reread the message on his desk. It lay there flat, clean and succinct. Frank Strickland had just been awarded the Navy Cross for actions with RCT-31 and RCT-32. Also mentioned was Strickland's courageous efforts at saving his executive officer's life during that march.

The pipe started to dwindle and no amount of heavy puffing would get it reignited. He flamed the Zippo again, sucked in a few times and then exhaled the entire batch of thick, bluish smoke while he watched it climb to the pyramidal's smoke exhaust, an opening above the top of the center pole that kept the tent at peak height.

He returned his attention to his scribbling on a piece of notepaper that lay next to Strickland's award notice. He reread his own note. Something was missing. "Hell, a lot is probably missing," he muttered aloud.

The plywood door popped open. "You called, sir?" It was Karoly.

Bradford jerked the pipe out of his mouth. "You heard that?"

"I heard your voice, sir. Not exactly what you said."

Brad stared at the young captain a moment then waved him in. "I'll keep that in mind." He paused for a moment then added, "I've a question. About this message." He was referring to the Navy Cross.

"Sir, if I can help."

"Yes. Do you know who recommended Captain Strickland for this?"

Karoly didn't like the military's internal politics and wondered if that's where this conversation was going. His expressive pause caused Bradford to let loose with one of his deep chuckles. "Just for me, Captain. Strickland is an old friend of mine. He deserves it."

Karoly relaxed, but not completely. "Sir. The request went upstairs from General Smith." He meant that the general had recommended it to Headquarters Marine Corps.

Bradford nodded. Of course it did. But who in the ranks suggested it? Karoly was good. He read Bradford's expression and answered the question before Bradford could speak.

"It originally came from Colonel Puller. In writing."

Bradford thanked Karoly and the captain happily returned to his office, making note that he'd never respond to the colonel's voice again unless he heard his own name.

Bradford kept busy for a few minutes restocking his pipe and making it work for him the way he liked. His mind wasn't really on the pipe, though. Instead it was on his notes. He'd done his best to build a chronology of what had taken place with Frank Strickland from his release at the hospital until now.

What he'd not mentioned to Hawk and Drier was that he'd visited directly with the CIA director in Korea the day before they met. Hans Tofte. The only thing he'd learned was that Hans Tofte was either the world's biggest liar or the smoothest salesman west of the Mississippi. He had not yet learned that Tofte was history.

Tofte outlined Dutch Kramer's job and made it sound as though Colonel Kramer was America's biggest asset to the war. When Brad argued that point, Tofte merely blew him off with a wave of the hand. Then he started to explain how Strickland was an adjunct to Kramer's work. That, "Captain Strickland's service to his country as both a Marine and an expediter for our rebel friends in the north might go down in the anal of Corps history as a great contribution."

Bradford thought he'd learned a lot when he served the Commandant of the Corps directly as a counter-intelligence officer. He'd learned from the CIA, the FBI and international agencies. He'd also participated with the Army, Navy and Air Force investigators.

When Tofte explained to him that their conversation was "ultra top secret," he concluded rightly he thought, that something fishy was going on. He wasn't able to put his finger on it yet, but he thought he could figure it out.

Tofte had told him that the president had authorized the CIA to develop NK spies out of North Korean expatriates. To then reinsert them into North Korea fully armed to fight as rebels or guerillas. That it was those arms and weapons the CIA was providing for "rebels in the north" that Frank Strickland was "in charge of."

And then he had said, "Strickland was ordered to remain silent. He could not tell even you, Colonel."

Bradford felt his anger rise, but he held it and wasn't sure why or how. He knew that if he blew his top here, the CIA guys would just pick him up and throw him out. That also contributed to his anger. Just thinking about these assholes having their own secret army in the midst of a war that had cost so many good young American lives made his throat tighten and his heart pound. He took a breath and said, "You were an army officer you say. Well, put yourself in my shoes and ask yourself just how well that would sit with you."

Tofte rocked his chair back and glanced at his watch with his arm raised high enough to make it a point. He was obviously telling Bradford that it was time for him to go. "That's moot. I will tell you that your captain disobeyed my orders. More than once. I ask you, how would you react if all your Marines were independent operators?"

He rocked forward and came to his feet. Sticking his hand out to shake Bradford's, he said, "Thanks for coming Colonel. Now, if you don't mind, I'm really very busy at the moment." He failed to explain that he was busy packing his bags.

Arms to the north. That was the key. Therein lay the answers to his questions.

He fingered the Navy Cross message. How could he give this to Frank Strickland, if indeed his friend had betrayed America and fallen into a trap that was appearing more and more to look like treason? His counter-intelligence experience had shown him that many undercover agents had smoothly converted their jobs to roles of self enhancement. In other words, their bank accounts had gotten very fat.

He shook the thought off. Not Frank, he counseled himself. He would never do that. Then a light bulb went on. But he would take those weapons to the Seventh. And he would defend himself against the NKs driving those trucks if they turned on him.

Karoly knocked on the plywood door. Bradford nearly fell out of his chair. Nobody had ever knocked on that facade before. Smith had trained this guy well. "Enter."

The plywood seemed to morph into Karoly as though he'd been standing there all the while. "Sir, a fresh crypto from EUSAK." He handed it to Bradford when he got to his desk. "Will you need anything else, sir?"

Bradford shook his head. "Not now, thanks."

Karoly left.

Bradford unfolded the message. He disliked crypto notes. His small crypto machine was a new toy for him but still, it was a pain in the ass. He moved to the Steelcase cabinet that housed his machine. He twirled the Master combo lock and easily opened the cabinet door.

After a few moments inputting codes into the machine he realized that the message was to him only. It had come from O.P. himself. When he read it he felt his face pale and his heart murmur act up.

Hans Tofte had been fired for misuses of CIA funds and other matters before he'd spoken with Bradford. As though he'd just stuck his finger in an electrical socket, his memory was jolted into action.

Tofte was the CIA director.

He knew from his experiences with the intel world that CIA types felt no qualms in eradicating witnesses to their illicit efforts.

Strickland was a witness. And Tofte had eluded to Strickland having "disobeyed" his orders.

Elation was his first emotion. His boy had not become one of them.

Fear was his next emotion.

Just as he had thought earlier, Strickland's life was in danger.

"Karoly!"

Drier raced into the parking area and braked hard, causing his jeep to veer sideways on the loose gravel. It came to rest within inches of the med tent.

He glanced upward to the sky. Dark clouds were showing up. Bad timing, he thought.

When he stepped out he caught sight of Corpsman Dobbins staggering out of the sickbay tent near the mess hall. Donovan and Winfield were missing. "Shit," he moaned as he took off after him. "What now?"

Dobbins knelt slowly down on both knees while grabbing his head. For Drier it all seemed in slow motion. The man was bleeding badly and he was going down. Just like men he'd seen when shot in the neck or right through their helmets.

"Where you hit?" Drier called out as he got there.

Dobbins just stared up at him. He was in deep shock already. But he had enough consciousness to say, "It was her. She shot me." Then fell forward flat on his face. His hands landed away from his head. They were solid red with blood. Drier went down and rolled Dobbins over enough to get his face off the ground. He wasn't sure if his friend was dead or alive.

Drier looked up into the tent. "Peggy," he shouted. He jumped up and yanked his .45 from it's holster when he dashed into the sickbay tent. First thing he saw was blood everywhere. Who else?

"Doc! Anyone. God damn it." He shouted loud enough to be heard throughout the camp.

He dashed from the tent to find Donovan and Winfield helping Dobbins. Doc McPherson had also come running. He instructed Donovan to get a stretcher.

Good Drier thought. He's alive. He left Winfield with Dobbins and dashed from med-1 to med-5 to find Peggy, but the tents were empty. Nobody. He ran from section to section again to check for human life of any kind, dead or alive. Still nobody.

When he landed back outside, Winfield and Donovan had Dobbins on the stretcher and were headed back into the tent. McPherson said, "I've got help coming. He's alive, but he needs help and blood."

"Sir," Donovan said. "We were relieving each other like we always do. Then the girl and that armorer guy, Bowers, they ripped outta here and took a jeep and sped away. We tried to catch 'em but they was too fast."

Drier would deal with their method of changing post later. "Bowers? The Army guy?"

"Yes, sir. They headed north, Lieutenant."

Drier left them and ran up Baker Company's street, which was more like an alley between rows of tents, only to find them empty except for a few men who were unfurling the tent sides and securing them for the upcoming storm.

"Winfield," he called back to the med tents. He knew Winfield was inside and could still hear his voice. "Where's your company?"

"In the field, sir," Winfield shouted back. "Captain took 'em out for training."

"Shit," he said to himself. He ran back to the med tent shouting louder to Winfield. "Get a BAR. You're going with me. Both of you."

Inside the tent Winfield and Donovan had just secured Dobbins for the doctors. McPherson no longer needed them and told them to go help the lieutenant. Winfield and Donovan rushed out of the tent. Winfield gave Drier a thumbs up and dashed off for the armory throwing back, "I'll get some grenades, too."

"Donovan, grab anyone including the cooks in the mess hall and get them outfitted for a fight. Now! You got two minutes."

Donovan took off at high port.

Bradford came alongside in his jeep. Before he could say anything, Drier explained his situation and what had just happened. Bradford nodded to a row of six-bys parked in front of the battalion supply tents.

"Put your men in one of those trucks and let's get up there. Let's get a roll on. Captain Strickland's life is in danger."

"The captain may be at the port south of the bunker. Colonel Hawk and Sergeant Fraker are at the bunker. That's where Delaplane is." Drier referred to the Q-hut as a bunker.

Donovan showed up with a handful of cooks and servers who had done their damnedest to look combat ready. Drier almost laughed but didn't. Two of them had their M-1s and a bandoleer of ammo. But they also had their chef caps on under their pith helmets. They had forgotten their steel pots. Too late now.

Winfield returned with two BARs and a pocket full of grenades and three of Baker Company's personnel who Drier had just seen working in their tents. They were much better prepared, just as Drier would expect.

Bradford came out of his jeep. "Cooks, into the first truck there." He pointed. "The rest into the second truck." Bradford knew the names of every man in his outfit. He ordered the head cook, Sergeant Spooner, into the cab of the truck he'd take and the others into the back.

To Drier he said, "I'll take the port. You get help back to Hawk."

Drier could not hold back a knowing grin. "You know the way to the port, Colonel?"

"There's only one road north, Lieutenant."

"Yes, sir. Six miles up that road, Colonel, turn left. It's a bumpy, twisting ride to the port from there. There's a sign there with one letter on it. P. Fraker put it there this morning. We'll be another mile up the main road, a left turn, same kind of road to the bunker. It's a Quonset hut."

Bradford started to leave but turned back. "Lieutenant. Captain Strickland is a straight arrow. He's on our team."

"I know that, Colonel," Drier said solemnly. "Never doubted it."

"Right now a few people want him dead. I'll explain later. And one more thing. They probably want Delaplane dead, too. Get to him. Keep him alive. We'll need him." He took off.

"Colonel," Drier called out to him.

Bradford turned back and waited.

"It's the girl, sir. She's going to try to kill him."

Winfield was next to Drier. In a low voice he said, "And Bowers, sir. He's with her."

Heavier than usual winds scattered the dust created by the trucks when they rolled out on to the dirt road that would take them north. Drier's truck took the lead at the camp, so Bradford dropped back about a quarter mile to avoid eating the billowing powder. The road had more problems than just potholes and ruts. Tracked vehicles had used it too many times which gave it a washboard effect. Bradford looked skyward. If that storm brings rain, he thought, we're likely to get bogged down in mud. Not a good thing.

Captain Black pressed his crazy hat to his head while Admiral Bird shot his hand a loving peck. "Wind's up, yawk," Admiral Bird cawed.

Indeed, Black thought. The wind was picking up and that bothered him. Not because of his hat, but because he was now looking at leaving at low tide with rougher waters.

His pigtail slapped around his neck with the wind, too. "Shit," he muttered. He tucked the damned thing under his hat and, grabbing the brim at the sides, he pulled down on his head even harder. The admiral was clawing deeper into his perch than normally. The wind was affecting him enough to make the bird want to go below deck.

"Boats," Black yelled to his first mate. "Prepare t' cast off."

"Boats," the parrot mimicked. "Cast off Ya lily livered swabbie!"

Black mumbled, "Ye keep talkin' like that bird an' he'll eat ye fer dinner."

Boats'n mate Olivet Narley, a man so black that Captain Black often kidded him about switching their names to match their appearances and attitudes, weighed about two-hundred and fifty pounds. Most of that weight was muscle. He was about six feet six inches tall, barely clothed and as agile as a mountain goat.

Narley's first days at sea had been on four masted rigs that sailed out of his home port in Haiti. His name wasn't really Olivet nor was it Narley. In fact, he had no idea what his real name was. His first seagoing captain had given him his name and he never asked why. After a few years with Black he'd come to like being called "Boats."

He loved working for Black, too. The man paid more and gave him more time to do what he liked doing, which was to play his drums. Two bongo drums that reminded Black of small kegs of beer.

Narley responded to Black with a nod and a thumbs up. Getting the JR ready to sail out of this country was the best news he'd had in a few days. Black turned back to him after checking the sky once again.

"We're goin' t' get rough ou' there," he said. "Batten th' hatches. Secure th' galley an' Boats—"

Boats paused. He was already calling the engine room to fire up the boilers.

"Load th' canon an' get yer rifle."

Boats looked ashore. His heart raced with excitement. The canon. Great good lord he'd been wantin' to shoot them scallywags ashore. The Koreans were still there with their 3.5 launcher. He knew why the rifle was needed as well. "Aye, Cap. On th' way." While listening to Admiral Bird repeat his response, he ducked into the hatchway nearest him and headed to his quarters for the best damned gun he'd ever owned. One of them American Winchesters. He knew it better by its model number of 94. He loved lever action weapons and this one was straight out of the American cowboy era. In Haiti, that was a big thing.

Black turned his attention to the Koreans. That's when his heart sank. The Marine captain had returned. He pulled his timepiece from his pocket and checked it. Sixteen thirty hours. He glanced behind to see if Boats had returned, but he hadn't.

Strickland approached the boat and stood on the dock just a few yards distance from the hull. His feet were planted with spread legs, his toes pointed perfectly forward. His hands were on his hips, a holster hanging on each side with his pistols aboard. He appeared ready for a fight. "You're not going anywhere tonight Mr. Black. You'll be staying right where you are."

Black's response was to shout to his crew along the starboard rail amidships. "Cast off the gangway," he ordered. Then to himself he audibly said, "Hork ye Marine. We're ou' o' here."

Strickland made a dash to the gangway but he was too late. The crew had been ready and they easily raised it and then pulled it aboard the boat.

Strickland turned back to the Koreans. The man with the 3.5 had taken the proper position for firing the weapon. Strickland held his hand up to him to hold on. If the guy actually fired that right now, he knew he'd take most of the explosion from the ship being hit. The JR was a floating bomb ready to be triggered.

Black's ship gave off with belches of rotten diesel smoke when the engine room finally got the boilers up to speed. Boats returned to the gunnel with his 94 in hand. He stood ready at the canon holding a punk in one hand and the rifle in the other. Black came alongside. Boats shouted to the dock men, "Cast off th' aft line. Cast off th' bow line. Cast off all lines."

Above them, at the crest of the hill where the road dropped down to the dock, an American six-by appeared. Nobody noticed it.

Bradford slowed to take in what lay ahead. The sun was reaching for the horizon and had turned the black clouds into golden balls of anger. He could see Frank Strickland on the dock pointing a Colt at the ship with his right arm stretched out. On board the ship he saw men who seemed frozen in place. "There," he said to Sergeant Spooner. "Ship's captain."

What they couldn't see were the Koreans with the launcher. The loader had accomplished his task, the gunner was ready to fire when commanded.

Bradford gunned the truck and headed down the road at a clip that forced the three men in the back to grab the rail siding of the six-by to keep from being catapulted out of the vehicle.

"Don't do anything foolish, Mr. Black. Tell your man to put the rifle down. One round from that launcher behind me and you're hell bound."

Black kept his hard stare on Strickland but under his breath he said to Boats, "List 't against th' gunnel. Brin' yer hands aft up t' th' rail. Be ready t' use 't."

Boats obeyed. He already had one in the chamber with the hammer back. He held on to the hot punk.

"That's better," Strickland said. "Now, drop the gangway back to the dock, Mr. Black. We're going to chart how you're going to deliver your cargo back to American authorities in Pusan."

Black had already made up his mind and his decision did not

include returning his cargo to those assholes in Pusan. "You're ou' o' yer element, Captain. Ye can't hijack a man's boat an' get away wi' 't."

Drops of rain could be felt by both men. Black also detected his ship was beginning to move with the flow of the river. The Korean dock men, two of Delaplane's Koreans, had let go the lines and Black's crew had pulled them in.

The river was a power he could not control and neither could the Marine. The ship was free to sail and the river was trying to grab hold of her. Black knew it was imperceptible to Strickland at the moment, but in a minute or two he would figure it out. He looked up at the stacks. The black smoke created by the diesel engines told him he was ready to get the hell out of there as fast as his screws could spin up.

He glanced to Boats. A grin crossed his crusty face. In a low voice, and without moving his lips he said, "Lower th' gangplank. Let th' lad' think he can come aboard."

"All the way?"

Black nodded. "Aye. We've moved a bit. River's workin' on us. If he's dumb enough t' board them assholes wi' th' launcher won't fire." Then, he added, "Sbung hole on down thar wi' yer hands up. That'll keep im thar. Hatchway. Use th' tube t' tell engines t' be ready." He glanced to the dock area then back to Boats. "I don't think them assholes will fire that launcher wi' th' lad's lookin' like he's gonna board."

Boats understood that he shouldn't acknowledge Black's orders visibly or audibly. He laid the punk across the canon and held his hands up for Strickland to see while he slowly drifted backwards until he got to the hatchway.

"Me boats will meet ye at th' gangway," Black called out to Strickland. He needed to buy a few minutes. His legs could feel the boat reaching. He grabbed up his megaphone and ordered his men amidships to lower the gangway.

Four confused deckhands obeyed orders without questioning their captain. They too could feel the ship reaching. But the gangway went out as ordered.

In the truck Bradford was beginning to understand Drier's warning. The road from the crest to the dock was awful. And it still had twists that caused him to slow down. He was coming to a curve where it appeared he'd lose sight of the dock for a few seconds or moments. He entered the curve and held his breath.

Strickland kept his position. He was seeing something that at first he didn't compute. Then it struck him. The goddamned ship was moving.

"Mr. Black. Tie to, sir. Now!"

Admiral Bird called out, "Avast. Avast." It was the first time in a long time that his master had slapped at him for crying out. He jumped up and let out a low screech and then settled back on the pirate's shoulder. He'd keep quiet.

Black ground his teeth together and pursed his lips. Dammit, he thought. I need another minute. He knew it would be impossible to tie the ship to the dock now. It would only rip the dock away from it's shoring. He could give the order to engines to power back, but dammit, he thought. He would make the time. He would give an order that would be impossible to fill. "All hands, tie to," he commanded. He raised his megaphone to the bow. "Bow lay ou' th' lines." He turned to the after section and called for the same order. The lines were cast back toward the dock. The men knew there was now way the dock hands would ever get them tied to.

They were right. The Korean dock men refused to lash a moving ship to the cleats of a weakened dock. They shook their heads and their hands at the captain.

Just then the gangway hit the dock and started to scrape along the surface sideways. Strickland went to it and started up but the ship began to pick up speed. Then it happened. The ship was with the wind and that caused the black diesel smoke to fall to the deck in a cloud like black fog. The men were all engulfed in the smoke and hidden from each other for a few moments.

"Reverse your course, Mr. Black. Dock this boat," Strickland shouted from the moving gangway. He tried to hike farther up the gangway, but it was bouncing and jerking radically and the goddamned smoke was blocking his vision.

"Hork ye, Marine. Up gangway."

The crew, many of whom were coughing and hacking out smoke particles, cranked on the retract wheel and the gangway started up with Strickland still on it. The boat at the same time thrust forward with both the river catching it and the ship's screws grabbing hold. It was now quicker than the wind and the smoke cleared the deck.

Strickland found himself over the water and moving quickly away from the dock. He dove for the boat and landed on the deck upright.

Then the rain began.

All he could hear when he made the decision to jump aboard the boat was Captain Black laughing with a deep guttural sound that pierced the rain and the smoke. He could hear the engine room working at full power.

And Admiral Bird screeched, "Fire! Fire!"

And the first mate with the rifle was aiming toward the shore.

Strickland looked back to see a six-by screaming into the open area near the two Koreans with the launcher.

At the same time he heard the rifle fire, he saw the 3.5-launcher let go a round.

And a punk ignited the canon.

A missile was coming right at the boat while a canon ball headed for the two Koreans.

CHAPTER 29

AT FIRST GLANCE you'd think they hadn't made a dent in the bunker's supplies. Somehow, Delaplane thought, they should have been able to get more of this crap on Black's boat. He looked at Kyoo and Chong and wondered if he could trust them with the transfer of supplies to the clients in the north. He shook his head. Hell no, he told himself. They'd go for the money just like anyone else.

He did a quick inventory of the hut. He was surprised to find that most of the remaining cases were loaded with explosives, not the weapons that fired them or used them. Mortar rounds, C-3, rockets, satchel charges, thermite grenades as well as frags. Along the south bulkhead he counted forty cases of 185 grain 30-06 AP rounds for M-1s.

There were four cases of rifles and two cases of Colts nested with the ammo as well as four cases of Browning Automatic Rifles. That was it for weapons. Not much. He called Kyoo over.

"Why do we have only explosive devices?"

"We ship others," Kyoo answered as though the question was stupid.

Delaplane rolled his head to stretch his stressed out neck and decided to not pursue the matter. He was frustrated more about not having enough trucks than about explosives being stacked in one spot. "The trucks are full," he said. "We need four more, maybe five."

Kyoo shrugged. He had no idea how to get trucks. "We wait here. You get."

Delaplane considered his options. Either release the convoy he had or scare up four more trucks and everyone goes at the same time. While staring without purpose at a crate of thermite grenades he remembered seeing a half dozen trucks at the supply tent. Army trucks. He smiled at his thought that they were real Army trucks. He snapped his fingers and said, "Got it. Can you drive a truck?"

Kyoo shook his head. "Not me."

Delaplane went outside to the leader of the trucks that had been loaded. He noted the drivers were huddled together under the lean-to alongside the hut, already ducking the light bit of rain that had fallen. "Joe," he said to the convoy leader who gave no other name for himself, "Tell your men to get inside. They can wait out the storm there."

"How long we wait?"

"I have to find four more trucks." He looked west toward the sky that was no longer golden but a dark purplish color. The sun was disappearing rapidly. "It'll be dark."

Joe was upset. "No. No way. We not drive north in dark. No way. You want load rest on trucks? We can do."

Delaplane shook his head. "You're already overloaded."

"No problem, soldier. We can do."

Drier parked his truck about a quarter mile back from Hawk and Snake's position. His shorthanded squad of armed cooks quietly advanced to the two men.

Drier looked like old "iron tits" with the two grenades he'd hung from his neck by using boot laces. Iron tits was the nickname given General Ridgway by his men. Ridgway always wore what appeared to be two grenades hanging from his neck, each one over his breast pockets. The problem was, one of them was a first aid kit, although the other was indeed a live grenade.

"Delaplane still there?" Drier asked.

"Yes. He's in the hut right now. They're loading more stuff on the trucks," Snake said. "Man Lieutenant, no way they gonna get out of here in the mud that's formin' up. Not with those loads."

Drier nodded. "We have to keep him alive. No matter what happens here, he's got to go back with us."

Hawk looked at Drier as though there was a chance Delaplane would be killed. "We'd like to do this without firing a shot, Lieutenant. So, what's up?"

"Not sure. I think Colonel Bradford knows things we don't." To Fraker he said, "He's cleared the skipper. Said he's a straight shooter."

"Never doubted it," Fraker said.

"The girl shot Dobbins and headed this way in a jeep with Bowers. The Army guy."

Hawk wheeled around. "Bowers?"

"Yes, sir. Looks like he's part of whatever's going on. Colonel Bradford told me that the CIA probably wants both the captain and Delaplane dead."

"Where's Colonel Bradford now?" Hawk asked.

"The port down stream."

Hawk suddenly felt left out of the loop. "Whoa. Let's slow down Lieutenant." Hawk was just now registering that Strickland had been cleared by Bradford. He said as much to Drier.

"All I know is he went to help him."

But Hawk remained confused. "Sergeant Fraker tells me about a boat south of here that Delaplane loaded up this morning. You tell me that's where Captain Strickland is." Hawk motioned to the group at the hut, "Now, we got a bunch of trucks being loaded by what appear to be North Koreans and one Army sergeant."

Before Hawk tried to implicate Strickland with association with Delaplane, Drier said, "The captain's trying to stop the boat from leaving port."

"I think, sir, we better take care of this situation real quick so's we can go help the Skipper," Fraker said.

It was the first time Hawk had heard these man refer to Strickland as their skipper. That was a term used with some endearment. That, he knew, also put him on thin ice with these two infantry types. "Well. We've been on the high side of this debacle for an hour now and it's perfectly clear we're watching a serious crime. I hope your captain returns with the goods." Then it struck him. "I sent you in for a rifle platoon. What's this?" He nodded to the five men Drier had brought with him.

"Baker company's in the field sir. There was no time to find them. This is all I could round up. Well, four cooks went with Colonel Bradford."

"The girl didn't come down this road."

"Most likely the back way in, Colonel," Snake said. "Path from main road to back of hut. Walked it this morning. Come out at the trees back there. Hardly notice it along the main route. Locals probly used it."

Hawk sighed heavily. It was getting to be darker and the drizzle seemed to be turning into rain. They had unconsciously donned their ponchos. If they were going to wade into the group below, they'd have to dump the ponchos and be prepared for a hell of a fight.

Hawk motioned Drier to follow him. The two men walked about twenty feet back down the road to an area where they could speak privately.

"What's up? Tell me everything you know."

Drier explained the ground Bradford had covered and exactly why the colonel wanted Delaplane alive. He told Hawk about Dobbins and the missing girl and that the armorer seemed somehow to be involved. He tried to explain what Strickland was up to, but wasn't himself one-hundred percent sure of that. So, he ended by saying, "So, we gotta stop these guys. Arrest them. Go help the captain."

Hawk pondered his words for a few moments, then said, "Lieutenant, I'm a pilot."

"Yes, sir."

"And you're an experienced infantry man."

"Yes, sir."

"Well, then you know that pilots peel over, drop a bomb or strafe and go home. You however, get into the trenches and know how to fight. Face to face as it were."

Drier said nothing but nodded his acknowledgement of the Colonel's correct analysis.

"Now, we have what?" he glanced to the new men and back to Drier. "We have five young men who've not seen combat or ever shot anyone or been shot at, an old top sergeant, a pilot and you, and we're going to just walk in and take these well-armed guys down?"

"Yes, sir. I think that's the plan."

Snake interrupted them. "Lieutenant, they's moved inside." He pointed to the hut. "All of 'em. And sir, they took their weapons with 'em."

Hawk looked into David's eyes and said, "Take us in, Lieutenant."

They failed to see Bowers and Peggy who were neatly tucked into a pocket of trees at the rear of the hut.

The pistol trainer for the CIA in Korea was a former Army master sergeant who'd been court martialed out of the Army for selling

Army goods from Camp Irwin, California to buyers in the city of San Bernardino, referred to by locals as San Ber-do. Camp Irwin was in the middle of the Mojave Desert and considered an isolated outpost for tank training and some foot training.

Master Sergeant Piccolo had had an average career up to his court martial. Average in that he'd fought in World War I and World War II. He'd been in the European Theater twice and gotten through each war without earning a Purple Heart or a hero's medal. He knew how to shoot and how to duck and when not to stick his head up. Lessons he would end up teaching others by the end of each war.

He'd learned to shoot a military pistol so well that he'd signed on with the Army's official rifle and pistol team and he made it to the annual matches three times. He never topped the competition though, always coming in behind the winners. But still, on a good day he could shoot as well as anyone.

His military life ended without full retirement benefits when he'd decided to sell tank parts to the folks in San Berdo who in turn would sell them back to the Army or to another country. Unfortunately for him his buyers for two complete sets of tracks sold them back to the Army at Camp Irwin and the Army, albeit unusual, traced the numbers to Piccolo's outfit. Twenty-nine years of Piccolo's life had been flushed down the drain.

Within days of his boot from the Army, he was approached by an agent from the still new CIA. Would he like to teach pistol shooting to CIA agents?

He already possessed some of the requirements to join the elite, clandestine corps of covert operations. His dishonorable discharge proved that.

That's how he found himself in South Korea, exactly where he'd rather not be. He got there after the Marines had pushed the North Koreans northward from Pusan to Teagu and with the Army's late help, created the "Pusan Perimeter."

He would be safe, he'd been told by Army Lt. Colonel Horace Taylor. He just had to teach each new agent they brought on board how to shoot the 1911-A1 Colt .45.

And more importantly, according to Taylor, "When to use it."

Piccolo also gave indoctrination classes to his charges for each and every NATO weapon and U.S. military weapon in the theater.

His first class was made up entirely of Koreans. Three of them spoke English better than he did. They, for that reason only, got the best of the training of his first class.

And the best graduate turned out to be a young woman they called only, Peggy.

Corporal Bowers entered the med tents alone. He had slipped past Donovan and Winfield who were going through their changing of the guard routine. He thought the Marines were peculiar in that regard, but for now it worked for him.

Dobbins was aboard along with Doctor McPherson, a young resident surgeon who'd volunteered for duty in Korea. McPherson however was just leaving, heading over to the mess hall to get something to eat. He hadn't eaten since the night before due to three emergency surgeries, the last of which he wrapped only a half-hour before Bowers showed up.

Dobbins nodded to McPherson that Bowers was okay. McPherson left them alone. Dobbins checked his watch. Donovan was due to take the watch. He was anxious for him to come in. He too wanted to eat. It wasn't just the doctors who worked long hours, their nurses and corpsmen worked right alongside them.

He glanced over to Peggy's enclosed space but she wasn't visible. He'd rigged a space for her just like he would a pull-around-curtain for a patient. She wanted privacy and he understood. So far it had worked out.

Bowers said, "She here?"

Dobbins tilted his head forward and looked through the top of his eyes. "She's off limits, Bowers. You know that. Told you that before. What do you need?"

"Right now I need her." He seemed high strung to Dobbins, maybe on too much caffeine or too many Bennies.

Dobbins left the gurney he was cleaning up and went to Bowers. "Can't do that, man. I'm not usually her bodyguard, but right now I can't do that. Maybe when Donovan gets here."

Bowers caught a glimpse of Peggy pulling the curtain back. His eyes bulged open as wide as a full moon. Peggy was lifting a pistol into the air in their direction. Bowers was a shooter. He recognized the pistol. It was a German Luger. "No. Peggy," Bowers yelled out. He leaped toward her thinking she was going to shoot Dobbins. "Not him." He grabbed for her arm but when he got it the pistol fired.

Dobbins had turned to see what Bowers was so excited about and that's when the bullet from the 7.65 mm pistol knocked him down.

With a cold chill in her voice Peggy said to Bowers, "Let's go. We don't have much time."

The "Q," the name Fraker had given the bunker, seemed quietly at rest. The canvas shells of the trucks seemed heavily soaked by now, and the Q itself was slicked clean by what had become a heavy rainfall. They knew the rain might not last more than a half-hour, so moving in it now was important. Although the rain had come from the south, and therefore was warm, the NKs and Delaplane had huddled inside for protection.

Delaplane was upset about the rain. His instincts told him that it was a foreboding shower. Not only would it create the deep kind of mud that clay soil produced, but the North Korean rebels manning the trucks didn't want to drive at night. Experience ensured that the Chinese or their own country's Army would probably attack their convoy in the dark. Most of the existing patrols stayed away from daylight attacks for reasons that seemed more obvious to them than to the drivers.

Also, the lead driver, the one Delaplane had nicknamed Tom Mix, was to meet their contact north of the MLR about ten miles into enemy territory. The contact was to provide some sort of guidance for Tom Mix to find him—they were accustomed to the signals. Usually they consisted of a simple road sign or an indicator of where to make a turn or to drop off the cargo. The finality of this trip, however, was that all the drivers were to remain in North Korea and help fight for their country.

At least that's what he believed.

He was nervous about it all though. The whole thing had been set up so quickly that for Tom Mix, finding the contact in daylight seemed tenuous at best. At night it would certainly all fall apart, and with it their hopes for getting together with their comrades. So it was Tom Mix who decided they'd wait until dawn for the journey.

Outside, at the back of the hut, Peggy and Bowers waited in the same clump of trees where Kyo and Chong used to relieve themselves. They didn't speak to each other except to confirm where Delaplane was. Their primary target was missing. Until he showed up, they thought it best to hide quietly. Better they spot him before he spots them. Bowers had already accepted his plight. Strickland was a damned good pistol shooter, but so was Peggy. They could only wonder whether the armed Korean soldiers would interfere or not. No matter they had decided, this would be their only chance.

For Bowers though, Peggy had been acting peculiarly. He had not considered that she would try to kill Dobbins. And she'd fallen completely silent and seemed terribly despondent over it. Something was wrong here.

The fact that she'd shot Dobbins, a good man in the eyes of the errant Bowers, suggested that her goals might be a bit different than his and her motives hidden from even Tofte and Taylor.

He winced internally. The boredom of waiting was forcing questions into his thoughts. Questions he would rather not have to deal with. Just the same they were there. The big one, the question he found most disturbing was not a new one. He'd been bothered by it before. It was a basic question, but one that he'd never been able to answer.

What kind of package was she with the CIA? Neither Tofte nor Taylor had ever claimed bringing her into her role. But here she was. His breathing became irregular and he needed to pee. Dammit, not now he told himself. He looked down at the girl and wondered more about her.

Taylor wanted all witnesses killed, but he named only four of them. Delaplane, Strickland and the two Koreans in the bunker. But wasn't Bowers himself a witness also? And the girl? Who is she, really?

He figured that she knew even more than he did. So, why wouldn't she be a target as well? Taylor hadn't ordered him to kill her. Then paranoia struck him for a moment. Had Taylor ordered her to kill him after he took out the Marine?

He kicked himself in his mental ass. He'd dipped into the devil's workshop again. His mother always told him that an idle mind was the devil's workshop. Until he got this job, he never fully understood the meaning. It was the wait. Always the wait, just like now. Hang out and do what? Think. Think about what the hell was about to happen.

What had happened. Who was who and all that. Yeah, it's just the devil's workshop. So, forget it, he demanded of himself. It's just a job.

He glanced to Peggy. She was squatted on the ground, legs crossed, her body curled to minimize the mist and drops of rain that worked through the trees. He didn't know much about her. Only that she was an operative of the Agency. He assumed that she was a native, which clearly meant to him that she knew how to take care of herself in this environment.

Her gaze was locked to the bunker. The hut they called it. She was so perfectly still he wondered if she was breathing. He looked down and saw that she had a tight grip on her pistol. It wasn't the same as the .45 he had. It was that damned Luger she'd probably gotten from someone in Seoul. A cop was it? No wait, holy Jesus. From Taylor maybe?

He inhaled deeply and let the air out slowly, pushing it between tightened lips and clenched teeth.

Devil's workshop, he concluded. Stop thinking about all this. You aren't being paid to think, he reminded himself. He leaned back against the tree where he stood. This night might take a while. He checked the horizon beyond the hut. He gave the sun another few minutes to sink. He thought he could see where it was. The clouds looked brighter there. Then a hole appeared and light streaked down in a broad beam. The storm was parting. The rain would soon stop and they'd have night. Dark. He smiled. It would be better to do all this in the dark. Yes, he thought. The wait is worth it.

When the 3.5 let fly with the rocket, the Korean standing behind it was blown back into the metal door of the port's storage building. The exhaust blast from a 3.5 recoilless tube was enough to kill you, but for this Korean his death happened when his head smashed hard against the corrugated metal. His body quickly slumped to the ground. His friend just as quickly was killed by the non-explosive six-inch canon ball that crashed into his chest and forced him back against the building where he ended up next to his friend.

At the same moment the six-by driven by Bradford came to a screeching stop at the edge of the pad next to the dock. Bradford had come into the area at full speed, slammed on the brakes, which barely took hold. That forced him to swing the truck to the left to avoid flying off the dock, and let it stop at its own will with one of the duo wheels in the rear just off the dock over the water.

The men in the back were happy to leap down from the back of the six-by onto the dock, although the sight of a burning boat loaded with rockets and other explosives within just a few feet, wasn't too encouraging. If it blew now, they'd all be checking in with St. Peter.

On board the JR, Strickland found himself diving and rolling across the deck and then jumping to his feet. The rocket had smashed into the wheelhouse and blown the lid off of it. A fire had quickly ensued. The old wooden ship could easily become a giant Roman candle.

He dashed into the burning wheelhouse to find Captain Black already with an old extinguisher in his hands. It refused to work. "Get th' pump going," he yelled to the engine room through his communication tube.

He pointed first to Strickland and then to a water hydrant. "The hose is in the locker," he yelled.

The locker was locked. Strickland grabbed an ax mounted on the aft bulkhead of the wheelhouse. He smashed open the locker. The connector end of the hose was on the top of the coil. He yanked it over to the hydrant connection and with a quick twist it was mounted. He pulled on the lever that opened the water but nothing came out.

"Shit," Black yelled. "They got th' pump."

The fire was more expansive now. It was lapping at the forehead of the wheelhouse all the way back to the main stack. Black yelled into the tube again. "The pump. God damn 't, fire up th' pump."

Admiral Bird was besides himself. He went airborne, then crashed back onto the top of Black's head. "Pump. Awk. Pump mate. Awk."

Strickland heard the reply from below. "Aye. Workin' on it." And just then water poured from the nozzle of the hose.

Black came over and grabbed the nozzle without speaking and started spraying water at the fire's root.

Aft of them, the engine room hatch popped open. Black smoke billowed out as though the engine room itself was on fire. The chief engineer popped up and yelled, "Too late Cap. The son o' a bitch is on fire down here." He came to the deck and was quickly followed by his two boiler men.

"Fire in the hold," Admiral Bird screeched. "Abandon ship."

Bradford watched helplessly from the dock. His men stood around him waiting for an order from their commander. The boat was about two-hundred feet downstream in the center of the river. The boat's engines had stopped, so it was the river itself taking the boat with its flow.

"She's gonna blow, Colonel," Sergeant Spooner said.

Strickland pointed to the only life boat on the JR. "Abandon ship, Mr. Black."

But Black's intense behavior was aimed at putting out his fire. He had a cargo hold full of a few million dollars and nobody was going to take that away from him. Instead, he yelled to the engineer, "Aft t' work, mates. Put that fire ou'."

"Back to work you scallywags," the parrot translated.

But the engineers bolted. They brushed their arms through the air as though to say to their captain, "Screw you," and started lowering the lifeboat.

They were too late.

The first thing that blew was an oil drum aft of the cargo hold. It didn't exactly look like the whole ship was going, just that part where the engines and the fantail used to be.

At first it felt to Strickland like an earthquake, the kind he felt in southern California. Then it made a muffled sound and that's when he knew the hold was about to explode. It was time to put his old college water polo swimming days to a test. He yelled to Black, "Get your ass off the boat. It's going to blow."

"Abandon ship. Abandon ship you lubbers," the parrot cried out. He was looking down at his captain. "Screw the boat, mate."

Black waved Strickland off. Strickland tried to grab at him, wanted to take him over the side with him, but Black just turned the hose on the Marine and yelled, "Get th' hork off me boat."

Strickland saw the fire in the man's eyes. It seemed certain to him that Black was going to go down with his boat and nothing was going to stop that. He dashed for the port side, the side the dock was on and dove straight down into the river. At about fifteen feet below the surface he started kicking his way back toward the shore. When he played water polo at USC, he could stay under for up to a minute and a half, maybe a bit longer. But he was older now, not in the same condition, and he wondered if he had enough to stay down long enough to get away from the explosion and the fire that was sure to follow.

Just then he could feel it. Concussion pressure pushed him as though a giant wave had come from nowhere.

The ship had blown.

Bradford was the first to spot a sad looking whale boat tied to the south end of the dock. By the time the ship's after section lifted into the air, he and two of his men were already fifty feet into the river. He would do his damnedest to find Frank Strickland and bring him back alive.

But first, they would have to survive the ultimate force from the explosion that was about to engulf them.

None of them noticed Captain Black swimming strongly downstream toward the shore with the parrot clinging on for dear life and crying out, "Swim mate. Awk."

CHAPTER 30

IT WAS TIME. A few more seconds and he'd drown. Strickland bolted to the surface as though he was about to slam the ball into the net. He burst upwards so high above the surface that he nearly landed in the two-oar skiff that was clipping past him.

He looked around for the JR. He saw it, but only the last of it. It had moved farther downstream with the current, but only it's bow was visible, jutting upwards like one of those Japanese ships at Wake that they'd sunk from the shore with Howitzers. They'd hit those boats amidships, blew up their fuel and cargo and the then they'd sink ass-end and bow apart from each other. The JR had apparently blown up as well. No flames anywhere, no smoke. Just the bow slipping under.

"Frank," Bradford shouted from behind him. "For chrissakes get in the boat."

Bradford's men had tacked the skiff around and they came alongside Strickland. The two Marines manning the oars quickly pulled Strickland into the boat.

"I don't know how you guys got here, but your timing is perfect."

The two grunts returned to the oars and headed upstream back to the dock. While they rowed, Strickland filled Bradford in on what happened aboard the JR.

He also suggested they make tracks to the Quonset hut.

Drier placed his men as best as he thought they would serve them. They crept closer to the building in relays with one element of his tiny force covering the other as they moved up. It quickly became obvious that nobody was outside, not even a guard.

444

"They aren't expecting company," Snake said to Drier.

Drier looked back for Hawk. The Colonel was with three of the Marines. He waved to them to come forward.

Snake said the obvious. "Getting darker."

Drier nodded. "Might be better for us. They have a light on inside."

"I seen it, sir. Coleman lantern. Their generator's out of fuel."

Hawk arrived. "Any surprises?"

Drier shook his head in response. He eyed the hut carefully. He didn't want to blow this, his first assignment as a unit commander. Small unit, he admitted, but in this man's outfit, all sizes counted.

"Snake," he said, "what should we know? Inside the hut."

Snake thought a moment. "Back end. Wood door. Warped, out of plumb. Doesn't shut easily. It's probably open. Windows all locked. Mid-section has a door this side. Squared off with the hut. Door didn't seem to be used much. Straight ahead door, the fore hatch, on hinges that swing in, instead of out. Poor shape, but it closes and opens without much effort."

"What's behind the hut?"

"A small shed. It was locked. Trees, brush. Open area big enough for a truck or maybe a couple jeeps. Gravel on the ground. All sides."

"That it?"

Snake thought a moment. "The trail leading out the back through the trees and up the hill I mentioned."

Hawk said, "We need to see if anyone's hanging out around the trucks."

Drier sent two Marines around the back side of them, the side away from the hut to check them out. Were they locked? Could they be started and driven? He also wanted them to check the struts to see if the trucks were sitting on their springs—a sign that they were very much overloaded and might not move in the mud, not even with six wheel drive.

"Rain's stopped," Snake said, once again speaking the obvious.

"What's your plan, Lieutenant?" Hawk asked.

Drier mulled over the question for a few seconds and said, "It's really quiet right now. There are ten or more armed men in that hut. I'm thinking they might be wanting to leave in the early morning. So, maybe they're tucking in to get some shut eye."

Hawk saw the wisdom. "Good idea. I like it."

"We'll wait to see about the trucks. And give Captain Strickland and Colonel Bradford time to get here."

Hawk glanced to his young lieutenant and only nodded. He didn't expect to see either one of them.

CHAPTER 31

STRICKLAND TRIED TO DRY OUT in the truck while Bradford drove it as quickly as the road allowed. Bradford explained to Strickland his role in Korea and what he'd learned during the past twenty-four hours.

He then acknowledged that he believed Strickland's life was in danger but from whom or where he wasn't sure. He did know, he told Strickland, that the CIA was a "sneaky bunch of bastards." It was a lesson Strickland had already learned.

At that point their truck hit a huge hole and nearly tipped them over at the curve in the road they'd just entered. Bradford braked hard and then slowed down after that. "Damn road is not a road," he muttered.

Silence ensued for a few minutes. Finally, Strickland figured it was his turn to speak. "I believed it was legit. I got suckered."

"You fell into a pit of snakes. And that part of moving arms to Vietnam? That was legit. I learned about if from O.P. It remains top secret." He thought about it a moment and then added with commitment. "It also stinks to hell."

Strickland rolled his head on his neck and said, "What stinks is that Tofte and Taylor were delivering used junk to the French. I swear they were selling the good stuff to the NKs. It was a big double-cross."

"And you're a witness. So's Sergeant Delaplane."

Strickland felt flushed, his face became hot even though he was chilled from his soaking. He was still angry. But he held it in. He was a Marine, even though a very pissed off Marine. Before he could think of anything to say, Bradford continued.

"Frank, I've known you a long time. When I first heard you'd reupped for Korea I wanted to grab your ass and put you into a safe assignment. I dropped the ball. And then I got my orders to move north. I suspected right away that you had become involved with Tofte's peculiar army during those two weeks of R&R."

"All along?"

"I suspected it was you when I heard about the arms drop off at the Seventh." He hesitated but then popped the big question. "Why did you shoot those Koreans?"

"They shot at me. With a rifle. Point blank range. I had no choice." Strickland knew Bradford's history just as well as Bradford knew his. The old man had been a rebel in his younger days and during the big war. He'd even been court martialed once for losing his copy of the unit's code book during combat. It had been a shitty deal, too. The guys pressing the charges had never been in a fight. They were damned lucky the camp didn't shoot them while they tried to railroad the aggressive yet very much loved officer into the brig.

Bradford braced for the mud hole he'd just spotted with one of the blackout lights. The truck hit it and both men bounced off the seat.

After adjusting his position in front of the steering wheel Bradford said, "So, I have some explaining to do tomorrow. I'll call O.P. directly. Not to worry too much about it. You're going to fill me in on what just happened back there. And what lies ahead."

Strickland kept his eyes glued to the road in front of them. It was dark and he didn't want to miss the turn. It bothered him as well that he still felt wet and cold, as though he'd just come out of an Alaskan river. His boots sloshed with sea water. And his pistols were gone. Lost forever. Dumped into the river when he dived. They would have been too heavy to swim with at any rate. Hell, his boots nearly pulled him down.

Bradford noted his discomfort. "You want me to pull over? You can always grab utilities off one of those cooks in the back."

"No, sir." What he'd love at the moment was a hot cup of coffee, a good cigarette and to be with Juliana again. Then it smacked him solid across his head like a DI might do with screwed up recruits. Who had the job to kill him?

Bradford asked, "Did you blow up the truck with the NKs in it?"

"They tried to run me down. I had no choice. Grenade at the fuel tank."

It got silent for a while after that. After a few minutes of bouncing along the road Strickland said, "You said the girl and Bowers are suspects?"

Bradford coughed out a yes when the truck hit another bump in the road.

"Where are they now?"

Bradford shook his head. "We don't know. They took off in a jeep." It got quiet for a while. Then Bradford asked, "The dum dums? Those were yours."

"I know they're illegal. Guess I'll bite the dust over that."

Bradford considered asking if Strickland had used them in combat and then decided he didn't want to know. If his friend had made deep cuts into the tip of the bullets, then they would fragment and tear the hell out his enemy. And any knowledge about him having possibly done all that would put Bradford himself into a terrible hole. He didn't want to go there.

"You said you lost your pistols in the river."

Strickland nodded. Then it struck him. No pistols, no ballistic checks. "Yes, sir."

Bradford sped up a bit faster.

Strickland moved ahead. He explained having loaned his .45 to Delaplane and that the army sergeant must have taken the ammo then. He couldn't figure how the ladies were shot though, since he'd left them there exactly in the same condition as when he and Delaplane arrived. "Barely alive. Obviously beaten by Korean cops a few days before."

"Or one of ours?"

"I doubt ours. The local cops terrorize their hookers."

"The girl. Did you see here there?"

Strickland thought a moment then said, "No. No we didn't."

"She may have seen you," Bradford said with a monotone.

Silence dominated again like the fog that blocked his thinking before. He narrowed his eyes when his mind's eye grabbed Peggy's image again. He hadn't seen her there but she told Drier she had seen her sister killed by an American. Except that according to the doc, her sister had died at least 48 hours before that maybe longer. Something was coming together in his mind but it still didn't turn any lights on. Why hadn't he thought all this through before? Maybe she did see her sister killed by an American. Earlier. A civilian maybe?

Or maybe she's an agent. Is everyone this god forsaken country an agent? He laughed at himself. But wait?

He turned to Bradford. "You think maybe the girl is the one who's supposed to kill me?"

"Possibly. Or Corporal Bowers." He coughed and added, "Or maybe both of them."

Strickland spotted the turn off. "Left turn here," he said.

Bradford grabbed the turn onto a road that was rougher with ruts and holes than the one they left. He started up a steep slope.

"Slow, Colonel. Maybe switch off the lights. It's just over the crest."

Fraker noticed the beam of light at the crest of the road, but before he could get Hawk and Drier's attention the beam disappeared.

"Vehicle comin'," he said in an almost inaudible tone.

The two officers turned their attention to the road, which was lost in the darkness. It felt like looking into an abyss of black tar. "Send two men up there, Snake. Tell 'em safety's on."

That meant live ammo into the chamber, safety on, but still ready to fire at the flex of a forefinger. The command generally give was "Lock and load."

Fraker chose Donovan and Winfield for the job of investigating who had come up on their rear. The two country boys took off with rifles at port. They would be ready if they ran into a challenge.

Bradford and Strickland went to the back of the truck and peeled the canvas flaps back. "Silently," Strickland ordered.

The men came out, making sure they didn't bang their rifles against the metal of the truck.

"Locked and loaded," he ordered. "But be ready."

Donovan was the first to hear them coming. The sound was soft, sounding more like men were walking in sand than on the dirt and gravel road. For Donovan, a youngster not bent on similes, that meant nothing other than someone was coming. He tapped Winfield on the shoulder and whispered, "Someone coming."

They were not accustomed to such conditions, neither man never having been thrust into a potential night time firefight. Consequently, they failed to muffle the sound of their safeties going into the off position. Generally the sound was so low few could hear it, but this was a dark and silent night and the sound of anything to do with a rifle could be heard by an experienced ear. The muffled footsteps ahead, stopped.

Strickland held his hand up. He'd heard the clicks. He also recognized them as clicks of M-1 rifle safeties. "M-ones," he said with a whisper that sounded almost haunting to the others. He knew the NKs had gotten hold of a lot of M-1s. He was aware too, that Delaplane's small army of trucker-soldiers might still be in the area. They had M-1s and as he'd learned before, some knew how to use them.

He guided each of his cooks to the side of the road, spreading them apart. He then motioned them down to the kneeling position for firing rifles. He then led Bradford to the west side of the road.

Heavy brush and a few stumps that exhibited the locals' need for firewood, along with tall dead grass, framed the road on each side. The Marine cooks, themselves head-high with the grass and prickly brush, tensed. It was only natural that they wondered on a dark night what the hell else might be in the brush with them.

Strickland advanced a few yards, knelt down low, understanding that most riflemen challenged by soneone in the dark would fire high, "Advance and be recognized."

Donovan's heart nearly stopped. "It's him," he said, still whispering. He yanked his finger away from the trigger.

"What if it isn't?"

Donovan thought a moment then called back, "Pfc. Donovan."

"What's your real name?" Bowers asked.

Peggy sat motionless on the wet ground and remained silent.

Bowers sat down alongside her. He was ready to accept that nothing was going to happen soon. "I know it's not Peggy."

"Huenyrsook."

Bowers bought it but didn't try to pronounce it. "First or last?"

"Last name is—" She stopped. "Not needed."

He nodded even though she couldn't see him. It was a war without last names. A time for privacy in the middle of chaos. He understood.

The Coleman lantern in the hut was working. It provided just barely enough light to cast a ghostly hue so that their silhouettes could be seen when close up to each other. She was a tall girl for a Korean he thought. And he noted again for himself only, that she didn't look as Korean as the others in the country did. Slender, yes. But sitting here in the moist shadows of a Korean night, she seemed fragile. "You speak good English," he said quietly.

"I also speak French," she volunteered. She startled him. "I grew up there. Paris. Learned English in Catholic school." She told the truth this time.

"How old are you?"

"I am twenty."

Bowers was taken aback. How in the hell did such a smart cookie who had apparently been educated in Paris get into this stupid war? And why is she now talking? He knew before he finished answering his question. He knew because he felt the same way. This was probably a suicide mission. She wanted someone to know her.

"Why? Why this?"

She didn't reply. Her own thoughts were turning to the same questions Bowers had. Instead, she shifted on the ground a little without exposing her pistol, a World War II Parabellum-Pistole, known otherwise as a Luger. Hers fired a 7.65 mm round. She had carried it in her backpack. She had gotten it from the CID officer. The man she'd known for a long time.

Her knees, drawn up to her chest in a natural huddle, had effectively concealed the weapon. She knew she didn't have to hide it from the American corporal, but it had become a habit through the past few years to hide anything of value and right now the pistol represented the only value she had left. Surviving threats and hunters had developed her instincts sharply. Her hand went to it and she rotated it a bit to make sure she could grab it when she needed to.

And on this night she knew that she would.

CHAPTER 32

"THEY HAVE TWO SENTRIES guarding the trucks," Drier said.

They were huddled together each man down on one knee. Their eyes had adjusted to the dark, but still there was very little light. They were about a hundred feet from the first truck, which was parked closer to the river on the old road than the side where the hut stood. The trucks had pulled off the road more than they'd stayed on it, getting their right wheels into sandier soil than the wheels still on the road. There was enough room between each truck for one man to walk through, but not much more.

"Where are they headed, Frank," Bradford asked.

"North."

"I learned about air drops to guerillas in the north. Boats have also been taking arms and food to them," Bradford said.

"But never by truck," Strickland replied. "They were used to take the materiel to boats in Inchon." He was no longer surprised at Bradford's knowledge of CIA activities. Still, he felt a new anger building in him. His face had flushed even in the cold night's air. All this, he figured, was caused by his own stupidity. He had crossed the line, gone over the edge. Quite suddenly and without warning, he'd been slapped hard on the side of his head by a sleeping conscience. What the fuck had he done? He had blown it. It wasn't just his career at stake here, either. It was the lives of his friends and his own character. He went blank for a moment and when he came to, his mind was clear. He knew what to do. He knew how to stop the men in the hut and how to bring Taylor and his gang to justice. The others couldn't see him nod involuntarily to himself. The whole mess they were dealing with wasn't just Tofte's creation. More than likely

Taylor had been the instigator of the illicit arms for sale program. He snapped to attention when Drier broke into the silence.

"How do we take these men alive?" Drier asked, sticking to the job at hand. Bradford had already informed them he wanted living POWs. Therefore, caution would rule their plans.

The score was ten of them to at least fourteen riflemen for the Hut. There were fourteen trucks and two jeeps out front. One of the jeeps belonged to Delaplane according to Fraker. The other jeep remained a mystery.

Strickland guessed it belonged to the convoy leader.

"The moon," Fraker whispered.

It seemed like frosted glass shattering over their heads in slow motion. Cumulus clouds were thinning and splitting open as though a map of bright lines were being drawn by nature's artist. It gave just enough illumination for them to make out the trucks and the outline of the hut.

"Nobody visible," Snake said.

"Yes, there is," Drier replied. He pointed halfway down the line of trucks. "Must have been sleeping in a truck. Check out four trucks down. Watch the glow when someone pulls on a butt." He meant a cigarette.

Then it happened. An orange hue as though someone had flicked on a night light followed by its fading disappearance, all happening in the same short span of someone inhaling a cigarette.

"Got it," Snake said.

Bradford said, "We need to take them out first."

Snake motioned for Donovan and Winfield to come front and center.

No one noticed Frank Strickland slip away.

Inside the hut eight Korean soldier-drivers slept at the far end on cots that Delaplane had pulled from a crate that had remained behind with the launchers and rockets stacked in the center of the hut. Another six slept in cots at the front of the hut, right at the bulkhead.

Military cots were made of green canvas and wood braces with three sets of legs that were two sticks hinged together at their center. These were spread apart with yet another wooden stick about one-inch by one-inch where recess holes at each end were shoved through a slot sewn into the canvas for them. The cot package starts out as a tri-folded unit with three sections each about two-feet in length. The user pulls the hinged sections out and it spreads to about six-feet in length. Wood braces are sewn along the side edges. When set up correctly it becomes taut enough to comfortably hold a human.

Kyoo and Chong were also present.

Delaplane had elected to stand night watch inside the hut. For that reason and only one other he could think of, he knew he would never go to sleep on this night. To make sure, he was consuming coffee as though it were intravenous. He'd had to use his portable coffeemaker, which meant the coffee would not taste good. It didn't.

Soon after the others crashed into their cots, he found himself staring at a man he had not invited to his party.

Horace Taylor had flown over the area and seen the loaded trucks parked bumper to bumper. He'd not been able to make out all the personnel on the ground due to the rain or he might have seen the Marines. The pilot was forced to fly against a stiff breeze, and when they landed on an abandoned field that was once a rice growing area the Cessna's wheels cocked for the cross wind. It took an excellent pilot to fly the 195 and land on a rough field in such conditions.

Taylor ordered the pilot to set up for a night takeoff when he returned. The pilot would wait.

Dressed in the wrong clothes for his mission, and in polished shoes instead of combat boots, Taylor had to hike the half-mile to the hut along the rocky shoreline. Fortunately he'd done that once before in daylight and knew his way. Tripping and falling twice however, did not make him a happy man. His civilian clothes had taken a hit with each fall and so had his ego. He'd been infantry before his CIA life, which had begun under William Donovan. He realized with each stumble to the ground that he'd lost a lot of his past, and probably wasn't looking at a great future.

When he got to the hut, he was unaware of Bowers and the Korean girl with a French last name. A name he would never forget. Francois DeHavilland had been a good spy in France. At least for a while.

Bowers had seen him though and kept his weapon trained on Taylor for a few seconds. Peggy had not seen him since she was sitting with her head down between her knees.

Taylor had barged into the hut and immediately dragged Delaplane to the coffee machine area – only to learn they were without power.

Delaplane found himself speechless at first. But Taylor was just the opposite.

"You better have a damned good reason why you haven't left here yet."

Delaplane glanced to the drivers to gain some thinking time, then back to Taylor. "I do," he said. Then he fell silent.

"Well? What could lead you to jeopardize our goddamned retirement?"

"It was rainin'. The mud in this area would sink every truck out there. They are way overloaded. That and darkness in enemy territory. We ain't got no shotgun riders, ya know. That puts fear into the drivers' hearts."

Taylor bit his lower lip with his teeth and gritted out, "Are you aware the JR has been sunk?"

Delaplane wasn't aware. "He didn't sink it. He just shot a rocket across the man's bow. Forced Black to the dock south of here to load half the stock aboard and take it to Pusan. We done that all day and came back for the other half. We needed twenty or more trucks to empty this place all at once and another boat."

Taylor pondered Delaplane's answer then said, "Why the JR?"

"Cap'n wanted to take that stuff right to your front door and dump it in your laps before you two split for the states."

"You should have sent me a message."

"What? You want everyone in Korea to know what's goin' on?"

The absence of the word "sir" was noticeable to Taylor. He decided that Delaplane had lost all respect for him, or the sergeant was planning on bugging out on him and ratting on the whole deal. He shook his head. No, he told himself. Don't get paranoid like Hans.

"Why are you here?" Delaplane asked.

Taylor stepped back and sat on the double set of rocket crates. He seemed dejected. "Among other things, we have to take out the Marine and get this crap out of here. All before sunrise."

Delaplane was happy that he didn't know where Strickland was.

It was as though on cue. The sound of a large truck roaring down the road to the hut caused the two men to look into each other's eyes with a question. What in the hell is that?

The answer came so abruptly that no one inside the hut was able to comprehend events in time to react in defense. A heavy six-by crashed through the front end of the hut sending the wooden front section flying off in splinters. Corrugated steel collapsed at the front side walls while North Korean were flung like rag dolls through the air in front of the truck. Blazing headlights blinded everyone inside. The truck skidded to a stop at the stack of launchers. The driver's door opened and Frank Strickland dropped down, holding two Colt .45s in his hands. One from Drier, one from Fraker.

"Don't anyone move," he commanded.

But only Kyoo and Chong among the Koreans understood his command. Before they could translate to the drivers, one had his rifle up and popped off a shot that hit the truck door within inches of Strickland.

Strickland's right hand .45 blasted loudly when he dropped the Korean whose name was Hyun-Ki, in his place.

"Anyo, Anyo," Kyoo shouted to the driver's with his hands waving frantically. His body language told them to stop, stay put. Don't shoot. Anyo meaning, No!

Delaplane turned his attention from Kyoo to Strickland. He palmed his eyes to cut the glare from the high intensity headlights from the truck. He could barely make out Strickland's silhouette. The Marine stood braced, both hands up with Colts in them, as though he were Wyatt Earp at the OK Corral.

Delaplane cried out, "You fucking nuts, Cap'n? What in the hell was that all about?"

Taylor, now alongside Delaplane shook his head. "You're finished, Frank."

Kyoo piped up from the background. "He kill Hyun-Ki." The remaining soldiers seemed tense to Strickland, like men ready to enter battle.

"Shut up, Kyoo," Strickland said. "Tell your men to put their weapons down. Now!"

Kyoo turned to the soldiers and did as commanded. Slowly each soldier laid his M-1 on the deck and backed off one step.

"Let's put an end to this now," Taylor said into the lights. He too, palmed his eyes to be able to focus on the dark silhouette of Strickland. Strickland stood between both headlights, which caused his frame to flare the luminance in such a manner that he appeared to be coming from a tunnel with the brilliance of huge Klieg lights pushing him.

"By that you mean let's put an end to my life." He turned to Delaplane, "And to yours Sergeant. He intends for you to die as well."

Delaplane had suspected as much but not quite accepted it yet. He glanced to Taylor and without realizing it, backed away from him a few steps.

"Bullshit," Taylor said.

"Where are you taking the trucks, Colonel?"

"Agency business."

Strickland leveled a pistol at Taylor. Although Taylor couldn't see Strickland, he could see the man's arms jamming out of the light with a pistol in each hand. "Better tell me. I've pretty much lost my patience with you assholes."

"You're speaking to a superior officer, Captain."

Strickland waved the pistol as though he meant to use it. "There's nothing superior about you, Taylor. Now answer my question."

Taylor's anger became instantly visible. It was as though he'd just morphed from a clothing store customer into one of the mannequins. "Can't do that."

Strickland pulled the hammer on his Colt back. "I think you'd better."

Taylor squinted into the light. A sharp pain seemed to crease along his forehead just above his eyes. "North. Guerillas. You know that."

"You're planning on selling them to the commies, aren't you?"

"We have a mission over here. Train North Korean rebels and then supply them."

Strickland nearly laughed. "From the air, Taylor. So, where's this shit going?"

Delaplane could barely deal with the tension and he knew Strickland was capable of dropping both of them to the deck right there. "He was gonna sell 'em, Cap'n. Just like you said. They was going to take the money and stuff it into a Swiss account."

Strickland eased the hand that pointed a Colt at Taylor. While he did that, the other Colt kept its position facing the Korean soldiers.

"That's treason, Taylor. That's good enough to get you hanged."

"You won't get out of here alive to tell anyone, Frank."

"Another reason for them to kill you as well, Sergeant. Tell us Taylor, you got a contract out on both of us?"

Taylor shook his head. He lowered his hands from shading his eyes and waved them off as though the idea was ridiculous.

"Tell me, Colonel. Tell me who killed the ladies in Seoul. I'm the one taking the hit for it, so if you're going to have me killed, at least let me know who murdered the prostitutes."

Taylor's face flushed red. His lips tightened to match his already narrowed eyes. The bright lights were taking a toll on his eyes as well. He blinked a few times and then said, "It doesn't matter."

Without warning Strickland fired a round at Taylor's feet. "It does to me. Now talk before I cut your shoe size down."

When the round bounced off the concrete pad at Taylor's feet, it sailed down the hut and through the bulkhead. The ammo was military issue. A copper jacket round with more strength than his own lead bullets. Taylor jumped upwards when the shot was fired but he would have been too late had the round been aimed at his feet. His reflexes had proved slow.

"Makimoto."

"Your idea or Tofte's?"

"Look, why are we doing this? It just doesn't matter."

"Answer me. Yours or Tofte's?"

"Hans wanted me to set you up so that we could control you more. You're wild, Frank. Way too wild for our mission."

"Delaplane. You know about that?"

Delaplane shook his head wildly. "No sir. Did not know that. Tofte wanted it to be me. Wanted me to be a witness. I agreed with 'em, Cap'n. They was blamin' you when I was in their office after. So, I told 'em you didn't do it." He looked to Taylor. "I led them on to believe I'd be the one. Jest to get Tofte off'n my back." He looked back into the bright lights. "But you know I didn't do it, Cap'n."

"He wasn't a part of the set up," Taylor said. "The sergeant here doesn't really play with a full deck, Frank."

"Ironic, wouldn't you say, Colonel. The sergeant here was lying to you that he'd done it, and you were lying to him about not knowing about the ammo."

"Look. Tofte is gone. It's all over for him. I'll leave shortly. History will little note our presence here. So, why don't we just look the other way and everyone walk off into the sunset."

He sounded like he was sniveling, but Strickland and Delaplane both knew Taylor was too conniving to give up that easily. Strickland didn't respond to Taylor but instead asked Delaplane, "Sergeant. Did you give them ammo from my pistol?"

Delaplane gulped visibly. "Yes, sir. After we saw the ladies. They wanted it."

Strickland pointed the Colt in his left hand directly at Taylor's head and asked, "So, Colonel, how did you get my ammo before we were there?"

"We had our source."

Strickland counted down from five. He clearly meant he would pull the trigger at the bottom of the count if Taylor didn't answer him.

"He'll shoot you," Delaplane said matter of factually.

Taylor put his hands with palms up toward Strickland. "Okay. Okay. I'll explain it to you. Just calm down with that pistol."

"Talk."

"Makimoto killed the ladies. He was supposed to retrieve two of the rounds that killed them. He had only enough to do the job. But when we got the rounds, we discovered that forensics couldn't ID a weapon from lead rounds that had hit anything more than a pile of feathers."

"So, you needed more rounds from the pistol I loaned the sergeant."

"Yes."

Strickland marveled at their stupidity. "Where did Makimoto get my pistol to kill the ladies?"

Taylor stared hard at him and didn't reply.

Strickland wiggled his Colt at Taylor.

"Okay. Okay. It doesn't matter. You'll be dead before anyone ever hears this from you."

"Talk. Without the threats."

The back door exploded open and Strickland was startled enough to be jolted back against the truck by it. Bowers appeared with his pistol hand held straight up at Strickland. "It was me, Captain. You should have cleaned your own weapons." Even though all Bowers could see was Strickland's silhouette, he fired his .45 directly at him.

A split second before he fired, the lights went out. Snake had reached into the truck and snapped them off.

And at that same moment, at least six M-1s returned fire to Bowers, each rifle firing with only the Coleman lantern as their source of light.

Everyone hit the deck. Delaplane flattened out only a few feet from where Strickland lay. Delaplane looked around for Taylor but the Army officer wasn't to be seen.

Kyoo and Chong tried to get to the exit but found themselves wrapped up in dead or wounded soldiers. Then they heard a woman's voice.

"This way," she said in Korean.

Kyoo and Chong had been blinded by the truck lights so everything was still very, very dark. Kyoo wasn't ready to question the pretty voice so he grabbed Chong's hand and following the seductive lady, led Chong out the hatch keeping as snug to the deck as possible since bullets still sailed overhead. To get out of the hut, they had to crawl over the corpse of the American Army guy named Bowers.

One of the Korean soldiers stood and fired two tracers at the Americans before he was dropped by return fire.

"Cease fire," Hawk commanded.

Silence same quickly.

"Frank, you okay?"

There was no reply.

"Lights back on Sergeant Fraker," Bradford ordered.

When the headlights came on the Marines who had been there to witness Strickland's conversation with Taylor nearly dropped their weapons. A pile of eight dead Korean soldiers were stacked directly in front of the truck. They had apparently bunched together to fire at the Marines and fallen inwardly, making it look like a stack of football players who'd tried to guard the goal line.

"Jesus," Snake said in a low tone that resembled a prayer of respect.

They noticed the back hatch open. Bowers lay dead alongside the Koreans. About ten feet in front of the truck Delaplane was sprawled out face down with blood pooled near his abdomen. Both Taylor and Strickland were missing.

"Where's Strickland?" Bradford demanded, breaking into their momentary shock.

"Medic," Delaplane called. He was unable to move. He'd been hit badly and probably paralyzed, at least that's what he thought.

Hawk looked over to Donovan. "Take one of those jeeps out front and hucklebuck back to camp. Bring a meat wagon and the corpsmen."

Donovan gave him a wave for a salute and said, "Aye, aye, sir." He took off through the jumbled mess of metal and wood created by the six-by.

Drier was down on one knee at Delaplane's side. "Where you hit, Sarge?"

Delaplane had very little energy left. "Gut. Leg."

Drier checked the pool of blood. It had stopped building. "Pain?"

"Uh, huh."

They weren't in battle here. They had not brought their duty emergency aid kits. "Corpsman will be here shortly."

Delaplane knew that to be about an hour. He didn't know if he could make it.

"Where'd Strickland go?" Bradford asked Delaplane.

But the sergeant didn't know and all he could do to answer was squeeze his left fist closed a little.

Drier looked up at Bradford. "Taylor's gone, too, sir."

Hawk and Snake came alongside Bradford.

Bradford scanned the entire hut for the first time since the lights went on. His cooks and infantry types had done well. None of them had backed down from the fight. If there was a problem it was probably that they reacted with a little bit of overkill. He smirked at his poor effort at a pun. Better overkill than be killed.

"Hawk. You and Fraker set up a perimeter guard. Post the men in case there are others around here we don't know about. Lieutenant Drier, take Donovan and Winfield and search for Captain Strickland."

Hawk and Snake nodded agreement and took the riflemen out of the hut into the dark surroundings. He'd first cover the back of the hut as well as the side areas.

CHAPTER 33

A MOMENT AFTER Strickland plowed into the building, a moment needed for them to comprehend what had just happened, Peggy and Bowers slipped silently up to the small window. The truck that smashed through the front end had now given them the light they needed to see their intended target clearly. Bowers had told her to keep one eye closed before they got to the small window. "That way when you back away you'll still have night vision in the closed eye."

She chose to shut her right eye. She'd need it to sight her pistol and kill her subject. She refused to reconsider her goal, had accepted her fate along with her target's. A tear appeared at her open eye and she wiped it away quickly. She could not allow that to happen. She could not fail now.

Two men were speaking. She edged up to the window carefully and peered inside. She could see the soldiers in the foreground, and the American sergeant between them and the bright lights, but that was it. The lights seemed like the searchlights she'd seen in Paris after the war. Lights that pierced the sky and lit up the Eiffel Tower when the Americans came and freed them from the Nazis.

They were lights that could blind you if you looked into them. Lights that she thought about back then with the same tears, the same emotions. Her vision of that past would never leave her. It haunted her. Now, maybe the ghosts would go away.

She suddenly realized that her eye seemed to be blurred. But instead it was the dirty window diffusing the light from inside. Her open eye refused to stop tearing. She wiped it again.

"Too bright," she whispered to Bowers. Then she saw him. The man she had come to kill. He was speaking. He was silhouetted against the headlights.

Bowers eased her away from the window. "Let me take a look." He believed in his mission. His target had screwed up the works, cost him the promised future. "Shit, it's him and he's a perfect target."

Peggy tugged at him and regained her position. The window was large enough for only one of them. Her vision once inside would be vivid, sharp. She would not miss her chance.

Bowers had not wanted to be pulled away from the window. "Hey, sister, let me back there," Bowers said. "We're after the same guy."

"He is mine. Not yours." She looked at him, and in that moment he understood.

The tall Korean girl sought revenge. Hers was a personal war.

It was time for him to act. "Okay," he said simply. He braced himself for the unknown like every soldier before him had done before battle and walked to the door. He pulled his .45 up with both hands. He eased the round forward quietly, seating it into the chamber rather than letting the slide noisily slam itself home as it usually did. Eight more rounds securely nestled in the clip that was housed in the pistol's grip. They served as back up if there was a need. He figured there wouldn't be one. This was a sure thing.

Then taking a deep breath, he raised his right leg and with powerful force he kicked the door open.

At that instant, Peggy, still at the window, saw her target duck to her left just before the lights went out. She knew there was a side door and she knew she better get the hell away from the window since a whole lot of bullets were going to be heading that way. She took off, directly for the side. The experienced American would know to go there.

Just when the lights went out, Strickland saw Taylor jump toward his right. He also recognized Bowers at the door, but it was too late for him to comprehend that Bowers had come to kill him. Instead, he bolted for Taylor, only to be knocked sideways by the round that Bowers got off. He doubled down to his knees, fell to his hands but stopped there. He calculated in that instant what was happening, pushed himself back up against the pain at his right hip. He knew from experience that the bullet had hit something hard on him, either a bone or his canteen or maybe even his holster. He felt for the area and blood married to his hand. "Shit," he muttered.

Live rounds zipped back and forth above him with the noise of the rifles tearing at his senses. The Marines and the Koreans were having it out at close range. The flashes from the weapons provided him a psychedelic look toward the door. He headed there, hoping he could grab hold of Taylor. But Taylor was much quicker than Strickland figured. He chased after him but his wound slowed him. It burned like hell. He transferred the pistol from his right hand to his left again and felt for the wound one more time. The blood had not increased. He kept moving, now realizing that his web belt had been hit. The fabric was still hanging together, but his holster was flopping around. Didn't matter, they'd probably saved him. The pistols were under control.

He returned the pistol to his right hand and kept after Taylor. They were outside now. It was dark again, with very little help from the moon or the hut. Clouds had returned. The chill was deeper. He stopped running. He listened. His trained eyes were adapting to the darkness quickly.

In the distance, near the head of the trucks he heard someone stumbling, running and cursing. It had to be Taylor.

He headed for the sound, trying to keep quieter than the Army colonel was. It occurred to him that possibly Taylor had also been hit in the hut.

He paused again. Taylor must have stopped running. A slight breeze gusted past him and then died down. No sounds yet. He wondered if the colonel had gone down.

The roar of a truck's engine pierced the night as though the results of incoming. The sound was the answer to his question.

"Damn," he said aloud. He headed for the first truck. But he was too late. Taylor had geared it and cranked it to life and the six-by was ready to roll.

But Strickland understood what Taylor might not have. The trucks were overloaded and the ground was still too wet and muddy for Taylor to move out quickly or get too far before he could catch him. If he tried to run at him now, Taylor would probably have a target from his position.

He looked back toward the hut. Two jeeps parked to the side of the hut. He ran to the first one and jumped in. He cranked it over and backed up in a circle with the jeep gripping the soft ground much better than the trucks would, and then jammed the gear shift into first and headed for the truck that Taylor had cranked up. It hadn't moved.

The gunfire in the hut stopped. He didn't know when, but it stopped. He saw light coming from behind him. Someone had snapped the truck lights on in the hut again.

He made it to the unmoving lead truck and skidded to a stop in front of it with the jeep sliding in the mud into the brush.

He got out and went to the cab. The truck engine was idling. He yanked the door open only to find the truck empty. "Shit," he muttered. Taylor couldn't get the truck to move up the slippery incline.

He jumped off the running board. If Taylor was trying to escape through the brush, he'd hear him. But silence is all that met his ears.

"Right here, Captain," Taylor called out.

Strickland whirled around. Taylor had slipped up behind him and was waving an 8-inch long pipe at Strickland. Frank could see that the pipe was a standard looking galvanized water pipe. It was capped at each end.

"Don't move," Taylor said. "This is a piss bomb. Ever hear of one? No. I didn't think so. It's a combination of my urine and nitric acid. I drop this and we're both blown to kingdom come." He sounded like he was laughing when he said, "It's a new CIA weapon. Works very well."

Strickland held his hands still. "You're going to hang, Taylor. You know that don't you?"

Taylor gave a hoarse laugh. "You're a real prize, Frank. A rough jewel that will always need polishing. No, I'm not going to hang. But you? You messed up a lot of people. Probably all the way to the top. I should think that they'd hang you first. But," he said, dragging it out, "there's not much chance you'll live to see that."

They were in a dark area, but because of the light in the hut they could see each other's shadowy figure. Apparently Donovan couldn't see either one of them when he raced by in the other jeep headed back to the base for help.

"No one is ever going to know the truth, Frank. It will leave with us."

Strickland glanced back to the hut, then to Taylor. He needed to hold Taylor in place, at least he thought, until help arrives. Drier and Fraker and the others. "And what's the truth, Taylor?" he asked.

Taylor checked the hut as well. He had seen Strickland look back. He was wary. Strickland's pals were down there. The one who just raced by was probably searching for him already. No one there. So far so good. He returned his attention to Strickland. "We were at the president's bidding. Arms for the French. Bribes for the NKs to get our pilots back. Train guerrillas. All ultra top stuff, Frank."

"Only you got greedy, right?"

Taylor fiddled with the pipe bomb, glanced around as though he could see in the dark and then looking back into Strickland's eyes he said, "It's hard not to. You put your life on the line, you live on the edge every day, and you know your career will be just for a few years." He sighed, seeking the right words to explain his actions to someone he was about to kill. His stress level had risen and blocked his brain from its usually perfect cognitive thinking powers. Why did he care now? He shook the questions off and said, "And money and gold bars are sitting on your desk. All of it unaccounted for. Hard. Too hard to turn down that opportunity."

"All at the president's will?"

"Don't be a smart ass. You knew what you were getting into."

"No. You lied to me. And probably everyone else you suckered into the Agency." He thought he saw Taylor flinch. He grabbed the moment, needed more time to hold the errant colonel, and said, "Tell me something?"

Taylor seemed short of patience. He motioned the pipe indicating to Strickland to ask his question.

"Why did you kill the prostitutes?"

Taylor glanced toward the hut again, he could swear he heard someone walking, but nobody was there. He turned back to Strickland. "I told you, Makimoto did that."

Strickland didn't believe him, but let the line drop. Instead, he asked, "I asked why."

"Tofte wanted them silenced. They had found out about our program from one of Colonel Kramer's men. But after we made the plan to ace them, Hans thought it a handy chance to set you up. He wanted you dead or thrown away at Leavenworth for life. You know, you really pissed him off."

Strickland considered that. Was he the reason twelve women died? "So, you arranged for the message from headquarters to Bradford that whores were giving out secrets for ammo dumps."

Taylor smiled. "You're smarter than I gave you credit for. Yes. I did that. But the truth is, some whores were doing that. So, it was a viable way of getting your attention."

A noise behind Strickland made him tense up. He hoped he hadn't shown Taylor his reaction. But Taylor heard it, too. Taylor's eyes narrowed in an effort to bring the background into focus.

Strickland turned around. When his eyes adjusted he saw the girl Drier had brought to camp standing behind him. She was directly in front of the truck. He recognized the pistol she held as a German Luger. Both hands gripped it in a shooter's style, held straight up and pointed right between his eyes.

"You will die tonight," she said.

Strickland shook his head. Her pistol was aimed right at him. But before he could speak, Peggy slowly moved her arms to his right until her sights set directly at Taylor.

"You must die, M'sieur Taylor."

"Peggy," Strickland said. "Hand me the gun."

She shook her head. "No. He must die. He has killed too many people."

Taylor held his pipe up high. "You shoot me Huenyrsook and this will blow us all to hell."

Strickland turned rapidly back to Taylor. "Honorsook?"

"My real name," Peggy said. "Huenyrsook DeHavilland."

"You know this girl, Taylor?"

"I know that whatever she tells you Frank, is a lie." He moved toward the jeep and got nearly to it when Peggy waved the pistol more strongly at him.

"Stop." A tear appeared below her right eye. Then another from her left. She just couldn't seem to stop them. She would let them flow. She couldn't wipe them away anyway, not now with two men who could rush her when her Luger wasn't aimed at Taylor. "Vous les avez tués," she said. She spoke to Taylor in French because she knew that Taylor also spoke the language.

Strickland turned back to Peggy. He didn't have to ask aloud. His expression did it for him.

"He killed them. Not the Japanese man. Him."

Taylor spoke to her in French. "Vous lui dites et tout est fini. Vous mourrez et lui aussi."

Peggy kept her pistol rigidly aimed at Taylor's heart. He had just threatened her, telling her that if she exposed the past to Strickland, each of them would die.

"Both of you. Speak English," Strickland ordered.

"Oui, Capitaine. Nous irons faire. Yes, Captain. I will," she quickly translated. She took a few deep breaths before she spoke again. Strickland could see that she was trying to keep herself from sobbing.

"He was American OSS during the war."

"Arrêter," Taylor ordered her. He had told her to stop.

"No," she said to him. She tightened her sighting eye as though she was about to pull the trigger. "He must know." She glanced to Strickland then while turning back to Taylor she said, "My father was with the French underground during the war. He worked with the OSS to help free France. He helped save American pilots and prisoners. After the war M'sieur Major Taylor here should have been hanged for his crimes. My father was going to the Americans, you know, the war crimes people, to report Taylor's activities."

"But instead, Taylor killed him," Strickland said.

Taylor waved the bomb around again. "She lies, Frank. You can stop now. Both of you. You've gone too far with this." He stepped closer to the jeep but Peggy moved a few steps closer to him.

"You stop. Or I will kill you now."

Taylor held the bomb up but said nothing. He froze in place to see which way it was going to play out.

"You stole money from France and from your own people. Now you steal from Korea."

"Not provable," Taylor said.

"You killed Frenchmen and Americans. My father knew it all. He had the papers, records. He was a witness."

Taylor appeared frantic. He wanted at once to throw the bomb at the two, but then realized it would kill them all. It wasn't a concussion bomb but instead a shrapnel weapon. His eyes darted from Strickland to Peggy and back. At the moment the girl was the most dangerous.

Strickland searched through the past few days. Peggy had just stunned him with her exposure. He couldn't believe that he had not thought of interviewing this girl right away. He had thought she was just another prostitute and Drier and Hawk had gotten all they could from her. The sister, what about the corpse they brought back?

"Peggy," he said. "Your sister. Did he kill her?"

She nodded and appeared to Strickland as though she was ready to pull the trigger right then. Taylor felt it also. "He killed her for my father's records."

He moved right to the jeep. "I'm leaving, Peggy. Go ahead and shoot me. You do and this bomb will drop and kill both of you."

"Stop, Taylor," Strickland said. To Peggy he said, "Don't shoot, Peggy."

Peggy glanced to him then back to Taylor. "Tell him, M'Sieur Taylor. Tell him now."

"She lied to you, Frank. She's working for the Army CID. They inserted her as a spy against the Agency. I'm sure of it." He looked from Strickland to her and said, "A double agent as it were." Looking back to Strickland he said, "The waiter. The Imperial Hotel? The Geisha bar? Makimoto did it. Tofte assigned this girl to kill you, but she obviously had her own plans."

"Makimoto killed who?" Strickland asked.

"Not Makimoto," Peggy said. "Him." She jammed the pistol straight at Taylor. "Tell him," she shouted.

"Go to hell."

Peggy sobbed, finally. Strickland watched the pistol more than he did her while she regained control. When she had it back together she said, "It is true. He killed my father." Strickland understood. He remembered his own father's death in that violent plane crash so long ago.

She sobbed lightly now, but continued on. "And now he has killed my sister. She was older than me. She helped my father during the war. She knew everything he knew. She had records." He stopped abruptly, wiped tears away with the back of her free hand and then said, "He wanted the records. He killed her for those. But she didn't have them. So he looked for me."

Peggy looked to Strickland while keeping the pistol trained on Taylor. Their eyes met. But Strickland saw something in the girl he'd seen only one other time in his life. It was the look a woman gave a man when instead of hating them, they loved them for having done something for them that they considered deeply important. But what had he done? He took his eyes away from hers and turned to Taylor. It became obvious. She'd cornered her family's killer.

"How long have you been chasing him?"

She pursed her lips, then said, "Six years. But he has been very hard to find. A few months ago M'Sieur Reineke sent us a message. He'd found him. Here. The Agency has an office in the army CID building. So, we came." She stepped even closer to Taylor keeping the Luger pointed at him. "When he killed my sister he saw the other ladies there. Three days later he came back and killed them. With the

Japanese man." She turned to Strickland, shook her head as though she was trying to erase the memory. Then she looked Taylor in the eyes and said, "I want to see you hang, M'Sieur." She wave the Luger from eye to eye and said, "This pistol, do you recognize it?"

Taylor seemed bewildered. "What?"

"It is the gun you killed my father with."

Taylor felt anger and frustration and fear all at the same time. "Reineke!" he called out, as though the man was hiding near them.

"Oui, M'sieur Taylor. You gave it to him to destroy. But as you see," She pushed the pistol a bit too close to Taylor, "it is about to destroy you."

"Sweet irony wouldn't you say, Taylor? Your Luger comes back to kill you," Strickland said.

But Peggy had gotten too close. In one swift move Taylor pulled her around and twisted her with his arm until he had a choke hold with her neck tightened in the crutch of his right elbow. Her hand gripped tightly to the pistol but she felt herself weakening. Taylor held his bomb up with his free hand and ordered Strickland to back off.

Peggy struggled to break loose but Taylor proved to be very strong. She was able to squeak out, "He killed them all."

Taylor tightened his grip on her effectively shutting her up. He sat backwards into the jeep and pulled her across the passenger seat while he worked his way to the driver's seat. "Back off Frank. I'm taking her with me."

"No you aren't," Drier said from the other side. He held his pistol to Taylor's head.

"Tell him, Frank. The bomb. Tell him."

Strickland was at the jeep at the moment Drier spoke up. Taylor hadn't seen him coming. "Go ahead," he said, "drop the bomb."

When Taylor twisted around to look for Strickland he found himself looking down the barrel of Peggy's pistol and Peggy was the one holding it. She'd worked her arm up past her left shoulder and into his face.

Drier saw the gun was aimed his way and moved quickly toward the rear of the jeep but kept his .45 against Taylor's skull.

Strickland saw the determination in Peggy's eyes. There would be no way to stop her. Taylor let go of the girl and dropped the piss bomb when the Lugar fired.

CHAPTER 34

NAVY PETTY OFFICER Walter "Whitey" Forbes, one helluva banjo picker, was the first corpsman to arrive with medical aid. Donovan had driven his heart out to get to the village and returned with one ambulance and one corpsman. Coming behind them though, he explained, "is an army of help."

Forbes started working on Delaplane first while Strickland, Drier and Snake checked through the dead Koreans for any evidence that might help the CID build a case for the government to prosecute Taylor and hopefully Tofte, Makimoto and the others.

Drier was first to find an I.D. on one of them. He pulled a small leather packet not unlike his own ID carrier from a dead soldier's breast pocket and flipped it open. When he seemed to freeze Snake asked, "What?"

Drier handed the leather pouch to him. "Pretty. Think it's his wife?"

Snake made a clicking sound with his tongue snapping against the side of his mouth and said, "War's hell, kid."

Drier checked through the rest of the billfold. He found a small piece of paper and opened it. It was all written in Korean. He looked back at the girl who was sitting in the chair by what used to be a coffee machine but now looked more like a sieve created by crossfire. Winfield stood guard over her. He motioned for Winfield to bring the girl over. When she arrived he held the wallet shaped folder up and asked, "Can you read this, Peggy?"

She liked Drier. It was him who helped her. The younger good looking one. She squinted at the print and said, "He was a North Korean soldier. Name was Chin-Hwa Park. He is from Pyongyang. Nineteen years old."

Drier nodded, folded the paper back to its original form and slipped it back into the holder. "Thanks," he said. "We'll be done here shortly. I'll make sure they take good care of you."

She nodded. She knew her fate had been written a long time ago. "I know," she said softly. She looked down at the body of Corporal Bowers who was just being covered by another medic.

Strickland came to her and nodded toward Bowers. "Did he come here to kill one of us? Maybe the sergeant there? Or me?"

She thought a moment and then shook her head. Bowers was a mixed up kid, she thought. He's dead. Why hurt him now? "He came to kill Taylor."

Strickland felt his hip where Forbes had patched him up. "Is that what they wanted you to do?"

She shook her head. "I came on my own."

Strickland saw a hole in her answers and wanted to plug it. "Bowers wasn't after me?"

She bent her head down and appeared to be studying the body of Bowers. "At first, yes. They told him a few days ago to kill you. He liked you, but I think he liked money more." She looked up into Strickland's eyes. "When they told him there would be no money, he got very angry. So, he came to kill Taylor instead."

"So, Taylor came here tonight to kill us himself."

Peggy could only nod. She didn't know why he came but that sounded good enough.

"Who is Reineke," Strickland asked.

Drier's ears perked up waiting for Peggy's answer. "He was a German officer who hated Hitler. He wanted Germany back for the people. He came to France for Germany but then found the French underground and worked with them. Then the OSS found him and they put him and my father together. They worked for Taylor. But they both hated Taylor because Taylor was a thief. A bad man. But Reineke? He is my friend."

When she looked up she noticed that all of them nodded with her even though they may not have recognized it themselves. She relaxed when they did. Maybe things wouldn't go so bad for her after all.

Hawk held his hands up. "Gents, let's stop there. We'll have to sort this out later."

* * * *

The following day Drier's duffel bag was jammed full of his personal gear. He had checked in on Dobbins and the man was doing well, although he'd be in pain for a long time. He also cleared Peggy of shooting him with intent. He was convinced that Bowers had caused the accident.

Drier would have to find out about Delaplane when he passed through Japan. They'd flown him there immediately. It was for curiosity only.

He dumped his bag into the back of a jeep that had been brought to his quarters by Donovan. Before he could climb into the passenger seat he was stopped by Fraker.

"You leavin' us, Lieutenant?"

Drier nodded. "Yes." He grabbed Snake's right hand and shook it. He then led him away from all ears. "I'm being transferred."

"And you were gonna leave without saying goodbye?"

Drier glanced around the camp. He had been ordered to not speak to anyone about his departure. So had Hawk and Strickland. But Snake was a friend. A life saver. He looked back into Snake's eyes. "I'm going to naval intelligence school."

Snake caught on. "Shit. Another good infantryman down the drain." His brow furrowed and he asked, "The Skipper?"

Drier shook his head lightly. "Barstow supply center. Can you believe that? They're going to dump him at Barstow. That's an end of the road assignment."

"No sir. Not necessarily. Remember the skipper swore he'd try to fix the supply system when we got out of that inferno up there. Well, maybe that's just what he's up to."

Drier smiled. "You're right again, Snake," he said. He saluted Fraker and headed back to his jeep.

"Lieutenant," Snake said like a D.I. might.

Drier turned back to him. "Yes?" Drier could see that Snake was not a happy camper and that the man probably wanted to know what the hell was going on. "Snake, I think you'll be seeing the colonel shortly." It wasn't his job to tell the sergeant that he was about to be promoted to sergeant major of the Marine Corps.

And that he would forever have to keep his mouth shut about recent events.

Acknowledgments

I want to thank all my military friends and a couple of CIA types who helped with this story. Unfortunately, too many of them are no longer with us and although I thanked them in person when each provided me important knowledge, I want to thank each and all again. Since the list is long and I've lost contact with a few, I'll say Thank You From The Bottom Of My Heart and hope you are able to receive this.

Collectively you provided insight to things we only suspect until we learn the truth. Although this tale is wrapped around true events and actions, some of the characters are fictional, introduced to the story to help carry the plot. The tale of the president pushing forward the CIA and shipping weaponry through Korea to Vietnam is true. The battles in this book are as accurate as military historical sources could provide me. The conscription of military personnel by the CIA was also true. Hans Tofte existed and ended up in Columbia as an agent for the U.S. General O. P. Smith became assistant commandant of the Marine Corps and retired with four stars, the highest rank in the Marine Corps. He was credited with responding to the media with "Retreat, hell! We're not retreating, we're just advancing in a different direction."

Frank Strickland existed but with a different name, and his friend Drier is a compilation of half a dozen young officers with whom I served.

The history of the Vietnam episodes and references to the CIA's growth is accurate and from detailed records obtainable from the Department of Defense, the Central Intelligence Agency, and the national archives.

Also, I deeply thank Tony DiMarco for editing, Rebecca Gazzaniga and William Gentry for their editing for typos and much else, and each and everyone of you who have read all 474 pages.

Other books by Donald A Gazzaniga

A Few Good Men, The Marines
Who Killed Rita Colleridge
Air France One
G*A*M*E*S

And from Macmillan St. Martin's Press

The No-Salt, Lowest-Sodium Cookbook
The No-Salt, Lowest-Sodium Baking Book
The No-Salt, Lowest-Sodium Light
The No-Salt, Lowest-Sodium Intern

And from Arrowhead Classics Publishing

Living Well Without Salt